Double Barrel

MICHELLE NAOMI MOSLEY

Double Barrel

A RED MOUNTAIN NOVEL

Publisher: Mariposa Books, LLC

Cover designer: Lia Ramirez

Editor: Editing by Andrea

Spanish editor: LC Editing

Proofreaders: Kari LeAnn and Lauren Rossi

 Formatted with Vellum

For every woman who can do it herself, here's the man who says, "I know you can, but let me do it for you."

"Your lips are like wine, and I want to get drunk."

— WILLIAM SHAKESPEARE

Author's Note

Dear Reader,

First of all, thank you so much for picking up this book and choosing to read Elyse and Dominic's story. While this is the second book in the *Red Mountain Series*, it can be enjoyed as a complete standalone. However, for a richer reading experience, I recommend starting with *Rare Blend*.

Dominic, the main male character, is a deputy sheriff. Multiple law enforcement professionals were consulted to help ensure accuracy in depicting Dominic's career, but ultimately this is a work of fiction. Some creative liberties were taken in service of the story. Please keep in mind that laws, policies, procedures, and law enforcement culture can vary widely between agencies, counties, and states. Fiction is meant to entertain—not serve as a precise or definitive portrayal of a real-life deputy sheriff.

In addition to his career in law enforcement, Dominic is a first-generation Mexican-American. As a biracial, first-generation Mexican-American myself, many of my own experiences are reflected in his character. It's important to remember that there are many subcultures within the Latinx community, and there is no single "right way" to be Latinx—it's in your DNA. Informal Mexican Spanish is used and translated throughout the book for your benefit. As with any language, idioms and nuances can vary from region to region.

This book is intended for adult audiences and contains sexually explicit content as well as emotional themes that may be sensitive for some readers. To avoid spoilers, I've listed content warnings at the back of the book.

You can also find them at www.authormichellenaomi-mosley.com

I hope you enjoy Elyse and Dominic's journey.

Happy reading. ¡Salud! (*Cheers!*)

Michelle

Glossary

Cruiser/Patrol SUV: Interchangeably used to describe a deputy sheriff's vehicle.

FTO: Field Training Officer

Kevlar vest: Bullet-resistant vest made from Kevlar.

Lateral: A law enforcement officer who moves from one agency to another as a lateral transfer. This can be in and out of state.

MDT: Mobile Data Terminal (a laptop-like device kept in law enforcement vehicles)

Sarge: Slang for sergeant.

Spanish 101

Dialogue spoken in Spanish is directly translated on the page, however there are some terms and phrases littered throughout that are not defined or translated. For your convenience, I have listed them below.

- **'Amá** - Slang for "mamá"
- **'Apá** - Slang for "papá"
- **Ay** - used to express "oh," "ouch," or "ah"
- **Barbacoa** - A Mexican dish made of meat that's slow-cooked until tender
- **Dios** - God
- **Chorizo con huevo** - spicy, seasoned sausage and eggs
- **Flaquita** - Skinny girl/little skinny one
- **Mijo** - Term of endearment meaning my son
- **Querida mía** - My darling/My dear

Playlist

I Love You, I'm Sorry - Gracie Abrams
You Belong With Me - Taylor Swift
Messy - Lola Young
THE GREATEST - Billie Eilish
Yonaguni - Bad Bunny
the 1 - Taylor Swift
Somewhere Only We Know - Keane
Do I Wanna Know - Hozier
To Build a Home - The Cinematic Orchestra
Stop Crying Your Heart Out - Oasis
Silver Springs - Fleetwood Mac
The Only Exception - Paramore
Red (Taylor's Version) - Taylor Swift
WILDFLOWER - Billie Eilish
Perfect - Ed Sheeran
Burning Desire - Lana Del Rey
Greatest Love Story - LANCO
Wine After Whiskey - Carrie Underwood
Motivation - Kelly Rowland (feat. Lil Wayne)
MIA - Bad Bunny (feat. Drake)

Kiss It Better - Rihanna
Begin Again (Taylor's Version) - Taylor Swift
21 - Gracie Abrams
Vindicated - Dashboard Confessional
Breathe (Taylor's Version) - Taylor Swift
Indigo - Sam Barber (feat. Avery Anna)
I Remember Everything - Zach Bryan (feat. Kacey Musgraves)
Your Graduation - Modern Baseball
Falling Asleep at the Wheel - Holly Humberstone
Pointless - Lewis Capaldi
West Coast - Lana Del Rey
Arms - Christina Perri
Sailor Song - Gigi Perez
Stay With Me - Sam Smith
Die For You - The Weeknd
BIRDS OF A FEATHER - Billie Eilish
The Bones - Maren Morris

About This Book

Elyse Ledger doesn't do love—not anymore. Her focus is firmly on her career and family. Between managing her parents and siblings and planning elaborate weddings at her family's winery, her schedule is packed, leaving no room for a personal life. So when her high school sweetheart returns to Red Mountain as the town's new deputy sheriff, she's determined to keep her distance—no matter how good he looks in uniform.

Dominic Alvarez doesn't make many mistakes, but losing Elyse was the biggest one of his life. A brush with death and a devastating loss have shifted his priorities, fueling his resolve to right the wrongs of his past. Now that he's back in his hometown, Dominic is determined to show Elyse he's not the same man who let her slip away. When a series of threats put her at risk, he's intent on protecting the woman he's never stopped loving.

As danger closes in, Dominic is determined to prove he's worth a second chance—like a double-barrel vintage, stronger and more complex with time. Yet Elyse's reluctance to open her heart again may keep them from savoring a future together.

Some loves, like the finest wine, become richer with age.

Character Catch-Up

The Red Mountain Series is an interconnected standalone series that can be read in any order. However, since the family at the center of it all is a big one (six siblings!), I thought it might be helpful to give you a little background before you dive in—especially if this is your first book in the series or if it's been a while since you last visited Red Mountain.

If you're new here, welcome! I'm so happy to have you and to share the Red Mountain universe with you.

Ethan Ledger and Marisa Castilla's story kicks off the series in *Rare Blend* (Book One). It's a grumpy/sunshine, dislike-to-love romance with male anxiety rep, a loyal German Shepherd named Goose, and plenty of banter and spice. These two lived in my head for so long that they hold a special place in my heart. Both characters appear in *Double Barrel*.

Double Barrel picks up shortly after the epilogue in *Rare Blend*, but before the bonus epilogue. You don't need to read either to understand the events in this story.

I'll be dropping a few hints about which characters are up next in the series, so if you like to guess ahead, keep your eyes open!

Happy reading, and welcome back to Red Mountain.

Prologue

DOMINIC

I didn't see the end coming until it was too late.

Ellie had been acting off all weekend, but I'd chalked it up to stress. Spring finals were around the corner, and after we got through them, everything would be fine. We'd spend the summer traversing Western Europe, just the two of us, soaking up every moment together before the next school year began. I let her pick each stop, curating our itinerary, because I didn't give a shit where we went—wherever she was, I wanted to be.

Life and circumstances forced us to attend different colleges. Ellie tried to convince me it would be fun, that we would have more authentic college experiences apart. I didn't care about an authentic college experience when it meant being away from her. Despite the distance, we'd found a way to stay connected. Our universities shared a study abroad program, and from the moment we discovered it, we'd made a pact: every summer would be an adventure, together.

Sometimes, I miss the version of me who believed that was enough. Who thought we'd always be enough.

"Bro, there's something wrong with your girl," Brett, my

1

roommate, announced from the doorway of our dorm. His eyes were glazed and heavy-lidded from his standard beer and blunt for breakfast.

"What do you mean, 'wrong'? Like, sick?" My lips pressed together as a gnawing sensation creeped into my chest.

He shrugged. "Tiff saw her crying in the bathroom."

That got my attention. Ellie wasn't a crier. I'd seen her cry before, but as we had gotten older, she'd gotten in the habit of locking those feelings away—until the pressure built too much, and she finally broke. If she was crying now, something was seriously wrong.

"When the fuck was this?" I snapped, already on edge.

Brett blinked, startled. "Don't shoot the messenger, Dom."

I was out of my chair before he finished speaking. It clattered to the floor behind me, but I didn't care. If Ellie was upset, I needed to find her.

I was done tiptoeing around whatever was going on with her this weekend. Honesty had always been the foundation of our relationship—since the beginning, back when we were just kids.

When I was seven, my parents finally achieved their American dream of owning a home. I didn't want to move because it meant starting over at a new school. They bought an old farmhouse with a couple hundred acres of neglected land. The house was crumbling, the fields overgrown, and to me and my older brother, Adrian, the whole place looked like a dump. But to my parents, it was full of potential—something they saw clearly, even if we couldn't.

The day we moved in, I set out to explore what I reluctantly considered my new playground. What I found instead was the most stunning pair of green eyes I'd ever seen, as translucent as green sea glass. To this day, those eyes are impossible to forget.

Crouched by the weathered railroad tie fence dividing our properties, tall, gangly, all elbows and attitude, was Elyse Ledger, the girl next door.

We became friends that day—or, more accurately, I said hi, and she promptly decided we were going to be best friends. And we were, despite our differences. My parents were immigrants, and our life was modest. The Ledgers, on the other hand, were practically local royalty—wealthy, well-connected, and pillars of the community. Ellie could've easily been a spoiled brat, but she wasn't.

Instead of just growing up alongside one another, we grew into each other. Our lives wove together so tightly that I couldn't imagine mine without her. As kids, we spent every free moment playing. As we got older, our parents started enforcing rules about how much time we spent alone and keeping doors open when we hung out. Our innocent minds didn't understand what our parents clearly saw coming. Even then, they couldn't stop the inevitable.

In seventh grade, we went to our first boy-girl party. Ellie was a bundle of nerves, convinced by teen movies it would devolve into a game of Seven Minutes in Heaven. We both knew everything about each other—including the fact that neither of us had been kissed. I don't think I had fully processed my feelings for her at the time, but the thought of another boy getting to be her first kiss made my chest ache in a way I couldn't grasp yet. So, I suggested we get it over with—kiss each other.

To my surprise, she didn't argue. She agreed like it was the best idea in the world. And so, at the very fence where we'd first met, it happened. It was awkward and barely lasted a second, but I was her first, and she was mine. I liked that more than I was ready to admit. In true Ellie fashion, she brushed it off like it was no big deal and acted as if it never happened for over two years.

It wasn't until an upperclassman invited her to prom at the end of our freshman year of high school that something in me finally snapped. It was hard enough watching my friends start to notice her, seeing her go on dates, but this was different. He was older, popular, and Ellie was easily the most beautiful girl in school.

I couldn't stop her from going, but I spent the entire night pacing the road in front of the Ledger house, imagining the worst. Was he touching her? Kissing her? Did she like him? I was spiraling, and I think her parents knew it because they didn't throw me off their property, like they should have.

When the limo finally pulled up at midnight, I exhaled a sigh of relief as she stepped out alone. The moment her eyes found mine, her shoulders dropped, noticeably releasing tension. And I stood suspended in time, unable to tear my eyes off her—she was breathtaking. The dress hugged her body in all the places I'd only dreamed of touching, her hair and makeup flawless, like she'd walked straight out of a dream. The sight of her hit me hard, stealing the air from my lungs.

"What are you doing here?" she asked, not at all surprised to see me, in fact it looked like she was expecting me.

I shrugged, attempting to play it cool. "I wanted to make sure you made it home okay."

She laughed quietly as her heels echoed against the pavement the closer she got to me.

"Where's your date?" I tried my best to not make the word date sound like a bad word, but I'm sure it came out sounding something close to disgust.

Her forehead creased. "He got sick. It was super weird, one minute he was fine, and the next he was puking his guts out."

I wasn't as religious as my extremely Catholic upbringing would suggest, but I thanked God in that moment, that the big man upstairs had been looking out for me, and gave her date a stomach bug, or more likely a mild case of alcohol poisoning.

"That's too bad. I'm sorry to hear that."

She scoffed. "No you're not."

Her head tilted, assessing me, as if those clear green eyes of hers could see right through me. And maybe they could, maybe I wasn't as good at hiding it as I thought I was.

A rush of nerves coursed within me. I couldn't remember a time when I didn't have feelings for Ellie, but a shift had happened recently. It changed from a mild crush on my best friend, to full-blown feelings. I thought about her constantly, wanted her constantly, but there was a lot of risk in making it known—in crossing the line. I didn't want to lose her as my best friend, and she'd never given me any indication there were feelings on her end.

"Seriously, I wanted you to have fun."

She came closer, close enough for me to get clouded with the smell of warm amber coming off her skin. "Why are you waiting for me?"

I swallowed the non-existent saliva in my mouth. "I told you, to make sure—"

"Tell me the truth," she whispered. Her glowing gaze locked with mine, refusing to let go.

The tension between us felt thicker than it had ever felt before. She got even closer to me and the beads of her dress made contact with my T-shirt. My fingers twitched, itching to touch her.

"If I tell you the truth," I said quietly. "You might not like it. It might change everything."

She dipped her chin, studying me with a curious expression. Then she smiled—a smile so different from any I'd ever gotten from her before, it might as well have set me on fire. My skin burned under its warmth. "I think I'll like it," she said.

Either I was imagining things, or she was giving me a clear

opening. Before I could second-guess it and risk losing my window, I closed the space between us and kissed her. The weight of every worst-case scenario I'd imagined had been driving me insane, and I couldn't hold back any longer. This time, it wasn't awkward or fleeting. She froze for a moment, then melted into me like it was the most natural thing in the world. Her arms wound around my neck, pulling me closer, and I was completely gone.

We kissed slowly, exploring each other, testing boundaries. I wanted all of her at once, and it took every ounce of self-discipline I possessed to not go further.

After hours or minutes—I wasn't sure because time lost all meaning with my axis completely tilted in this new world—she pulled back, smiling softly at me, her eyes dazzling under the starry sky.

"Took you long enough."

Before I could reply, she yanked me by my T-shirt and crashed her lips to mine. Not slow, not exploratory, she knew exactly what she wanted. And I wanted it too. Badly.

That night changed everything. I'd been terrified my feelings would ruin our friendship, only to realize her feelings were just as strong. From then on, we were together. There was no awkward transition, no questioning what we were—it was seamless. The only thing that changed was my relationship with her brothers, who weren't thrilled their buddy was now their sister's boyfriend. It took some time, but eventually they realized I was pathetically in love with her, that I wanted to marry her one day, even though we were so young.

Forever with Ellie felt destined. There wasn't a doubt in my mind she was the one. And while I still held strong to the belief we were forever, I couldn't ignore that something was going on with her. And I didn't have a good feeling about it.

We needed to talk before she left to go back to school. I wasn't going to let her go without understanding why she'd been distant since she had arrived. If I was being honest, it wasn't just this visit—she'd been acting strange for the past month. Little pieces of her had been slipping away, just beyond my reach, no matter how hard I tried to hold on.

After storming out of my dorm, I found her in the bathroom, hunched over the sink. Her hands gripped the edges of the counter like it was the only thing holding her up. When she looked at me in the mirror, her red, swollen eyes nearly stopped me in my tracks. I couldn't tell if she'd been crying, or puking, or both.

"What's wrong, Ellie girl?" I asked, my voice quiet, worried if I spoke too loudly she'd spook.

She shook her head, breaking eye contact. "I think I'm going to go," she murmured.

"Go?" I repeated, confused. "It's late. You're not feeling well. You're not driving anywhere tonight."

Her eyes darted around the room, looking anywhere but at me. Unable to stand the space between us, I wrapped her in my arms. I told myself it was to comfort her, but really, I was the one who needed the comfort, trying to hold on to her as best as I could.

Everyone warned us long distance would be hard, but fuck, it was so hard. Every other weekend, we traded off who would make the five-hour drive across the state. On top of being exhausting and expensive, it was stressful, juggling school on top of all of it. Every time we had to go our separate ways, I questioned if my scholarship was even worth it. Transferring schools and taking on a student loan seemed a lot easier than being away from each other. Even though I knew my parents were set on me staying and graduating from WSU, I'd already started looking into transferring. I couldn't do four years of this—we couldn't withstand it.

"Talk to me. I can't fix it if I don't know what's wrong." I held her tightly, breathing her in.

7

For a beat, the tension uncoiled from her, and she relaxed into me, only to stiffen back up just as quickly.

She pulled away and took a noticeable step back. "And that's the problem. You can't fix it, and I don't want you to."

"I don't understand." I raked a hand through my hair, wanting so badly to see things through her eyes.

"There's nothing to understand. I just—I just can't. I can't breathe." She took a deep, choking breath, her chest trembling between inhales.

I'd never seen her this way and it was terrifying. I went to rub her shoulder, trying to offer comfort, but she brushed me away.

She'd never resisted my touch. The sting of her rejection felt like a stab.

"Ellie, you're scaring me." My own voice shook. My entire body was shaking. I thought I knew everything about her. I'd spent years learning to decipher her veiled expressions, read between the lines, and see through her carefully constructed walls. I knew Ellie, but I didn't know *this* Ellie.

"Why don't you go lie down and rest, you're clearly not feeling well."

Her head snapped at me. "So now you think you can tell me what to do?"

Her tone was unrecognizable. She was a force, never one to back down, but we didn't speak to each other like this. This wasn't her. It wasn't us.

"Ellie, talk to me. Please." I stepped closer. "I want to understand. Help me understand so we can figure this out." Gathering her face in my hands, I stroked my thumbs over her tear-stained cheekbones. "Querida mía, let me in," I rasped.

Her eyes were pleading at me even if her body was retreating. A war was raging inside of her, but I was feeling more and more like the casualty.

Slipping away from me again, her expression hardened as

she moved away. I followed her back to my dorm room, my stomach sinking deeper with every step.

When she turned to face me, her glassy eyes were distant, looking at me, but not really.

"I can't do this anymore," she said quietly.

Her words hit like a punch, taking my breath. "What are you saying? Are you breaking up with me?" I said it almost like a joke, because it seemed ridiculous, despite my pulse heating in panic beneath my skin.

She didn't answer, but the slow nod of her head was deafening.

My voice cracked. "Is there someone else?"

Her eyes flashed to mine, red and full of hurt. "What?! No, never. There's no one else," she said firmly. "I just...I can't be with you. I need to be alone."

I couldn't process it. There was no world where Ellie and I weren't together.

But when I looked around my dorm, I saw it—her stuff was gone. Even the stuff she usually kept here. She'd packed while I wasn't paying attention, removing every trace of herself from my life. The necklace I bought her with our initials—the one she never took off—was sitting on my night-stand. This wasn't impulsive. She'd planned to leave. To leave me.

My blood turned to ice, the shock of what I was seeing—what I knew was happening without fully realizing it yet.

"I love you," I choked out, desperation creeping into my voice.

"I love you, too," she said with a quiver, heavy tears streaming down her face—dropping her head, still avoiding my gaze.

And then she walked out the door. I stood stunned, in disbelief at what had just happened.

By the time I came to my senses and chased after her, she

was already in her car. I banged on her window, begging her to stop, to stay, to explain. She didn't.

And just like that, she was gone.

I didn't know she would cut me out of her life completely. I didn't know the gravity of what had occurred.

Not yet.

Six years passed before I saw her again.

It would take another four years before I'd get the chance to fight for her. And this time, I wouldn't let her go.

CHAPTER 1

Elyse

THIS ISN'T PERSONAL

PRESENT

Some couples are built to stand the test of time; others remind me why I don't offer refunds. As much as I'd like to be proven wrong, these two are destined for the big D within five years, if not sooner—the big D being divorce, not dick.

It's not that I don't want to believe in them—it's just that my instincts, honed over time, are rarely ever wrong. One—his annoyingly affectionate nickname for her. Now, I am not a nickname hater; love a good nickname. But "baby" pronounced "bee bee" might be my thirteenth reason. It takes everything in me not to gag when I hear it. Two—she looks to him before answering any of my questions, like he's her keeper. I can't. What in *The Handmaid's Tale* is this shit? And finally, three—at the cake tasting, he broke the cardinal rule of feeding your partner cake. He smushed it in her face. Everyone, and I mean *everyone* knows it's the number one sign of a future divorce. I don't make the rules, but they never fail me.

"Thank you so much for suggesting this bakery, the cakes

were all delicious," Jenna, my client says as she clings to her fiancé Matt like a barnacle on a sinking ship.

"Good thing the pieces were small," he looks at Jenna with a misleading smile. "Wouldn't want you gaining any weight before the wedding."

I clamp down on my lips tightly to keep from screaming. Matt is the absolute worst. He was a douche in high school and clearly hasn't changed much since then.

Jenna giggles as if he said a joke and continues beaming at him with so much happiness, it makes me want to slap some sense into her. I don't, obviously. I am a professional.

After several years as a wedding planner, I've seen it all—including men who have no business getting married.

"You can't go wrong with Layered. They're the best in town for sure."

Matt checks his watch, and I don't miss the twitch in his hardened jaw, though Jenna's too busy mooning over him to notice.

"Baby, let's get going. I have that thing I need to get to."

My face involuntarily scrunches hearing "bee bee" again while Jenna's shoulders fall.

We were supposed to grab apps and drinks across the street. Either Matt has conveniently forgotten, or he's blatantly going against our plans.

Instead of bringing it up and making things awkward, I tell them both goodbye and give her a reassuring smile before we part ways.

The change in plans actually works better for my schedule. At the end of last year's wedding season, my trusted intern-turned-assistant, Bella, decided it was time to venture out on her own—which I fully supported—but the result has been a gaping hole, nearly impossible to fill. Bella ran all the administrative tasks, freeing me up to spend more time on designs and tending to my couples needs. I ended up hiring three interns to fill her role and it's been rough, to say the least. One of them—Faith, didn't even know how to use Word. I assumed they taught that in school.

In an attempt to get a handle on their lack of skills before my schedule gets out of hand, I put together a training packet and will be meeting with them later to go through it. I can't have interns who make my job harder once the season gets busy. But before that, I have a linen order to pickup for a micro wedding next week, a meeting with a seamstress because she made one of my bride's cry, and somehow I have to pick up my niece, Lily, from ballet and squeeze in grocery shopping.

With my mom recovering from a partial hysterectomy, I've taken it upon myself to shoulder some of the weight. My plan is to stock my parents' freezer with meals that will make life just a little bit easier while she heals—one less thing for them to worry about in the midst of it all.

In between everything, the day moves at a steady pace. The linen order was packaged and ready for pickup, the seamstress meeting went far more smoothly than expected, and I made it to ballet class right on time. With a few minutes to spare, I even swung by Novel Teas and Coffee—my sister Ariana's shop—to grab drinks for Lily and me. Since Lily's only six, her "coffee" was a hot chocolate, but I love making her feel like one of the girls. My brother Gavin, her dad, is raising her solo, so I take every chance to be the cool aunt. After dropping her off at home, happily sugared up, I hightailed it back to town.

Just as I'm about to pull into the parking lot of Harvest Grocers, red and blue lights flash in my rearview mirror. I keep driving, missing the turn in my distraction, even though there's no way they're for me. Continuing to drive, my eyes flick to the mirror, expecting to see the cruiser moving around me. It's not, it's still right on my tail.

You're fucking kidding me.

The siren goes off, and I let out a long exhale as I pull over.

Please don't be who I think it is.

My gaze rolls up toward the sky, begging in silent prayer that I'm being pulled over by literally anyone else. I wasn't even speeding and have no idea what's warranted me getting pulled over.

A thrum jumps in my neck as I wait with a held breath to see who's going to exit the patrol SUV.

Please. Please. Please.

The door swings open slowly before someone steps out. I desperately want to whip my head around to get a better look but force my eyes to remain trained on the rearview mirror instead. Unfortunately, what I manage to make out is confirmation enough. Olive skin, corded arms covered in tattoos, and that familiar, cocky walk.

Fuck me.

I steal a quick glance at my reflection, making sure my lipstick is in place and there's nothing in my teeth. I won't give him the upper hand, not even in something as trivial as my appearance.

His shadow looms over me as he waits for me to roll down my window.

With a few deep breaths, my disinterested expression is firmly in place and ready to face him.

Normally, I love how small Red Mountain is, but getting pulled over by my ex makes me wish it was much larger, lessening my chances of running into him. Ever.

I roll down my window at the same time that Dominic bends at the waist and leans his elbows over the door—his veiny arms practically taunting me. He's so close now I wish I didn't need oxygen to stay alive, because I just know the next time I risk an intake of air it's going to smell like him and wreck me.

14

"Look who it is," he says, humor lacing his words. The dusting of his breath warms my left cheek, sending an unwelcome trail of heat down the side of my neck.

He chuckles, likely amused at my refusal to look at him. "Still stubborn as ever, huh, Ellie girl?"

Wonderful. He finds this hilarious.

I don't.

And he really shouldn't call me that. It's too familiar.

"Is there a problem, officer?" My voice is dull and flat, hopefully proving how unaffected I am by his presence.

Because I totally am.

Reluctantly I turn my head, refusing to actually make eye contact, but I still notice his hand move to the silver star pinned to his chest. He taps the metal with his index finger.

"It's Deputy Alvarez, actually."

Fighting an eye roll, I breathe out an audibly annoyed sigh as I try to ignore the way blood is rapidly running through my veins.

"Okay then, *Deputy Alvarez*, is there a reason you pulled me over?"

He clears his throat, and then pauses, letting silence linger between us as the ghost of a smile plays on his lips. I hate it.

"You have a taillight out. Might want to get that fixed."

All this for a stupid taillight? Ridiculous. "Good to know." I reach for the gear shift, but the disapproving sound coming from Dominic stops me.

"You can't leave yet. I need your license and registration."

My head jerks at him. "Seriously?"

He nods, the corner of his mouth twitching as he stares at me. The air inside the car thickens, the space shrinking as his gaze holds steady, pressing in with a heaviness I can't escape. His eyes are hidden beneath sunglasses, and I can see my reflection in them. It's unsettling, like he can see more than I want to show. I need to get out of here. This is unbearable.

"Seriously. Have to follow procedure."

Quickly, I reach into my glove box for the registration and grab my license from my wallet, handing it to him in a way that prevents our hands from touching.

He shoots me a smug grin. "Be right back."

Once he's gone, I let myself collapse into the seat, my body sinking like the air's been knocked out of me. His scent lingers —a maddening blend, both new and familiar. It's so good, I can't decide if I want to breathe it in or hold my breath and suffocate instead. He wears a different cologne now, but he still smells like him—like cedarwood and soap—spicy, clean, and undeniably Dominic.

My hands clench at my sides, knuckles white, as memories claw their way to the surface—memories I've spent years trying to lock away. Being near him again is like standing on uneven ground, my footing slipping with every passing second. We've crossed paths more times than I'd prefer since he returned, but this is the first time it's been just the two of us. No buffer, no distractions, no audience.

Just those few minutes between us had felt too over-whelming. Now, the empty space he's left behind lingers with a gravity I'm trying my best to not acknowledge, but it clings to me like a second skin. It was easier to push him out of my mind when he wasn't at every corner I turned—he's inescapable.

Dominic moved back to our small town, Red Mountain, about a month ago. And true to form, had to make a big whoop about his return, showing up uninvited to my parents' anniversary party.

As the town's former golden boy, he's been welcomed back with open arms. The charming, state-winning quarter-back turned deputy sheriff.

Now, he's acting like he can just waltz back into my life like a decade hasn't passed since we've been anything more than strangers. I wish I could say I'm immune to him with years and distance having hardened me, but my pulse quickens in a way that betrays every lie I tell myself.

I think it's more of a muscle memory thing, like when someone has amnesia, but their body remembers how to do everything. That's all this is. That's all it can ever be.

Minutes pass before gravel crunches under steady steps, the closer it gets, the more anxious I feel.

He's holding my license and registration, but makes no move to hand it to me.

"Am I free to go now?"

Rather than answer me, he stays silent, his posture rigid, his stance unnervingly formal. It's almost as if he's slipped into another persona—detached, professional. This must be how he carries himself on duty. And fuck, is it hot. *Why is it so hot?* It shouldn't make my stomach flip. It definitely shouldn't make my skin tingle. And yet here I am, gripping the steering wheel so tightly, I'm surprised it hasn't cracked in my hands. I thought there was a universal rule that exes are supposed to get less attractive as the years go by.

Dominic didn't get the memo.

Clearing my throat, I shift in my seat, willing away the heat spreading across my chest.

"I don't have all day. Either give me a ticket or let me go." My bite is forced, lacking the grit I intended.

An unreadable expression twists his features, and he looks to either side before speaking, like he's checking to see if anyone is listening. He removes his sunglasses, slipping them into his front pocket where his name is stitched *D. Alvarez.*

"I'm going to need you to step out of the vehicle."

His already deep voice sounds foreign in the professional tone he's trying to exude.

My head falls back, colliding with the headrest, and a laugh barks out of me. It's unhinged and slightly manic sounding; I let it flow, nonetheless. I don't know what game he's trying to play, but if he meant to rile me up, he failed. He's acting like he's going to arrest me or something. Hell, this is the first time I've ever been pulled over. Apart from some stupid antics as a teenager, which Dominic was part of, I've never been in real trouble.

"Don't make this harder than it has to be, Elyse."

The last bits of my laughter bubble out, and I clear my throat to stop it completely. He called me *Elyse*. I don't think he's ever called me by my full name.

I make the mistake of meeting his stare, and he locks me in place as my stomach barrels down to the floorboards.

I've been doing so well—avoiding truly looking at him. Clinging to every shred of determination not to study him, not to sink into his eyes the way every instinct in me has begged to. But all that effort vanishes in a heartbeat.

Instantly, I'm hit with every detail of him at once. Deep brown eyes under dark, thick brows. There's the start of wrinkles on the outer edges, ones that weren't there ten years ago. His pupils are consuming all the bits of gold flecks that are normally present when they aren't so dilated. Smooth-shaven cheeks sit above faint creases on either side of his mouth, laugh lines likely caused from that contagious smile of his. There's a new scar above his upper lip—well new to me. And a gold chain is peeking out from beneath the collar of his uniform. Despite it all, he's just how I remember him, but filtered through age, with sharpened features, and somehow even more good-looking than he was when we were younger. Now that I've really looked at him, I don't want to look anywhere else. It's only the seriousness in his eyes that keeps me from getting lost in him completely.

"Ellie, please get out of the car." He sounds almost pleading, the strain in his voice louder than anything he's actually saying.

Is he not joking?

As if he can hear my thoughts, he slowly shakes his head. "It's not a joke. I'm wearing a body cam and the dash cam is recording."

Dumbfounded, I stare at him open-mouthed.

"Step out of the vehicle, ma'am," he says loudly, like it's for someone else.

My hands grip the steering wheel harder, tightening as his words sink in. He's serious. Dead serious. My heartbeat picks up, banging against my ribs, trying to escape, and I realize this isn't just Dominic trying to mess with me. I sit there, frozen, trying to convince myself this is some kind of elaborate prank, and the universe really isn't this cruel.

"Dominic." I force his name out like a plea, even though I hate the desperation in my voice. "You can't be serious. You're not actually going to do what I think you are, are you? You don't even have jurisdiction, this is a city road, and you're not a city cop."

A glimpse of something that looks like regret passes over his face, but it's gone before I can decipher it.

"Jurisdiction or not, I'm obligated to proceed." His tone is clipped, but his eyes are rapidly blinking, as if he's wrestling with every decision he's making. "I'll explain once you're out of the car."

"Explain now," I counter, my voice rising despite the lump forming in my throat. "This is ridiculous!"

"Ellie," he says softly, trying to soothe me, and that only makes it worse.

"Don't 'Ellie' me! You can't just—"

"Step out of the car," he cuts me off, firmer now, his gaze darting to the dash cam on the cruiser behind him. "Please."

And then it hits me—he has no choice. Whatever this is, it's bigger than just us.

Swallowing hard, I unbuckle my seatbelt and open the

door. The spring air smacks me as I step out, and I'm suddenly aware of how exposed I feel under his unwavering stare.

"Turn around," he says, reaching for the handcuffs on his belt.

My breath catches. "You're actually arresting me?"

He hits a switch on a device on his Kevlar vest—I'm assuming it's his body cam.

"We're muted, just for a minute. Can you keep your face neutral and calm while I explain?"

I nod wordlessly, my mind still spinning in shock.

"There's a bench warrant out for your arrest. You didn't show up for jury duty, and now I have no choice. I'm sorry, but I have to do this."

Fucking jury duty?!

"Do what you have to do," I force out through clenched teeth, knowing there's no point trying to argue with him. It's been years, but I think I still know him well enough to know he wouldn't be doing this unless he absolutely had to.

At least I hope.

His Adam's apple bobs in his throat. "Given our history, I can't show you any favoritism."

History. Such a simple word. It doesn't feel complex enough to explain *us*. I don't think a word exists to describe all the intricacies of who we've been to each other. Best friends— until it wasn't enough. Even before we crossed the line, our relationship was always more. Deeper. Undefinable. Dominic has been everything to me. And now...he's nothing.

The harshness in his jaw eases, and his mouth softens. "This isn't personal, querida mía."

My eyes fall shut, both hating and loving the old term of endearment. I was always *Ellie girl*, but *querida mía* came later. It came with the *more*.

He hesitates, only for a fraction of a second, but it's

enough for me to see the flare of guilt in his eyes before he switches off the mute on his body cam and moves behind me.

Fighting the shiver rolling over my body at his proximity, my gaze dips, unsure of where else to look except down at the cracked asphalt as the cold metal snaps around my wrists.

His thumb brushes lightly over the inside of my left wrist, so soft I almost question if I imagined it, but I'm certain of what I felt.

"Elyse Ledger, you're under arrest for failure to appear. You have the right to remain silent. Anything you say can and will be used against you in a court of law. You have the right to an attorney. If you cannot afford an attorney, one will be provided for you. Do you understand these rights as I've explained them?" His voice is monotone and distant. Robotic.

A surge of hot anger crashes through me. How dare he not only move back here, but then be the one to arrest me? Publicly. Humiliatingly.

None of this would be happening if he'd just stayed wherever the hell he's been all these years. The truth is, he's the last thing I need right now.

I whirl my head back to meet his gaze, my side-eye sharpening into a glare. His brows are tilted in, skin flushed like he's embarrassed.

The audacity.

If anyone has the right to be embarrassed in this situation, it's me.

"Just so you know, I'm never going to forgive you for this," I grind the words out embarrassingly shaky.

"Careful, Ellie girl. It's a crime to lie to a member of law enforcement."

CHAPTER 2

Elyse

REALLY HATE THE PEE

PRESENT

The Clore County Detention Center reeks of things I'd rather not identify—one smell, in particular, overpowering the rest. Why do the worst situations always smell like pee? A fuckboy's headboard-less bedroom, the backseat of a minivan, cheap motels, hospitals, and now jail—it's like life's most cringe-worthy moments come with their own urine-scented air freshener.

"You got a smoke on ya, sweetie?"

Sherry, a frequent flyer around these parts, asks while lounging on the bottom bunk.

She's in for slashing her husband's tires. Again. He has a bad habit of sticking his dick in women who aren't his wife. And Sherry is just crazy enough to destroy the only thing he actually loves, his big, red souped-up truck. I support it.

"Sorry Sherr, not on me." I unfold my arms and show her my open palms. "They took everything I had on hand when I was booked."

She shrugs and returns to eating her bologna sandwich.

I'm not a smoker, unless I've had a few drinks, and then I dabble. It's not the sexiest habit, but I don't really give a shit what the male gaze deems attractive. Most have proven they'll fuck anything with a hole, anyway.

As my fingers rub together, coincidentally craving the comfort of a cigarette, the electronic beep of our jail cell chimes and the door swings open.

When I notice who it is, I lock my arms over my chest and cross my legs, not bothering to look up and give Dominic the satisfaction of my attention.

After our incredibly silent drive to the county detention center, Dominic passed me off to another deputy without so much as a glance back. I didn't think I'd see him again until some unfortunate run-in in town.

But now he's here.

I may not be looking at him, but that doesn't mean I'm not taking in every detail through my periphery. He's practically under a spotlight with the harsh fluorescents shining down on him.

I guess the saying about a man in uniform is true—he wears it really well. Annoyingly well. He had to have gotten it tailored because no one else's fits as snug as his does—tight on his biceps, stretching taut across his broad chest, every ridge of his chiseled abdomen on full display. Tattoos litter his corded, muscular arms, some I recognize and some I don't. A pang hits my sternum, the unfamiliar tattoos a stark reminder that we don't know each other anymore.

He catches the corner of my gaze and, in return, gives me a subtle yet appreciative once-over. My skin warms under his stare, completely beyond my control.

Had I known I'd be spending my afternoon in jail, I probably would've chosen something slightly less revealing. The thin black slip dress paired with a blazer does little to hide my legs, given how short the hem is and how high the slit sits.

Quickly, I jerk my head away, desperate to regain some composure. This is exactly why we can't be around each other—our chemistry is combustible enough to ignite with the slightest spark.

"There was an initial bail set on your warrant. Lucky for you, someone paid it." I can hear his smile—know exactly how it curves on one side first. I hate that I still remember that.

I was expecting him to tell me I could make a phone call, not that I could leave.

The relief I should feel to be getting out of this cesspool of piss, is dimmed by the uneasy rolling of my stomach. If my bail was paid, that means Dominic called someone, and I'm not sure I want to find out who.

My forehead creases as I begrudgingly face him. "Who posted it? Don't tell me you called—"

"Elyse Meredith Ledger."

I close my eyes, a shudder running through me at the familiar voice in that familiar tone I thought I'd outgrown.

I'm going to kill him.

He couldn't have called one of my brothers—Gavin, Ethan, or even Shane? God knows they all owe me at least a favor or two.

A tall frame fills the doorway, his expression unreadable. Great. It's like my high school graduation night all over again, yet somehow more embarrassing.

I stand, squaring my shoulders. I'm not going to whither like a child. "Hi, Dad."

I highly doubt civilians are allowed in this part of the county jail, but rules have never really applied to Jack Ledger. Not because he demands special treatment, but because he's so highly regarded, he may as well be the mayor.

My dad is trying his best to give me his stern, disappointed look, but his lips keep tugging upward like he wants to laugh. I wasn't quite expecting *that* reaction.

At least someone finds this funny.

"Really, Elyse? Skipping out on jury duty, of all things?"

"I never received a summons," I defend.

He shakes his head, more amused than upset. He's gone soft in his older age. I'm also nearly thirty—far too old to be scolded. Yet that same surge of teenage dread, like I'm about to be grounded, still grips me the same.

I give Sherry a wave and join my dad on the other side of the jail cell—the free side.

"Thanks for calling me, son," my dad tells Dominic as they shake hands. He's always called him son, but that doesn't stop the word from sounding like a betrayal.

That's the problem with Dominic—everyone likes him, especially my family.

"Of course, Jack." Dominic nods at him, giving him the level of respect a soldier would give his superior, without all the formalities.

I can't even begin to explain how much I hate this entire situation. More than the pee, and I really, really hate the pee.

"We should go." My voice is overly-cheerful.

"How are your folks?" my dad asks Dominic, ignoring me.

Did he not hear me say we should leave?

I expect an animated, long-winded answer and instead, an eerie quiet settles, my dad waiting expectantly and Dominic falling silent.

Going against all my instincts, I risk a glance at Dominic, and my stomach plummets the moment our eyes lock.

His expression is pained, hands twisted, eyes hollow. Every single facet stealing more of my breath the longer he goes without speaking.

Something is wrong.

A tightness grabs hold of my chest, and my body tenses as a knot forms, rolling up my throat. Whatever he has to say, it's not good.

Fuck. Fuck. Fuck.

"My mom's doing okay," he says, with his eyes firmly fixed on me while speaking around the audible catch in his voice.

A gulping breath escapes me at the same moment the pieces fall together.

His dad.

A man I loved like a father.

My head is already shaking, refusing to accept the words I know are coming. I want to hit rewind, retreat into the blissful ignorance I had just moments ago.

Dominic clears his throat, an obvious mask to conceal his emotions. "My dad passed in January. Heart attack." It comes out strained, like it physically pains him to say it. And maybe it does, because *hearing* it hurts. It hurts everywhere, all at once, a thousand pinpricks, jabbing over and over again. Survivable, yet torturous.

Whether it's years of ingrained instinct from knowing each other since we were kids, or the fact that neither time nor distance has dulled our connection, every fractured piece of our past reconnects for a brief moment. I have to physically hold myself back from collapsing into his chest, from burying myself in him until there's no space left between us. Wanting to comfort him and being unable to feels like defying something written into my bones. Denying it is like trying to unlearn breathing.

"Why didn't you call me?" The accusation flies out of my mouth before I can think to hold it back.

Dominic's brows raise, eyes widening. I've shocked him—stunned him to the point that he blinks at me several times, his head rearing back slightly.

It's too late to take it back now, as much as I wish I could.

"Ellie—I—I—"

I put my hand up to stop him. "You don't owe me an explanation, I shouldn't have said that. I'm sorry."

He nods, clearly not wanting to press the matter.

In different circumstances, I wouldn't be so quick to eat my words, but I'm not such a monster I can't admit when I'm in the wrong. Why would he call me? It's not as if I've ever given any indication in the past ten years I want to hear from him.

Still, the relentless pounding of my heart against my chest leaves behind an ache—a hollow, empty void. It's as if an unwelcome seed is trying to take root—a seed that feels a lot like regret. But my reasons for breaking up with Dominic were valid then and remain valid now. Any hint of regret is likely grief manifesting where it doesn't belong. Letting go of Dominic meant losing his family, and after years of feeling like they were my family too, it was an entirely different kind of breakup to get over.

My dad, ever the perceptive one, saves us both from opening the Pandora's Box that is our complicated relationship. He comes forward and wraps Dominic in the kind of hug men so rarely receive.

"I'm sorry to hear that." His voice is muffled as he holds Dominic, whose body has gone rigid from the unexpected affection, until it seems he's reached the point he can no longer carry the weight of his grief. I watch as his shoulders sag, accepting the embrace.

Witnessing the strongest man I know comfort the boy I used to love is almost too much to bear. Watching them share in their mourning may be one of the few things sharp enough to chip away at the hardened shell I work so hard to maintain. I hate feelings. And most of all, I hate *feeling* feelings, because once you let one in, the rest find your cracks and seep through.

My vision blurs, moisture burning my eyes. I look away before the tears find their way out. Luckily, a few rapid blinks later, and they're dissolved. I rarely cry, and I'm not about to cry in front of Dominic. His emotions are warranted, he just

27

lost his dad. I don't deserve to cry over a man I haven't spoken to since we cut ties.

This day has taken so many unexpected turns; I'm ready to cocoon myself in bed until the universe balances out whatever this is. Because I sure as shit didn't wake up with jail and death on my bingo card for the day.

"I'll pay you back," I tell my dad as we pull out of the parking lot. We have to get my car at the impound lot, across town.

He nods easily, already past his emotional moment with Dominic. An expert at compartmentalizing—I would know since I inherited that useful little skill. "I'm not worried about it. It was only $100." Chuckling, he shakes his head. "Want to explain to me how you unknowingly had a bench warrant out for your arrest?"

"Apparently I didn't change my address from my college one, so the jury duty summons went there without me knowing anything about it."

He exhales deeply before his lips straighten into a thin line, and like a frayed string on an old sweater, the work I put in to turn my parents' opinion of me from wild teenager to dependable adult, starts to unravel. He's probably been sitting back and waiting for me to reveal I hadn't changed at all. My blood turns hot as it pumps through my veins. Years of work, years of proving myself. And for what? So one measly little arrest could undo it all. I'm not sure who I'm even mad at right now. Me? Dominic? Past me? My dad, for his obvious lack of faith in me? The world?

I'm going to go with Dominic because it's easier to be mad at him. It's actually better if I'm mad at him, because I can already feel myself sliding back into old patterns, and I can't go there. I refuse. Besides, the asshole arrested me. Asshole.

"Elle did you hear me?"

My dad stares at me like he's waiting for an answer to a question I clearly wasn't paying attention to. "I'm sorry, I zoned out. What were you saying?"

"Your mother. You should call her."

My back presses further into the seat, defeat finally overtaking my last bits of resilience. "You told her!" I blurt out, internally cringing. I'm not trying to sound like a petulant teenager, but the way my voice pitches up says otherwise.

He tosses me a scrunched expression. "We don't keep secrets. If I didn't tell her, someone else would have."

That's the shitty part about Red Mountain. Big enough to not feel suffocating, small enough that gossip is the town's number one form of entertainment.

"I'm sure she's thrilled," I tell him as I dig through the ziplock bag full of the stuff the jail confiscated from me. My phone is buried at the bottom.

The moment I pick up my phone, the screen lights up with a flood of notifications—texts, missed calls, emails, and more. Among them are half a dozen missed calls from a number I'm certain I'd already blocked. Not wanting to encourage any further contact, I block the number again. Ignoring the mess for now—I'll deal with it when I get home —I dial my mom.

She picks up after the first ring but stays quiet. Dragged out seconds go by before she speaks. "Oh, Elyse. You've had a day, haven't you?"

The breath I didn't realize I was holding, releases. I don't know what to say, I feel foolish. It was a stupid reason to be arrested, but in the end I feel a million times more stupid that I allowed it to happen in the first place. I'm organized, dependable—not someone who lets details like this slide and ends up screwed.

"Sorry, Mom."

She sighs a resigned, heavy breath, and I can picture the slow shake of her head, the unspoken disappointment flowing through the phone.

"You're an adult, there's nothing to apologize for."

"I'm sure you're ashamed of me. Embarrassed at the very least." I'm aware being a Ledger there's a certain expectation to uphold a good image. As one of the town's founding families, we're scrutinized under a much harsher lens.

"Elle, you're being too hard on yourself. Gossip will make the rounds, as it does, and then next week someone will cheat on their husband or steal mascara from the pharmacy, and you'll be old news."

"You think so?" I hate how weak I sound; how childish I feel.

She laughs lightly. "I know so." My dad gives my shoulder a squeeze, not that he can hear what she's saying but can probably guess. "Is it true? Is *he* the one who arrested you?"

At least she has the decency to pretend she doesn't already know. I let out a humorless laugh. "Yeah, believe me, no one is more shocked than I am."

The click of her tongue sounds. "He always did have a way of catching your attention."

"Mom," I warn. "That's not what that was." My cheeks heat in spite of my protest, defensiveness sending my heartbeat thrumming.

"Then what was it?" She's smiling, I can tell. Since when did my strict parents become so relaxed?

I groan, frustrated that I'll likely be retelling this story for years to come. "He was doing his job. Dominic and I are nothing. We don't even know each other anymore. If it wasn't him, it would've been some other cop."

"Hmm, I don't know about that. You two know each other better than anyone."

"Knew, Mom," I quip back. "Past tense."

"Elle, I—"

"We just got to the impound lot, I'll call you later."

"You—"

I hang up before she can finish her sentence. I don't know what she was going to say, but I'm sure I have no interest in hearing it.

"I can handle it from here," I tell my dad while I unbuckle.

"Alrighty," he sings. "I can stick around, make sure there aren't any hiccups."

I flash him an assuaging smile. "Not necessary, I've got it." I lean over and give his cheek a brief kiss. "Thanks Dad, I promise I'll pay you back this week."

He leaves with a wave, and I stay unmoving with my arms crossed until his car rounds the corner, out of sight. I wouldn't put it past him to turn around and spy, so I remain rooted for a few minutes longer before going inside the ramshackle building.

The impound lot is exactly as bleak as I imagined it would be—cracked pavement, a rusting chain-link fence, and an office that smells like stale coffee and old motor oil. The guy behind the counter doesn't look up when I walk in, too busy scrolling on his phone.

"Hi," I start, my voice tight with discomfort, "I'm here to pick up my car."

He glances up, his attention bouncing between me and the paperwork I'm sliding across the counter.

"Driver's license?"

I pull it from my wallet, and he snatches it up like I might bolt for the gate. After typing something into the computer, he nods. "Yeah, it's here. Black Mercedes, right?"

"That's the one," I reply, with a fake smile and a squeaky voice to match.

He practically throws my license back to me. Once I grab it, I start to move, but he lets out a whistle, raising his brows with a bored expression. "Not so fast there, Ma'am. Gotta pay up first."

After he tells me the fee, I'm nearly seeing red. I could buy a designer bag for what today has cost me.

Reluctantly, I hand over my credit card, ignoring his evil little smirk. This place is a rip-off, and he knows it. Seems proud of it, too.

He hands me my card back and jerks his thumb toward the yard. "You're clear. Spot 47. Keys are in it."

I push out the back exit, the heat of the afternoon sun beating down on me, burning past the layer of my blazer. Rows of cars stretch across the lot, each one covered in a thin coating of dust. Near the back, my black car waits, its once-sleek surface faded, now sinking into the bleakness that surrounds it.

The moment I reach it, I yank the door open, brushing away the grime on the handle. Sliding into the driver's seat, I slump back and sigh, closing my eyes. The last few hours blurring together like a fever dream.

But as I press the start button, the engine sputtering to life, my mind wanders back to Dominic—those deep, searching eyes, the way my name rolled off his lips like it still carried meaning, like I still mean something. My chest constricts, a twist of emotion settling in my ribs, impossible to swallow. With my fists clenched, my nails dig into my palms, as if the pain is enough to deter my intrusive thoughts.

Easing out of the lot, I pull onto the main road, exhaling with relief. At least now, I'm back in the driver's seat—literally and figuratively.

CHAPTER 3

Dominic

HUMBLE-BRAGGING ASSHOLE

PRESENT

I don't know which is worse—the dull ache behind my eyelids, a testament to a shit night's sleep, or the relentless throb in my cock from tossing and turning all night as my thoughts were consumed solely of Ellie.

Every time I closed my eyes, her piercing gaze would pull me back, a weave of desire and torment so tangled, I'm pretty sure it was her anger that turned me on. I couldn't get over how damn beautiful she looked—even pissed. Hell, maybe especially pissed, with her cheeks flushed and her voice cutting like a whip.

All these years later, and I'm still just as pathetic for her as I was when we were teenagers. I'm not sure what that says about me.

Rather than question my sanity this early in the morning, I groan and swing my legs out of bed, rubbing the sleep—or lack thereof—out of my face. Before standing, I work out the stiffness in my shoulder. The pain is always worse in the mornings, tender, like the wound is still fresh even though it's been months.

For a moment, as I sit on the edge of the bed, visions of the incident rotate through my mind. For some fucked up reason, it helps if I get it all out now—get it over with—rather than a memory hitting me when I need to be on my game. Sometimes a memory will hit me regardless, but this helps. Facing it head-on helps.

Breathing deeply, I take in my space, grounding myself. Slowly, the images fade into the distant reaches of my mind. Far enough away to move forward with enough clarity to get through the day.

The faint morning light spills through the makeshift curtains, painting the room in muted shades of gray. My bedroom is the only livable part of the house. Buying a fixer-upper seemed exciting at first—full of possibilities—but that excitement faded fast after my first night here. Growing up, my dad made renovations look easy, and I'm quickly realizing I didn't inherit his knack for it. Progress has been slower than I expected, the to-do list just keeps getting longer. But, I chose this place for a reason. It has history, and that makes all the hassle worth it.

My uniform hangs neatly on the chair by the window, a silent reminder that the world doesn't stop for sleepless nights or complicated ex-girlfriends. Nothing about this job gives a shit about what's going on inside your head. There isn't suddenly a lack of crime just because I'm distracted.

And yet, I wouldn't have it any other way. Even after leaving the chaos of Los Angeles for the sleepy calm of Red Mountain, the unpredictable nature of this job still sends a rush of adrenaline through me.

After a groggy, quick shower, I slip into my uniform, tugging my boots on with a groan. Ryker—the sheriff and an old buddy from high school—is going to take one look at me and know I didn't sleep a lick. Unfortunately for him, he can't afford to send me home because of it.

I grab my keys off the counter and head out, the crisp morning air nips at my skin, the scent of sour grapes infiltrating my nose. The smell brings on a wave of comforting nostalgia. Some things never change, even when it feels like everything has.

As I slide into my patrol SUV, I catch my reflection in the rearview mirror—dark circles under my eyes, my jaw set tight. I look like shit, feel like shit, and now I have to work a twelve hour shift masking all of it.

This job may not be as high-risk as my last one, but it only takes one misstep for things to take a turn. Still, in all my attempts to remain focused, as I start the engine and pull onto the road, Ellie's voice echoes in my head, so full of anger and hurt, I nearly broke protocol. *I'm never going to forgive you for this.*

I have no idea how I'm going to fix the mess I made yesterday. Is there even a way to apologize to someone after arresting them? Nothing I come up with seems good enough—but doing nothing feels just as wrong. I'm not sure I've made one right decision since moving back. Starting with the move itself —a choice I made in the aftermath of two life-altering events. Every day since, it's felt more and more like a lapse in judgment.

I'm not slipping into the job as easily as I thought I would have. Connecting with old friends has been more like a chore than anything else. And then there's Ellie. She can't stand me, can barely look at me.

Pulling her over was supposed to be funny—an icebreaker to get past her cold exterior. And in my defense, she really did have a taillight out. Having to fucking arrest her was not part of the plan.

I should've just let her go and ignored the bench warrant,

but I'm too much of a rule follower to let it slide, even for her. If she didn't already hate me, she sure as hell does now. Maybe coming back was a mistake, a romanticized idea I let get out of hand.

The scent of burnt coffee greets me as I step into the station, mingling with the hum of conversation and the faint clatter of keyboards. The station is lively, churning like it always is on a weekday morning. Ryker leans against the corner of the front desk, mug in hand, shooting the breeze with the public records clerk, Nicky. He grins when he spots me.

"Morning, Dom. You look like hell."

"Good morning to you, too," I reply, dropping my keys onto the communal hook. "Your coffee still taste like black tar?"

He raises his mug with a smirk. "Wouldn't have it any other way. Man's coffee, puts hair on your chest."

I glance toward the break room, debating whether to risk a cup or stick with water. Last time I had a cup of his lethal coffee it ripped my stomach to shreds. I have no idea how he drinks that poison.

"Alvarez!" a voice calls out. "You're late."

Turning, I see Deputy Morales standing by a cluster of filing cabinets, she's sorting through a stack of paperwork, her dark ponytail swaying as she moves. She casts me an overly bright smile, her cheeks looking slightly flushed. I'm surprised she's still here since her shift ended over an hour ago.

She was my FTO when I first started, AKA my babysitter, and I couldn't stand her. She lacks the concept of personal space, and her eager personality grated at me, especially in the mornings. Somehow, though, she's started worming her way under my skin and kind of growing on me. Kind of.

"On time isn't late," I say, snagging a donut from the box on the front desk. Some stereotypes exist for a reason, donuts included. But I'll be damned if I let them move my belt notch. I already increased my workouts when I realized how much more sedentary this job is compared to my last one. It might seem action-packed, but the reality is a lot of sitting around—way more than when I worked in L.A..

In a small town like Red Mountain, crime tends to be quieter, and the job moves at a slower pace. Most of what we deal with involves domestics, bar fights, or the occasional property crime. Anything within city limits is technically handled by the Red Mountain Police Department, but since we're the sheriff's office for the entire county, there's plenty of overlap.

"Any later and you'd miss out on the hot new case we just got," Morales shoots back. Her eyes widen to saucers as if she's trying to have a silent conversation with me, but I don't understand.

It's Clore County, how exciting can the case be?

Ryker steps closer, likely drawn by the tail end of Morales's words. The station isn't exactly spacious, and quiet conversations are nearly impossible. His shoulders straighten as his grin fades slightly. "She's not kidding. We've got something weird on our hands this morning. Might be your kind of thing."

I arch a brow, donut halfway to my mouth. "Define 'weird.'"

He gestures toward the hallway. "Better if you see for yourself. Team huddle in the training room at six thirty."

Glancing at the clock, I have just enough time to set my stuff down at my desk before the meeting starts. Normally, our huddles happen in the conference room. But if we're in the training room instead, it means one thing—all hands on deck. That space is double the size for a reason.

The door creaks open, and the low murmur of voices quiets as I step inside. There are two large TV screens on. One is displaying a map of Clore County, the other displaying an image of a parked vehicle in what looks like Juniper Bluffs. Morales follows close behind me, dropping a thin case file onto the conference table before taking a seat.

Uniformed bodies continue to filter in until it seems the room has reached its capacity.

Ryker clears his throat to get everyone's attention before nodding at Under Sheriff Doyle to proceed.

Doyle rises and walks to the front, standing at the podium. "We got a call from a camper at 5:00 a.m.," he begins, gesturing at the image with the vehicle. "Spotted a car abandoned near Juniper Bluffs hiking trail—doors unlocked, no sign of the owner. Looked like it had been there overnight."

He keeps talking as the case file makes its way around the room. When it reaches me, I scan the photos—a close-up of the weathered sedan parked at an odd angle on a dirt trail, and several shots of a woman running errands, seemingly unaware she was being photographed.

"Deputy Morales," Doyle calls out. "Can you tell us what was found in the trunk of the abandoned vehicle, since you were first on the scene?"

Morales lifts her chin, loving being the center of attention. "I was initially going to have the vehicle towed, but after doing a 360-degree walkaround, I noticed what appeared to be blood on the rear bumper and initiated a search. The trunk was unlocked. Along with the photographs in the case file, there was also a duffle bag containing duct tape, rope, and zip ties."

Is it suspicious? Yes. Does it scream foul play? Not necessarily. People have a tendency to see what they want to see—

without considering all the angles. So far, I'm intrigued. I'll admit that much.

Keeping my thoughts to myself, I glance around the room, trying to gauge reactions. Everyone is mostly stoic, hard to read. This could all mean nothing, but a jolt of excitement hits me regardless. I'll take anything even remotely different than our usual stack of cases.

At my last job, after years of working patrol and climbing the ranks, I had just passed my exam and completed the interview process to become an entry-level detective in the homicide unit. Little did I know, I'd be walking away from my dream job before I ever got a chance to do it.

"Sounds like someone's prepping for a DIY project," Deputy Cooke barks out with a laugh. A few of his buddies fist bump him. Idiots.

Morales breathes out an annoyed smile. "Except," she continues, an edge creeping into her voice, "that doesn't explain the photographs."

The disruptive deputies quiet down after Doyle pins them with a look. They wouldn't have said shit if a man had been speaking, but since Morales is a woman, the disrespect is second-nature to them. It's one of the reasons, despite how annoying she is, I can't fully dislike her. She already has it hard enough.

"Tell us more about the photos," I say, as all heads snap to me.

I've been fairly quiet since I started, so they're probably surprised to hear me speak, let alone speak out during a meeting.

Morales gives me a grateful smile. Using the remote, she starts flipping through the images, the ones from the case file, stopping on one of the same woman, except it's her photograph from the DMV.

"This is Victoria Delmar. Two months ago, she went

missing from Badger Canyon. Her family reported it within 24 hours, and they told BCPD she had a stalker. Prior to her disappearance, she made several attempts to file a report, but there was never enough evidence to proceed. It appears the reports weren't taken seriously, possibly due to her prior involvement in sex work. She hasn't been seen or heard from since."

The room falls silent. It's too soon to jump to conclusions, but I think we all know what this is starting to look like.

"Any thoughts, lateral?" Doyle asks.

Lateral.

I fucking hate that nickname. It's super original, considering I'm a lateral transfer. My previous agency would never refer to a fellow uniform that way, but it's a lot more of a frat-bro environment here than I was expecting. Pretty sure this is their version of hazing.

All eyes land on me, expectant—like I'm supposed to solve the case on the spot. That's the trouble with joining this station with my background. People assume I'm some kind of big shot. And that comes with a double-edged sword—some of my coworkers admire me; the rest can't stand me.

I'm not anyone special, but saying that out loud just makes me sound like a humble-bragging asshole. So I keep my mouth shut. Not that it's doing me much good.

I glance at the screen, where all the photos of Victoria are now displayed for everyone to see—Victoria at the grocery store, walking to her car, sitting at an outdoor café. The images feel invasive, like glimpsing into someone else's private life. There's a familiarity about her I can't wrap my head around. It makes my stomach sink. I'm sure I've never met her, yet if she's from around here, maybe I have. Regardless, something about this whole thing feels...off. I can't pinpoint it, but whatever it is, it isn't sitting well.

I look back at Doyle. "The evidence is pointing toward

this abandoned vehicle being tied to her disappearance. I'm assuming the plates were ran."

Ryker joins Doyle at the front. "That's where it gets trickier. The car's registered to a fake name, and we've got no ID on who actually left it there."

"So, what's our next move?" Morales asks to both Ryker and Doyle.

"Red Mountain PD is assisting C-Shift, as they canvass the area near the ridge," Ryker says. "Seeing if we can turn up any witnesses. Meanwhile, the evidence is headed to forensics. We're hoping the bag or the car itself gives us something to go on."

Jesus Christ, the last people who should be canvassing are the deputies on C-Shift. They just worked a 12-hour shift, and now they're expected to work OT on something this important. They're probably all exhausted. It's not my place, but some of the decisions this office makes are mind-boggling.

I shake my head while scrubbing a hand over my face, and continue to stare at the images on the screens. It seems almost too convenient for this to have all been found, with what looks like no attempt to conceal anything.

"What is it?" Ryker asks, noticing the questioning look on my face.

I hesitate, not wanting to overstep. I'm still new and there's a lot of politics at play. Ryker is an old friend, but not the kind of friend I kept in touch with. We ran in the same circle but were never particularly close. And now he's my boss.

"I don't know...doesn't it all feel a little fabricated?"

The atmosphere grows stilted, focus firmly on me.

"Keep going," Ryker insists.

My hand drags down my face again, nerves coursing through me. "It's just that, what year is it? Doesn't this all seem like an old *CSI* episode? Who still uses printed

41

photographs? And they conveniently left behind their 'stalker kit'? To me, it feels like a setup."

Ryker's brows furrow as he listens, clearly considering my take.

Morales nods in agreement, crossing her arms over her chest. I don't miss the eyes around the room that briefly flash to her cleavage. She leans forward, almost as if she's aware of it.

I keep my focus on Ryker.

"I get what you're saying," Ryker says finally. "The setup theory is one we've considered, but we can't rule out the possibility of it being real just yet. Sometimes a case can appear too neat, too convenient, but that doesn't necessarily mean it's fake. We need to look at the evidence objectively, keep an open mind."

Doyle steps in. "Agreed. We're not ruling anything out. But we have to be careful not to jump to conclusions. We need more evidence before we make any assumptions."

I nod, still suspicious. "I'm just worried that someone's trying to manipulate us. The timing of Victoria being missing at the same time a bag of photographs of her are found, the way everything's laid out—it just seems too perfect."

Ryker pauses a moment, staring at me with an unreadable expression. "It's a valid concern. We'll double-check everything, make sure we're not missing anything. But for now, we proceed as planned."

The meeting comes to a close, and everyone starts dispersing. As I move to stand, Morales claps me on the shoulder, her hand lingering a second too long. "Good eye Alvarez. I knew I liked you."

She saunters off, and I look around to see if anyone noticed our interaction.

Ryker taps my arm with the file in his hands. "Let's have a chat in my office."

I freeze, unsure if it's a good thing or a bad thing that he wants to meet. I answer with a nod before he exits the training room.

Cooke and Deputy Gerard—one of Cooke's buddies— walk out in front of me. Gerard whispers something that sounds a lot like "show off", eliciting a hearty chuckle from Cooke.

Dicks.

I should've just kept my mouth shut, instead I got carried away.

My heart thrashes in my chest as I make my way to Ryker's office. I'm either about to be reprimanded or praised. With Ryker, you can never tell.

"Is it true you had to arrest Elyse?" Ryker asks, as I take the seat across from him.

He's asking like he doesn't already know the answer, holding back a laugh.

Since the door is closed and it's just us two, I shoot a glare at him, not bothering to hide my irritation.

"You're an asshole," I say under my breath, laughing.

His head falls back, a deep chuckle rumbling out of him. "I just can't believe you did it. You could've let her go as a favor and then ran it by me. It's not like I'm worried she'll skip town."

I'm used to following the rules by the book. The casual- ness of this department is still something I'm getting used to, and it didn't even occur to me I had the option to let her go. It goes directly against procedure to let someone go with an active warrant unless there are extenuating circumstances. In this case, there weren't.

I should've called him, then maybe Elyse wouldn't completely hate me.

Fuck, I'm an idiot. I panicked the second the MDT flagged her name after I ran her license. She looked so damn beautiful, my brain short-circuited. I was running on autopilot. And maybe some messed-up part of me liked having an excuse to touch her, to pull her in close.

She was mad as hell, but the moment I laid a hand on her, goosebumps rose on her skin. She still reacted to me. And that alone? That was enough to spark a little hope.

"I didn't consider involving you. I should have."

His lips curl up in a condescending smile. His politician's smile.

"Well, hopefully there isn't a next time, but just know you can always come to me."

This is why I'm never sure which Ryker I'm going to get. Ryker, my buddy or Ryker, Sheriff Tapert. The line gets blurrier and blurrier.

Before I can respond, there's a knock on the door. In walks Detective Sergeant Vorheis.

I stand and greet him, shaking his hand.

Ryker didn't mention Vorheis would be joining us. I can't even begin to think what this could be about, I doubt Vorheis knows who I am, seeing as we've never interacted.

Ryker gestures for him to take the seat next to mine.

"Well, I'm sure you're wondering what this is about," Ryker starts.

"Just a bit." I glance over at Vorheis, assuming he's going to explain.

"I spoke with your old captain," Vorheis says, angling toward me. "He had nothing but high praises to say about you. Said you were on track to becoming a detective."

I nod, still unsure of where this is going. "That's correct."

"Given today's event's, we could really use the extra

support. Someone with your experience might be just what we need to not let this case go cold. How would you feel about temporarily transferring over to the detective's unit while we work the Delmar Case? Unfortunately, due to budget constraints this doesn't come with a pay increase, but it'll be taken into consideration next time the unit has an opening for a detective, and of course during your annual review."

More work and no extra pay? Most people would turn that down. I'm not most people.

Maybe this is what I need to start turning things around and actually make a life for myself here. I've been so focused on trying to repair the past. Somewhere along the line, I forgot about my future.

"I'd say it sounds like a very enticing offer." My eyes flit to Ryker, who looks eager for my answer. "And I'd be honored to assist on the case."

An hour later, I'm so engrossed in finishing up paperwork from Elyse's arrest, it isn't until Morales's shadow casts behind me that I notice she's still at the station.

"Heard about your promotion," she whisper-sings before hopping up on the edge of my desk, her ass way too close to my keyboard.

"That was fast," I mutter, sliding back in my chair to put some distance between us.

I haven't said a word to anyone yet, so I'm not sure how she found out.

"Nicky heard it from Vorheis and then told me." She looks around to see if anyone is listening. "Don't worry, I won't say anything."

I'm not trying to keep it a secret, it'll get out eventually I just haven't really found my spot within the group yet, and feel weird announcing anything.

CHAPTER 4

Elyse

FULL-ON CUFFS

PRESENT

I drag myself into work, still feeling exhausted from yesterday's shit show.

My office sits on the second floor of my family's winery, Ledger Estate Winery and Vineyards, tucked near the balcony of the ballroom. Instead of my usual route through the main entrance, I slip in through the back, wearing my most over-sized sunglasses, as if they will somehow disguise me. I'd rather not deal with the staff's curious looks—or worse, their questions—after the rumor mill has no doubt been churning about my arrest.

Once I reach the second floor, I make sure to steer clear of Ethan's side of the office. I really don't have it in me to sit through one of my brother's lectures.

Setting my bag on the desk, I roll my shoulders, the tension from the last twenty-four hours refusing to ease. It's going to be a long day. But before I can power up my laptop, the faint sound of footsteps approaching makes me pause.

"Morning, Elyse!" Faith's voice cuts through the silence, a

wide grin on her face. My other two interns, Ben and Paisley, follow behind her, all three of them looking far too chipper for this early hour.

"Morning, guys." I force a smile, bracing myself for what's coming. These kids have been a handful, but they mean well. And I forgot, Fridays are when they spend the entire morning in the office. "What's up?"

Faith smirks and nods toward my desk. "Notice anything different?"

I furrow my brows in confusion, roaming my eyes across the wooden desk. "Why? What did you guys do?"

Paisley laughs, shaking her head. "To your left."

And that's when I see it, my eyes snag on it, not sure if I should be embarrassed or impressed.

It's a framed copy of my mugshot sitting amongst the cluster of family photographs I have displayed. How they managed to get it so quickly is beyond me. I doubt it's even hit public records yet. I pluck it, staring at it more closely. My bright red lipstick only draws more attention to the corner of my mouth lifting in a *fuck you* smirk. It's got that messy, early-2000s celebrity mugshot vibe—and I kind of love it. For as pissed off as I was about the whole thing, I actually look pretty good.

"Oh my gosh." I turn back to them, trying to keep my voice stern, but my lips twitch despite myself.

Faith's smile widens. "We thought you'd appreciate some humor after yesterday's...events."

Ben snickers, leaning against the doorframe. "My cousin Nicky works for the sheriff's office; she did me a solid."

Well, that explains how they were able to get ahold of the picture so quickly.

Paisley chuckles. "Plus, it's kind of iconic now. I mean, you look like a Hollywood actress."

I shake my head, trying not to smile. "You guys got me," I admit.

I'm almost thankful they broke the ice. The last thing I'm in the mood for is explaining every detail of what occurred. I'm glad they're lightening the mood. After all, they could've been annoying about it, but they chose to playfully tease me instead.

I laugh, setting the picture down. "It's creative, I'll give you that."

The irony of it sitting between my college graduation photo and a family portrait from a charity gala the winery hosted—forever the bad seed in my family, no matter how hard I try to hide it.

"Oh, and these came for you." Ben hands me a vase of red roses. My favorite.

I set them down and immediately grab the card nestled in the arrangement. I don't often get flower deliveries.

The card reads: "Thinking of you. S."

S?

I have to think for a moment, and then laugh for not realizing it sooner.

"Who are they from? Secret admirer?" Faith asks.

"My best friend, Scottie. She's just being a brat."

I'll have to remember to text her later, but right now I need to get into work mode.

To keep the interns from getting further distracted by my embarrassing arrest, I hand them the training packets I meant to give out yesterday. That should keep them preoccupied for the time being—my brain is too scattered to dole out assignments.

They head back to their desks and get to work before leaving for their afternoon classes at the local community college.

Meanwhile, I spend the next few hours buried in mindless

tasks, my inbox overflowing with client inquiries and questions from vendors. We're one of the only wedding venues in the area to offer full planning services—something I implemented when I took over. Most venues only provide a day-of coordinator, making Ledger one of the more desirable places to host a wedding. With it being nearly wedding season, it seems everyone picked today to start their planning in earnest. I'm answering emails, confirming appointments, and sorting through vendor contracts when the phone rings.

"Elyse Ledger, Event Coordinator."

"Hi, it's me." I immediately recognize Marisa's voice. She's my brother, Ethan's girlfriend, but she was my friend first, so I still claim her.

My forehead creases. "Why are you calling my work phone?"

"I tried your cell, you didn't answer and your voicemail box is full."

Picking up my phone, I notice it's on silent and littered with missed calls. Fuck me. I must've switched it to silent after everyone kept blowing me up last night—everyone being my siblings and Scottie because they lost their minds when they heard about the arrest.

"Oh, sorry. What's up?"

"I'm picking up lunch at the diner for Ethan and wondered if you want me to grab you something. My treat."

Marisa doesn't have a sly bone in her body. "Are you offering out of kindness or because you want details?"

She laughs. "Can it be both?"

Snorting, I shake my head. "Sure. Get me the club sandwich with a side salad."

Thirty minutes later, Marisa waltzes in with a takeout bag in tow, her lipstick smeared, hair tangled, and her top looks twisted. She obviously stopped by Ethan's office first. I don't even want to think about what those two were up to. She's already told me more than I wish I knew.

She notices my pinched face as she hands me the bag. "What? Do I have something on my face?"

I huff a laugh. "Yeah, my brother's spit."

After settling in the chair across from me, she whips out a compact, fixing her makeup and smoothing her hair. "Sorry." She giggles, not looking the least bit sorry. "We got a little caught up."

"I don't need to know," I sing-song.

Although acting annoyed, I'm actually very happy for them. If it weren't for me, they'd never be together. When Marisa temporarily moved to Red Mountain from Seattle, she ended up stuck living next door to my grumpy-ass brother. I saw the sparks between them immediately, but they took a while to catch on. All the tiptoeing those two were doing around each other was driving me up a wall, so I used my Cupid powers for good and encouraged them along. Now, they're madly in love, and my punishment is having to hear all the sordid stories.

Marisa eyes me suspiciously as I dig into my sandwich, her lips curling into a smirk. "So...are we going to ignore the fact that you were arrested yesterday?"

I freeze, the lettuce from my club sandwich halfway to my mouth. "Just diving right in, aren't you? This is off the record, right?"

Marisa works for the *Red Mountain Herald*, so it's not insensitive of me to ask. Her eyes roll, annoyed.

"Like I would ever do that to you. Of course it's off the record, it's always off the record."

"Fine," I relent with a sigh, knowing if I don't tell her, she'll eventually drag it out of me.

She claps excitedly. "Now, spill. What did you do to get hauled off in handcuffs?"

I groan, setting the sandwich down and rubbing the bridge of my nose. "It wasn't even a real arrest. There was a bench warrant because I missed a jury duty summons. My address was outdated—not exactly scandalous behavior."

Marisa gasps dramatically, clutching imaginary pearls. "Elyse Ledger, hardened criminal. You would've been a hot commodity on one of those date-a-prisoner sites."

"Shut up," I mutter, fighting a laugh as I take a generous bite, buying myself time before I need to speak. "It was a mistake. I'll see the judge soon, and I'm sure it'll be a fine or some expedited jury duty assignment. I'm not a criminal."

"But Dom was the one who arrested you?" she asks, her eyes lighting up with glee. "Like, full-on cuffs and everything?"

I let out a breath, deeply regretting this conversation. After Dominic crashed my parents' anniversary celebration last month, Marisa was full of questions. A girl's night and a few bottles of wine later, and she's now fully up to speed on our very long history. She even managed to convince my mom to whip out some old photos at a recent family dinner, and I'm almost positive she pocketed the one of me in my cheerleading uniform and Dominic in his football one. So high school it's disgusting.

"Yes, full-on cuffs. It was humiliating. He put me in the back of his cruiser and everything."

Marisa lets out an amused laugh, covering her mouth as she chews. "Oh my God, you must've been losing your mind."

"You have no idea," I say, shaking my head. "After I was booked, they threw me in a holding cell with Slashing Sherry. All I could think was, 'This cannot be my life right now.'"

She grins wickedly, resting her chin in her hands. "I can't get over the fact that he actually did it. Do you think he planned it or something to get your attention?"

I glare at her with a deadpan expression. "He looked just as surprised as I was about the warrant. I doubt he planned it, and I doubt he wants my attention."

"Oh, I don't know," she says dripping with false innocence. "I think he wants more than your attention."

I groan again, louder this time. "You're just as bad as my mother. There's nothing there. Ancient history."

Marisa's smirk grows impossibly wider. "You know, he was the one who called Ethan to tell him what happened. Then Ethan told him to call Jack and fill him in."

"So much for sibling code," I mutter before taking another bite, busying myself with my food.

We sit in comfortable silence for a stretch, both of us focused on our meals. If I focus on my food, then I won't think about him. I won't replay in my head over and over again the feel of his warm sturdy hands, his breath on my skin, how he felt familiar and new all at once. I don't know why he moved back, but I've been off-balance ever since. There was a time when I couldn't imagine living without him, until I forced myself to. But now? Living in the same town as nothing but strangers, with enough history to fill a text-book, it's somehow worse.

Marisa's face flushes as she looks at me through her lashes, her phone clutched in her hands. So much for comfortable silence.

"Was it hot...when he cuffed you?" she whispers, glancing at the doorway as if someone might hear her.

I drop my head into my hands, a combination of frustration and wanting to laugh, because what the hell kind of question is that?

"No, it's not like I was checking him out while he was *arresting* me!"

She giggles and turns her phone to face me. On it are several different kinds of handcuffs. The furry kind. The kind not used by cops.

That's when it dawns on me—she's asking for herself.

"How many times do I have to remind you to not tell me about the freaky shit you guys are into? I'd rather not lose my lunch."

She snickers. "It's not my fault my only friends here are related to my boyfriend. You guys just need to suck it up."

"Whatever." I roll my eyes at her, shaking my head with a laugh.

Obviously, I was too angry with Dominic to think beyond the shock of being arrested, but later that night, once I was home, yeah...it was pretty hot. Not that I'll ever admit it out loud. I hate myself for that. And I hate myself even more that I thought about it while using one of the several battery powered boyfriends I keep in my nightstand. There's something seriously wrong with me.

Marisa raises a brow at me, her tone losing its teasing edge. "You know, if he still cared enough to call someone for you, maybe it's not exactly ancient history. He could've just let you rot. Who knows how long it would've taken for them to give you your one phone call if he hadn't been there?"

She's trying to make him seem like the hero, when really I should've been allowed a phone call after I was processed, but for whatever reason a deputy took me straight back to a cell. I'm not super well-versed in criminal law, but I know that much at least. Being a documentary connoisseur like myself will teach you a thing or two.

Marisa is being way too reasonable and logical about this whole thing, when I would much rather stew about it until I turn bitter and no longer fantasize about Dominic in that skin-tight uniform. It's like he knows he looks good in it. If she keeps talking, my already thin resolve will crumble—and I can't let that happen.

"I'm sure Ethan is super sad that you're with me instead of him. Maybe you should go cheer him up."

Her lips purse slightly as she levels me with a pointed stare, but she's smart enough to take the hint, and stands to leave. "Alright, I'll leave you alone."

"Bye, Marisa." I flash her a smile.

She stands in the doorway, her probing gaze seeing beyond my false easiness. "If the roles were reversed, you would be relentless."

As she turns to go down the hallway, I shout out, "good thing you're not me, then!"

Rather than be alone with my thoughts, I text Scottie.

> Thank you for the flowers!!

SCOTTIE
What flowers?

> The roses…

SCOTTIE
Babe I didn't send you any flowers. Must be from a secret admirer 😉

My stomach sinks. That's not exactly what I wanted to hear. Fuck.

> Or your prison lover 😒

The front door clicks shut behind me, the sound bouncing off the quiet walls of my townhouse. I press my back against it, exhaling a dragged, quiet breath as the long day finally slips from my shoulders. Home. At last.

I drop my bag onto the entry table, wincing as it tips over, spilling its contents—several lip products, contracts, bridal magazines, a half-empty bottle of ibuprofen.

Whatever. I'm too tired to care.

Kicking off my heels, I leave them where they land and head straight to the kitchen. It's almost a ritual at this point: pour a glass of wine, microwave whatever leftovers I can scrounge up, and pretend I don't mind eating alone. Tonight's gourmet feast is two-day-old pasta and a wilted salad that should've been thrown out yesterday.

I rest against the counter as the microwave roars, staring out the window at the quiet street below. The glow of the corner lamppost drapes across the pavement, illuminating the row of small shops closed for the evening. Sagebrush Diner, Layered Bakery, Trove and Treasure Antiques—they all look like they belong on a postcard. The kind people send from charming little towns where everyone knows everyone, and no one is lonely.

Lonely is a feeling I'm all too familiar with—it's my normal. I'm perpetually dateless for big events. Having given up on dating after realizing I'd be resigned to a dating pool filled with incels living in their mom's basements, guys I grew up with who peaked in high school, and divorcés looking for a wife to take care of them.

On occasion, I'll entertain a casual fling, but only long enough to scratch the itch, and then I'm done. I like being alone. I like that my choices are my own, and I never have to defend or explain why I needed to order sushi and *Taco Bell* in one night.

But for every good day alone, it only takes one bad one to derail me. To make me question all the choices I've made leading up to this point in my life. And lately? It's been more often than not.

Everything is too quiet, too still. I can see through the windows of a wine bar across the street where a couple lingers over a cheeseboard. Outside of it, there's a bench where teenagers are hanging out, laughing and scrolling through their phones. Beside them, the darkened windows of Wildflower Bookshop stand, still smelling like old pages and weathered wood despite a recent remodel. It's picturesque. Perfect, even.

And yet, all I feel is how small it all is. How big the empty silence feels in comparison.

By the time the microwave beeps, I'm already regretting not stopping for something fresh on the way home. I eat standing up, fork in one hand, wine glass in the other, flipping through emails on my phone between sips and bites.

Another bride wants to change her floral arrangements—again. The mother of a groom has questions about seating charts, which really means she wants me to referee a family feud. And my favorite—a last-minute cancellation from a DJ who "apologizes for the inconvenience."

I close my phone with a sigh and set it on the counter. For all its chaos, I love my job. But sometimes, it feels like everyone else is celebrating something—love, family, milestones—and I'm just the facilitator. I make the magic happen, but never get to actually experience it for myself.

After finishing my sad excuse for a dinner, I shuffle into the living room and sink onto the couch. My feet throb from hours in heels, and I stretch them out, wiggling my toes like it'll somehow undo the damage.

The remote sits on the coffee table next to a stack of new books I wish I could dive into if my eyes weren't so dry and tired. I know if I turn on the TV, I'll fall asleep halfway through whatever I'm watching. I grab it anyway, flipping aimlessly through streaming services, the silence is unbearable. Romance movies, wedding shows, reality dramas about couples finding love—it's like the universe is taunting me.

I settle on a documentary about a woman who killed her

husband, something neutral and unromantic. As the narrator drones on, I'm reminded of my jail cellmate and wonder if I'll ever see her in a documentary one day.

Glancing at the empty spot on the couch next to me, for a second, I imagine what it would be like to come home to someone. To share the leftover pasta, complain about work, and laugh about all my weird work emergencies.

Shaking my head, I push the thought away, fixing my gaze back to the TV. Not sure where that came from.

When even the wife's murderous confession can't grab my attention, I reach for my phone, needing a change of plans.

Ignoring the string of missed calls from a number I don't recognize again, I send a message in the group chat with my sisters, our cousin Tawny, and Marisa, to see if anyone's up for a drink at The Jackalope. Sometimes, being out in a crowd helps quiet my overactive mind, offering a welcome escape from the solitude of my townhouse.

> Anyone free for a drink? On me.

LAYLA

Ugh wish I could. I have a practicum to study for ☹

ARIANA

I'm already in bed for the night. Sorry Elle ☺

MARISA

We're getting ready for bed. Rain check?

TAWNY

Girl, I'm too old and tired.

With no replies worth following up on, I block the unknown number and flip my phone over, trying to return my focus on the documentary. Though, I'm quickly realizing it was a mistake to put this on when there's nothing but men in uniform all over the screen. Great, like I need yet another reminder. I let out something close to a growl and flick the TV off.

Padding to the kitchen, I refill my wine glass to the brim, put my earbuds in, and slip into my pajamas before getting in bed. Who needs men, anyway? Not when there's an endless supply of smutty audiobooks and wine to keep me company.

CHAPTER 5

Dominic

FUCK IT

PRESENT

Harvest Grocers hasn't changed a bit, and I'm not sure that's a good thing. The place is definitely in need of a face-lift. Cracked tiles, outdated signage, and the same cashier that has been working here since I was a kid.

I push the cart down the canned food aisle, eyes scanning the shelves for something that looks appetizing. With a non-working kitchen, I'm limited to a mini fridge and a microwave.

As I turn the corner, I nearly bump into someone's cart. "Sorry," I say automatically, glancing up—and freeze.

"Look who it is," Leanne Ledger greets me with a warm smile, the kind only a mom could manage. Her cart is full, overflowing with fresh produce and a bouquet of daisies poking out the top. Jack stands beside her with his arm looped around her lower back, like he's holding her steady.

"Leanne." I nod at Jack. "Jack, good to see you again."

Jack nods back and Leanne comes forward, walking carefully, and wraps me in a hug. As she pulls away, she grabs hold of my shoulders. "I probably look breakable right now, just recovering from a minor surgery."

"You look great, Leanne." She smiles and blushes, reminding me of a time when my compliments used to emit the same reaction from her daughter.

Her smile evens out, turning down at the corners as she tilts her head slightly. "I heard about your dad. I'm so sorry. He was a good man."

"Thank you." My throat begins to tighten. "I appreciate that."

Will the day ever come that I'm not on the edge of a breakdown any time someone mentions my dad? People say time makes it easier, but if anything, it continues to feel worse and worse.

Leanne steps back, returning to stand at the cart. "Next time you talk to your mom, would you ask her if it's okay if I reach out? It's been so long since we last spoke, but we used to be great friends when you guys lived next door."

"I'm sure she'd love to hear from you."

She hesitates for a moment, exchanging a glance with Jack. "You know, we're having our usual Sunday dinner tonight. You should come."

The invitation catches me off guard. "I...I don't know if that's a good idea." My brain immediately flashes to Ellie, and I can't decide if she'd be shocked or more irritated to see me sitting at her family's table. Probably both. "I'm sure Jack filled you in on the incident that occurred..." I trail off, embarrassed to even bring it up.

She laughs and waves her hand through the air, her smile widening just slightly. "Oh, don't worry about Elyse," she says dismissively. "She'll be fine. Besides, the guys would love to see you."

Ellie's brothers may have been my friends at one point, but they'll always have their sister's back. I wouldn't be surprised if they gave me the cold shoulder. Ethan is the only one who's been mildly welcoming since I moved back.

I raise an eyebrow, skeptical. "Are you sure about that?"

"Of course," she insists, as if it's the most obvious thing in the world. "You've always been welcome. That hasn't changed."

I'm not so sure Ellie would agree with that sentiment, but Leanne's expression leaves no room for argument.

"I'll think about it," I say finally, which is code for probably not.

"Good," she says, patting my arm lightly before pushing her cart past me while Jack offers me a parting nod. "Dinner's at five. You know the address."

I stand there for a moment, watching her and Jack walk away, the scent of daisies lingering in the air. Part of me feels like a teenager again, awkwardly navigating my way through the Ledger family's orbit. And part of me wonders if showing up at Sunday dinner isn't the worst idea after all.

The groceries I bought earlier still sit on the makeshift counter, a slab of plywood perched on cinder blocks. I only put away the two perishable items I bought, and the rest I was too lazy to deal with. It's not as if I have cabinets anyway. Glancing around at my half-gutted kitchen, I take in the disaster that it is. The drywall is exposed in patches, wires snake out from where outlets should be, and a stack of cabinets in parts leans against the far wall.

The place looks more like a construction zone than a home. It was supposed to be a project to get buried in, a way to keep my hands busy after my dad died. Something to fix when I couldn't fix anything else. Only now, almost two months later, the kitchen still looks like this, and I can't remember the last time I cooked a real meal.

I pull out the ingredients to make a sandwich for dinner— bread, deli turkey, and a six-pack of beer. Not exactly the most nutritious thing I've ever consumed, but then again, beggars can't be choosers. After cracking open a beer, I hold it to my lips, debating on whether I even want it or not. None of this shit sounds appetizing, beer included.

Instead, I set the can down and lean against the plywood counter, letting out a breath as I put together the sandwich. This house was supposed to be a step forward, a fresh start, but all I've managed to do is collect more unfinished projects. Leanne's voice replays in my head. *You've always been welcome. That hasn't changed.*

The idea of Sunday dinner at the Ledger's stirs something in my chest—nostalgia, maybe, or just dread. Nostalgia for the way it used to feel like family. Dread because I know Ellie will be upset by my presence.

I bite into the dry turkey sandwich and stare at the hole in the drywall above the sink, my mind already playing out the scene. Me, walking into their dining room like a decade hasn't passed since I've been there. Leanne greeting me with a hug, Jack with a clap on the back. And Ellie, shooting me a death glare, or worse, being perfectly polite. Lately, I never know which version of her I'm going to get. It's never the good one, that's for sure. After the arrest, I'm not sure I'll ever be graced with her good side again.

I take another unsatisfying bite and toss it back down on the paper plate, abandoning it, and walking into what's supposed to be the living room. Right now, the only furniture is a camping chair and an oversized, mounted TV. Fuck, this place is depressing as hell.

I can either spend the rest of my night working on this shit show, or I can go face the other mess I'm trying to repair.

Fuck it.

I'm going, and Ellie is just going to have to deal with it. If I have any chance of getting past the walls she's built up, I'm going to have to do things that make us uncomfortable. She needs to know I'm not going anywhere.

CHAPTER 6

Elyse

WHOLLY UNPREPARED

PRESENT

S undays at my parents' house always feel the same, same people, same rotation of meals, same everything. But not this time—this time Shane is the one behind the stove instead of my mom. He never thought he'd see the day, and I can tell my mom is hating every minute of it. Not because Shane is a bad cook—he's actually amazing, classically trained and all—but because she always has to be in control, and right now she can't be. Though, she did manage to convince my dad to take her grocery shopping in an attempt to cook tonight. We put a stop to that quicker than she could crank on the stove.

She's been sulking about it ever since, shooting mom death glares our way.

The whole house smells like roasted chicken and fresh baked bread, with a hint of sweetness from whatever dessert Shane has going in the oven.

"What did you make?" I ask Shane as I ruffle his hair.

He shoos my hand away. "Bruh! Watch the hair."

"I didn't realize you were so vain." I tease. "Why even try? We both know Gavin is the one who inherited Dad's good hair."

At the same time, we both turn to look at an oblivious Gavin, whose dark brown, shiny, locks are pulled back into a haphazard low bun. It's honestly not even fair, he probably uses off-brand shampoo without conditioner. Genetics are such a bitch.

Gavin catches us both staring. "Why are you guys looking at me like that?"

"No reason," we say in unison.

His nose scrunches. "You guys are weirdos."

Gavin walks away and scoops Lily up, slinging her on his back for a piggyback ride. Her loud giggles fade, as they wander outside.

"I made a spatchcock roasted chicken, herby focaccia, and roasted garlic parmesan asparagus," Shane finally answers, speaking animatedly as he points to the dishes.

He starts droning on about the dessert, but I tune him out as I open the freezer. Due to my untimely arrest, I never did get around to making those freezer meals I'd planned on. I expect to find it empty, with maybe a few packages of random frozen vegetables, but instead find it stocked to the brim with various freezer bags and meal prep containers.

"Who made all this food?" I ask, cutting Shane off from his chocolate soufflé speech.

He scoffs. "Who do you think?"

"I was going to make them," I say, my voice pitching higher as my defenses kick in.

Shaking his head at me, he laughs. "Yeah, well then you became a little jailbird and someone had to step up to the plate."

"I *said* I was going to make them," I grit through a tightened jaw as I slam the freezer shut.

65

Shane halts. "Wait, are you actually pissed? I did you a favor and now you want to throw a fit about it? Who cares who made the food, either way Mom and Dad are good to go."

I cross my arms, the heat of embarrassment mangling with frustration. "It's not about who made the food. It's about the fact that it's always me. I'm the dependable one—the one they can count on. And now I can't even do that right."

A thick, heavy feeling sinks in my stomach. I said I would handle something, and I failed. And I hate failing. The arrest has been like a domino effect—one wrong move and everything is falling over.

Shane raises an eyebrow while resting against the counter. "So you're mad because you're not playing martyr this week? Jesus, Elle, maybe it's okay to let someone else handle things for once."

I narrow my eyes at him, my jaw clamping down further. "You don't get it."

When you're part of a big family, something has to be your *thing*. Gavin is the oldest—the good child and the calm, rational one of the bunch. Ethan's running the family business. Shane is a goof-off and a manwhore, but the boy can cook. Layla's probably the smartest of all of us. Ariana is the sweet, caring one.

And me? I'm the one everyone relies on. Need a party thrown together last minute? A babysitter in a pinch? An ex's social media stalked? I'm your girl.

Because if I'm not the one holding everything together, then who am I?

"No, I think I do," Shane says flatly. "You've tied your whole identity to being the one who does everything. It's like you think the rest of us are useless. You bitch about not getting help, and then complain when someone does. God forbid anyone else takes the reins."

His insinuation lands like a blow, twisting my stomach. I know he's right. He knows he's right. But admitting that feels like surrender, so I don't. Instead, I let out a clipped sigh and grab a glass from the cupboard, pouring myself some water to distract from Shane's assessment.

"Well, congratulations." My voice is harsh. "Enjoy doing all the things. Don't come to me and start complaining when you start to drown."

He groans, running a hand through his hair, ruining the careful styling he'd whined about earlier. "You're so goddamn territorial. I'm not trying to take over. I'm just trying to help. And maybe—just maybe—you need to let people do that every once in a while. Why is it always a fight? I'm just as capable as anyone else, but you treat me like a fucking kid. I can do things too, you know?"

I stare at him, his words stinging painfully. And from Shane of all people, which makes it worse. I didn't realize he even cared about stuff like this. The kitchen is quiet now, the tension heavy.

Before I can come up with a retort, Ariana and Layla walk in.

"What's all this bickering?" Ariana asks. The look of concern on her face has gnawing guilt starting to claw at my spine. Ariana hates it when any of us fight, always trying to be the mediator.

Shane and I exchange a look, and for a moment, the irritation between us dissipates. He gestures toward the dining room. "Come on, let's eat. You can be mad at me after dessert."

I roll my eyes, but follow him out of the kitchen. I don't want to fight, but I don't know what to do with all the bottled up pressure I've been feeling lately. I'm out of sorts. Everything feels out of control.

"We're fine, Ari," I tell her as I brush past her to get to the dining room.

"Set an extra place," my mom calls from the living room. "I invited a guest."

Before I can question who this so-called guest is, there's a knock at the front door. Only a guest would knock, the rest of us barge in.

"Elle, be a doll, and get that for me please," my mom says.

She's acting odd, her voice carrying a conspiratorial lilt.

"Okayyy," I drag while I pad to the front door. The last time she acted this suspicious she invited a "nice girl" over to get to know Gavin. It didn't go well.

My head is down as I turn the knob, eyes catching on the bits of grease Shane splattered on me when he was gesturing to all of his dishes earlier. *Freaking Shane! I just bought these shoes.*

When I finally do look up, the air whooshes out of me the moment I realize who's on the other side of the door. Our eyes collide. Dominic's pensive, penetrating brown ones hold mine captive.

You're kidding me. Is there no escaping this man?

"Hey, Ellie girl."

My stomach flips. I wish he would stop calling me that.

He smiles sheepishly, like he's aware that I'm less than pleased by his presence.

With a silent shrug, he tucks both hands in the front pockets of his jeans, managing to look boyishly innocent and stupidly cocky all at once.

I glance over my shoulder, confirming no one is watching, and quickly slip outside, closing the door behind me. Now it's just me and Dominic on the porch.

Alone.

He steps back, likely taken by surprise that I would choose to be alone with him.

"You're the guest my mom invited."

It's not a question, but he nods, answering it anyway.

I cross my arms over my chest, the need to protect the heart hammering under it is instinctual. "I don't know what game you're playing, but it needs to stop. It's not funny." My eyes dart down, hating the vulnerable wave about to break over me any moment now.

Forcing myself to look back up, I watch the playful smile he was sporting drop as he steps forward.

I step back.

He sighs, but remains still. "You think I would play games with you? There's no game. You know me better than that."

"I don't know you. Not anymore." It comes out hushed and ragged, revealing too much emotion when I was aiming for indifference. "You can't just show up here like this."

His brows fall into a single line, the softness in his gaze replaced by something heavier, harder. "Your mom invited me. Not the other way around. I wasn't planning to crash Sunday dinner just to mess with you."

I scoff, even though a small part of me feels stupid for assuming it was his idea. Of course it was my mom's idea, she doesn't know when to mind her own business. "So, what, you're just here to...what? Make nice with my family?"

Dominic rubs the back of his neck, the movement drawing my attention to the way his shirt stretches across his shoulders, to the veins branching down his inked arms.

Damn it. Focus.

"I don't know what I'm doing here," he admits, quietly, unsure. "Your mom asked, and I didn't have a reason to say no." He hesitates. "And maybe I wanted to see you."

My insides somersault. I can't decide if it's from anger or something else. Something I'm sure as shit not going to name.

We stare, studying each other. No matter how badly I try not to feel it, the ever-present thread between us pulls tight. It's always there, tugging.

"Well, you've seen me," I say, trying to sound cold, though my voice wavers. "Now you can leave."

He flinches at that, and for a second, I regret my bitchiness. But before either of us can say more, the sound of a truck pulling into the driveway snaps the tension.

Dominic glances over his shoulder as Ethan's truck rolls to a stop. Marisa hops out of the passenger seat with a wave.

"Dom, good to see you, man," Ethan calls, grinning as he rounds the walkway.

Marisa jogs up to us, her hand brushing my arm as she passes, giving it a double-squeeze. "Are you joining us? Oh, this is going to be fun." She beams at both of us. Either she's not picking up on the strain crackling in the silence, or she's choosing to not acknowledge it.

Dominic bro hugs Ethan, his easy smile sliding back into place. "Your mom invited me, and I couldn't pass it up." His eyes briefly swivel to me before Marisa greets him with a hug.

Shane's voice calls from inside. "The food is getting cold!"

I glare at Dominic one last time before sighing and opening the door. "Let's get this over with."

Dominic follows close behind me, the heat radiating off him penetrating my skin as if we're touching. I feel him everywhere and nowhere at once, a special kind of torture. As we get closer to the dining room, I brace myself for an evening I'm wholly unprepared for.

CHAPTER 7

Dominic

SULLIVAN RIDGE HOUSE

PRESENT

I expected dinner to be awkward, but somewhere between parking and walking to the door, I convinced myself it wouldn't be as bad as I feared. I was wrong. It's worse.

I'm sitting at the Ledger family table, surrounded by a chorus of voices speaking over each other and the loud clink of plates, struggling not to choke on the tension swirling from Ellie across the table.

She hasn't looked at me once since we left the porch. Not really. A quick glance—more out of necessity than acknowledgment. Now, she's doing an admirable job of pretending I don't exist, laughing a little too brightly at whatever Lily, her niece, is chattering on about.

"How are you liking working for the sheriff's office?" Leanne's question jolts me out of my thoughts.

I clear my throat. "I love it, actually. It's a nice change of pace from LA, that's for sure."

Ellie's eyes rove over to mine for a split-second. Since we

didn't keep in touch, she likely didn't know I'd been living in California up until recently.

"That's wonderful. They really needed some fresh blood." Leanne looks over to Ellie, who's scowling, and her smile slightly falls before she puts it back in place. "I had a nice chat with your mom after running into you, and she filled me in on you and Adrian. It was so great catching up." She breathes a soft laugh my way. "She's very proud of you."

My face flushes hot. I look down at my food and when I look back up, my eyes can't help but find Ellie's. I've always been drawn to her—searching for her in crowded rooms, even ones I know she couldn't possibly be in. Now she's right in front of me, and all I want to do is stare. Is it the same for her? Has she been looking for me the way I've always looked for her?

She's not regarding me with hurt or sadness or anger. More like curiosity, like she can't quite figure me out.

I stare back, because I think if I looked away, so would she.

Neither one of us blinks.

Or moves.

"I'm glad you could join us tonight." Leanne continues, breaking the spell.

Ellie snaps her neck down, suddenly fascinated by her plate. A beat later, I turn my focus back to Leanne.

"It's been too long since we've had you over."

"Yeah," I say, too bright to sound genuine. "Thanks for inviting me."

Ethan, seated next to me, nudges my shoulder. "About time. I've hardly seen you since you moved back."

"Been busy with the house."

I was hoping my vague answer would suffice, but based on Ethan's expression it had the opposite effect.

Ethan's head cocks. "You bought a house?"

I should've rehearsed this, come up with a story. But I didn't.

"Yeah."

He waits for me to elaborate and the rest of the table follows suit. When I don't speak, Ethan pushes on. "What house? One of the new developments?"

Well, fuck. I guess the truth was going to come out eventually.

My throat clears before speaking, buying myself time. "Sullivan Ridge House."

Like a record scratch cutting through the noise, all eye snap to me.

I never really got the saying you could hear a pin drop—until now.

The silence stretches, heavy and suffocating, until Ethan cuts through it like a dull knife. "That's great." His smile is tight, his eyes darting to Ellie, checking for fallout.

My stomach twists. I should've kept my mouth shut.

Across the table, Ellie grips her napkin like it's the only thing keeping her from launching it—or maybe herself—at me. Her knuckles whiten as she twists the fabric tighter, her jaw locked so hard I can almost hear her teeth grinding. If looks could kill, I'd already be six feet under.

An uncomfortable quiet grabs hold of the room until Marisa shatters it with a question about Lily's upcoming dance recital. The conversation shifts, flowing around like a current about to drown me.

I focus on the food I barely taste, because of the pressure building in my chest from the unspoken animosity coming from the woman across the table.

When dinner ends, everyone moves to the living room for dessert, but I linger in the dining room, helping clear plates. Ellie breezes past me in the dining room to grab a stack of dishes, her shoulder brushing mine. It's the first time

73

I've gotten her alone since the porch and the closest we've been all evening. Being this close feels like static crackling in the air.

"I should've told you...privately. About the house. I'm sorry you found out that way." My voice is low, for her ears only.

She doesn't look at me. "It's fine."

And just like that, she's gone again, disappearing into the kitchen where Shane and Marisa are putting together dessert plates.

Not wanting to torture her any further, I keep my distance and chat with Ethan and Gavin. Shane hasn't so much as greeted me, giving me a cold shoulder almost as bad as Ellie's. We used to be friends, but I can see now that he's drawn a line, and it's firmly on Ellie's side.

By the time I'm outside, saying my goodbyes to everyone, dinner feels like a blur of forced smiles and awkward conversations. I'm halfway to my cruiser when I hear a frustrated groan behind me.

Turning, I see Ellie standing by her car, the hood popped and her phone flashlight aimed into the engine.

"Everything okay?" I ask, walking toward her.

"Does it look like everything's okay?" she hisses, then immediately sighs, pinching the bridge of her nose. "Sorry. That was uncalled for."

"What's wrong?"

"It won't start." She moves to step back as I peer under the hood, and I catch the faintest trace of her perfume.

"Battery's probably dead," I say after a moment. "You need a jump?"

"Don't have cables," she mutters, crossing her arms.

I don't have cables on me either, though there are likely some in her dad's garage. If there are, I don't bring it up.

"I'll give you a ride," I offer, already knowing she's going to argue. "I'm heading into town to pick up a few things, if that's where you live."

I'm actually not heading into town, and like a total creep I already know where she lives. I've never driven by, I'm not *that* creepy I was more curious to see what kind of place she chose and if she lived in it alone. City records confirmed she's the only occupant.

She hesitates, her lips settling into a thin line. "I can call someone—"

Gavin and Ethan live on the estate property, and Shane and Layla and Ariana just left. I'm her only option unless she wants to ask her parents, which knowing her, she doesn't.

"It's late, and I'm here," I cut in. "Let me drive you home."

Her shoulders sag in reluctant defeat. "Fine."

Fine seems to be her word of the day. Frankly I don't care what words she says, as long as she's still speaking to me, I'll take it as a win.

As she settles in, more of her perfume reaches me, warm and intoxicating. She still smells like amber—deep, rich, and slightly sweet with an edge. It's not overpowering—just enough to lead me down memory lane, to a time when that smell lingered on me and anything she came into contact with.

"Why aren't you driving?"

Her voice pulls me out of the daze I didn't realize I was in. It takes me a second to process that she was speaking, too drugged by her scent and still a little stunned by the fact that she willingly got into my truck without a fight.

"Earth to Dominic? Are you even listening to me?"

I blink, shaking off the haze clouding my thoughts. "What?"

She sighs, her head tilting slightly as if debating whether I'm worth repeating herself for. "I said I live at the townhouses on Second Street."

"Right," I mutter, turning the key in the ignition. The groan of the engine is the only sound as we pull out of the Ledger driveway and head toward town.

The silence between us is unbearably awkward, broken only by the rolling of tires against the road. Every so often, I glance over, hoping to catch her eye, but she keeps her gaze fixed out the window. The passing streetlights trace over her profile, illuminating her features in soft, glowing light—plump lips captured with a nervous bite, sharp, high cheekbones that give her an effortlessly regal air, and delicate shadows cast by her long, dark lashes. Her skin, smooth and creamy, shimmers, and a loose strand of her dark hair brushes against her cheek, catching just enough light to gleam. She looks untouchable. So fucking beautiful it hurts.

"You know," I start, desperate to fill the silent void, "this is the quietest I think I've ever seen you. It's a little unsettling."

Her lips twitch, and for a second, I think I've imagined it, but then a soft, reluctant laugh escapes her. "Don't get used to it."

"I'll try not to," I say, the corner of my mouth lifting.

The atmosphere between us shifts slightly, the awkwardness lifting just enough to breathe. But by the time we pull into the driveway of her townhouse, the distance is back. She unbuckles her seatbelt, one hand already on the door handle as she pauses to look at me.

"Why did you buy Sullivan Ridge House?"

Her question suspends in the air, taking me aback. Not because it's accusatory, like I would've expected, but because it's sad—sad in a way that makes my heart hurt. It's as if it burns with every beat. She wants an answer, but maybe not the real answer.

I turn to meet her eyes, my voice steady but barely above a whisper. "You know why."

Her breath hitches, and for a moment, I see a flash of

something raw beneath her perfectly cold exterior. But then she pushes the door open and steps out, her expression hardening like a slammed door.

"Goodnight, Dominic," she says, not waiting for a response before shutting the door softer than I expected and walking toward her front porch steps.

I sit there for a moment, watching her retreating figure, her shoulders squared against whatever storm she thinks I've brought back into her life.

"Goodnight, Ellie," I murmur to the empty seat next to me. Once she's safely inside, I shift the cruiser into reverse and drive away.

One step forward, two steps back.

CHAPTER 8

Elyse

BETWEEN NOW AND FOREVER

17 YEARS OLD

"**E**arth to Dominic? You're not paying attention."

His head tilts, pretending to be annoyed, but I know better.

Smiling, I lean in close, resting against his shoulder and snap the picture. The rough brush of his scruff against my cheek sends a sprinkle of shivers down my spine.

Not that I need another photo—my phone is already filled with pictures of us. But with the sunset painting the sky behind us, I can't resist capturing just one more.

Seated in the passenger seat of Dominic's old Honda, I feel the vibration of the engine beneath my feet. We're heading to our special spot—the old mansion on Sullivan Ridge. A discovery we stumbled upon as kids after wandering too far one day, and it's been ours ever since.

Crumbling and forgotten, its paint peels in brittle sheets, and its shattered windows gape like hollow eyes. The only way to get there is by walking or driving the barely-there path between our property lines that snakes over the far side of Red Mountain.

Dominic's fingers drum against the steering wheel to the beat of the song on the radio. His jaw locked, his focus intent as he navigates the uneven terrain that can't really be considered a road.

I can't stop myself from staring. There's just something about watching him drive that makes my pulse race. The way his dark hair falls over his forehead, the crease of concentration in his brown eyes, and the way his toned arms flex when he grips the wheel—it's all so...hot. Especially hotter with the new tattoo wrapping around his forearm.

He catches me staring, and a slow smirk spreads across his face.

"See something you like, querida mía?"

"Wrong question," I reply without hesitation. "What don't I like about you?"

He laughs, tipping his head back as he rolls his eyes. I unbuckle my seatbelt, leaning across the console to cuddle up against his side.

Dominic let's out a low tsk, eyes flicking to the unfastened seatbelt. "Ellie girl, I'm driving. It's not safe if you're not buckled up."

I ignore him, brushing my nose against his neck and breathe him in. His cologne mixes with a scent that's clean, yet spicy, pure Dominic. Indescribable, but completely addictive.

"What if I don't want to be safe?" I murmur, my lips brushing his skin. "What if I want to be reckless?"

He exhales, long and drawn out, before pulling the car to a stop and putting it in park. His hand finds my hip, and before I know it, he's tugged me across the console and onto his lap. My legs straddle him, arms looping around his neck.

"You're a bad influence," he teases, his lips trailing featherlight kisses along my neck, up to my jaw, and finally capturing my mouth with his. His kiss is gentle, but mine isn't. I deepen it, slipping my tongue against his, and he moans, pulling me tighter.

My hips instinctively roll against him, the heat between us building until it's almost too much to stand.

"Mmm-mmm." Dominic pulls back, his forehead pressing against mine as his hands cradle my jaw, holding me still. "I'm not fucking you in this piece-of-shit car, in the middle of a field, surrounded by manure."

I whine, not caring at all how desperate I sound.

A sighing groan escapes my lips as I roll my hips again. "But I'm so horny. I want you." I kiss up his jaw. "We've never had sex in your car." My whisper in his ear forces the skin right below it to scatter in goosebumps. I dust my breath over the area and watch the goosebumps spread.

Dominic practically squirms like he can't stand it, but the growing hardness between his legs says otherwise.

"You make saying no to you very hard," he rasps.

I giggle, swiveling my hips playfully. "You're definitely hard."

He throws his head back against the headrest, huffing. "What am I going to do with you?"

I take it as a challenge, letting my hands drift down his chest until they reach the waistband of his jeans. "We could..." My words trail off as my fingers find the button on his fly.

Before I can make any real progress, he captures my wrist, stopping me.

"We're almost there, Ellie," he says. The gruffness in his tone is filled with both desperation and resolve. "Just a little longer."

His restraint makes me grin. I know he's hanging on by a thread, and sometimes I make it my mission to drive him wild —but I never push too far.

Taking pity on him, I climb back into my seat, buckling

up as his shoulders sag. I can't tell if he's relieved or frustrated. Likely both.

I figured we'd have sex pretty quickly after our relationship shifted from friendship to something more, but Dominic had other ideas. He wanted to wait—not because he didn't want me, but because we were both virgins, and he wanted it to be special for me. It was very sweet, yet incredibly excruciating.

Somehow, by sheer willpower—and maybe a few well-timed interruptions—we made it nearly two years before giving in. And when we finally did, it was everything I'd hoped for. He made it special, just like he promised. Every time since then, he's treated me with a level of care I've come to realize is rare. If my friends' stories are anything to go by, I got lucky—because all my firsts belong to him. And I wouldn't change a single one.

As the car continues on its journey, I glance out the window, the fading sunlight casting golden streaks across the hills. It doesn't matter how many times we make the drive, the view never gets old. The hills look as if they go on forever, like it's just us and them—our own little world. Sometimes it's like life is spinning too fast, change is on the horizon, it's inevitable, but then we come here, and I can breathe again.

"We're here," Dominic announces.

The car rolls to a stop, the tires crunching over gravel as Dominic kills the engine. A soft silence settles, broken only by the distant rustle of leaves in the breeze and the faint hum of crickets.

I stare out the windshield at the dilapidated house. It looks even more haunting in the fading light, the last rays of the sun catching the jagged edges of broken windows and highlighting the overgrown vines that cling to its stone facade. Despite its decay, there's something magical about it too.

Dominic opens his car door, and the creak of the hinges

echoes in the quiet. He holds my door open, the cool spring air kissing my skin as I step out.

"Still as creepy as ever," I say, squinting up at the house.

"Creepy?" Dominic smirks, walking around the car. "More like mysterious."

I laugh, the sound bouncing off the empty space around us. He grabs a blanket from the back seat, slinging it over his shoulder before offering me his hand.

"Come on, Ellie girl. Let's see the view before we lose the light."

Sometimes, we come here to escape our parents; other times, we come just for us. For talks, for silence, for the freedom of being alone together. This long-abandoned house has become our unexpected sanctuary.

Hand in hand, we make our way up the familiar path, the cheatgrass breaking underfoot. The mansion looms larger with each step, its darkened windows seeming to watch us approach.

As we round the side of the house, the ridge opens up before us, the valley below bathed in shades of gold and orange. It's breathtaking, even after years of seeing the familiar view. Dominic spreads the blanket over a flattened patch of grass near the edge, and we settle down together.

The silence between us is comfortable as we take in the dips of the valley. He leans back on his elbows, and I rest my head against his shoulder. The heat of his body against mine is soothing in comparison to the growing chill, and for a while, we don't need words.

"So, separate schools, huh?" Dominic says suddenly, his voice quiet.

I lift my head to look at him. "Separate schools," I echo, confirming his question.

Today was the deadline—college decision day—and we both confirmed to different schools—me to the University of

Washington and Dominic to Washington State University. Opposite ends of the state, with a five-hour drive between us. It will be the first time since we met that we'll be apart.

Dominic received a full ride to WSU, something his parents are insanely proud of since he'll be the first in his family to attend college. His brother Adrian has plans to attend school, but he joined the army, with the hope he'll receive a G.I. Bill to pay for it.

I confirmed my acceptance to UW, a Ledger legacy, one I'm expected to uphold. I'm not even sure what I want to do with the rest of my life, but college always felt like the path I would take. My parents highly regard education, and though they're not pushy, it's heavily implied and expected for each of us to get a degree. As the eldest daughter, I set the tone for my younger siblings and won't allow myself to be the one who fucks up tradition.

I tried to tell Dominic it would be good for us, that we have the rest of our lives to be together, and that four years will fly by. But in the end, I'm not sure who I was trying to convince—him or me.

"I'm scared," he admits softly, and his admission pokes at my heart like a hot needle.

I'm scared too. Terrified, even. But I don't want to acknowledge it.

"What are you scared of?" I ask, hoping he doesn't catch the shake in my voice.

"Losing you," he responds in a heartbeat, staring off into the distance.

Curling myself closer, I rest my cheek on his chest. "You're never going to lose me."

Dominic stays quiet for a long moment before speaking. "We don't know what the future holds, querida mía. A lot can happen between now and forever."

Instead of continuing on with this depressing conversation, I move to sit on my knees and press Dominic onto his back. It takes him a second to catch on, but then he's gripping my hips, digging in as I make my intentions clear. I want to get lost in him. I don't want to think about the future, because it's enough unknowns to make me spiral. I'd rather feel Dominic's body against mine, a reminder of how well we fit together. Made for each other.

"What about this room?"

Dominic gestures widely, showing me a space I'm guessing was once the parlor.

After the sun went down, we made our way inside. The few candles we leave here are our only light.

When we're here, we daydream—about giving new life to this old house, maybe remodeling it one day. It's a pipe dream, something that will likely never happen because it would probably be easier to tear the whole thing down and start fresh. And honestly, the last thing I want is to spend the rest of my life in Red Mountain, but it's fun to imagine. Maybe one day, when we're older and have lived in other cities, we'll come back and raise a family here. By then, though, this place will likely be a pile of collapsed wood. It's barely standing now.

"I want a library." I give him a playful grin. "Bookshelves from floor to ceiling, with a ladder so I can reach the top ones. Like Belle from *Beauty and the Beast*."

He laughs. "Ellie girl, you don't even read. The last book you read was *The Scarlet Letter*, and you watched the movie and called it 'reading.'"

Spinning around, I shoot him a half-hearted glare—or an attempt at one. "So? Maybe when I'm older, I'll be sophisticated and worldly, and read novels and go to art museums. You never know."

Dominic's eyes light up, matching my playful tone. "I'll build it for you," he says without missing a beat. "Bookcases, ladders, the whole damn thing." Coming up to me, he kisses my forehead gently. "And you're going to be anything you want. Definitely sexy." He kisses my collarbone. "You're already sophisticated." He drags the strap of my tank top down my shoulder. "Titties out of this world, a work of art." His head dips, and I feel his tongue glide across the swell of my breast.

Laughing, I gently shove him away. "Liar. I have the tiniest boobs ever."

Not letting me get away, he pulls me back, spinning me around so his front is to my back, completely encasing me. His hot breath fans over the shell of my ear, and I sink into his embrace. "Querida mía, your tits are perfect. Your body,"—he moans, thrusting his hips against me so I can feel his erection—"always has me hard."

"You're a horndog," I tease.

He scoffs as his hands roam over my body. "Were you or were you not trying to ride my dick on the way over here?" His teeth tug at my ear, sending a delicious jolt down my body. "And were you or were you not full of me just a few minutes ago?"

I whirl around to face him and cross my arms behind his neck. With the added height of my wedges, we're almost at eye level. Dominic is 6'2", but I'm taller than most of the girls we grew up with at 5'9.

"What can I say? You're a very cute boy."

Shaking his head, he pulls his lips into a smug smile. "Ellie girl, I'm all man."

My own grin widens. "Whatever you say."

He's quiet for a stretch, just staring at me as the smile on his face slowly eases—looking at me with a seriousness that wasn't there before. "One day, I'm going to do it—the house, the library. Whether it's this place or somewhere else, anything you want."

"Promise?" I tease, raising an eyebrow to break through the tension that's joined us.

"Promise," he replies, looking so determined I can't help but let out a huff through my smile, even though I think I might cry if he keeps talking like this. "We'll come back here one day and make it happen. It'll be like those HGTV shows, but with lots of sex."

I giggle, grateful he's pivoting the conversation to something lighter. "You're such a sap."

"I'm whatever you want me to be." He pulls me close, capturing my lips with his, and I lose myself.

CHAPTER 9

Dominic

HAVING LOTS OF SEX

PRESENT

A nother night of sleeping like shit. Except this time, it wasn't Ellie haunting me—it was the nightmare. The same one I've had since the shooting.

It always plays out the same way. I step into the convenience store, my eyes locked in on the perp, his back is turned to me. Then he spins around, and I recognize him instantly.

He recognizes me, too.

My gun is raised. So is his.

And he's just a fucking kid.

I wake up the second my gun goes off.

The sheets are soaked from the sweat coming off my body, and it takes me a few deep breaths before I feel ready to move. I glance at the clock on my nightstand, seeing it reads three in the morning. *Fuck me.* Flopping back onto my damp pillow, I groan, staring up at the ceiling. My heart is practically banging against my chest, racing so fast it feels like I just worked out. *Why won't this go away?*

I went through the mandatory counseling, passed my fit-for-duty eval—this shit should be over. But it's not.

The counselor suggested I keep seeing a therapist, but for what? Talking about it isn't going to change anything. It's not like I'm Adrian, who's been in the Middle East, in active combat and witnessed things no human should ever have to see. I was in one messy shooting, and somehow, it's still fucking with me. Not just physically—mentally, too. And that's the part I can't stand. The part that makes me feel weak.

Forcing myself, I get up out of bed, I slip on a fresh T-shirt, but I don't make it two feet out of my bedroom before I hear it. The *drip, drip, drip* coming from the bathroom across the hall, the one right above the kitchen.

Gritting my teeth, I scrub a hand over my face as I head for the bathroom. Fuck this fucking house. The damn faucet has been dripping for days, and I've ignored it, thinking I'd get to it, eventually. But now, with my nerves already shot and my skin slick with sweat, the sound is unbearable—like a ticking clock counting down to my breaking point.

I flip on the light, step inside, and glare at the sink. The steady *drip, drip, drip* taunts me.

With a sigh, I reach under the cabinet, grab the wrench, and crouch down, twisting at the pipes. It doesn't budge. I adjust my grip and try again, harder this time. Nothing.

My jaw clenches. My pulse pounds in my ears as I try again. Harder.

Still nothing.

"Goddamnit!"

I slam the wrench down on the tile, chest heaving, frustration crawling up my spine like a vise. I should be asleep.

The drip continues.

I grab the mallet from the cabinet.

One hit. *Clang.*

Two. *Crack.*

Three—then the faucet breaks clean off, and a burst of water explodes in my face, soaking my shirt, spraying across the bathroom like a goddamn fire hydrant.

"Shit!"

I scramble back, slipping slightly on the wet tile, lunging toward the pipes to try and stop the flow. Water is everywhere, pooling, dripping down into the vent that leads straight to the kitchen.

Fuck. Fuck. Fuck.

I leap up, tear out of the bathroom, and bolt downstairs, nearly eating shit on the soaked floor. I skid into the kitchen and drop to my knees, yanking open the cabinet beneath the sink and frantically twisting the shut-off valve.

The pipes groan. The water slows.

Then, finally—mercifully—it stops.

I sit back on my heels, drenched, breathing hard, the house silent except for the distant drip of water making its way down from the bathroom.

I run a hand through my wet hair and let out a bitter, breathless laugh.

Perfect. Just fucking perfect. One more thing to add to the list of things I haven't quite figured out how to fix.

By four, it's too late to go back to bed and too early to get ready for the day. Despite exhaustion creating a mental fog I can't seem to shake, I get to work on the kitchen.

With the water shut off, I'm not in danger of anything leaking again. I hope.

I strip the old, bottom cabinets and properly seal the ancient pipes so I don't risk another leak before the plumber can come out and modernize the plumbing. Once that's complete, I work at forming the boxes for the new cabinetry. In an attempt to save money, I opted out of the premade ones, and now I'm regretting having to tediously put together each one.

Halfway through the first one—because I'm still on the first one and it's been over an hour—my mom calls.

Before answering, I check my watch, calculating the time in Monterrey. It's two hours ahead but still early, even there. Ever since my dad died, a knot of dread coils in my chest whenever my mom or Adrian calls, like I'm on the verge of hearing the worst news of my life and tumbling into a black abyss.

Still, no matter the panic simmering beneath the surface, I always answer with an intentional lightness in my voice. My mom doesn't need to worry about me; she doesn't need to know I'm still deep in the trenches of grief. I lost my dad, but she lost the love of her life. A loss I understand, though in a different way.

"You're up early," I greet.

She blows out an exasperated breath. "It's so hot here. Has it always been this hot?"

The tension in my spine immediately dissipates. She's in a good mood, and that's good enough for me. "I don't know 'amá, you tell me. You're the one who grew up there. You should be used to the heat, it's hotter than hell in Phoenix most of the year, can't be much hotter there."

She laughs softly and the sound fills me with relief. She's starting to come back into herself.

"Maybe I'll cut the trip short, go back home."

I'm predicting a phone call with Adrian soon. Neither of us wants her to go back to an empty house without family nearby. Adrian and his wife Celia live in Portland, and now

I'm even further than I was from her when I lived in L.A.. She shouldn't be alone.

"I think my tía would be upset if you left early."

She sighs, but I hear her agreement.

After my dad passed, my mom's sister invited her to come stay in Mexico for an extended visit. It's been good for her.

"How's your shoulder?"

As if my body heard the question, a heated jolt radiates through the area—painful and nearly impossible to ignore. I shift slightly, wincing as I try to find a more comfortable position.

"Still hurts," I admit, because there's no sense in lying. "It's worse in the mornings, but gets better once I start moving."

She exhales loudly. "Mijo, you need to keep doing the exercises the physical therapist told you to do. What if something happens at work and you can't defend yourself?"

I want to argue, but she has a point. I can't afford for my shoulder to get locked up in an altercation. Not that I'm anticipating anything happening, the crime rate is very low throughout the county.

"I know. I've been slacking lately, but I'll get back into the routine."

I know she hates that I'm in law enforcement, and she hates it more now after what happened. It's part of why I decided to relocate somewhere smaller, a small part, but it still factored in. The bigger reason can't seem to stand the sight of me. I can't fix the house, and I can't fix the past. I'm fucked.

"Mijo, are you still there?"

She was speaking, and I was too buried in my thoughts. "Sorry, yeah, I'm here. What were you saying?"

The other end of the phone is quiet, a silent eye roll passing between the line. "I was saying that I talked to your brother, and I guess they're trying for a baby."

Now my eyes roll. Adrian has been married for five minutes. Not only that, they met less than two months ago. I shouldn't be surprised he's already trying to get her pregnant. He said *when you know you know*, and even though I get it, I still think it's too fast.

"What am I supposed to say to that? Thanks for telling me they're having lots of sex, I guess."

She makes a disgusted sound. "Ay, why would you say it like that?"

She's probably twisting the gold cross around her neck, too Catholic for such crude conversation.

I snicker. "Sorry 'amá."

The noise of a vehicle approaching makes me pause. The only traffic I get is from delivery drivers. I flick my wrist, checking my watch. It's seven in the morning—way too early for something like that.

"I have to go. I'll call you later."

We say our goodbyes, and I slip on a hoodie and sneakers. Whoever it is, they weren't invited.

CHAPTER 10

Dominic

PUTRID FLORAL SMELL

PRESENT

There's a woman on my porch.

My door creaks open, the sound grating like nails on a chalkboard. I make a mental note to grab some WD-40 the next time I'm in town. But the thought disappears the moment I see who's standing in front of me.

What the hell?

"Morales?"

"Hi!" she replies, a little too friendly. Noticing my expression, her smile drops as her eyes sweep over me. "Did I wake you up?"

I drag a hand down my face. "Uh...no. I'm just confused why you're here."

It's my day off, and I also have no recollection of telling Morales, or anyone at work, where I live.

"Can I come in?" she asks, while brushing past me.

I remain still, trying to figure out what the fuck is going on. "Sure, come right in." I can't help the sarcasm in my voice.

She walks ahead of me, admiring the disaster. "Didn't take you for a DIY guy."

A noncommittal grunt is my only response. It's not that I dislike Morales, exactly, but I don't like her enough to invite her over or socialize with her outside of work. I have nothing against a woman in law enforcement—I know it's still very much a good ol' boys' club—but boundaries need to be maintained when working with the opposite sex. People talk, and the last thing I need is a rumor going around that Morales and I are getting *too friendly*.

"Is there a reason you're here on my day off? And how do you know where I live?"

I'm not trying to be a dick, but there's no reason to beat around the bush with her. I have a lot of shit to get done and really don't appreciate the unexpected visit.

She laughs like I said something funny. "You're so hospitable."

I don't laugh or smile. In fact, now I'm kind of pissed. She noticeably didn't answer my questions either.

"Morales," I say as my arms cross and shoulders square.

She plops down on a turned over bucket in the middle of the room. "Dominic, you can call me Talia, it's not like we're at work."

My stare narrows. I'm not going to call her Talia. "It's Dom or Alvarez. Not Dominic." I correct.

Only a few select people in my life call me by my full name —Ellie being one of them. It's not for Morales to use.

Her smile strains before she reaches into her shoulder bag and produces a file folder. "I was hoping I could run a few things by you, related to the JB Stalker."

"JB Stalker?"

She blows out a puff of air. "The Juniper Bluffs Stalker." She says this like it should've been my first conclusion.

I rake a hand through my hair, exhaling a slow breath. "You gave the stalker a nickname?"

She shrugs, unfazed. "It's catchy. Easier than saying, 'That guy who left a bunch of creepy pictures in a duffle bag'—assuming it's a guy. For all I know it's a woman, not likely, but still."

I grab a rag off the workbench and wipe my hands, stalling. She's clearly not leaving until she gets what she wants.

"And you couldn't have called me about this? Or, I don't know, waited until tomorrow?"

Her lips quirk up in a grin. "Would you have answered?"

I glare. She knows the answer.

"I'll take that as a no," she says with a satisfied smirk, leaning back on the bucket.

"Why not go to Sergeant Vorheis about this?"

She lets out a breath, revealing a crack in her usual confidence. "Because he doesn't respect me. I've been trying to get in the detective's unit for almost two years, and I'm not making any headway. He seems to like you more than me."

Well, fuck. Talk about feeling like a dick.

I gesture vaguely at the folder. "Fine. What do you need from me?"

She flips it open and starts rifling through papers. "Just your insight. I figured your fancy LAPD job might provide a different perspective."

"Wasn't really that fancy," I mutter, but I pull up another bucket and sit across from her anyway.

She's likely being honest about Vorheis. I'm not about to question her experiences, but my gut is telling me Morales came here with intentions that have nothing to do with work. If I'm right, it's really going to mess up our already fragile work relationship.

She spreads a few photos across the makeshift table between us. Grainy images of a man standing just beyond the light of someone's front porch, his face obscured by shadows. The timestamps show the photos were taken a few nights ago.

"There's a Peeping Tom case in Coyote Creek Junction. This is the third house he's hit this month," Morales says, her voice dropping into a more serious tone. "Same pattern. He watches for hours, just standing there. Leaves no trace. No prints, no hair, nothing."

I study the photos, an unease curling in my stomach. It's the same feeling I got when I was looking through the Delmar file. The timing is too suspect.

"You think this is our guy?" I ask.

Her expression hardens. "What are the odds of a Peeping Tom case, potential stalker and missing woman all happening at the same time in our county?"

She's right. Things like this don't happen in Clore County. It's sleepy and touristy with more land covered in agriculture than people. It's not impossible for it to all be a coincidence, but it's also not likely that it is.

"Alright," I finally say, rubbing the back of my neck. "I see your point. If you want me to present this to Vorheis, I will and I'll make sure to tell him it came from you." I stand, and nod to indicate her time is up. "But next time, Morales? Call first."

She grins, sauntering ahead of me toward the door. It's only now that I actually take in what she's wearing—jeans so tight they might as well be painted on, hugging curves her work uniform usually keeps under wraps. Her top isn't much better, clinging in a way that leaves little to the imagination. Unlike the ponytail she wears at work, her hair is down in soft waves, and she's wearing more makeup than usual. She's not unattractive. But she's not Ellie.

She pauses at the door and a wave of unease rolls through me. I'm hoping like hell she's not about to make things fucking awkward.

"Next time let's wait for work. I like my days off."

She bats her eyelashes. "Where's the fun in that?"

Leaning closer, she invades me with a putrid floral smell.

Fuck.

I pull the door open, all but pushing her out, when she suddenly stops short. Confused, I glance over to see what's holding her up.

My heart drops like a brick.

It's Ellie.

CHAPTER 11

Elyse

DELICATE CURSIVE LETTERS

PRESENT

S omeone needs to commit me, because I have lost my fucking mind.

Dominic stands there, jaw slack, while his little girlfriend shoots me a gloating smirk.

This was a mistake.

My lips turn up, in what I hope is a smile, but I'm sure looks more like a grimace. A gasp floats up my throat and my chest heaves, trying to take in air that isn't coming. *Am I hyperventilating?*

"I'll come back another time," I choke out, and sprint toward my car.

Over the crunching of gravel under my shoes, I hear Dominic behind me, but I don't turn around. This is mortifying.

"Wait! Wait! Wait!" Dominic shouts.

I keep walking, my skin burning redder with each step.

"Morales, I'll see you at work," he tells the woman who was just in his house.

My ears snag on the mention of work, but I'm too focused on how pretty, and flushed, and thoroughly satisfied she looked, to fully comprehend the scene I stumbled upon. They were probably saying their goodbyes after fucking all night, and I'm so lucky I got to witness it.

I've never felt so embarrassed in my life.

And, God, she's pretty. *So pretty.*

I'm sure every woman he's been with since me has been gorgeous. I wouldn't expect anything less. Dominic has only gotten better with age.

"Ellie, wait!" I feel him right at my heels, the pounding of his steps moves the ground beneath mine.

Still not looking back, I reach for the handle of my car door, but before I can pull it open, his hand slams against the window, holding it shut. His arm grazes against my shoulder, and he's so close now I can feel the puff of his breath on the back of my neck.

"Ellie," Dominic says, his voice low and steady. Too steady, considering the way my chest is rising and falling like I've just run a marathon.

I keep my gaze fixed on my car door, refusing to turn and meet his eyes. Every time I look into his melty brown eyes, my defenses evaporate to dust. "Move," I manage, though it comes out more like a plea than a demand.

"Not until you talk to me and tell me why you're here," he counters, his hand still pressed firmly against the window.

"There's nothing to talk about," I grumble, wishing I could disappear into thin air. "I didn't mean to intrude. I just got curious—" My voice catches, and I bite down hard on my lip. "I haven't been by in years...And I'm sorry for ruining your date, or whatever."

Why am I explaining?

He exhales sharply, the frustration in the sound rippling over my skin. "Ellie, Morales isn't—"

"I don't want to hear it." My grip tightens on the door handle—trying to pull it, but his weight keeps it in place. My stare flicks straight ahead, landing on the woman. Morales. Our eyes meet—hers narrowed, assessing.

Her stare is cold, not so much as an attempt at feigning friendliness. I guess I would be upset too if another woman showed up at my man's place in the early hours of the morning.

She pins me with one more glare before getting in her car.

If she's not his girlfriend, she wants to be. I know that look.

Dominic and I remain unmoving as she peels out of the driveway without a glance back.

And then it's just us.

"You don't owe me an explanation," I start, trying to keep my delivery breezy despite the pressure building in my ribs. "You can date whoever you want. It's none of my business. Just let me go."

I mean it. I do. But the words taste bitter, and my pulse thrums painfully in my ears.

This is uncharted territory. Outside whatever my imagination could cook up, I've never seen him with another woman. It's unsettling.

"Ellie girl." He softens, in that low, patient tone that used to make me melt. It's making me melt now, but I'm choosing to ignore it.

Finally, I spin around, ready to confront him, but I freeze when I see the look on his face—he's amused, smiling.

I find nothing about this situation funny.

"She's my coworker," he says quietly, his all-knowing eyes shining with glee. "We're not together. Morales stopped by to talk about a case, that's all."

My cheeks flame, and I drop my gaze to the ground,

suddenly very aware of how ridiculous I must look right now. "Oh," I mumble.

"Yeah. Oh." His lips twitch like he's holding back a laugh, which only makes me more defensive.

"Well, how was I supposed to know that? She was in your house. I just assumed—"

"That we're together?" he interrupts, his eyebrows lifting.

"Well, yeah," I admit, focusing my attention on a rogue wildflower instead of him.

A beat of silence passes before he chuckles, and I whip my head up to scowl at him.

"This isn't funny!"

"Ellie," he says, that damn grin still plastered on his face. "You're jealous. It's cute."

My head jerks back, hot embarrassment crawling up my neck. "I am NOT jealous." It comes out sharper than I intended, but I double down, crossing my arms. "What I am, is too curious for my own good. I only wanted to see the house, see if you made any changes. Your personal life doesn't concern me."

His smirk deepens, slow and deliberate, the kind that creates a coil low in my stomach. A wicked, almost teasing curve settles on his lips.

"Admit it."

Before I can quip back, he comes forward, leaning his body close, forcing me against my car. For a moment I think he's going to kiss me, but at the last second turns his head to whisper in my ear.

"You're so jealous."

The dusting of his breath caresses the shell of my ear. I swallow hard. If I wasn't resting against my car, my knees would've given out by now.

How does he still have so much power over me? I'm turning to putty in his hands, and he's barely touched me.

It would be so easy to give in to this overwhelming want for him—a want that just won't die. I've starved it, smothered it, neglected it, yet it still breathes. In his presence, it blooms as brightly as the wildflower at my feet, tangling with the weeds but refusing to let them win. So resilient, it makes you wonder how it survives.

But then I remember how quickly I withered without him. And just like that, reality comes crashing down.

Sidestepping, I put some needed space between us. "I'm not going to admit to something that isn't true. And let's not pretend like we both haven't seen other people. I highly doubt you've been celibate all these years." I square my shoulders, false confidence surging through me. "I know I haven't."

His smile falls in an instant. My words hit the nerve I was aiming for, but it doesn't feel as satisfying as I thought it would.

He clears his throat and takes a measured step back, straightening his stance. "So, that's what we're going to do? Petty jabs? I'm aware time didn't stand still."

The hurt in his eyes is unmistakable—hurt I caused on purpose. Further proof I'm exactly the monster I always knew I was.

"I'm sorry, I shouldn't have said that."

He nods, looking like he wants to say more but doesn't.

Coming here was a mistake. I don't know what I was thinking. "I'm leaving."

He reaches out, stopping me, his fingers wrapping gently around my wrist. His thumb brushes over the soft skin on the inside, sending a shuddering warmth through me. Slowly, he turns my hand palm-up, revealing something I usually keep hidden beneath a stack of bracelets. But not today.

"You kept it," he murmurs low, almost reverent.

"Kind of hard to get rid of something permanent," I reply just as softly, not sure why we're whispering.

It's been there so long, I barely think about it anymore. The delicate cursive letters etched into the inside of my wrist spell out one name: *Dominic*.

Still holding my wrist in his right hand, he lifts his left arm and turns it, revealing the matching tattoo inked on his skin. The script is identical, but his reads *Elyse*.

"Why did you keep it?" he asks.

I yank my arm away, pushing the sleeve of my shirt down to cover it.

"I really should go." My voice wavers as I turn toward my car, my fight or flight instincts battling for control.

"Ellie. Why. Did. You. Keep. It."

Each word lands like the steady pounding of a drum as he inches closer until his chest is brushing my back, his heat penetrating through the thin barrier of my top.

I should move. Say something.

But I don't.

Because all I really want to do is give into him, let the weight of whatever this is—whatever it's always been—consume me.

My fingers twitch at my sides, nails digging into my palms. "It doesn't matter."

His breath hitches, a beat of silence stretching between us before he exhales. "It matters to me."

I squeeze my eyes shut. "That's the problem."

"Have dinner with me," he says quietly.

My chest caves in. "I can't." It's a knee-jerk reaction answer, and if I wasn't already so tense, I'd likely be shaking.

"Can't or won't."

"Both," I tell him, honestly.

His hand skims down my arm, fingers just barely grazing my wrist. A touch so light, so careful, it makes my heart squeeze.

"Ellie—"

I pull away before he can finish. Before I do something reckless. Before I lose what little sense I have left.

Instead, I do the responsible thing and get inside my car.

"Why did you keep it?" he repeats. "Please."

Before closing the door, my eyes lock with his one last time. "Like I said, some things are permanent."

"You did what?!" Scottie screeches over FaceTime later that night, her voice piercing even through the connection. Still wearing her stage makeup, she looks half-crazed, her wide, blue eyes glued to the screen.

"Scotland, stop yelling!" I snap, wincing.

"Oh, I'm sorry," she sings with a sardonic edge. "It's just that you went to Dom's house after being adamant that you were going to avoid him at all costs. Excuse me for needing a moment to process this!"

I sigh, regretting the decision to bring it up at all, but grateful I left some parts out—like the part where I think he asked me out on a date. I'm keeping that one to myself.

Scottie and I barely have time to catch up these days, and I'm wasting our call talking about Dominic. We've been best friends since elementary school. A boy shoved her, so then I shoved him and made him cry, the rest is history. She's the only one who knows everything that happened between me and Dominic. She's been there for me through being blissfully in love to devastatingly heartbroken, and everything in between.

Coming closer to the camera, her expression turns sly, her red hair falling in wisps as it unravels from a ballerina-esque bun. "Well? Don't leave me hanging. What happened? Did you two finally have it out? Did he grovel? Did you grovel?"

"None of the above," I mutter, shifting uncomfortably on the couch.

Her brows shoot up. "Wait. You said he had a girl over. Was she just some badge bunny or...?"

My forehead creases. "I literally have no idea what that means."

Scottie laughs through her teeth. "It's women who go after police officers, you know 'guys with badges.'"

I shake my head. "No, he said she was a coworker. Not a badge bunny, more like she's one of the badges."

Scottie throws her hands in the air, nearly sending her phone flying. "Tell me everything. What does she look like? Is she pretty? I mean, probably not. You're gorgeous, but, like, objectively."

This is the downside of having a best friend who's an actress. Scottie doesn't just talk—she performs, every word infused with enough energy to power a small city. People think I'm dramatic, but then they meet Scottie and quickly realize I'm the calm one by comparison.

"She's...pretty," I admit reluctantly, picking at a loose thread on my sleeve. "Like the kind of girl you'd expect him to be with. Petite, fit, huge boobs. She looked Latina, likely Mexican, so I'm sure his mom will love that."

Her eyes pinch. "But she's just a coworker. If there was something going on between them, I think it would've been more obvious when you showed up. So, what if she's pretty, she's not you."

"Yeah, I don't know," I sigh, slumping back into the cushions. "I shouldn't even care. We're not together. We haven't been for years. For all I know, he's had tons of girlfriends since me."

"But it still stings," Scottie finishes for me, her voice losing some of its enthusiasm.

I nod, biting my lip. "It does. And I hate that it does. I'm so stupid for even going over there."

"Stop it." Her tone is resolute. "You're not stupid." She pauses a beat, and her head cocks to the side. "Why *did* you go? It's very unlike you."

My shoulders lift as I try to look uninterested. Sadly, I'm not as good of an actress as Scottie so she doesn't buy my act for a second. "I wanted to see what the house looked like. And I thought because it's a weekday, that he would be on duty. I figured I'd get a quick peek at it before heading into work."

Her brows furrow. "So, the plan was to sneak around his house? That's not weird at all."

I roll my eyes. "Well, when you say it like that. It was going to be a simple drive by."

Her lips twitch like she wants to laugh. "But you didn't just drive bye, you got out of your car."

"Okayyy," I draw out the word. "That's enough Dominic talk for tonight. Let's focus on you—tell me everything."

She looks like she wants to press further, but knows me well enough to let it go. After a brief hesitation, she gives in and starts telling me about her latest performance and the improv group she's been working with. She's been in Chicago for the past five years, fully immersed in the city's stage and improv scene.

We don't get to see each other as often these days, with her across the country, but I usually make it out to visit a couple of times a year. Her parents still live in Red Mountain so she's always back in town for the holidays. It doesn't matter how much time passes between visits or calls—it always feels like we pick up right where we left off.

Eventually we call it a night, it's late for me and even later for her.

As I finally crawl into bed, my gaze lingers on my wrist. I trace the letters with my fingertip, Dominic's question hauntingly replaying. *Why did you keep it?* It's not like it's ever done me any favors in the dating department. Most men aren't exactly thrilled about being with a woman literally branded with another man's name. Probably why I've been ghosted more times than I can count.

I sigh, letting my hand fall to my stomach as I stare at the ceiling. Maybe I should have gotten rid of it years ago. Covered it up. Removed the evidence that, at one point, I was so in love with a guy I got my first and only tattoo. But every time I tried, I couldn't bring myself to do it.

If I'm honest with myself, I think part of me feels like getting rid of it would be like erasing us. I'll never love anyone the way I loved him—so free, so brave. A long time ago, I was a girl who was fearless enough to love with her whole heart, and every time I look at Dominic's name on my wrist, I'm reminded of her, and I smile.

CHAPTER 12

Dominic

THE VIRGIN'S DISCOUNT

17 YEARS OLD

"I'm warning you now, it's going to hurt like a bitch," Ray says, holding the tattoo gun like it's a loaded pistol. "Are you a bitch, Dom?"

Ellie snorts, trying to stifle her giggle, but it spills out anyway. She's perched on a stool a few feet away, flipping through a binder stuffed with Polaroids of Ray's work. "Oh, he's definitely a bitch," she teases without looking up.

I roll my eyes, leaning back in the chair like I'm completely unbothered. "Just stick me, asshole."

"Don't say I didn't warn you." Ray laughs to himself.

He loves to give me shit. It's only my second tattoo, but he was even worse during the first one.

The needle touches my skin, and fuck, does it sting like hell, but I keep my face neutral. Out of the corner of my eye, Ellie's watching, clearly waiting for me to flinch. No way am I flinching in front of my girl.

When she sees that I won't be bursting into tears anytime soon, she returns her focus back to the Polaroids.

To distract myself from the pain, I stare unabashedly at her. Her long legs are on display in the red cheerleading uniform she wore today for Senior Day, one of the rare times she wears bright colors. It might be my last time seeing her in it, so I commit the picture to memory. I know she can feel my stare because her creamy skin starts to turn pink, a slight flush overtaking her face.

"You're awfully quiet over there." Her eyes slide to mine, her blush darkening. "Feeling inspired to get one yourself?"

She's not the type to get a tattoo. She'll do other reckless shit, but nothing permanent. I'm kind of the opposite, more of a rule follower, and this is my rebellious outlet.

Arching a brow, she casts me a flat look. "Not a chance. My body's a church...or whatever the saying is."

Ray snorts. "Temple. The saying is 'my body is a temple.'"

We both turn to look at him, blinking in unison.

"What?" he says, pausing to look between us. "I grew up Mormon."

Ellie and I exchange a glance before looking back at Ray. At his wild hair spilling past his shoulders, tattoos covering nearly every inch of visible skin, and a leather cut hanging on the wall behind him, proudly displaying the patch of his motorcycle club. Nothing about him screams Mormon.

He notices our expressions and bursts out laughing. "No longer practicing, of course."

"Yeah, no kidding," Ellie says under her breath, shaking her head as she flips the page.

As Ray works, I clench my jaw so tightly, I expect it to throb for the next few days. We're only doing the outlining of the skull today, which means it'll be a short session. Shading will be another session.

"Just about done," Ray announces.

Ellie walks over to inspect his handiwork, leaning in close to get a better look.

"So, does the missus approve?" Ray asks, smirking.

Her smile turns shy as her eyes dart to mine, locking there. Ray knows we're not even out of high school yet, nowhere near married, but I can see it—the way she likes being called mine. My wife.

And that's the plan. Someday.

She lifts her shoulders in a shrug. "It's alright."

I shake my head, laughing. She knows it's good but has to be a little brat about it.

Ray looks at her with narrowed, amused eyes. "This is my last appointment for the day. You sure you don't want a little something? Most girls your age like butterflies. I'll even give you the virgin's discount."

Her face flames bright red, misunderstanding him. She thinks he's calling her a virgin, when really he means tattoo virgin.

"He means tattoos, querida mía," I tell her quietly and her shoulders drop in relief.

"I don't really like butterflies." Her bottom lip catches between her teeth, clearly wanting to say no, but not wanting to be rude either.

"Don't waste your time," I tell him, grinning. "She'll never get a tattoo."

Ellie's head snaps up, her competitive streak igniting in an instant. "Excuse me?"

I smile, already knowing I've pushed her buttons. "You heard me. You'd never actually do it. You hate pain. You can barely stand a flu shot. Besides, you change your mind every five minutes. There's nothing you love enough that you could stand being permanently on your body."

Her lips lift, eyes disarming me as they narrow. "I guess the only thing I love permanently is you."

For a second, I'm stunned, her words catching me off

guard. She's smiling, but there's a flicker of vulnerability in her eyes, like she's daring me to say something.

Ray lets out a low whistle, enjoying the entertainment. "Damn, kid. She's good. A little cheesy, but I like it."

Ellie steps closer, her chin lifted in that stubborn, confident way she gets when she's ready to prove someone wrong.

"You think I won't do it? Fine. Let's go, Ray. I'll get *Dominic* tattooed on my wrist right now."

Shit.

That is not where I was going with the teasing. I was thinking a flower, not my fucking name. "Ellie, you don't have to—"

She cuts me off with a wave of her hand. "Oh, don't backpedal now. You wanted to say I'd never do it, so let's see if you're right."

Ray laughs a deep rumble, already reaching for his tools. "Alright, I'm in. Sit your little ass down, sweetheart."

She hops onto the chair with an air of nonchalance, though I know her well enough to see the slight tremor in her hands.

Panic rises within me. "Ellie, it's permanent. You don't have to do this to prove a point."

She ignores me. "Just make it small," she tells Ray, holding out her wrist. "And pretty. I want it in script."

How the hell did she go from not wanting a tattoo, to now knowing exactly where she wants it and how she wants it to look?

I stand there, dumfounded, watching as Ray gets to work. He traces it out first, confirming she likes the size and script style. Any minute now, she's going to back out. No way is she actually going to follow through.

We're not even eighteen yet, but Ray isn't the most law-abiding citizen. If she actually does it, her parents are going to lose it.

"Seriously, Ellie, don't do this. It's not like you're going to be able to hide it easily. I believe you, let's just go."

She looks up at me with raised brows. "Nope. I'm doing it."

I can tell by her tone that she's set on it, and arguing with her won't get me anywhere.

Holy shit. Jack is going to kill me. I rub the back of my neck, already feeling the ghost of his hands around it, as a trickle of fear works its way down my spine. My chest simultaneously swells knowing my name will be on her skin. I didn't think it was possible to be both terrified and turned on at once.

Ray starts in on the first letter and Ellie flinches as the needle touches her skin, her free hand gripping the arm of the chair, but she doesn't say a word.

Wordlessly, I snag the seat nearby, scooting it until I'm next to her, grabbing her hand in mine. She instantly tightens her grip, letting out the pain the only way she can.

"You good?" I ask. I hate it when she's hurting, even if it's over something harmless.

She glares at me, pressing her lips together as she tries to tough it out. "I'm fine. Don't even think about gloating."

"Never," I say, but the grin tugging at my lips gives me away.

My girl is getting my name tattooed on her.

I like the thought of my name on her skin. It's almost barbaric how much I fucking like the thought of it. But I like something else even more—the idea that any asshole who thinks about hitting on her will see it and know she's mine.

Ellie's stubborn as hell, wild in a way that doesn't ask for permission. She does what she wants, when she wants, and there's no changing her mind once it's made up. I'd never try to control her. But this is a possessiveness she'll allow. And I'll take it.

When Ray finishes, she lifts her wrist to inspect the delicate script of my name branded on her flawless skin. "Well?" Ray asks, wiping it down.

Ellie beams, holding it up for me to see. "Guess I'm the tattoo type after all."

I shake my head, an erratic laugh tumbling out of me. "You're full of surprises, Ellie girl."

She shrugs, her chin dipping, pinning me in place with her pale eyes. "Your turn."

"What?" I laugh. "You want me to get one too? Like a matching one?"

She gestures to the chair. "Only seems fair, don't you think?"

Ray bursts out laughing. "I see what you did there, sweetheart. Smart girl."

I sigh, but take a seat with zero hesitation. As if every tattoo I have—and every one I plan to get—isn't already inspired by her. The roses etched on my forearm are her favorite flower, and the skull I had outlined today is a nod to the way she loves the dark and the beautiful—always dressed in black, listening to emo songs on repeat. She probably doesn't even realize it, but she's inked into my skin as much as she's embedded in my bones. "Alright, fine. But if we're doing this, I'm getting *Elyse* in the exact same spot. I'm doing your government name, Ellie girl."

She smirks, looking far too pleased with herself. "Good choice, sounds more official."

Once I'm settled, Ray gets to work, tracing quickly. As soon as the needle hits, the sting is sharp, but I barely notice. Out of the corner of my eye, Ellie watches intently, her face softening. She's so beautiful, the way she takes everything in, the way her smile says so much, but only for me. I'll gladly walk around with her name marking me like I'm the luckiest fucking guy to belong to her.

When it's over, we stand side by side, wrists extended, her name inked on me and mine on her.

Ray shakes his head, chuckling as he cleans up. "You kids are either the dumbest or the most romantic people I've ever met."

Ellie glances at me, her eyes shining with mischief. "We'll go with romantic."

I grin, pulling her wrist to my lips and press a kiss above the fresh tattoo. "Definitely romantic."

When I go to pay Ray, I know for certain he's undercharging me. My brows lift in question as he tells me the total.

"Just charging you for the skull. My cold, dead heart is throwing the names in for free."

I'd argue, but I'm not exactly rolling in it. Instead, I make a mental note to make things right one day.

Ellie grabs onto my arm, dragging me out of the shop and onto the quiet, dark street toward my car. Her face is bright as she looks at me, a surge of adrenaline no doubt running through her. Fuck, I'm like a moth to a flame when she gets like this—powerless against the magnetic pull of her energy. I can't wait for the day I never have to leave her side again. Until then, though, it's late, almost her curfew, so I drive a little faster than normal, grinning like an idiot the whole drive there.

Getting the tattoos probably wasn't the best idea, yet I can't bring myself to regret it. It's stupid, impulsive, and maybe a little reckless.

But it feels perfect. It feels like us.

CHAPTER 13

Elyse

HARMLESS LITTLE PRANKS

PRESENT

Something about my office feels wrong, though I can't quite put my finger on it. It's not something obvious —more like a sixth sense nagging at me.

I glance around, taking inventory. Calendar? Meticulously organized and untouched. Framed photographs, including the mugshot? Exactly as I left them. Perfectly curated decor? Immaculate, as always.

Still, the unease lingers. I scan the room again, slower this time, but everything looks perfectly in place. Maybe it's all in my head. Shaking it off, I settle into my chair and power up my computer.

That's when I see it.

Those little shits.

My monitors. The images on both screens are flipped upside down. *How?*

I stare in disbelief for a moment, fucking interns. I thought they looked a little too smug when I came in this morning, but I chalked it up to their excitement for spring break.

Ever since the mugshot incident, they've been pulling harmless little pranks. At first, it was annoying—between my siblings, I get enough grief without adding them to the mix. But after a while, I started to feel like a grumpy old witch, ruining their fun. Besides, it's all good-natured, and I have to admit, they're pretty creative.

"Faith!" I call out. "How the hell am I supposed to fix this?"

I've deemed Faith the leader of the three since she seems to be the most responsible.

Instead of Faith, Ben strolls in, hands in his pockets, a devious smile plastered across his face.

"What seems to be the problem, boss?" he asks, all mock innocence.

I level him with a frown. "You know exactly what the problem is."

He bites back a laugh, clearly enjoying himself. "Oh, that. Yeah, you're gonna want to press Ctrl + Alt + Down Arrow to flip it back. Unless you'd prefer to work upside down—might be good for blood flow."

"Ben," I warn, but he's already crossing the room, stepping behind my desk to fix it himself.

I reluctantly scoot back to give him room, but it's not enough distance to stop me from nearly choking on his cologne.

Young boys and their cheap cologne.

"You know," I start, inching away even more. "You weren't my first pick when it came to hiring interns," I grouse, watching as his fingers fly across the keyboard.

In truth, I felt a little strange hiring a male. Especially one who isn't interested in working in the wedding industry. But he needed the hours, and I needed someone savvy on the computer. So far it seems to be working out, even if he is a little *Dennis the Menace* at times.

"Oh, I'm well aware," he says, not even looking up.

"But I've got to admit," I continue, "your computer skills are useful. Too bad you use them for evil."

He glances up with a smirk, eyes giving me a once-over. "I wouldn't call it evil. I just like keeping things interesting."

I shake my head, unable to suppress a small grin. "That you do."

With a few keystrokes, the screens return to normal. Ben steps back, looking way too pleased with himself.

"Anything else I can do for you?" he asks, his tone overly polite.

"Yeah," I say dryly. "Tell Faith she owes me coffee for letting this happen on her watch."

Ben chuckles. "Will do, boss."

As he heads for the door, I call after him, "And I'm going to need a tutorial so I can mess with my brother's monitors."

"How many times do I have to tell you? I'm not charging you." Ariana swats my card away from the reader and slides a sixteen-ounce latte into my hands.

I needed an afternoon pick me up after one of my brides had a meltdown with me over gold chia chairs being the wrong shade of gold. She wanted a hideous yellow-gold, whereas the ones I already have on hand are a brassy-gold, which is much more elegant. It took an hour to convince her I was right without making her think I was trying to convince her of anything. I swear this job is two parts therapist, one part actual wedding planning.

"I'm trying to be supportive, and you won't let me," I say, exasperated.

"You being here is support enough."

Ariana is the baby of the family—technically. She's a twin, but Layla, her other half, managed to beat her into the world by a whole twelve minutes. She smiles in that soft way that makes her dimples show, and dusts her flour-covered hands on her apron.

Layla is more like me. It's not unusual for the two of us to be impulsive, speak without thinking, or do something completely rash just for the thrill of it. But Ariana is nothing like us. She's the calm to our chaos, pure goodness wrapped in an apron. She's the one you go to when life falls apart and you need a steady shoulder to lean on. Her hugs could fix anything, and she pours every ounce of that sweetness and care into her baking.

I take a sip of the latte, savoring the rich, creamy warmth. "You're too good, you know that? Makes the rest of us look bad."

Ariana grins, tying her apron tighter around her waist. "Someone has to balance out the family. Now, sit down and let me grab you a scone before Layla comes in and steals them all. I made the cranberry-orange ones you like."

She wanders off to the back, and I settle into an empty bistro table. It's quiet today, as expected—once Spring Release weekend hits, though, it'll be packed until winter. Spring Release marks the local wineries' big reveal of new vintages, and it's considered the unofficial kickoff to tourist season. My family's winery is usually the main attraction and draws in crowds from all over the country.

I stare out the window facing Main Street while I sip on my drink. Since it's finally feeling like spring, large hanging pots, overflowing with colorful flowers, adorn the lampposts lining the cobblestone sidewalks. The storefronts are decorated with window box arrangements, drawing attention to new window displays. Everyone can smell tourist season coming, doing everything they can to generate business. If there's one thing I love about my small town, she knows how to put on a show. Red Mountain is easily the cutest town in the county, and even though the younger version of me turned my nose up at the thought of calling Red Mountain home forever, the older, wiser version of me today knows it's a little slice of heaven.

The bell on the front door jingles, forcing my eyes to rove over as a man walks in wearing an olive-green sheriff's uniform. My breathing falters as I hold it, only to release it when I realize it's not Dominic, it's Ryker. A rush of disappointment hits me, but I shake it off. Considering how we left things the other day, he's the last person I should be hoping to run into.

Ryker flashes me a friendly smile as he approaches. I stand, meeting him halfway for a brief hug. It isn't until I pull away that I see he's not alone. Morales is with him. She ignores me, brushing past us to the counter to place her order.

Okay then. Kind of a bitch move.

Ignoring her obvious snub, I focus my attention back on Ryker. "How's it going, *Sheriff Tapert*?"

He blushes slightly, obviously still not used to the title. "Oh, you know, same stuff, different day." he says, cheerfully, as he joins me at my table.

I've always liked Ryker. Most people do—he's proof of that, being the youngest sheriff ever elected in the county. He also holds a special place in my heart since his wedding was one of the first I planned after taking over as the winery's event coordinator.

He married Claire Landry—now Tapert—five years ago, and they've been a beloved couple in town ever since. I felt awful when I heard about their struggles with infertility, but recently heard the good news that Claire is expecting. She's due in just a few months.

"Congratulations, by the way." I offer him a smile. "I heard about Claire."

His face lights up with pride. "Thank you. We're pretty excited. It's been a long time coming."

There's a glimmer of something that looks like sadness, but it's gone in an instant, replaced by his usual positive smile.

Ariana returns with a tray of scones and sets one down for each of us.

"Afternoon, Sheriff," Ariana greets, her face blushing pink, and Ryker tips his head at her.

I take a bite even though they're piping hot. "How's Claire doing? I feel like I haven't seen her in months," I ask Ryker, talking around a mouthful of scone.

His shoulders drop as his mouth presses into a line. "Well, the baby is good. Strong and healthy, but Claire has been sicker than hell. The doctor diagnosed her with HG, she's practically been on bed rest."

A bittersweet curve of my lips appears as I look at him. "I'm sorry to hear that, but happy the baby is staying healthy. If you two need anything at all let me know. I'm great at organizing meal trains and all sorts of stuff like that."

He smiles wistfully. "Thanks. I just might take you up on that one of these days. You've always been so great to us." His hands clasp over the table as he regards me thoughtfully. "I'm glad we ran into each other; I've been meaning to have a chat with you."

I take a small sip of my latte. "Oh, yeah? What about?"

His head lolls to the side. He's smiling, but it's strained. "I wanted to formally apologize to you over the arrest. I already spoke with Dominic, reprimanding him. You're a respected member of the community, and the entire matter could've been handled differently."

I don't like the idea of Ryker reprimanding Dominic. I may not agree with the whole arrest situation, but Dominic followed the law—that much I know. "I appreciate the apology, but it's completely unnecessary. I had a warrant out, and Dominic was just doing his job. It's water under the bridge now."

Ryker shakes his head with a light chuckle. "Can't help but defend him, can you?"

"I'm not defending him," I say, sounding very much defensive.

His smile turns knowing. "Whatever you say. We all know it's only a matter of time."

Before I can respond, his phone rings. He answers, only giving a few 'mm-hmms' in response before rushing to stand. "Morales," he calls out. "We've got a call."

Morales nods immediately, slapping a twenty on the counter as the barista hands her a drink.

On his way out, Ryker tosses me a wave, shooting me an apologetic smile.

"That man is going to be such a DILF," Ariana says quietly, checking out Ryker as he and Morales jog across the street to a cruiser.

I whip my head at her, shocked little miss innocent would say such a thing. "Ariana! He's married."

"What?" She laughs. "I can still look. It's not like I would actually act on anything."

My head cocks as I stare at her wide-eyed. "He's too old for you. You shouldn't even be looking at guys his age."

Ariana is only twenty-two, a child if you ask me.

Her face twists. "He's only a little older than you, and like I said, I'm not actually going to do anything. It's like having a celebrity crush."

She busies herself, setting scones in the display case, avoiding looking at me. Ariana has never brought a guy home before, and I worry about all the creeps out there, just chomping at the bit to take advantage of her naivety. The fact she admitted Ryker is attractive has my head spinning, worried she's setting her sights on unavailable men to avoid anything real.

It's not that I disagree. Ryker is handsome, in an—American-apple-pie-could-run-for-president—kind of way. Blond hair, cut high and tight, blue eyes, and he clearly puts in a lot of time at the gym. He's classically good-looking and rarely lacked for company when he was single. But I've never seen him as anything more than a friend.

I'm not sure why my stomach is souring. It's not as if he would ever leave Claire, and Ariana is way too shy to act on a crush, inappropriate or not.

"Just stick to guys your own age. We both know Layla is probably going to show up one day with a guy three times her age, and Dad will lose his shit. You have to be the good one."

She spins to face me, rolling her eyes, looking like the child she is. "I know. I'm always the good one."

> PSA Dad's birthday is coming up. We need to start brainstorming gift ideas.

SHANE

Easy. Boys trip to Vegas

LAYLA

Just because you want a free trip to Vegas doesn't mean that's what Dad wants. You're dumb.

GAVIN

Gift card?

ETHAN

I second the gift card idea.

> A gift card isn't a present.

> We want to give him something meaningful.

SHANE

Ok then what's your stellar idea genius

> We could all pitch in for a tandem kayak so
> he and Mom can go out on the river
> together.

SHANE

BOO. Pass. Vegas or bust!

ETHAN

He has a bad shoulder.

ARIANA

What about a weekend getaway?
Leavenworth?

LAYLA

What Ariana said

SHANE

How rich are you guys? I can barely afford
my own vacation.

LAYLA

Says the guy pushing for Vegas.

SHANE

It was worth a shot

ETHAN

Just tell me what I owe. I don't have time
for hours of back and forth texting.

GAVIN

> Ditto.

I toss my phone onto my desk with a groan. It pings again, but I don't even bother looking. This is exactly why I usually just handle this stuff myself. I ask for their input, and get nothing but bad ideas, sarcasm, and zero cooperation.

They'll complain later when I pick something out on my own, but what choice do I have? Dad's birthday isn't going to plan itself, and someone has to step up and make sure plans are executed. If I don't handle it, no one else will.

The buzz of the air conditioning is the only sound as I close my laptop and stretch my arms above my head. It's the tail end of the day, and I'm the last one here. Besides Ethan, but he's all the way over in his wing.

The interns left a mess in the break room with their green juice—again. I decided to let it slide this time. My patience isn't endless, but it's been a long week, and I don't have the energy to play the role of the office drill sergeant today.

Grabbing my bag, I power off the lights and lock the door behind me, my heels clicking against the pavement as I make my way to my car in the parking lot. The sky is painted with streaks of orange and pink, the kind of sunset that would make my mom gasp and reach for her phone.

As I get closer to my car, something catches my eye—a piece of paper tucked under the windshield wiper.

I frown. A flyer?

I pull the paper free, my fingers brushing against the cool glass of the windshield. It's not a flyer. It's a note.

Elyse, you have me tied up in knots. One day, I'll repay the favor.

My brow furrows as I read it again. The handwriting is unfamiliar, neat but rushed, like the writer was in a hurry. A chill creeps up my spine.

What the fuck?

It's probably the interns. It has to be.

They've been ramping up their pranks lately, and this has their fingerprints all over it. They're probably trying to freak me out after their upside-down monitor stunt earlier today.

I glance around the parking lot, half-expecting to catch one of them crouched behind a bush, snickering. But there's no one, just a mostly empty parking lot, looking slightly eerie as the last lights of day start to disappear beyond the horizon.

Sliding in behind the wheel, I toss the note onto the passenger seat. It lands face up, the words glaring at me. The phrase is strange, like maybe it's a joke or a pun but I'm missing the punchline.

I take a steadying breath. It's just a prank. They're kids with too much free time and not enough supervision. My stomach feels uneasy, the way it does when the house creaks in the middle of the night, but I shove the feeling down.

Once I get on the main road, I crank up the music, letting the familiar beat drown out my thoughts.

But as I continue driving, the note lingers in the back of my mind, unsettling in a way I can't fully explain. And for the first time in a long while, I double-check that my car doors are locked after I pull into my driveway.

It's probably nothing. Still, as I step into the house and bolt the door behind me, a pit in my stomach grows.

CHAPTER 14

Dominic

PRESENT

The morning air is cool, the sky just starting to brighten as I drive to work. I go through the usual routine—coffee in the cupholder, radio turned low, mind cycling through renovation tasks. It's a welcome distraction, a way to keep from thinking about today. It's my first day with the detective's unit. I'm so nervous; I'm pretty sure I've already sweat through my uniform.

I'm more nervous about this than I ever was at my last job. It's the pressure. It's the fear of failure.

A jolt shoots up my shoulder, as if my body is reminding me that maybe I'm not ready yet. Maybe I'll never be ready.

My thoughts are interrupted when dispatch cuts in with instructions to switch to a private channel.

"All units, report to Canyon Ridge, coordinates sent. Possible 10-54."

I nearly slam on the breaks. *What?*

That can't be right, it's the radio code for a possible dead body, foul play suspected.

My heart starts to race with a rush of adrenaline as I flip on the lights and sirens, making a sharp U-turn toward the location. Canyon Ridge isn't far, but the isolation of the area has alarm bells going off in my head. It's too early for most hikers, too late for late-night wanderers. Whatever is waiting for us there, it won't be good.

By the time I arrive, the scene is already swarming. Patrol cars, both city and county, line the dirt road, their lights casting an eerie glow against the trees. Ryker stands near the perimeter, talking to Corporal Keene.

For a moment, I stay frozen, gripping the wheel so tightly my knuckles ache. *Breathe in. Breathe out.*

It's been a while since I've rolled up on a scene like this. And even though it's not the same—not the same location, not the same circumstances—it still feels the same.

This is my first time responding to a big incident since the shooting, and I'm struggling to separate the two.

The swarm of officers moving with practiced efficiency. The low murmur of radios crackling over the chatter. Forensic tech's cameras click as they document everything.

It's only a matter of time before the press shows up, and starts crowding behind the barricades.

It all blurs together, the sights and sounds folding over me like a tide, pulling me under. My throat is dry. My pulse pounds. My shoulder burns.

Breathe.

I flex my fingers, willing the tremor in them to stop as I peel my hands off the wheel. They still shake as I open the door, still shake as I step onto solid ground.

But by the time I reach Ryker, my hands are steady. My breathing is even.

Under control.

For now.

The moment our eyes meet, his expression tells me everything I need to know.

"Morning." He looks uncharacteristically grim.

"Who's the vic? Have they been identified?"

He nods slowly, while scanning the scene. "It's Victoria Delmar."

The evidence was leading to this, but that doesn't stop the sense of shock radiating through me. This wasn't the outcome any of us were hoping for.

"Who called it in?"

Ryker gives me a baffled look. "Anonymous tip." He lets out a wry laugh and shakes his head. It's not funny, and we both know it. It's the kind of laugh you give when you know you're fucked.

"Shit," I mutter, glancing toward the taped-off area where crime scene techs are already at work. "What's the condition?"

Ryker exhales heavily. "Looks like she was dumped here. CSI hasn't found much so far. The medical examiner estimates she's only been dead a few hours."

She's been missing for a while but only died recently. Was she with the perpetrator the entire time? A million questions are rifling through my mind at once.

I follow his gaze to the cluster of trees ahead. Even from a distance, I can make out the dark shape lying on the ground, partially covered by a tarp. My jaw clenches.

So much for low crime. I thought I was getting away from this kind of shit.

"Still think it's all fabricated?" Ryker throws me a pointed, *I told you so* glare.

I don't respond. A dead body doesn't change the fact that this case feels strange—off in a way I can't logically explain without sounding like a woo-woo conspiracy theorist. But now, it's urgent. We need to figure out what the hell is going on before someone else ends up like her.

"We'll need to notify her family," Ryker says, his voice quieter now. "But first, we have to manage the scene."

"Are you going to call in the feds? We're not exactly equipped to take on an investigation of this caliber."

His spine straightens like a rod, eyes pinching. "No feds. And should that change, I'll be the one who makes the determination."

Clearly, I hit a nerve. Rather than argue, I nod. I know when to pick my battles with Ryker, and now isn't the time. Even though I'm fucking right. We're not equipped for this. For most of these uniforms, it's their first time seeing a murder victim up close.

As we move closer to the scene, I catch sight of Morales by the patrol cars. She's chipper, as usual, chatting with a city cop and gesturing animatedly. Even a dead body can't rattle her, apparently.

It's been over a week since she showed up at my house unannounced, and I've been actively avoiding her with little success.

She hasn't tried anything and the more time that passes the more I think I'm overreacting. But the personal attention she's been giving me lately, trying to get me to engage with her, it's too much. Her bubbly demeanor is grating at the best of times, and now it's just...awkward.

I told myself I'd keep things professional, but every time I see her, there's this undercurrent of something I don't want to deal with. A crush I don't reciprocate, a situation I don't want to navigate. So, I've been distant.

She notices me now, waving enthusiastically. I pretend not to see her, walking toward the scene instead.

Ryker casts me a look, but I ignore it, focusing on the task at hand. There's a killer out there, and this could just be the beginning. Whatever Morales's feelings are can wait.

I join Sergeant Vorheis and the rest of the detective's unit on shift. We're standing over the body, and I take a deep breath, letting the weight of the situation settle in. It never gets easier—seeing someone's lifeless form, especially when it's obvious she didn't die of natural causes, the marred skin around her neck giving me a clue at cause of death.

Acid creeps up my throat, caused by the stench of decomposition. Taking a few steps back, I force a swallow. There's nothing quite like starting the day with a dead body. My old captain used to say that the day it gets easy to see the bad shit, is the day you're no longer fit for the job.

Feeling more composed, I step forward, crouching down, inspecting her closely, but making sure to keep enough distance so I don't interfere with forensics. Ryker was right, definitely dumped. There's only a small amount of blood, small enough to make me think the perp left it there on purpose.

Vorheis gathers us off to the side.

"What's our next move, Sarge?" Detective Kincaid asks.

Vorheis exhales through his nose, scanning the stretch of dirt road. "This wasn't where it happened. Body was dumped. Clean, intentional. They knew this place."

He gestures to Kincaid. "Check for tire tracks, drag marks —anything that tells us what kind of vehicle we're dealing with."

Then to me: "Alvarez, we need to know who has access out here. Rangers, hunters, anyone who might've stumbled onto this place. Start making calls."

Vorheis keeps rattling off assignments, but shouts from the press barricade pull my attention. Two vans from local news stations just rolled up. How they got here so fast is beyond me.

Fucking bloodhounds.

Homicide is rare in Clore County. It's going to have the whole community on edge until we get to the bottom of this.

"Heard they're dropping like flies over there," Adrian says through the speaker, his voice laced with dry humor.

"Jesus Christ, Adrian. Have a little decency," I grit, though there's nothing behind it, I'm too tired to argue. "Is it already on the news in Portland?"

"Not that I know of. Heard it on the police scanner app," he replies, as he crunches on—what I'm assuming is—a potato chip. "I'm always listening. Gotta make sure you're staying alive up there."

His tone is light, teasing, but I know better. We both do. It's not just a joke—it's his way of coping. Adrian probably does listen, every chance he gets, just to make sure a call doesn't come up to make him think something happened to me. To make sure he's not getting another call telling him I've landed in the hospital—or worse.

I know exactly how he feels too, because it's exactly what I went through watching the news while he was deployed. Thankfully, after serving six years, he's back to being a civilian, and the whole family breathes a lot easier.

I change the subject, steering us toward safer ground. "Mom mentioned cutting her trip short."

He sighs. "Yeah, she said the same thing to me."

"I don't like her being down there alone, without him."

"Neither do I," Adrian agrees before crunching loudly. "We need to talk her into moving up here. Portland's perfect —close to me and Celia, and not far enough from you for her to complain about the drive."

"She's set in her ways, though," I remind him. "Good luck convincing her to leave the house 'apá practically built with his bare hands."

After selling the house Adrian and I grew up in, our parents built their dream house in Phoenix. It was less work to maintain than the sprawling property they had before and conveniently closer to Mexico for quick trips to visit family. It was all part of their retirement plan.

Adrian chuckles, a sad kind of chuckle. "Yeah, she's tough, but I'm tougher. I'll wear her down eventually. Besides, you know how Celia is. She's already got Pinterest boards full of 'downsizing tips' and 'how to help parents relocate.'"

I don't actually know Celia all that well—I've only met her twice. Once when Adrian introduced us, and then again at the small family dinner they had to celebrate their marriage after eloping.

After our dad died, we both coped in our own ways. I quit my job and relocated, set on winning back the girl I could never let go, and using the small lump of life insurance money my dad left me to buy a house that's barely standing. Adrian married a woman he hardly knew, like he was trying to fast-forward through life to get to the good parts. I'm not sure if what either of us did is healthy, but I think 'apá would be proud of us, if not at least highly entertained.

"I'll let you do the talking. You're better at that shit than I am, anyway."

"So," Adrian starts. "Have you talked to her yet?"

I can hear his smile. Fucking dick. "Yeah."

He laughs. "Not going well I take it?"

I knew I shouldn't have told him the main reason I decided to move back to Red Mountain. He's been giving me a hard time about it ever since. At first, I was able to easily brush it off, but now that my encounters with Ellie have all gone to shit, his teasing is hitting like a punch to the stomach.

"Things could be better."

"She probably thinks you're psycho. It's not normal to

uproot your entire life just to chase after some girl you screwed things up with years ago."

He's always assumed I was the reason for our breakup, but to this day, I've never been able to figure out where exactly it all went wrong. We were so close to summer break—to having months of alone time. It didn't make sense to me then, and all these years later I have a hell of a lot more questions than answers.

"What did you even say to her when she asked why you moved back?" Adrian asks, breaking me out of my thoughts.

I clench my jaw, my grip tightening around my beer bottle. "She hasn't asked," I admit. "And if she does, I'll tell her it's for work until I think she's ready to hear the truth."

"Uh-huh," Adrian drawls, oozing sarcasm. "Because Red Mountain is just overflowing with opportunities. Come on, man."

Rubbing the spot between my brows does little to soothe the panic Adrian has induced. "You're not helping."

He howls with laughter, and I resist the urge to hang up the phone. "Elyse has never done anything she didn't already set her sights on. Not as a kid, and likely not now. I don't know what made you think showing up ten years later would warm her up to you."

"How about you focus on your love life, and I'll focus on mine. Stay out of it," I mumble.

"Look," Adrian says, his laughter finally tapering off. "You've got two options: either you give her space and let her come to you—which, let's be honest, might never happen—or you figure out a way to show her you're smarter than you were at nineteen."

I sigh, gliding my palm on the back of my neck. "Easier said than done. I thought I was making progress, but she's so quick to lash out at me, I can't get a read on her."

I was completely caught off guard when she showed up at

my place the other day, and I played it all wrong. I came on too strong, pushed her too far. It's so easy to go there with her, easily slipping into her gravitational pull—natural, effortless. Now I'm not sure how to recover from it. I don't know where to go from here.

Adrian snorts. "Not that you asked, but my advice would be to start small. You're always doing too much; you're too intense," he says, as if it's the most obvious thing in the world. "Show up, be consistent, and don't make it about you. Be laid back. And maybe if you're patient, and don't attack her like a dog in heat, she'll eventually come to you."

The irony of getting relationship advice from him is not lost on me. He used to be adamantly against marriage and anything close to a serious relationship.

I cut the call short, claiming something work related came up, when really I'm done talking about my recent string of failures involving Ellie. If I don't figure out how to make things right, I'm not sure I'll ever be able to move on.

I'm clinging onto one thread of hope, and one alone.

The tattoo.

She kept it.

CHAPTER 15

Dominic

RECKLESS DECISIONS

17 YEARS OLD

"**Y**ou're not allowed to see that boy anymore!" Jack yells at Ellie, as if I'm not standing right beside her. *That boy.*

Ellie stiffens, her fingers curling into fists at her sides, her whole body radiating pure rage. Jack has always liked me—I know that much. But right now, he's looking at me like I've just stolen his daughter's innocence and ran it through the dirt.

And he doesn't even know the half of it. He'd likely kill me if he knew his little girl is far from innocent.

Ellie tilts her chin up, defiant. "I'm not a kid! You don't get to tell me who I can and can't see, you can't control me."

Jack's face reddens, his jaw tight. "You are seventeen years old! You're a goddamn kid, and you live under my roof. You think this is about control? It's about you making reckless decisions! Tattooing a boy's name on your wrist is not what I would define as responsible behavior. Jesus, Elyse, what were you thinking?"

I knew they would discover the tattoo, but I didn't anticipate it being so quickly. It took them two weeks. I was hoping we could hide it for a year. Or even better—forever.

As I was saying my goodbyes to Ellie at the front door, Jack caught sight of her wrist as she hugged me, and that's when all hell broke loose.

Ellie crosses her arms, refusing to shrink under her Dad's stare. "I was thinking that it's my body and my choice. And that I love Dominic. And that maybe it's none of your freaking business."

Leanne steps in then, her voice calmer but still strained. "Sweetheart, no one is saying you don't love him. But this is permanent. Did you even think of what would happen if you two break up? You're so young—"

Ellie barks out a bitter laugh, cutting Leanne off. "Wow. Thanks for the vote of confidence. I thought you were on my side."

I stay quiet, feeling like I'm watching a car crash in slow motion. I don't blame them for freaking out—I get it. I knew Jack would be mad, but he's beyond mad. I've never seen him so angry, and it's fucking scary.

But Ellie isn't backing down.

Her dad looks ready to explode, hands firm on his hips, eyes locked on me now. "And you—"

I take a step back, my body bracing for a blow.

Ellie throws up her hands, moving to stand in front of me. "Oh, for God's sake, stop it! Stop looking at him like this is his fault. He didn't make me do it. In fact, he tried to talk me out of it. Newsflash—I didn't get it for him—I got it for me."

She reaches for my hand, and I hesitate for a fraction of a second, knowing walking out of here right now is only going to make this worse. But when she looks up at me, eyes blazing with determination, I know there's no stopping her.

I sigh and thread my fingers through hers. "Ellie—"

"No," she cuts me off, tugging me toward the door. "I'm done with this conversation."

Jack steps forward, but Ellie doesn't waver. "I am NOT a little kid. You don't get to make decisions for me, and you don't get to keep us apart. If you're going to try, then I don't want to be here right now."

With that, she yanks open the door, dragging me with her as she storms outside.

"Elyse Merideth Ledger, get back inside this house this instant!" Jack yells.

Leanne's softer voice comes through, almost out of ear shot. "Let her go, honey, she'll come back."

I cast one last glance at her parents—Jack looking furious, Leanne looking worried—but there's nothing I can say that will fix this right now.

So I do the only thing I can. I walk out with her.

Even if I know damn well, we'll pay for this.

CHAPTER 16

Elyse

MY TERRITORIAL SIDE

PRESENT

"Can I just pay for this now, and get it over with?"

The courthouse clerk types away on her computer, her long acrylics clacking on the keys.

I got lucky. The judge was really lenient and let me go with a fine. After some online research, I was expecting to be hit with community service.

"Hmm that's odd," she says, pinching her face as she stares at the screen.

My heart drops. If there's another bench warrant out for me, I'm going to lose my shit. "What? What is it?"

"Says here, your fine was already paid." Her hand reaches through the divider, long nails wiggling near me. "Let me see that paperwork again."

I hand it to her, feeling just as confused as she looks. After a few moments, she slaps the counter, forcing a jolt out of me. Just being near the jail has my nerves buzzing with unease.

"I see it now. According to the note in your file, your fine was taken care of by Deputy Alvarez." She looks up me through the glasses resting on her nose. "Must've done something super sweet for that kind of *favor*."

The way she says *favor* makes it sound like I sucked his dick so he'd pay my fine. I fight a scoff while willing away the red heat creeping up my neck. She probably thinks I just got done working the corner, and based on the way she's eyeing my black leather skirt and knee-high boots, I'm all but confirming her suspicions. Great.

"So, am I good to go?"

"Looks to be that way," she says, her voice deceptively nice.

Something tells me I'm going to be the topic of conversation amongst the courthouse clerks, the moment I hit the parking lot.

As I walk out the exit door with my head down, distracted by the red notifications littering my phone, my shoulder collides with something hard, setting me off balance, and I nearly trip.

Looking up, I find a set of narrowed brown eyes, blazing into me. It's Deputy Morales and she's giving me a smile that looks both syrupy-sweet and razor-sharp.

"Sorry," she says in a sing-song with a sheepish shrug. "Wasn't paying attention."

Yeah, right.

"Hi!" I say, forcibly upbeat. "You work with Dominic, right?"

Her smile drops, jaw tightening. "Yeah, why? You got a problem with that?"

What is wrong with this girl? "No, of course not," I say through a smirk. "Just like getting to know Dominic's coworkers, that's all."

My territorial side is coming out, but I can't help it. So, what if I'm making myself sound like his girlfriend? She's the one acting like she has some kind of claim over him.

"You know, it's really pathetic that you can't take a hint and leave him alone. Obviously, he doesn't want you."

This bitch...

"Sweetie, if he wanted you, you'd know it. Pretty sure drooling over him at work is more pathetic."

She scoffs, crossing her arms, and popping a hip.

I haven't wanted to lunge at someone this hard since I saw Ethan's skank ex-fiancé at the bar, but there was a little liquor in my system then. Right now, I'm totally sober, yet the same surge of anger is still taking hold of me.

"Sweetie," she says, throwing the word back at me. "If he really wanted *you*, he wouldn't be all over me at work."

I recoil, my head snapping back. I'm almost certain she's lying. Dominic doesn't strike me as the type to flirt with coworkers, but the image she just planted lodges itself at the forefront of my mind, and it's jarring. The thought of him touching her sends my heart into overdrive.

What if he does have feelings for her? What if they start dating? What if I have to see him with someone who isn't me?

I hate all of it. Selfishly. Completely.

Why did he have to come back?

My eyes slit, sizing her up. "What did you say your name was again?"

Her lips curl into a snarl. "Talia." She steps closer, trying to intimidate me it seems, but our height difference makes her attempt laughable. I tower over her by at least six inches, if not more. "If you know what's good for you, you'll stay away from him."

With that, she turns, joining a group of uniforms standing around chatting.

For a brief moment, I'm frozen. Was that an actual threat? From a cop, no less. There are a lot of things I'll let go, but not getting the last word isn't one of them.

"Hey, Talia," I call out. She turns her head, unable to hide the surprise in her expression.

"I'll let Dominic know how lovely it's been running into you. Tonight. When we're in bed."

I've crossed over into crazy ex territory, and it's not a good look. It's been hours, and I still can't stop thinking of what I told Morales. If it gets back to Dominic, he's going to see it exactly for what it is—marking my territory. He's not even my territory to mark.

I don't know how to coexist with him when we're nothing, but we've been *everything*.

"What do you think?" Layla, asks, showing me her right hand, freshly manicured.

I might've been inspired by the judgy clerk, because right after leaving the courthouse, I asked Layla if she was free for a manicure.

"Pretty," I tell her, distracted.

She frowns, admiring the peachy pale-pink polish. "I wanted to go brighter, but it's kind of frowned upon to wear polish while we're in the program, so I had to keep it subtle."

Shaking my head, I offer her a more genuine smile. "Sorry, no. It looks great; I just have a lot on my mind."

Layla shrugs, not one to pry, and resumes watching one of the several TVs in the nail salon, each one playing daytime TV —a few talk shows, soap operas, game shows, and an old sitcom rerun.

"Did you hear about the dead body?" Layla asks, so casually you'd think she was talking about the weather.

My lips turn downward. "Please don't tell me some nursing school cadaver story again." An uncomfortable shiver works its way through me. I usually get squeamish whenever Layla talks about school. I cannot handle medical stuff.

Her eyes bulge, as if I've sprouted a second head. "You seriously haven't heard? Do you live under a rock? It's been all over the news."

Since when does she watch the news? I never watch it. Occasionally, I'll read an article in the paper to support Marisa, but I find the news depressing. It seems more and more, some crime happens, large enough to become another chapter in the history books. I've lived through more historical events than I can count, and I'm not even thirty yet. It's exhausting.

"Well, are you going to enlighten me or keep making me feel guilty for preferring to stay under the safety of my rock?"

Her chin lifts to the screen directly in front of us. It's a commercial for the evening news airing later, showing Canyon Ridge. It's been taped off with yellow crime scene tape and Ryker is standing in front of it, being interviewed by a reporter. The footage is dark, with a time stamp in the corner dated for yesterday.

It's muted so I can't hear what's being said, but I can still put the pieces together. A missing woman, whose name sounds vaguely familiar, was found dead. The circumstances are suspicious enough the sheriff's office has declared her death a result of homicide, and the investigation is ongoing.

My eyes find him before I even realize I'm searching for him. I can barely make Dominic out, but I know his form. He's almost out of frame, hands tucked in his pockets while chatting with another deputy. His expression is tense, and the tension continues in his stance. Balled up fists, strained arms muscles, even his neck is fraught with tension.

"You know you don't always have to undress him with your eyes." Layla laughs, forcing me to blink.

I scrunch my nose at her. "I don't know what you're talking about." Maybe if I play dumb, she'll drop it.

"Mom said you left with him after that Sunday dinner he crashed." She pins me with a look, wagging her brows.

Rolling my eyes, my focus returns to the manicurist as she freshens up my usual red polish. "You're reaching. It was nothing, just a ride home."

"You're literally the worst liar. Just admit you still like him and get back together already. If you do it by next week, I win the bet."

Snapping my neck, I turn to face her. "You guys already have a bet going?"

My siblings are always betting on something. Usually, I'm at the helm of it. Never thought I'd be the subject.

She snorts. "Fuck yeah, we're betting. Do you even know us?"

We're quiet for a stretch, me mulling over my siblings turning my love life into a money grab, Layla engrossed in some random soap opera.

"She had a stalker, you know?" Layla says out of nowhere.

"Who had a stalker?"

"Victoria. The victim."

Oh, we're back on that subject?

"Weird," I tell her, disinterested.

"Yeah," she continues. "I guess he started leaving her these weird notes on her car, then he started sending her flowers. Eventually he got braver and—"

"Did you say notes on her car?"

Up until now, I'd convinced myself it was some kind of one off. Some prank from the interns. Now I'm not so sure.

"Where did you hear that?"

"Her mom was interviewed by some news station from Seattle. I listened to it while I was getting ready this morning."

My stomach sinks.

One note doesn't mean I have a stalker. Who the hell would want to stalk me, anyway? I barely have a social life. I'm boring.

It's the interns. It's definitely the interns.

I think I would know if I had a stalker.

CHAPTER 17

Elyse

EAT YOU ALIVE

PRESENT

You'd think that being a wedding planner would make me great at dealing with criers. Turns out, not so much. Which makes Jenna's full-on sobbing meltdown even more of a nightmare.

"There, there," I say, awkwardly patting her back like I'm burping a baby.

"What am I going to do?" she wails, hiccuping between words. "The dress is hideous! Matt's going to leave me at the altar!"

Honestly, would that be the worst thing?

"He's not going to leave you over a dress," I say, as soothing as possible. "And I happen to know an amazing seamstress who can fix this."

Jenna sniffles, lifting her tear-streaked face to look at me, her mascara smudged beyond recognition. "Really? You think they can fix it?"

"Absolutely," I say with a confidence I don't entirely feel.

"She's a miracle worker. If anyone can make your dress look exactly how you imagined, it's her."

There was a mix-up with Jenna's dress. Not only did it come three sizes too big, it also came backless and with a sheer bodice that's hideous.

She inhales shakily, clinging to the hope in my words. "Okay. Okay, yeah. That might work." She takes another deep breath and wipes her face with the tissue I handed her. "You're sure Matt won't notice?"

I stifle the urge to roll my eyes. "Jenna, Matt won't care if you're wearing a potato sack. He's going to be so overwhelmed seeing you walk down the aisle, the dress won't even register."

I'm completely pulling this out of my ass. Matt is a shallow douche.

Her lips twitch upward in the barest hint of a smile, believing my spiel.

"Besides," I add, "Men don't notice little details. He loves you. Let's focus on that, okay?"

Jenna nods, finally seeming to calm down, though her grip on my arm remains a little too tight. "Thank you, really. I don't know what I'd do without you."

"You would've figured it out, just not as quickly as me." I joke lightly, earning a trembling laugh from her. "Now, let's get that dress to the seamstress and keep this between us. No need for Matt—or anyone else—to know about this very fixable little mess up."

She nods again, her shoulders straightening as she stands. "You're the best. I don't know if I could plan this wedding without you."

I give her a forced smile. "It's what I'm here for."

After Jenna leaves, taking the last of my energy with her, I slump my back against the wall. The emotional capacity it takes to even attempt at being comforting is utterly exhausting.

Unfortunately, rest isn't an option—not with my mom heading straight for me, coming up the staircase that connects to the lobby.

"What are you doing here? Should you be walking up stairs yet?"

She levels me with an annoyed stare. "I can walk. It's been weeks since the surgery. And your dad wanted to chat with Ethan, so I tagged along."

She pulls me in for a hug, enveloping me in her signature Dior perfume.

When she steps back, her brows knit as her eyes take me in. "You look tired. Is everything okay?"

I manage a smile, hoping to deflect. "Just a long day, that's all. You know how busy this time of the year gets for me."

Her frown deepens, and I know she's not buying it. She has a sixth sense for sniffing out drama, especially when it involves her kids.

The truth is, I'm running on barely any sleep. After Layla brought up the dead body, I ended up watching the news special on it. Now that stupid note is haunting me even more. I can't get it out of my head, and since the interns have been on spring break, I haven't been able to confront them about it either. I was up all night last night, tossing and turning with ridiculous scenarios playing out in my head. Worse, my imagination insisted on casting Dominic as the hero—a detail I won't be sharing with anyone, but especially not my mom.

"Would this have anything to do with a certain someone?" Her brows waggle, her smile comically wide. She's about a subtle as a freight train.

I breathe out a groan, forcing myself to summon the restraint to keep my frustration in check. "You just had to invite him to dinner, didn't you?"

If she hadn't invited him to dinner, I never would've

147

found out about the house, and I never would've shown up, embarrassing myself more than I thought possible.

I'd still be completely content living without the knowledge that he bought *our* house.

I was honest when I told Dominic I hadn't been by in years—almost ten years.

When I think of Sullivan Ridge House, I think of us. A place where we shared everything, where we dreamed, where we made plans.

Since our breakup, it's stood in my mind as a representation of everywhere I fall short. Too cowardly to be honest. Too broken to ever be whole. Too stubborn to admit I'm wrong. And worst of all, too late.

I'm better off alone. At least then, there's no one to disappoint but myself.

My mom's expression softens. "I should have told you. It was wrong of me to go behind your back, but it's so hard not meddling. I know it's wrong, and I do it anyway."

I know she means well—she's not malicious—but she needs to leave this alone. She can't right my wrongs, as much as I know she wants to. The past is in the past, and that's where it needs to remain.

"Well, stop. Please. You can't push us together like we're puppets. Leave him alone. No one forced him to move back here; it's not your responsibility to lay out the welcome wagon for him."

As she crosses her arms, her expression hardens a fraction. "Elyse, he just lost his dad, and his family doesn't live in the area anymore. I would think you of all people would know how badly he needs some support."

I pinch the bridge of my nose, trying to ward off the guilt churning in my stomach. "Supporting him doesn't have to mean inserting him into every part of my life. He and I are... complicated."

She tilts her head, giving me the kind of look that leaves me feeling too exposed. "Complicated doesn't mean unsalvageable. Sometimes, it's just another word for unfinished."

I suck in a breath, hating how easily she can poke holes in my defenses. "I'm not interested in trying," I say, barely above a whisper, looking away.

I don't understand how I can hold so strong in my resolve to not let Dominic in, and my mom can wash it away in seconds, as if I was never strong to begin with.

"You can't avoid him forever, you need to talk to him, to tell him." she says, gentler than I deserve, running a reassuring hand up and down my arm.

I've blocked so much of that time out of my mind, the memories too painful to confront, sometimes I forget how much she knows—how much she was there for.

"Life is short," she continues. "And pretend all you want, but you and I both know you never got over that boy." I look down, anywhere to avoid my mom's eyes, my skin prickling from the intensity of this conversation. The urge to fake an appointment or phone call just to escape, pulls at me, but I resist it, knowing she would see right through it.

"I don't even know where to start—what to say."

Rather than answer me right away, she wraps me in a tight hug. Normally, too much affection overwhelms me, but in this instance, I don't resist it, letting myself sink into her embrace.

"You don't have to keep holding onto whatever hurt you're carrying." Her voice is muffled against me, but too clear to convince myself I didn't hear every word. "Getting it all out in the open will be relieving. Some things you can't avoid forever, they'll eat you alive otherwise."

CHAPTER 18

Dominic

PEOPLE YOU MAY KNOW

PRESENT

I can't do another night of cold dinner, alone in that empty house. Every day I come this much closer to cutting my losses and scrapping this whole remodel thing. I'm not nearly as skilled as I thought I was, and it's taking forever to gut and rebuild every inch of the house.

Work was stressful, so I'm treating myself to a hot meal at Sagebrush diner. I take up residence in a booth that's seen better days while I scroll through social media, waiting for my order to be done. There's a red notification, indicating I have an unread message. It's the same message that's been hanging out in my inbox since I was in the hospital. I wasn't ready to read it then, and I'm still not ready.

Ignoring it, I keep scrolling, in search of anything else.

After Ellie broke things off with me, she blocked me on everything, including social media. At the time, it hurt, because the message was clear—I wasn't welcome in her life anymore. The more time that passed, though, the more grateful I became. I never had to worry about depressingly looking at her happy life without me. There wasn't a fear that I'd drink too much one night and message her, likely making a fool of myself. Now, it's been so long, I'm not even sure she's on social media.

My eyes slide over to the kitchen to see if they're bagging up my food. By the looks of it, they're not. I stare back down at my phone and curiosity gets the best of me.

Quickly, I look around, as if someone is watching me about to creep on my ex. No one seems to be paying attention, so I proceed, and type in her name. To my surprise, she's the first to pop up in the search.

When did she unblock me?

I click her profile and get flooded with so many images at once, my eyes don't know where to settle. Ellie with her family. Ellie and Scottie in Chicago. Ellie in a bikini on the beach holding a margarita. My gaze snags on that one a little longer than it should.

So fucking beautiful.

Growing up, she was insecure about her height, always the tallest girl in our class. She takes after Jack's side of the family, tall and thin. My mom used to call her "flaquita" and would tease her that she needed to eat more. I had to have A LOT of talks with my mom to knock that shit off. She didn't mean it in a negative way, it's just common in Mexican culture to end up with a nickname that's usually your biggest insecurity.

Everything she was insecure about, I only thought made her more attractive. I liked that she was tall, that when I held her, I could stare into her eyes. I liked the way she fit against me, as if our bodies were meant to be intertwined, every curve aligning perfectly.

The more I scroll, the more it aches to see all the life she's lived without me. Every picture is a glimpse into a life I know nothing about. I heard through old buddies that she had moved back to Red Mountain after college, which surprised me because she was always adamant in having no interest in living in our small town. It seems even though her plans changed, her life looks anything but small. Filled with travel and adventures—everything she used to dream of. She looks happy. And I wonder if she is happy. It's easy to look happy for a snapshot that took a second to take, when in reality your life is falling apart.

None of her posts show her with another man, which, embarrassingly, brings me a sense of relief. But then again, she's the kind of person who erases someone completely once she's done with them—something I know all too well. I can only imagine the trail of broken hearts she's left behind since me.

"Order number ten," the teenager behind the counter calls out.

I stand, still distracted by my deep dive, and accidentally collide with something soft as a cloud of warm amber embraces me.

My obstacle makes a girlish grunting sound at the same time my phone crashes to the floor. "Sorry about that," I say before I realize who it is.

Ellie.

She stiffens and turns to me, her clear green eyes meeting mine. Then her gaze darts down, to my phone that's facing up. She bends down to retrieve it and stares at the screen.

"Is this my—"

I snatch the phone out of her hand, the tips of our fingers making the slightest contact, and it sends a shock up my arm. "Yep," I quip. "You came up under *People You May Know*."

Her brows raise and I know she knows I'm lying. "Sure," she teases, smiling.

Smiling...

Shaking my head, I look at her again to confirm I'm not imagining it.

I'm not. It's still there, and it's aimed at me.

It's the first genuine, full-fledged smile I've received from her, and fuck, was it worth the wait. I would've waited a lifetime for that smile if I had to.

"You caught me." My face heats, admitting the truth.

"Order number ten!" the worker repeats.

I nod, gesturing to the counter. "That's my order."

She steps aside and lets me pass by, the amber smell lingering off her skin infiltrates my senses as I do.

After grabbing my food, I turn back around and expect to see the spot she was standing in empty, since she's always trying to avoid me. Instead, I'm pleased to see she's still right where I left her.

Our eyes connect as I walk back with my takeout bag in hand. Just seeing her—in this old familiar place—it takes me back. The past and present collide, like no time has passed while simultaneously feeling the rigidness of when our relationship severed, sending us on opposite paths. It's a painful reality, forcing me to take a big inhale in an attempt to steady my erratic heartbeat.

Though a soft smile is resting on her red lips, her arms are crossed over her chest—an obvious wall, nearly impenetrable. I want to bulldoze right through it and get to the place where this isn't so hard. But I can't—I have to climb it instead.

On approach, her arms cross tighter as she steps back—the wall not budging.

"Picking up food?" I ask, like an idiot. Why else would she be here.

She breathes a laugh. Her eyes bounce around my face and to the surrounding restaurant. "Great work, detective. Yeah, I'm picking up food."

I shake my head and tsk, hitching a brow. "Not a detective, just a deputy."

Her tongue rolls over her teeth, drawing my attention

back to her pouty, crimson mouth as she works at holding back a playful grin. "Oh right, my mistake. Sorry, *Deputy Alvarez*."

The way she said *Deputy Alvarez*, with a sultry little edge, stirs something in me I haven't felt in a long while. It's not hard to imagine her calling me that in a difference scenario— one where she's under me, thighs spread open, pussy clenching around my cock as I fuck her so thoroughly she can't remember anyone but me—claimed. Mine. I want it so badly, the thought alone has my zipper straining. *God, I'm easy*.

Swallowing, I feel my Adam's apple bob painfully in my throat. I forgot the way she pulls at me, can put me under her spell in one look. My gaze trips up on her face—everywhere I land, I want to stay. She completely disarms me and has no idea.

I don't know how to be around her and not be *us*. Ten years didn't do shit to change that.

Now that I have my food, I have no reason to stick around, but the last thing I want is to lose out on time with her, even if it's only seconds.

"My goodness, look at you two," Marie, the owner of Sagebrush shouts from across the restaurant. She approaches us with quick steps, nearly bouncing, a wide smile splitting her face. "Well, if it isn't the star quarterback and head cheerleader. You two lovebirds back together? We all got such a kick out of hearing about the arrest."

We exchange glances, a silent conversation passing between us.

Ellie bites her lip, her fair skin noticeably flushed. "Just picking up food." Her voice is breathy.

She seems way more affected by Marie's nosiness than I would've expected.

It's no secret Ellie and I were every small town cliché—the

makings of your standard teen rom-com. Hell, we were even prom king and queen our senior year.

"So, then you're not together?" Marie, asks, almost sounding emotional, as if she might cry.

Oh, jeez.

"We're friends!" Ellie bursts out, looking to me with her gaze widened, silently pleading I save her.

"Yep," I speak up. "Great friends."

Marie frowns. "Oh. I see. Well, that's a shame." She turns her focus on Ellie. "You need to get him back. It's not like you've dated any winners since him."

Ellie's eyes bug out, her face blooming even redder than it already was.

I sure as shit don't like hearing about her dating other guys, but a surge of pride hits me knowing none have been better than me.

"Marie!" someone shouts from the back. "The fryer's acting up again."

She laughs, shrugging her shoulders. "Damn thing's on its last leg." She smiles warmly at us. "I'll see you kids later."

And then she's gone, just as quickly as she popped up, leaving behind a stilted air between us.

"So," I start. "That wasn't awkward at all."

Her eyes flash to mine, the redness slowly easing off her face. "Definitely not incredibly embarrassing." She laughs lightly through her smile.

I'm not sure what's brought on this side of her, but whatever it is, I'm here for it.

"Order number eleven!" a worker calls out.

Ellie starts to move, but then pauses and looks at me. There's a flicker of vulnerability in her expression, but it's gone before I can decide if I imagined it or not. "That's my order. Are you in a rush to get somewhere?"

At a loss for words, I simply shake my head.

"Okay, good. Do you mind waiting? There's something I'd like to talk to you about."

I nod, wordlessly, and she responds with a faint smile before continuing on to retrieve her order.

It's been so long since she's spoken to me with anything besides stiff conversation and animosity, I have no idea how to handle this version of her.

I watch her chitchat for a second with the boy behind the counter as she grabs the takeout bag.

"Walk me to my car," she tells me, breezing past me and leading the way, not bothering to look back to see if I'm following.

And like the whipped man I am, I'm in step right behind her, doing a piss-poor job of staring at anything but the sway of her hips.

The parking lot is mostly vacant. Sagebrush Diner isn't necessarily the most popular dinner spot in town, since they focus mostly on breakfast.

She lingers by her car, clutching onto the paper bag, looking almost nervous as she bites down on her plush bottom lip, averting her gaze.

I'm nervous too. So much so, the back of my neck is burning up, pulse beating rapidly beneath my skin.

We stand awkwardly, my brain in a spiral wondering what's shifted—why she suddenly wants to talk. And why the ever-present crease in her forehead that forms every time we've seen each other seems to have smoothed out.

Cutting into the silence, I clear my throat reflexively. "How's your car doing? I meant to ask you about it last time I saw you."

When she showed up at my house, and I fucked everything up like an idiot.

She looks at the car but doesn't look at me. "Fine. It needed a jump like you said. Ethan took care of it, and then I had the battery replaced after I left your place. The guy at the shop said my battery was too new to die. Said it was probably a manufacturing error." The corner of her lip lifts slightly. "Got the taillight fixed too," she adds, dropping her chin and playfully rolling her eyes.

At least it seems she's let go of some of the anger from the arrest.

I hate thinking of her having to shoulder the responsibilities I'd gladly take off her hands if I could. If she were mine, she'd never have to worry about shit like her car breaking down. When we were together, that's who I tried to be for her —someone she could rely on. I even had to give her a lesson in pumping gas before college started because she'd never done it.

While I'm glad she has brothers and a dad who step up and help when she needs it, it doesn't stop the jolt of jealousy that takes hold of me. I want to be that for her, and I can't.

"So," she begins. "I've been doing some thinking..." My breath freezes in my lungs. There are so many things that could be on the other side of that statement, most I'm sure aren't in my favor. "I owe you an apology," she finishes.

For an extended moment, I don't know what to say. Of all the things I was expecting, it definitely wasn't that. I rake a hand through my hair—something to preoccupy the hand closest to her, the one that wants to touch her. "An apology?"

She sighs through a smile. "Yeah. I'm not sure if you've noticed, but I haven't been the most welcoming person toward you."

I smother a grin. "Really? I hadn't noticed."

Her head falls back, a soft giggle escaping her lips. The sound of it sends a tingle down my spine.

I'm suddenly aware of how closely we're standing, like we both inched together without realizing it. Her eyes round, coming to the same conclusion, and she rears a step back.

Coughing, she turns her head to focus on a squawking

bird across the parking lot. Anything to not have to continue looking at me. Her smile has fallen, replaced with something wistful.

"Like I was saying, I've been a total bitch since you came back, and that's not fair. We have a lot of history, but it's no excuse to treat you the way I have been."

I have no idea what to say so I keep quiet.

"I was hoping we could try to be friends, like we used to be, before...you know."

Before we fell in love. I finish silently for her.

Her eyes swivel down as her throat works down a swallow, the delicate curve of her neck straining.

"I'd like that," I say quietly.

I'm an honest man, but in this moment, I know I'm lying. I don't want to be her friend—I want to be so much more. I always wanted to be more.

"I have to ask, where is this coming from? You've been close to biting my head off every time we've run into each other."

She laughs. "I'm not planning to leave Red Mountain, and by the looks of it, you don't have plans to leave anytime soon. It's a small town, and we used to be great friends. Plus, it's more exhausting avoiding you than it is to just suck it up and move past this awkward shit." She pauses for a moment, a knowing smirk on her lips. "And you paid for my fee, so I'm feeling a little more inclined to be nice."

I chuckle. "There it is, the real truth. Least I could do." I give her a teasing smile, and she rewards me with one of her own.

I'm still working out a way to make things up to her, but taking care of her fee was a start.

Her smile fades and her eyes regard me carefully. "I'm sorry about your dad." Her breath shakes for a moment before she exhales fully. "I—I wish I had known. I would've gone to the funeral, paid my respects. He was a good man, and he was always good to me."

My jaw tightens as my tongue rolls across my teeth to keep from doing something stupid like cry. I've done a tremendous job of keeping my emotions at bay, but Ellie has a way of dragging it all up to the surface, even if she doesn't intend to.

"Thanks," I rasp, my voice husky despite myself. "He always liked you—loved you, actually." Because he did. He never stopped talking about Ellie, making sure I never forgot about her. Not that I ever could, but I could tell it hurt him to lose her, and I think he hoped we'd find our way back to each other.

Her glassy, green eyes meet mine, a rare flicker of emotion passing through them.

Fuck, I want to hold her. But I think if I did, my emotions would break loose. It would be too much for me—everything I want, but nothing I can have.

She steps forward and then quickly steps back, shaking her head as she does.

I think she wants what I want. And she's fighting it.

A little seed of hope starts to take root.

After a brief moment, she smiles a soft smile, but her gaze looks brighter—at least brighter than its been when I'm on the other end of them. We're quiet for a stretch before she speaks.

"What did you get?" her eyes are fixed on my bag.

"Pancake special. You?"

"Pancake special," she breathes a laugh before biting her bottom lip to keep her smile from fully breaking free.

The same orders we've always gotten. I guess that's something that's never changed about me or Ellie—we both like breakfast for dinner.

CHAPTER 19

Elyse

EARN BACK OUR PRIVILEGES

17 YEARS OLD

"Who wants chorizo?" Raúl, Dominic's dad yells out as if we're not all in the same room.

He's lively today, dancing in place as he grounds the sausage into the pan. He's making one of my favorites, chorizo con huevo. It's not exactly a dinner meal, but he makes it for me no matter the time because he knows I like it.

"'Apá, you can stop dancing. We don't need dinner and a show," Dominic says, his skin flushed with embarrassment.

I swat his arm, but his dad seems unfazed. "Mijo, music is meant to be danced to. No te preocupes, no es mi intención hacerte pasar vergüenza." *(Don't worry, it's not my intention to embarrass you.)*

Dominic groans, pulling at his hair. "'Apá, she knows Spanish."

I giggle, exchanging a look with Raúl. He knows I know Spanish. Well—more like I understand it. Speaking it is a whole other thing. Ethan is way better, practically fluent.

Dominic's parents have always been more laid-back than mine. His mom, Silvia, is mostly quiet, but with a gentle sweetness, the kind that makes you feel at ease without a word needing to be spoken. I suspect her silence stems partly from not knowing English as well as Raúl, but with her, words feel unnecessary—we understand each other in ways that don't require translation.

She often teases me for being too skinny, but it doesn't bother me. If anything, it makes me feel like she's comfortable around me—like I'm part of the family. Dominic gets more worked up about it than I think is necessary.

Raúl is Silvia's complete opposite. He's a whirlwind of energy, always humming a tune, breaking into spontaneous dances, and cracking jokes that make Silvia shake her head with an exasperated but affectionate smile. Dominic is his mirror image in looks—the same strong jaw, the same deep brown eyes—but that's where the similarities end. Where Raúl fills a room with his presence, Dominic carries himself with a more subtle confidence, a steady energy that doesn't demand attention but commands it all the same.

Dominic and I are still on thin ice with my parents over the whole tattoo thing, and one of the conditions is that we're not allowed to hang out unsupervised. My parents talked to his, and everyone—and by everyone, I mean the old people—agreed we can't be trusted and have to earn back our privileges. I'm glad we don't have to sneak around, but we've barely been able to kiss, let alone do anything more.

"What time is the food going to be done?" Dominic asks.

Raúl glances at the clock on the microwave. "Veinte minutos." *(Twenty minutes.)*

"We have some vocab words to go over for a test. Is it okay if we go in my room? We'll keep the door open."

Raúl looks over at Silvia, and they both nod their heads in

161

agreement. Which is surprising since Dominic is lying. We don't even have any classes together this quarter.

I play along, more curious to see what Dominic has up his sleeve.

As we walk down the hallway toward his bedroom, Adrian passes us, exchanging a quick high-five with Dominic before heading in the opposite direction. "You owe me," he calls over his shoulder.

What was that about?

Adrian's voice is impossible to miss—deep, booming, always carrying no matter where he is. I catch the start of some animated story about basic training, his words full of energy, but I don't hear the rest. Because in the next second, Dominic's arms are around me, guiding me backward into his closet.

I barely have time to catch my breath before his lips crash into mine, hungry and demanding. He kisses me like he's starved, his tongue sweeping against mine, hands roaming greedily over my body. Every nerve ending ignites under his touch, setting my skin on fire.

When his lips move to my jaw and start working down my neck, I take in a few shallow breaths while trying to fight a moan.

"Fuck, I thought Adrian was never going to text me back," he whispers between kisses. "Been trying to get you alone since you got here."

My stomach dips, a familiar warmth pooling between my hips. It's only been a month, but it feels so much longer, and my body has been craving him, desperately.

I tug at his hair, needing his lips back on mine. If we only have twenty minutes, I'm not wasting them.

We make out like we haven't seen each other for weeks as I resist the urge to hike my leg up around his hip, the need for relief growing the longer we kiss.

Dominic drops his head, leaning against my forehead. Our ragged breaths mingle between us. "I'm going to talk to your dad," he says with an exhale. "With prom and graduation coming up, we have too much to celebrate. And I want you alone. I miss you, querida mía." He gathers my face in his hands, placing a soft kiss to my lips, soft enough for butterflies to take flight inside my chest. When he's this careful with me, I can't help but melt.

"What are you going to say?"

He steps back, straightening his stance. "I'm going to be a man and apologize."

CHAPTER 20

Dominic

THIS OUGHTA BE GOOD

17 YEARS OLD

"Elyse is picking up the twins from practice," Jack says, shutting the door in my face.

Right before it fully shuts, I stop it. "I know. I—I came to talk to you," I stammer.

Fuck, I'm nervous. My palms are slick, my heart feels like it's going to give out, it's beating so fast, and my knees would be shaking if I didn't have them locked. I don't think I've ever been this nervous in my life.

Jack swings the door open wide and stares at me, letting out a grunt as he gives me a once-over.

This is going to be a lot harder than I thought it would be.

"Can we talk, Ja— I mean sir—err...Mr. Ledger?"

God, I don't even know what I'm allowed to call him now.

He jerks his head with an eye roll. "Come on in."

As I follow behind him, I'm pretty sure he mutters, "This oughta be good."

He leads me to his office, which already feels like a bad sign. Not the welcoming living room, not the open kitchen.

His office. A room tucked away in the back, down a dark hallway. There's a good chance I'm not walking out of here alive.

He takes his seat behind the desk, and I take the one opposite of him, hoping the barrier of the desk buys me enough time to make a run for it if needed.

With a misleading smirk, he leans back in his chair, crossing his legs, and giving me his full attention. "You wanted to talk. So, talk."

Shit. Now I'm not sure what to say.

I open and close my mouth a few times, a nervous croak tumbling out of me.

He must take pity on me, because some of the stiffness in his jaw loosens, and he lets out a breath. "Jesus Christ," he mumbles. Rubbing the bridge of his nose, he lets out a strained sigh. "Listen, I probably came down a little too hard on you and Elyse, but you've got to see things from my perspective." Uncrossing his legs, he scoots closer, resting his elbows on the desk. "It's not that I don't like you. It's just that she's my little girl and well, if I'm being honest, you've scared the shit out of me since you were seven years old."

My head rears back, caught off guard. "What?"

He huffs a laugh. "The day Elle showed up with you trotting right behind her like a puppy, I knew."

"Knew what?" I ask, hesitantly.

"That she liked you. An innocent little crush, but you were the first boy she ever liked. The *only* boy she's ever liked. No dad is ready to see stars in his baby's eyes. And those stars just kept getting bigger and bigger, and here we are."

I work a swallow down, unsure of what to say. So I say the only thing I think can even salvage this mess. "I love your daughter, sir. I would never do anything to hurt her. We might do some stupid shi-- stuff, and I know we're young, but I fully intend to marry her one day." I pause, gauging him. "With your permission, of course." When he doesn't react or say anything, I keep going. "I would never do anything to get her in real trouble. I promise. I really did try to stop her from getting the tattoo, but you know how she gets and—"

He cuts me off by raising his hand. "I know. She's head-strong, takes after me I'm afraid," he says with a light laugh. "Did she have to get your name, though? Why not a butterfly?"

"She doesn't like butterflies."

Releasing an exhale, he groans. "I'm guessing you're here because you two want to enjoy prom and graduation and all the festivities. Am I right?"

I nod, words lodged in my throat.

"I'll make you a deal."

I lean forward, certain my eyes are practically bugging out of my head. "Yes, anything!"

He smiles, a genuine smile this time. "But first, you have to make me a promise."

"Whatever you want."

"You want to marry Elyse, correct?"

"Yes, sir," I reply in an instant, trying my best to not shake like a leaf in my seat.

He exhales, shaking his breath. "Can you just wait, please? Wait to propose. Can you two at least finish college before we start talking about marriage?"

"We'll wait!" I nearly scream before regaining my composure. "I promise. No wedding anytime soon. You have my word."

He smiles, satisfied with my answer. "Now, son, about that deal..."

CHAPTER 21

Elyse

I'M LOSING IT

PRESENT

T oday is wedding day. And naturally, everything is going wrong.

It's the first big wedding of the season, which means there are bound to be some kinks to work out. The first one is like the first pancake—edible, but not always pretty.

The ceremony is just hours away, and it's a madhouse. Faith, Ben, and Paisley are everywhere, buzzing like bees as they tackle the final touches—setting up chairs, arranging flowers, and triple-checking table settings. Their faces are flushed with effort, a sheen of sweat glistening as they haul centerpieces and hustle to get everything in place. Poor Ben is practically drenched because the girls keep sticking him with all the heavy lifting.

"Ben, could you carry that crate of candles to the altar?" Paisley calls out sweetly, batting her lashes in a way that makes me wonder if she's using more than charm to keep him working overtime.

Despite the frenzy, they somehow manage to laugh and

joke as they work, likely fueled by the unyielding energy of their early twenties. Meanwhile, I feel like I've been run over by a bus, and the day's barely started.

Tablet in hand, I'm directing the photographer where to set up for the first look while simultaneously cross-checking the timeline for the day. My phone buzzes incessantly in my pocket, notifications from vendors and questions from the wedding party all demanding my attention.

"Miss Elyse!" the caterer shouts as he jogs over, a tray of mini tacos in hand. "About the appetizers—you wanted spring rolls, right?"

I stare at the tray and bite back the scream building in my throat. "Yes, I wanted spring rolls. These are tacos."

He winces. "Well...we had a mixup with the menus."

"Spring rolls, Zach. Make it happen," I snap, already scrolling through my phone, wondering if I should start having Shane take on catering.

If it's not the caterer, it's the florist, who conveniently forgot the boutonnieres. Or the band, whose members are stuck in traffic on their way from Spokane with no ETA. Every time I think I've handled one crisis, another pops up. It's a game of whack-a-mole—exhausting and exhilarating all at once.

But I never let my bride see the chaos behind the scenes. From her perspective, the day is supposed to be pure magic— magic I make happen, even if it feels like I'm barely holding it together. That's the job.

As the sun begins to dip lower in the sky, casting a golden glow over the vineyard, it seems like things might actually start coming together. The ceremony space is beautiful—rows of white chairs adorned with greenery and tied with delicate satin ribbons, all leading to a breathtaking floral arch at the altar, backdropped by rolling hills of blooming grape vines. The guests are starting to arrive, dressed to the nines and blissfully unaware of all the moving parts that made this moment come together.

Finally, I allow myself a moment to step away. Just a quick breather before the ceremony kicks off.

I head toward my car, parked at the edge of the winery, hidden from the main area to keep the view picture-perfect. The walk feels longer than it should, and I'm already dreaming of the five minutes of quiet I'll get once I'm inside.

But when I approach, my steps falter, nearly tripping me.

There's a flower on my windshield. A single white rose, carefully placed, as if someone wanted to be sure I'd see it. Beneath it is a photograph—a candid shot of me taken earlier during the wedding preparations. It was taken hours ago, when I was fluffing out the greenery on the wedding arch.

My heart sinks down to my stomach.

I glance around, my pulse racing. In the distance, guests continue to filter in, but the employee-only parking lot is quiet. I study the crowd, searching for a logical explanation— for anything that might make sense. But nothing, and no one, seems out of place. The hairs on the back of my neck stand on end.

Picking up the flower, the thorns scrape against my fingertips. It's fresh, clearly plucked from one of the arrangements I'd spent hours overseeing earlier. My mind races. Was this some kind of prank? Another joke from one of the interns?

But then there's the photograph. That's what twists the sour knot in my stomach. It's not just a flower; it's the picture. Who took this? Why?

I pocket the photograph and grab the rose, crushing the delicate petals in my fist. White roses symbolize death, and while I'm not one to buy into omens, I can't shake the sense that this is more than just a harmless prank.

This ends now.

I straighten my shoulders and head back toward the ballroom, the sour feeling still stirring in my gut. Someone clearly thinks this is a game, but they're about to find out I'm not playing.

I think I've broken my interns.

To keep wedding things moving along, I decided not to bring up the flower incident until after clean-up.

"We have no idea what you're talking about," Faith says, finally speaking up.

"Yeah," Paisley chimes in. "All three of us have been together this whole time. And no one went out to the parking lot."

Ben looks pissed, while the girls appear more defensive. "If someone put a creepy flower on your windshield," Ben starts. "It wasn't us. You think I have time to take a picture, print it, and put a flower on your windshield? Bullshit. You're barking up the wrong tree."

He's right. And I basically had eyes on them the whole time. My face reddens, embarrassed that I automatically assumed it was one of them.

Ben gets up to leave, but then something else dawns on me.

"Wait! Did one of you leave a note on my windshield the other day?"

Ben groans, and Faith and Paisley shake their heads.

Faith has a silent conversation with Ben and Paisley before speaking. "We've only pulled a couple of innocent office pranks. We have no idea what you're talking about."

Shit.

This is much more serious than I thought.

I rub the back of my neck, feeling the tension knot in my shoulders. Something is definitely off here. All three are being upfront, and they seem genuinely confused. But if they didn't put the flower there, who did?

I let them leave early, mainly due to guilt. I direct and assist the cleaning crew for takedown, and once the ballroom is back to pristine condition, it's time to go home. Walking toward my car, I try to ignore the nagging sensation that I'm being watched. The wedding was a success, I should be relieved, but now everything feels tainted by the strange flower and picture.

As I unlock my car door, I glance over my shoulder. The mostly empty parking lot stretches out behind me, the pole lights casting long shadows across the gravel. My unease deepens. What if someone was lurking around? What if they saw me?

I glance at my phone. No missed calls, no new messages. I should be glad for that, but it only adds to the paranoia settling in my chest. What if someone knows I'm leaving the winery? What if they know where I live?

I take a deep breath, trying to steady my nerves. Maybe I'm overreacting. Maybe it's just someone trying to spook me in good fun, and I'm taking it the wrong way. But I can't let go of the suspicion that something more serious is at play, the feeling that someone is watching me.

As I get in my car and start the engine, I realize I don't even know what I'm going to do. I can't exactly call the cops and say, "Hey, I found a flower and a note, I think someone is trying to scare me." It sounds ridiculous, even to me.

I drive away slowly, scanning the streets as I go, half-expecting someone to jump out in front of me or worse; follow me. I need to get home, but I don't feel safe. Not really.

Pulling up to my townhouse, I park in the driveway and cut the engine. The headlights flicker off, leaving the yard in darkness. I sit there for a moment, staring at the front door, debating if I should go inside or stay in my car a little longer. I know I'm being paranoid, but I also have no clue how to handle this.

As I finally step out of my car and make my way to the front door, I spot a white envelope taped to my storm door. My chest tightens and stomach flops like I might puke. With shaking hands I grab the envelope and tear into it.

I'm an idiot.

Looking around, I check to make sure none of my neighbors were awake to watch me rip open the envelope like a crazy person.

It's a notice from the city that the water will be shut off for an hour next Wednesday.

The tightening in my chest uncoils for a moment, only to return when my mind is flooded with every bad thing that could be waiting on the other side of my door.

My heart races as I work to unlock the door. It's not until I hear the distinct sound of the latch clicking that I'm able to take a breath. Stepping inside, I immediately switch on the lights.

The great room is just as I left it, and there's a stillness in the air that tells me I'm alone. At least I think I'm alone.

Regardless, I don't trust my instincts at the moment. Instead, with my phone clutched in my hand, I race through my townhouse, checking every room and closet, even checking under the bed.

I'm losing it. Or worse, I'm not.

CHAPTER 22

Dominic

GORDON RAMSEY

PRESENT

"Y ou coming tonight?" Ryker asks on our way to a domestic call.

"No," I tell him, distracted. "Can't."

Normally Ryker wouldn't be coming on a call with me, but it's a domestic call for a city councilman in Badger Canyon; a little more than your run of the mill DV incident. He needs to manage the politics of it all.

"You used to be good back in the day. Not as good as my record, though," Ryker muses, trying to get a rise out of me, I think.

He's been trying to get me to join the recreational football team since I started. It's made up of a mix of the sheriff's department and RMPD. Usually they play against the fire department.

"My shoulder is still healing. The last thing I need is some hefty fireman tackling me to the ground."

He snorts. "It's flag football."

I toss him a wry glance. We both know nobody adheres to

the rules and mainly use the game as away to take out their aggressions. Aggressions that were probably caused because of their jobs. It's a toxic cycle.

"Ran into your girlfriend the other day," he says, pivoting the conversation. There's humor in his voice.

He must be in a shit mood, because he doesn't usually try to goad me twice in less than ten minutes.

I blow out an exhale. "She's not my girlfriend."

"Oh, I know."

I stay silent, because I'd rather not discuss Ellie. Especially at work. I'm a private guy, and Ellie is never a topic I feel comfortable discussing when she's not around.

"I can't believe a knockout like her is still single," he continues.

Yep, don't like that at all. Ryker is married, but he wouldn't be the first married guy I've worked with to stray. It's kind of a rampant epidemic in law enforcement.

"Relax." He must've noticed the tension in my shoulders, the way my fists are clenched. "Claire and I are happy. She's fucking pregnant, dude. I'm not looking at your girl like that, I'm just trying to figure out what's taking you so damn long. All it's going to take is the right guy coming around, and your window will close. Hell, it should've closed a long time ago. You're on borrowed time, my friend. Unless of course she's not interested in giving you another shot."

I grunt in response, hoping he drops the subject. And thankfully we're almost there.

The councilman lives on the outskirts of Badger Canyon, just outside city limits. When we arrive, the scene is about what I expect—two local patrol cars already parked out front, lights flashing, and a handful of neighbors loitering nearby, trying to look inconspicuous while blatantly watching.

"Borrowed time," I grumble under my breath, glaring at

Ryker as I put the car in park. "Since when do you give a shit about my personal life."

He shrugs, a shit eating grin plastered on his face. "Those Ledger sisters are something else. You seen the little one lately? Ariana? If I were ten years younger..."

He trails off, his eyebrows lifting suggestively. I know what he's doing. And I'm going to let him get to me.

"I'm just saying." He grins like a smug bastard. "A woman like Elyse doesn't stay single forever. Tick-tock." He points to his watch for dramatic effect.

I slam the car door harder than necessary and start toward the house. "Pretty sure there are more pressing matters than my love life, Sheriff."

He jogs to catch up, still chuckling. "I'm just giving you shit. You make it too easy—you're the most laid-back guy until someone mentions Elyse, then you turn into a damn bulldog. I want to see you two get back together. Hell, pretty sure the whole town wants that. Well, except Morales."

I ignore the Morales dig, not wanting to add fuel to the fire. It's bad enough the whole station found out she showed up to my house. That, paired with her blatant flirting, even Ryker's taken notice.

"Glad to know my personal life is keeping everyone entertained," I deadpan.

Ryker doesn't reply because the front door bursts open, and a man in his late forties storms out, waving his arms dramatically. He's dressed in a stained tank top and cargo shorts, and I can already tell this is going to be one of *those* calls.

"Officer, you need to arrest her!" he shouts, pointing toward the house like it's on fire. "She's unhinged! Destroyed my car with a baseball bat!"

"Holy shit," Ryker says quietly as we approach.

"Sir, why don't you calm down and tell us what happened?" I say, keeping my tone even.

"She lost her damn mind, that's what happened!" He flails a hand toward the driveway, where a red sedan is parked, its windshield shattered and several dents visible on the hood. "I told her I didn't like her cooking, and she—she went insane. She's possessed by a demon!"

Ryker raises an eyebrow at me. "Some days, this job isn't so bad," he says under his breath.

Before I can respond, a woman appears in the doorway, holding a...rolling pin? Yep. A literal rolling pin. She's short, wearing slippers, and her hair is pulled into a messy bun.

"Damn right, I went insane!" she shouts. "You've been complaining about my cooking for fifteen years, Ted. If you wanted a chef, you should've married Gordon Ramsey!"

I snort, but Ryker shoots me a warning look. "Ma'am, why don't you put the rolling pin down, and we'll have a calm discussion?"

Her eyes narrow. "I'm calm! I've never been calmer in my life!"

"Sure," Ryker says, biting his lips. "And the car just tripped and fell into your rolling pin, right?"

"Exactly," she snaps, clearly unamused. "It's a miracle I didn't aim for his head."

This time, I don't even bother hiding my sigh. Ryker nudges me with his elbow as I pull out my notepad.

"It's going to be a long day."

I groan in agreement and get to work.

Eight hours later, I need a drink. A strong one.

I push open the door to The Jackalope at five o'clock—too early for the usual drinking crowd and definitely not the go-to spot for a gourmet meal. Lucky for me, I'm in the mood for something greasy, washed down with a generous pour of tequila. Both are specialties at Red Mountain's beloved dive bar.

Behind the counter, the bartender is a fixture of the place, a woman who's been running the joint since before I was born. With her feathered hair, bold eyeliner, and oversized hoop earrings, she looks like she's stepped straight out of the 1980s.

"Hey, cutie," she greets in her signature deep smoker's voice. She calls every guy cutie, and every woman princess, so none of us feel too special about the nicknames.

"Hey, Rhonda. How's it going?"

She smirks as she wipes down the counter with a rag that's seen better days. "Oh, you know, livin' the dream, darlin'. Or somethin' close to it." She tosses the rag into a bucket and leans on the bar, one eyebrow arched. "What can I get you?"

I settle into a barstool. "Tequila, neat. And whatever's hot out of the fryer."

She whistles low. "Tequila before six? Either you're celebrating or you've had a helluva day. Which is it?"

"Let's just say, I'm not in a celebrating mood," I reply, avoiding her probing gaze.

After the domestic call in Badger Canyon, it was all downhill from there. If I was superstitious, I'd think it's because there's a full moon tonight.

Rhonda shrugs and grabs a bottle of well tequila, pouring generously into a tumbler. She sets it in front of me with a bowl of stale peanuts. "Suit yourself, cutie. But if you're gonna drink like that, you better be eatin' plenty. It's the rule."

"Since when does The Jackalope have rules?"

She laughs, loud and raspy, as she resumes wiping the counter. "You're the law, aren't you? You tell me."

"Good point."

She nods her head toward the kitchen. "Tony will bring you out a basket of fries here in a sec."

I nod my thanks and take a swig of the tequila. The instant is slides down my throat, I regret not opting for the top shelf shit. Nothing quite like the burn of cheap tequila.

The door creaks open behind me, and Rhonda looks to the entrance. "Looks like you're not the only one who needs a drink this early. Princess, what can I get ya?"

I look over my right shoulder, catching sight of a familiar face.

Ellie.

And she's not alone.

Next to her is a guy about my height, with a mop of curly, light brown hair and thick, black-framed glasses. He's standing close to her, too close.

Is she on a date?

The thought makes the tequila turn in my stomach. First of all, the last thing I want is to witness her on a date. But secondly—this is not the kind of place a man takes a woman like Elyse Ledger. What types of men has she been seeing that make her think this is appropriate for a date?

She hasn't noticed me yet, because the bar is so dimly lit I probably look more like a shadow than a person from where I'm seated. I take advantage of it and stare at her, letting my eyes roam over slowly. I'm so distracted, I barely give my thanks to Tony as he slides a basket of fries in front of me.

Absentmindedly I start in on the fries, continuing to admire her. She's wearing a dress, black and form-fitting, a little more dressed up than she usually is. Her shoulder-length brown hair is flowing in soft waves, lips painted in her signature red lipstick. Ellie has always exuded an easy elegance, but with an edge. There's always something a little wild about her. And those eyes, they may as well be glowing, always piercing, and more so with the coal-black liner drawing attention to them.

After Ellie places an order, she moves closer to my side of the bar, finally noticing me.

Her face lights up in surprise. "Hey! What are you doing here?"

I wipe my greasy hands on a napkin as she walks toward me, still a little in shock that she's greeting me so warmly. I like it. "Just grabbing a drink." My gaze shifts to her date, who is still standing where Ellie left him, back by the entrance.

She catches the look and smiles. "That's Ben—one of my interns."

I blink several times. "Your *intern?*"

It's embarrassing how relieved that makes me feel.

Ben waves at us awkwardly, and Ellie nudges her head for him to come join us.

"Hey. Uh, good to see you again, sir."

He extends his hand out to shake mine, and surprisingly has a strong grip. *Sir.* Way to make me feel like a crusty, old grandpa.

My eyes widen. I don't recall meeting him. "Have we met?"

He nods. "Yeah, I did some IT work at the station."

Now that he mentions it, he does look vaguely familiar.

The door swings open again and in walk two college-aged girls, a tall redhead and a shorter, dishwater blonde.

"I'll go grab a booth with the girls," Ben announces, before going up to meet them.

Once he's out of earshot, I turn my attention to Ellie. "What's with the field trip?"

She laughs and it's the kind of sound that makes my chest feel too full. Ellie's laugh always does that—makes the world feel lighter, brighter even because she's not the kind of person who freely gives it away. It has to be earned.

"I told them I'd treat them to dinner for," she pauses, choosing her words, "for basically being a bitch." She laughs again, making me want to lean into her to feel the vibration of it. "They *chose* this place. I offered an actual restaurant, but go-figure; the twenty somethings prefer a dive bar."

"It is top-tier bar food."

She huffs and looks over at them chatting in the booth. "Saves me money in the end, I guess."

I take a sip of tequila, my eyes on the booth as well. "So, how old is the boy?"

Her eyes narrow at me with laughter on the edges. "You sound like my dad," she snickers and then mocks me in a faux man-voice, 'How old is the boy'?"

Jesus, she's right.

"Oh my God," she blurts, giggling. "Did you think Ben was my *date?*"

My ears heat, but I shrug, trying to play it off. "I didn't think that."

She leans back, resting against the bar, still grinning. "Ben's twenty-one. If I was dating him, I'd be a cougar. I'm almost thirty."

"I know how old you are. And you'll be thirty next month."

Like I could ever forget her birthday. It's the same day as mine.

Our gazes latch and she swallows audibly before glancing away, directing her focus on my fry basket rather than me.

Her hand reaches over, grazing my arm as she sneaks a fry. Mesmerized, I watch her take an aggressive bite of it before plopping the second half of it in her mouth. Those red lips look even poutier with something between them.

I shake my head, trying to dislodge the image of her with

something else between her lips—on her knees, looking up at me with glassy, glowing eyes.

Her eyes pinch, forehead creasing adorably. "What's that look for?"

"Nothing," I say feigning innocence. "Tired. Long day."

"Heard that." Her shoulders drop as her eyes lose some of their luster. She looks tired.

"Everything okay?" I ask, risking setting her off. She's never been one to like being asked if she's okay or if she's tired, plus we're still on delicate footing in terms of this friendship.

She sighs and reaches for another fry. I nudge the basket closer to her. She can have the whole damn thing as long as it means keeping her talking, keeping her close.

"It's nothing. I haven't been sleeping well, that's all."

There's a hollowness in her voice, a downturn to her lips. Whatever it is, it's more than just not sleeping well. She forgets that I can tell when she's lying. I don't care if it's been ten minutes or ten years, I know all her tells. And her biggest tell is when her gaze darts down and to the left, avoiding eye contact.

"If you need anything, I'm here." My eyes latch to hers, trying to convey how serious I am. It's not a throw away statement. All she has to do is ask, and I'm there. Hell, I'm there even if she never does ask.

"I should go over there. Socialize. Try to be nice."

I don't want her to leave. The amount of times I've imagined coming home to her after a long day at work and losing myself in her, it's too many to count. Even now, in this shit bar, with only a brief conversation, I already feel a million times better. I feel revitalized, like she's breathed new life into me. She's fucking magic and has no idea. It's like I've been living in a decade-long fog of black and white, and the moment I'm back in her orbit, my life is in color.

Without considering the repercussions, I reach out for her,

wrapping my hand around her wrist. She looks down at where I'm holding her and then back up to my eyes.

"Want a drink first?"

Breathing out a sigh, her lips curl down. "I already ordered a cranberry juice. I don't like drinking when I'm still in work mode."

"Want the rest of my fries?" I'm acting desperate and I don't care. I want her to know I'm desperate for her.

"Dominic," she starts. It's a cautious whisper.

"I had a long day, but just getting to see you made it better."

She looks down at my hand still wrapped around her wrist and gently shakes it loose before crossing her arms tightly. "What are you doing?"

"I think you know what I'm doing."

I've been obvious. Embarrassingly obvious. At this point, my pride is nonexistent.

"Well, don't."

If the rejection didn't sting like a bitch, I'd probably laugh. She sounds like she did in high school, her claws coming out in defense.

"I don't know how to stop," I tell her honestly.

With her, I have no game. Any smoothness I possessed is gone.

She looks away, glancing back at her three interns and then locks eyes with me for a brief moment, before dropping her chin down. "I—I can't. We can't."

"Why?" I wish she would just talk to me.

Her hands start brushing up and down her arms like she's cold, but really I think she's just itching to get away from me —from this situation. It stabs at me, but I keep my face neutral. I don't like it, but I can take a hint. "It's fine, Ellie girl. Go ahead and enjoy some time with your interns. I'll leave you alone."

Closing her eyes, she lets out a long exhale. "I'm sorry—I'm not trying to—I'm sorry."

I take a sip of tequila to keep my voice from cracking. "Nothing to apologize for." I raise my hand at Rhonda to get her attention so I can close out my tab. "I'll leave. That way you can relax."

"Fuck," she hisses under her breath. "You don't have to go. I'm sor—"

"Stop apologizing." Risking even more rejection I stand and step close to her. "I'm the one who's sorry. I'm sorry I keep pushing you when you're clearly not interested."

Her shoulders slump, eyes meeting mine since we're nearly at eye level now. "So, are you giving up now?"

"No," I say, huffing a laugh. "Do you want me to?"

"I don't know." She looks down, swallowing harshly.

That's not a yes, but it's also not a no.

Rhonda slides the check across the bar to me, and I retrieve my card, setting it down without shifting my focus from Ellie.

"I'm not going anywhere, querida mía. I'll be here when you're ready."

"And if I'm never ready?"

I lean down to whisper in her ear. "I've never given up on us. I'm not about to start now."

CHAPTER 23

Elyse

BARELY SURVIVING MINUTES

17 YEARS OLD

"Never leave me."

Dominic is tagging along with me for my tour of UW. It's supposed to be for upcoming students only, but it's not like they're checking IDs. And since they already separated the parents for their own guided tour, it's just me and him and a bunch of future students I've never met before.

He runs a comforting hand up and down my back, his touch the only thing capable of soothing me. "I'm not going anywhere," he murmurs.

When I first signed up for this tour, I was riddled with excitement. UW is the school I always hoped to attend, and the one I was expected to get accepted in, despite their low acceptance rate. The grounds are beautiful, like the kind of college you see in movies—brick buildings, sprawling green spaces, a combination of dark academia and timeworn architecture. But now, standing in the middle of this massive campus with students bustling past like they know exactly where they're going, my chest tightens.

Seattle feels too big, too loud, too overwhelming. Everything is moving so fast, and I'm used to the quiet, slow lifestyle of Red Mountain. If Dominic wasn't by my side, I'm not sure how much longer I'd be able to keep going through this tour, pretending I'm not terrified out of my mind.

The tour guide is rambling about something—libraries or resources or something. I'm barely listening. My eyes keep darting around, trying to take everything in, but it's too much.

"You okay?" Dominic asks, leaning down so only I can hear him.

I nod quickly, but it's a lie. "Yeah, just...a lot to take in."

He doesn't push, just gives my shoulder a gentle squeeze and stays close. It's like he can sense I'm one wrong word away from bolting.

As we walk to the next stop, my steps are so shaky, I find myself clinging to his arm to keep from tripping over my own feet. He doesn't complain or pull away, just stays steady beside me, letting me hold on.

When the group pauses in front of the student union building, the guide starts talking about clubs and activities, but my attention drifts again. I glance at Dominic, and he catches my eye.

"You want to step away for a bit?" he asks quietly.

I know this tour is important, but the idea of sitting somewhere quiet sounds like heaven. "Maybe just for a second," I admit.

He steers me toward a bench nearby, away from the crowd but close enough to still hear the guide if I want to. I sink down and let out a shaky breath.

"You're allowed to feel overwhelmed," Dominic says, sitting beside me. "It's a big school."

"I just thought I'd feel more...ready," I admit, barely above a whisper.

I've dreamed of going to school here my whole life—of moving to the city and making a life for myself. The last thing I expected was to feel like maybe I'm not cut out for my own dreams.

"Feeling ready doesn't mean you're not allowed to be scared," he says. "If it wasn't scary, then it wouldn't be a change. It doesn't mean you can't handle it."

I blink back tears that catch me off guard since I rarely let myself get so emotional, especially in public. I hate how much I'm leaning on him, how dependent on him I am. But in this moment, I don't care.

"I don't know if I can do this without you," I whisper.

Dominic's face softens, and he reaches for my hand, lacing his fingers with mine. "You can," he says confidently. "It's only a few hours distance, and we'll see each other on the weekends."

I wish his words had the calming effect I know he intended, instead they have the opposite. We'll be hours apart, and I'm barely surviving minutes.

I can't do it.

CHAPTER 24

Elyse

FIVE-COURSE MEAL

PRESENT

"Elyse, you don't have to do this," my mom protests as I clean the living room of my childhood home.

She's lying on the couch, looking at me like she's contemplating ripping the hand-held vacuum out of my hands, if only to demonstrate I'm not doing it correctly.

"Well, you fired the cleaners I hired to help you out, so now I'm handling it." I can't help the annoyance in my voice. She's not supposed to lift more than ten pounds for six weeks, which means she really can't do much. To be nice, and help her out, I hired cleaners to come weekly for the next three months. They came one day, and she promptly let them go because they used chemicals she didn't like. Which is valid, I get it, but maybe communicate before straight up firing them, and then trying to take on the cleaning as if nothing has happened.

My dad's birthday celebration is today, and all of our family birthdays are at my parents' house. I tried to convince them that we should do this one at the winery since we do larger events there, but they both said no, that it wasn't homey enough.

My mom sighs and rolls her eyes, clearly not thrilled about being sidelined. "I just don't like feeling useless."

"You're not useless." I give her a reassuring smile. "But you need to rest and let me take care of things. We don't want you overdoing it today."

She sighs again, but nods in agreement. "I know, I know. I just hate being a burden."

"You're not a burden. And I'm not saying this to guilt you, but I need you to be healthy for the long haul. And besides, you've already done so much for us over the years. It's our turn to take care of you."

She studies me for a moment, her eyes softening. "You're right. Thank you, sweetie. I appreciate you doing this."

"Of course," I reply, slightly out of breath. My townhouse takes me an hour to clean, tops. I'm not used to taking on as big of a space as this one on my own. "Now, why don't you go relax and let me finish up in here?"

Standing, she gives my shoulder a squeeze before heading to her bedroom.

Before I can get lost in my task, the doorbell rings and rings and rings. I groan internally. *Who's here this early?* When I open the door, Shane is standing with his arms full of bags, using his hip to continue to ring the bell.

"Walk slower than a sloth, why don't you," he mumbles, stomping past me. "These bags are heavy as fuck."

"Hello to you, too. How's your day? Mine's great, I've only been cleaning for over an hour. By myself." I tell him through a clenched jaw as I follow him into the kitchen.

He sets the bags on the marble kitchen island with a groan. "I thought you hired cleaners. We all pitched in."

Crossing my arms, I rest my hip against the counter. "I did. Mom fired them."

He blows out a huff. "Of course she did."

Now that his arms aren't full, he's instantly in a much better mood.

"I've got the kitchen covered. Go back to doing your thing. And maybe call the twins, to get their asses over here and be useful. Or at least Marisa. Put that girl to work, she'll be family if Ethan ever grows the balls to ask."

"He's going to ask her. He's waiting for the timing to be right."

Shane scoffs as he begins prep work, and puts his earbuds in, effectively dropping the conversation.

Shane's insistence that Ethan needs to propose to Marisa has been an interesting development. For a man who's allergic to monogamy and proud of it, he's the last person I'd expect to give Ethan shit.

I smile to myself as I pad out of the kitchen, thinking Little Shane's frontal lobe must be close to being fully formed. I still won't hold my breath for him to settle down anytime soon, though.

Checking the clock, I see there's still four hours left before guests start arriving. Plenty of time, but there's still too much for me to get to and still have time to get ready.

With Ariana working and Layla at a nursing school lab, I decide to take Shane's advice and text Marisa to come help. She replies almost instantly, saying she'll be over in twenty-minutes.

I continue straightening the living room and fifteen minutes later, Marisa is at the front door, but she's not alone. Dominic is right beside her.

"Look who I ran into," Marisa says, her smile way too wide, brushing past me with Dominic following.

When I don't reply right away, because I'm afraid I'll say something mean, she continues on. "I was at the post office

189

when you texted me, and Dom was in front of me in line. I figured two hands are better than one."

"But *you* have two hands, Marisa," I grit with a forced smile.

Her grin fades. "Oh...right. You know what I mean."

She could've at least given me a heads up, girl code and all. Had I known Dominic was tagging along with her, I would've made an attempt at looking presentable. Instead, he looks effortlessly good in jeans and a green Clore County Sheriff's Office hoodie, his forearm tattoos peeking out over the pushed-up sleeves. Meanwhile, I'm wearing a ratty tank top, leggings with holes, and a musty flannel tied around my waist. Not to mention, the sweat soaking my scalp, makes my hair look greasy, without a lick of makeup on. No one should see me like this, least of all my ex.

Unable to control myself, my gaze moves to his, meeting his dark brown eyes, laser-focused on me.

I try to break the connection, but I'm held captive, unable to do anything but stare right back.

He shrugs, giving me a boyish smile that makes my stomach dip. "I'm at your service, Ellie girl."

"See," Marisa exclaims excitedly, nudging my shoulder. "He wants to help."

Her lack of subtly is enough to jolt my focus, and I cast her a strained glance, clearly communicating I'm less than pleased with her meddling.

With widened eyes, she inches away. "I'm just going to go set down my stuff." She fiddles with the strap of her purse, flashing a wink at me before rounding the hallway, out of sight.

The moment me and Dominic are alone, the foyer shrinks, the air between us inflating.

"Is it okay that I'm here?" There's an unease in his voice, his usual air of confidence slipping.

Something about his hesitancy has a tightness forming in my chest. We've moved past my hostility, but we still don't quite know how to act around each other. When I ran into him at The Jackalope, he made it pretty clear that he's interested in trying again.

I don't know if I am. Because trying again, means talking. It means explaining myself. And I think I'm too much of a coward to do it.

And what would be the point? He thinks I'm still the Ellie he's always known. He thinks I'm a good person. But I'm almost certain the moment I let him in, he'd see all the ugliness inside of me. And then he won't want me anymore. I'm not sure I'd survive that kind of pain.

I'd like to hope we can be friends, but I don't think it's possible.

Before we started dating, our friendship was laced with an undeniable current, an awareness that feelings were coming to the surface. We've never been just friends, even as kids, before either of us could comprehend it, Dominic always felt like more. Who are we to each other when more isn't an option?

"Yeah," I say nodding. "It's okay. As long as you're useful, you can stay."

With a chuckle, he tilts his head, regarding me with an assessing stare. "I can be useful."

A trickle of heat works its way down my spine, the atmosphere shifting in an instant.

He steps closer, his tongue rolling under his top lip, the tip just barely poking out as his eyes roam over me, so slowly I get a little dizzy. It's not until his eyes stop at my hips that I finally take a shallow breath.

"Is that mine?" The corner of his mouth lifts in that lopsided smirk I've never been able to resist.

I look down at the red and black checkered shirt he's staring at. I grabbed it out of the hall closet because I was freezing when I got here, only to get overheated while cleaning and tying it around my waist. I assumed it was my dad's.

Before I can answer he loops his thumb over the knot and tugs me forward, his forefingers rubbing against the fabric.

"It is," he says, a hint of amazement in his voice. His eyes lift to mine. "Funny that it's been here this whole time."

"Mmhmm," I manage, fighting the urge to squirm. I was already hot, but now I'm on fire.

Our gazes hold as he lets me go, and I can't decide if I'm relieved or—

"You always did look good in my clothes," he says while his eyes rake over me again, even more heated, if that's possible.

"Stop," I shout-whisper. It's not as if anyone can hear me anyway, it's just hard to speak normally when I'm being blatantly checked out. I'm fighting to not go in that direction but he's leaning all the way into it.

"Stop what?" he chuckles, knowing exactly what I'm talking about. He's doing this on purpose.

"Stop looking at me like that." I step back, folding my arms. "You're looking at me like I'm a five-course meal. And you're obviously doing it to get under my skin." I gesture to my outfit. "We both know I look terrible."

His smile eases as he shakes his head. "Ellie girl, you've never looked terrible a day in your life. Always the most beautiful woman in the room."

Not allowing me a chance to respond, he starts walking toward the hallway, leaving me with a slacked jaw and wrapped in his scent, only further turning me into an absolute puddle.

Just as he's about to turn the corner, he stops short, and glances back at me. "About that five-course meal," he begins, tugging on his bottom lip, his eyes staring at the increasingly wet spot between my thighs before his attention finally lands on my face. "I am starving for it."

CHAPTER 25

Dominic

WALK LIKE A MOUSE

PRESENT

"**E**xpect there to be payback for that little stunt," Ellie practically hisses at Marisa on the other side of the closed door, completely failing at keeping her voice from traveling. Marisa answers with a giggle, followed by Ellie groaning.

As soon as I entered the living room, Ellie was right behind me, grabbing hold of Marisa and dragging her into the bathroom. I'd feel bad, but I wouldn't have ended up here otherwise, so I can't help but be a little thankful for Marisa's meddling.

It's still surprising Ethan landed himself a bright ray of sunshine girlfriend, when the guy's usually a dark cloud. I like her, though. She's good for him.

And apparently good for Ellie, too.

Even if she is all worked up at the moment. It's my fault. I told myself I wouldn't be anything more than friendly, but the second I saw her, in my old shirt no less, I couldn't help myself. She brings it out of me, whether she means to or not.

Watching her react, getting to see that pretty pink flush take over her creamy skin because I'm affecting her, it's like a drug. And all I want is more of it. Somewhere in there, she still feels the pull between us, now I just have to figure out how to drag it up to the surface.

Ellie and Marisa walk out of the bathroom, Marisa whispering a sorry as Ellie hands her a toilet scrubber. "You're on bathroom duty."

Marisa's shoulders slump, but she reluctantly accepts the toilet brush. "Fine," she sighs and heads back toward the bathroom her and Ellie just exited.

"Where do you need me, Ellie girl? I'm all yours."

She coughs, a visible heat rising up her neck. She can deny this all she wants, convince herself she just wants to be friends, but her body is telling me everything she's refusing to admit.

I step closer, invading her space, and her breath hitches. "Tell me what you need?"

I'm pushing my luck, any minute now she's going to throw me out.

Her eyes narrow, shoulders straightening as our gazes clash.

"You can only stay and help if you stop flirting with me. *Friends* don't flirt."

My head falls back, a laugh escaping me. I've always loved how blunt she is, cutting right past all the bullshit. "I'll behave."

"Sure you will." She shakes her head like she's frustrated with me, but the corners of her lips are twitching, fighting like hell to not smile.

"I promise. Just give me a task." The flirting has been fun, like slipping back in time, but I really do want to help her. And helping her with cleaning will probably earn me more brownie points than getting her hot and bothered.

"You can vacuum the stairs." Her head gestures to the closet under the staircase. "The vacuum is in there."

"On it." I nod.

She steps back—two generous strides—and I instantly miss her scent. Warm and spicy, the kind that lingers, tempting me to lean in and breathe it in again.

The edge of her mouth quirks into a grin, her eyebrow arching. "Try not to moon over me while you're vacuuming. It would be really inconvenient if you fell down the stairs."

At that she struts away without another look, and I get to work.

I'd heard about Jack's birthday. The Ledgers are known for always having some event going on, whether it's personal or at the winery. I wasn't necessarily invited, but I wasn't not invited. Still, I know how upset Ellie was when I showed up to her family's dinner a few weeks ago, and I'm trying really hard to keep things moving forward.

I said I wouldn't moon over her, but my eyes flash to her briefly, getting a peek at her bending over to adjust a couch cushion.

For as far back as I can remember, she's always taken on more than she should, not letting her siblings pick up the slack. I love that she cares so much and loves so big, even though she'll never admit it. But it makes me sad to know she makes it her mission to shoulder everything, getting almost nothing in return. The Ledgers are good people, but they would crumble without her. She's the backbone of her family, and they don't even realize it. It was true when we were kids, and it obviously still rings true today.

She buzzes around, straightening and restraightening, the perfectionist in her is unable to see that the place is already immaculate.

Halfway through vacuuming, the smell of garlic starts to waft in the air. Whatever Shane is cooking, it smells good.

Once I'm done vacuuming, I put everything away and approach Ellie for my next task.

She doesn't see me at first, and it gives me a free moment to watch her without prying eyes, since it's just us two at the moment.

I can tell by the way she's holding her shoulders, tense, as if there's a weight on each one, pushing her down, that she's bone tired.

"Why don't you sit for a bit?"

She jumps at the sound of my voice, clearly not having heard me walk in. "You scared me. How long have you been standing there."

"A while," I tell her truthfully.

Her face scrunches. "They teach you how to walk like a mouse at the academy? I didn't even hear your footsteps."

"Among other things," my lips lift, amused at the mix of her disheveled appearance and attempt to be mad at me for no real reason. "Sit," I repeat. "Before you collapse."

Surprisingly, she nods, and then spins to flop down on the nearby couch. She lands with a sigh, followed by a groan as her body uncoils.

My brain knows she's just relieving the tension, but my dick has no idea those sounds aren't sexual and it jerks against my pants' zipper.

It's been a long time since I've let anyone close enough to even think about having sex—and now I'm standing in front of my dream girl, and my body's in overdrive, aching for her.

After we broke up, it took me a while to try to move on. Ellie had been my everything for pretty much my entire life, and it felt like cheating, even though she was long gone. It didn't take me long to realize no woman would ever compare to her, that she was the standard and everyone else was a place-holder. I tried, I really tried. I dated, had one-night stands, did the apps, I've even had a few girlfriends. None who lasted more than a couple months. When a woman realizes she's competing against a ghost, she's quickly out the door. It's a losing competition.

I should've come back for her sooner. I should've never let her get away in the first place. There's been a lot of could'ves, would'ves, should'ves when it comes to Ellie. I had to almost die to realize I'd wasted a decade trying to outrun the love of my life, when I should've been turning around and chasing her down.

"Why did I listen to you?" she mumbles, pulling me back to the present. "Now I don't want to get back up and finish."

I shrug. "So don't. The house is spotless. You should rest."

She scoffs. "I can't rest until everything is perfect."

I lean against the wall, crossing my arms, watching her. Her hair's falling out of its ponytail, wisps framing her flushed face, and her body is slouched in a way that's almost uncharacteristic. She's so used to holding herself together that seeing her like this—vulnerable, tired—is a rare sight.

"Ellie, the house is already perfect," I say softly. "You've done enough. You are enough."

Her head dips toward me, eyes pinching, "You're getting sappy on me. You know how I feel about feelings."

I hold my hands up in mock surrender, a grin tugging at my lips. "Can't have that, can we? But seriously, take a breath. Shane's cooking, Marisa's scrubbing tiles, and I've vacuumed the stairs so thoroughly they could star in a cleaning commercial. There's nothing left."

She stares at me, her lips pressing into a thin line. Finally, she exhales sharply. "Fine."

For a moment, we fall into silence.

"I don't know why you're here," she says suddenly, her voice quieter, almost unsure.

I'm not sure if she's asking why I'm here in her family's home, or why I moved back. I think it's both.

I step closer, sitting on the arm of the couch, careful not to crowd her, and answer the simplest question. "You can thank Marisa for that one."

She gives me a tight, resigned smile but remains quiet.

"You do too much, querida mía," I tell her under my breath, low so only she can hear me.

Her eyes lift up to meet mine. "I know," she admits. "Normally, I'm not this anal about things, but lately it's felt like everything is out of control. I can control this, though."

"Want to talk about it?"

She blows out a breath. "Not really."

I'll let it go for now, but she's not off the hook. Whatever it is that's bothering her is clearly taking a toll. The shadows under her eyes, the worry in her gaze—it looks worse now than it did at the bar.

"You do everything for everyone—take care of your whole family, but who takes care of you?"

Ellie releases a weary sigh, pushing herself up from the couch with a groan. "I don't let anyone take care of me."

I stand as she does, watching her carefully. She's good at deflecting—always has been—but I'm not letting her get away with it this time.

"Well, maybe you should start," I say gently.

She scoffs, brushing past me toward the kitchen. I follow in step behind her.

"Shane and Marisa are here. You're here. Clearly, I know how to accept help."

As I'm about to respond, we enter the kitchen and Shane spots me, leveling me with a glare. He's practically snarling as he removes his earbuds.

"The fuck's he doing here?"

Shit.

I suspected he didn't like me during dinner, but now it's confirmed.

Before moving back, the last time I saw Shane he was a teenager. Now he's very much a grown man who could probably kick my ass if he tried. He'd have to try pretty hard, but it wouldn't be a cakewalk.

"Be nice," Ellie tells him as she grabs a stack of mail and puts it in a drawer.

Shaking his head, he stirs something in a pot. "No can do. I'm a grudge holder. Especially when it comes to pieces of shit who hurt my sisters."

Ellie groans, tossing her head back. "Grow up, Shane."

This feels like a conversation I shouldn't be partaking in, no matter how badly I want to defend myself. Shane seems to be under the impression I did something to hurt his sister, and it couldn't be further from the truth.

Shane drops the whisk into the pot, causing a loud clang. "Just gonna stand there and not say anything?" He turns to face me, and even though we're on opposite ends of the kitchen, I have a feeling he'd reach me before I could get very far. "Always knew you were a bitch."

Well, now I'm getting pissed.

Ellie walks over to me, grabbing me by the arm, and starts dragging me out of the kitchen. "And we're leaving." She looks back over her shoulder at her brother. "I don't know what's wrong with you, but knock it off."

We're not even fully out of the kitchen before she starts trying to apologize.

"Hey, it's fine."

"It's not fine. He's being a dick. I don't know what's gotten into him."

I expected hostility from Ethan or Gavin, definitely not Shane. Of the three brothers, he's always been more of a goof off.

Ellie looks taken aback by Shane's outburst, and I wish I

could touch her to offer some comfort, but I don't think it'd be welcomed.

"He's protective of you. That's not a bad thing."

She shakes her head, her right hand rubbing at the center of her chest, like she's trying to soothe herself. "I'll talk to him."

"Don't. Let him be mad at me. I'd rather earn his respect. I'm not going to come between you and your family."

Her eyes squint, lips curling slightly. "I hate it when you do that."

I smile. "Do what?"

She cocks her head, barely holding back a grin. "Say all the right things."

Before I can respond, my phone buzzes in my pocket. I glance at it and curse under my breath. Vorheis just called an emergency meeting.

"I have to go. Something came up at work."

Ellie's lashes flutter as she blinks, her expression almost imperceptible. "Oh, right. Of course." Disappointment settles across her face.

For the first time in my entire career, I want to forget about my responsibilities. Even though I'm sure this has something to do with the Delmar case.

"If I didn't think it was something big, I'd probably ignore it."

Her eyes meet mine, so beautifully clear it almost hurts to stare into them. "Does that happen a lot? Getting called in for work."

This is the first time she's truly asked about my job. She almost looks worried, and it does something to my chest.

"No. We just have a big case at the moment."

She nods, chewing on her bottom lip. "Well, be careful."

What I wouldn't give to at least be able to kiss her goodbye. Anything to keep that look off her face.

"I'm always careful. Try not to miss me too much." I wink at her, trying to lighten the mood.

A hint of a smile plays on her lips. "Go...and thanks for helping."

"Give me your phone." I reach my hand out.

Her brows furrow. "Why?"

"Just hand it over," I reply, wiggling my fingers impatiently.

She hesitates, but eventually huffs and fishes her phone out of her pocket. "Fine. But if this is some weird—"

"It's not," I cut in, taking her phone. My fingers brush hers as I grab it, and the brief contact sends a jolt straight up my arm.

She hands it to me locked but doesn't give me the password. Without having to think, I punch it in. Her password is our birthday.

I toss her a small smirk, and she shakes her head but remains quiet. *That's right Ellie girl, I still know you better than anyone.* Quickly, I add my number to her contacts and hand the phone back.

"There. Now you have my number. Call me if you need anything. Seriously, Ellie. Anything."

She stares at the screen for a moment, then glances back up at me, her expression unreadable. "You put yourself in as *Deputy Alvarez*?"

I shrug, flashing her a knowing smile. "Figured you'd like that better. Maybe actually, I don't know, reach out some time."

"As a hardened criminal, I don't make it a habit to reach out to law enforcement."

I laugh, stepping back toward the door. "You're hardly a criminal. Besides, I'm sure the asshole who arrested you deeply regrets it and wishes there was something he could do to make it up to you."

Her plump lips roll, concealing a smile. "I'm sure I'll think of something."

Fuck, now I really don't want to leave. I'm pathetic for this side of her. It's like an addiction.

My phone buzzes again, reminding me of pressing matters.

"Don't overwork yourself while I'm gone. Promise me."

"No promises," she shoots back, but there's a hint of softness in her tone.

As I walk out, I glance back and catch her staring at her phone, wearing a faint smile, a small blush creeping across her cheeks. I hope it's because of me and not just from a day spent cleaning.

CHAPTER 26

Dominic

HAPPY BIRTHDAY

18 YEARS OLD

"What's all this?" Ellie's smiling brightly, blushing the prettiest shade of pink, as she takes it all in.

Strings of fairy lights are looped between trees, surrounding a picnic blanket. I skipped last period to race over here and get it set up. I'll probably get hit with detention for it, but the look on her face is more than worth it.

"Do you like it?" Normally, I ask for Scottie's opinion before surprising Ellie, but she's been out of town at an acting workshop.

Ellie comes up to me and wraps her arms around my neck, crashing her lips to mine.

After I met with Jack, he eased up on the rules and has allowed us to hang out alone again. We've been so busy with our senior projects though, this is our first time truly alone since we got in trouble. And, fuck, did I miss her.

I slip my tongue in, coaxing it to hers, and she moans into my mouth, opening up even more for me. My hands travel over her body, kneading her hips, grabbing handfuls of her breasts, before pinching her nipples through the thin fabric of the black cotton dress she's wearing.

I want her so badly, but if I don't stop now, we'll get too carried away.

With all the strength I can summon, I pull back, breaking our kiss.

Her lipstick is a little smeared, lips beautifully swollen. I love the way she looks after I've messied her up. And once she opens her birthday present, I plan to make her even messier.

My forehead rests against hers, our breaths tangling with each other.

"Ready for your present?"

Her smile stretches. "You mean there's more? You already did so much."

I grab her hand, guiding her over to the picnic blanket where we both sit.

She kicks off her sandals, tucking her legs under her as the blanket crinkles beneath us. The late afternoon light filters through the leaves, casting golden flecks across her shoulders, her cheeks, her hair. She looks unreal, like a dream, and every goddamn thing I've ever wished for.

"I couldn't let our first legal birthday pass without getting you a present," I say, reaching into the picnic basket for the little velvet box I've kept hidden.

Her eyes go wide with panic, lips parting just slightly. "Oh my god. Are you—?"

I bark out a laugh, shaking my head. "Just open it," I say quickly, grinning. "It's not what you think. Not yet."

Color blooms in her cheeks again, but she relaxes, biting her bottom lip she opens the box.

Inside, nestled in soft velvet, is a delicate gold chain. Two slender initials—an E and a D—are looped through the center.

"I know it's not that exciting," I say, suddenly self-conscious. "I just thought since we're going to be apart this next school year, it's like we're still—"

"It's perfect," she cuts me off, lifting the necklace out of the box. Her fingers tremble slightly as she tries to loop it around her neck, the thin chain slipping through her grasp.

She turns around without a word, sweeping her hair to the side. I step in, brushing my fingers lightly against the back of her neck as I fasten the clasp. The chain settles against her skin, the initials resting just below her collarbone.

She spins to face me, eyes shining as she lifts her chin. "I love it," she whispers, and then, softer, "and I love you."

"I love you too," I whisper back, capturing her lips in a kiss —slow, delicate, torturous—until she's breathless.

She laughs against my mouth, pulling back. "We must've been on the same train of thought."

"Oh, yeah? Why's that?"

Reaching into the pocket of her dress she produces a nearly identical velvet box.

I take it, opening it to reveal a gold chain.

"I know you're not really a jewelry guy, but I think it would look good on you." She blushes, chewing on her bottom lip. "You don't have to wear it all the time—"

I kiss her cutting her off.

"You like it when guys wear chain necklaces?"

"No." She giggles. "I like the idea of *you* wearing one. Only you."

If my girl wants me to wear a chain around my neck, looks like I'm wearing it for the rest of my damn life.

"Happy birthday, querida mía."

"Happy birthday, Dominic baby."

CHAPTER 27

Elyse

WRITE IT DOWN

PRESENT

My car is fucked.

Waking up to the sound of glass violently shattering is not how I thought my day would start.

I'm standing outside, waiting for the cops to show up, when a pair of headlights crest the hill in front of my townhouse, cutting through the dark morning. My hands tremble, and despite the cool temperature, I know it has everything to do with the adrenaline racing in my veins.

The car slows, my pulse spiking as it seems about to stop completely. But then, as quickly as it appeared, it picks up again and turns onto the main road. Just a passerby, probably on their way to work.

Tapping the screen of my phone, I check the time. *Again.* Where the hell are the cops? They should've been here by now. I called *911* over ten minutes ago.

Ten very long minutes ago.

Feels like an eternity.

When I realized the source of what jolted me awake, I ran outside—a stupid move on my part. By the time I reached my car, whoever had decided to take a beating to it was long gone.

Glancing around, my eyes search for something out of place. Someone who might be watching me. But there's nothing—no one.

I walk up to my car, inspecting the damage.

Every window is gone, reduced to shards scattered everywhere, sparkling like glitter over the asphalt. The doors are dented and the hood is caved in, as if someone took a bat to it.

A breeze sweeps past me, causing goosebumps to prickle my skin. It's eerily quiet, only adding to the knot of anxiety in my chest. Every sound—branches creaking, leaves rustling—feels amplified. The desire to jump out of my skin is incessant. My car is a wreck, and now my nerves are too.

Wrapping my arms tightly around myself, I try to stop the overwhelming feeling of violation from consuming me. It's just a car. No one was hurt, but that doesn't stop the creeping sense of vulnerability. My sense of security is as broken as the glass surrounding me.

I stare at my phone, my thumb hovering over Dominic's contact.

It's a bad idea.

He's probably asleep.

But I need someone to be here now.

And for reasons I'm too overwhelmed to question, he's the only person I want to call.

I press the call button before I lose the nerve.

The phone rings three times before a groggy voice answers, "Ellie?" His tone carries a hint of disbelief, as if he never expected to hear from me, let alone at this hour. I don't respond immediately—words are hard to find when my brain feels scrambled.

He clears his throat. "What's wrong?" His voice turns serious, a stark contrast to his grogginess a moment ago.

Hearing his instant concern creates a burning ache through my chest.

"Sorry for waking you up," I crack.

I was aiming for an air of detachment, maybe even professionalism. Instead, his voice is all it takes for tears to blur my vision. I blink them back, causing a painful pressure to build.

"What's going on? Talk to me."

Either he detected my veiled panic, or he's smart enough to know I'd never call him unless I absolutely had to.

"My car...someone smashed in the windows. I—"

"What?!" The sound of rustling blankets and his sharp intake of breath fills the line. "Are you okay? Where are you?"

"I'm fine. I'm home, waiting for the police, but they're taking forever. I just...I didn't know who else to call."

"I'm on my way," he declares, already sounding fully awake. "Stay put. Lock your door if you're not already inside."

"I'm outside," I admit, weakly.

"Well, go inside. Now. I'll be there in ten minutes, fifteen tops."

"Okay," I tell him, even though I have no plans to go inside.

The call ends, and I tuck my phone into the pocket of my robe, looking up at the empty street again. I pace along the sidewalk in front of my townhouse. The idea of being cooped up while someone out there has violated my space makes my skin crawl.

The headlights that passed earlier replay in my mind. What if it wasn't someone on their way to work? What if they were the vandal checking to see if I'd noticed their destruction?

Another chill races down my spine. I pull my robe tighter around me, but it doesn't help.

When I finally hear the low rumble of an engine approaching fast, I whip my head around. Dominic's patrol SUV barrels up the street, red and blue lights blasting through the dark. He parks haphazardly at the curb, barely shutting the engine off before he jumps out.

He said fifteen minutes, tops. He made it in five.

"Ellie!" He's out of the cruiser and closing the distance between us in seconds

"I'm fine," I say quickly, though the wobble in my voice betrays me. If I wasn't so shaken, I'd make sure to keep some space between us. But at this point, resisting the pull to seek comfort from Dominic is pointless.

His eyes sweep over me, searching for any sign that I'm not telling the truth. Only when he seems satisfied does he turn his attention to the car. His jaw tightens as he takes in the shattered windows, his hands curling into fists at his sides.

"Jesus Christ," he mutters. He crouches to look closer, his flashlight illuminating the shiny glass.

"I should've taken the note more seriously," I say under my breath. "Or at least reported the flower and picture. I knew it was weird, but I didn't take it seriously."

Dominic straightens and moves back to me, his expression strained. "What note? What flower? What are you talking about?"

I tell him about the note left on my windshield and then the picture and the flower.

The muscles in Dominic's jaw twitch with thin restraint, while his nostrils flare like a bull ready to charge. His eyes blaze with an angry intensity I've never seen in him before.

"I didn't think it was a big deal." I look down, ashamed.

Each instance raised alarm bells in my head, but enough time passed between them, I convinced myself they were nothing. That they were harmless.

I was wrong.

I've worked my whole life to not be *that girl*. And I became her in an instant—the brainless one in slasher films who runs toward the danger instead of away from it.

Tension radiates off Dominic, a vein pulsing at his temple. His voice is low, almost too calm, deceptive. "You didn't think it was a big deal?" Each word is clipped, like he's barely holding back the full force of his frustration.

I fold my arms defensively, my gaze darting away. "It was just one flower. A silly note. I didn't want to overreact."

He takes a step closer, his broad shoulders practically vibrating. "Ellie! Overreact. Always overreact." He runs a ragged hand through his hair. "This is someone crossing a line —a line they don't get to cross. You didn't think to tell anyone? To tell me?" His voice rises slightly, but it's not anger at me—it's fear, frustration, the protector in him.

I flinch at his tone. "I didn't want to bother anyone. I thought it would stop."

Even I can hear how idiotic I sound.

He exhales sharply, shaking his head. "Bother me! Call me! Come to me! Ellie, someone is threatening you. They're testing boundaries. That doesn't stop—it escalates. You've got to take this seriously. What if something happened to you?" His eyes search mine, desperate for me to understand the gravity of the situation.

Before I can respond, the distant sound of tires humming softly against the pavement has us both turning. A police cruiser finally pulls into view.

Two officers step out, their gait slow and casual, as if they're arriving to a non-emergent event. Dominic storms toward them, his entire frame morphing into someone I don't recognize.

"Thirty minutes!," he barks, his voice sharp and biting. "It took you thirty fucking minutes to respond to a call! What if something had happened in the meantime?"

I never told him when I called the cops.

The first officer, a middle-aged man with a slightly rumpled uniform, raises a placating hand. "We were tied up with another call. A neighbor dispute. Low resources tonight."

Dominic's nostrils flare. "A neighbor dispute?" I can see the effort it takes for him not to completely explode. "You couldn't have split up? There was a targeted attack against a woman, and instead of responding immediately, you two left her defenseless, in the dark like a sitting duck." He looks between the men, disgusted. "Your captain will be hearing from me. Completely inexcusable."

The older officer stiffens. "Look, man—"

"Deputy Alvarez," Dominic snaps, cutting him off. "Deputy Dominic Alvarez. Write it down and don't fucking forget it." He steps closer, his height and commanding presence making the officers shift uncomfortably. "And let me make something very clear; this case falls under our jurisdiction now. It's directly tied to an ongoing investigation."

It is?

The officer's lips curl down, clearly irritated. "This is city property. Our territory. We'll handle it from here."

"Your territory?" he huffs. "For someone suddenly feeling territorial, you failed to prioritize a clear and immediate threat. This isn't just a random act of vandalism. There's a pattern here, one the sheriff's office has been tracking. So no, you're not handling it."

The second officer clears his throat, clearly uncomfortable with the escalating tension. "Maybe we can coordinate—"

"Coordinate all you want," Dominic cuts in. "But the case is mine. You can file your reports, collect your data, and send it my way. But from this moment on, we're the lead agency. And if I hear even a whisper of someone dragging their feet again when her safety is at stake, I will personally make sure it doesn't happen twice."

The lead officer glares but doesn't argue further. "We'll be in touch."

Dominic turns his back on them without another word.

I think I'm having an out of body experience. I've never witnessed this side of him.

It was...It was really hot.

I must be in a state of shock, not thinking clearly. I've heard shock can do funny things to people. Like make them lose their minds.

Dominic approaches, close enough for his scent to travel around me. "Let's get you inside," he says softly. A gentle hand presses to my shoulder, steering me toward my front door. "Change into something comfortable. We're going to the station."

The sheriff's station is dimly lit, the flickering fluorescents casting uneven shadows across the cold, impersonal room. Though the space is packed with people, the noise feels distant, muffled, as if I'm submerged underwater. Dominic's pen taps sharply against the desk, snapping me back to the present. Suddenly, the sounds rush in—keyboards clacking, a printer humming, coffee dripping from a Keurig, voices overlapping in chaotic layers. The urge to rush for the exit churns in my stomach. What the hell is happening?

"Before we get started, can you think of anyone that would want to hurt you? Anyone that has it out for you?" He hesitates for moment, swallowing harshly. "An old boyfriend?"

I can't seem to concentrate. There are too many thoughts

racing and crashing together. My knees bounce frantically with my hands beneath my thighs to keep them from shaking.

"Ellie? Did you hear me?"

I take a breath. "Yeah—sorry. There was this guy..."

Months ago, on a dare from Scottie, I downloaded a dating app.

One date was all it took for me to swear them off completely.

The guy was...weird. Not cute-nerdy, anime-and-D&D kind of weird. Just weird.

"I'm such a nice guy" weird. "I'm a high-value man" weird.

He made me uncomfortable.

And the worst part wasn't even the date—it was everything that came after.

He was relentless. Harassing me. Blowing up my phone.

I had to block him—*multiple times*—because he kept getting new numbers.

I think the last time I blocked him was after my dad picked me up from jail.

Honestly, I forgot all about him.

Until now.

I tell Dominic any details I can think of, and he writes them down, listening intently. Not judging me. Not angry.

"I'm going to record our interview for the report." Dominic sets the body cam usually attached to his vest on the table between us, lying face up.

The worry is written all over his face, and I hate it.

A wave of discomfort creeps over me, prickling my skin. I cross my arms tightly, resisting the overwhelming urge to scratch. If I could crawl out of my body, I would. This feeling —it's familiar. Too familiar.

I was twelve the first time I felt it, sitting in a restaurant with my mom. It had been one of those rare, special days—

just the two of us. While she was in the restroom, a man at the next table leaned toward me. His smile was too wide, his eyes lingering too long. He asked questions that made my stomach twist: Did I have a boyfriend? Was I the prettiest girl in my class? I was always taught to be polite, so I answered as best as I could, even though I wanted to disappear. When my mom returned, the man straightened, pretending nothing had happened. I didn't tell her about it, not then or ever. But that encounter left a mark, a sour, exposed feeling I couldn't comprehend, yet knew it felt wrong.

Now, sitting in this sterile metal chair, surrounded by deputies in uniform, that same unease creeps over me again—violated, raw, and this time, unable to convince myself nothing happened.

"Ellie," Dominic says, drawing my attention back to him. "Do you agree? We can wait until tomorrow, but it's better to do this while it's fresh."

His tone—even, cautious—only makes me feel worse. I nod, blinking rapidly to fight back tears. When one escapes, sliding hotly down my cheek, Dominic pushes a tissue box toward me. "It's okay to cry," he says so gently it makes by tears burn hotter.

"I don't cry." My shaky voice betrays me. Another tear falls. He pulls a tissue from the box and presses it into my hand, knowing I'd never reach for one myself and admit defeat.

Dominic flicks a button on the cam. "This is Deputy Sheriff Dominic Alvarez of the Clore County Sheriff's Department. This will be a recorded conversation with..." He hesitates, his eyes flicking to mine. "With the victim, Elyse Ledger."

The word crashes over me like a tidal wave. *Victim.* It burns, stripping away the last threads of my composure. A gasp escapes me, and Dominic stops the recording in an instant. He's at my side, pulling me out of the chair and into his arms.

It's been so long since he's held me, a different surge hits me, spreading across my chest. And this time it has nothing to do with the situation at hand and everything to do with feeling like I've landed exactly where I belong.

His embrace is safe, grounding, his warmth pressing against my trembling body. He steers us into a vacant interview room, kicking the door shut. In the darkness, his arms stay wrapped around me, his hand running soothing circles on my back.

"You're safe," he whispers. "You're always safe with me."

And for the first time all night, I believe it. Wrapped in him, I'm safe.

I let go, my sobs breaking free as I cling to him. He holds me tighter, absorbing every tremor, every tear, until the overwhelming weight begins to lift.

Eventually, I step back, wiping my face as I try to collect myself. But his steady gaze tells me he's not letting go.

CHAPTER 28

Dominic

MY HOUSE. MY WINE.

PRESENT

The sun is beginning to rise by the time we return to Ellie's townhouse. Her head rests against the passenger door window, her gaze fixed blankly outside.

"I'm going to do a sweep inside, make sure the house is empty." It's not necessary, but it'll give me peace of mind, something I desperately need right now.

She nods, not protesting at all, which isn't a good sign. The Ellie I know would put up a fight, insist that she didn't need me or my help.

As I climb out of the cruiser, I gesture for her to stay put. She doesn't argue, confirming my suspicions that she's more shaken up than she's letting on.

The only reason I'm comfortable leaving her alone in the driveway is because there are two patrol cars parked out front, waiting for me to give the all-clear before returning to duty.

I head to the front door and quickly inspect the exterior. All the windows are intact, no sign of forced entry.

When I step inside, my nose is instantly flooded with her smell, and I can't help but breathe it deeply. Walking around with measured steps, I take in the small space; a two-story, three bedroom, two bathroom townhouse. It's older, but has clearly been well-maintained over the years.

We were so young when we broke up, I never got the chance to see her get an apartment or make a space her own. If I was forced to guess what kind of home Ellie would've made, the scene before me is nearly identical to the image in my head. Plush, velvet furniture, dark colors, art and photographs that shouldn't go together, yet appear meticulously curated. Everything is intentional, but looks as if it's not. Like Ellie, it's a juxtaposition of all the characteristics that make her unique. She doesn't conform, and her home is a reflection of that.

I listen carefully for any sounds that don't belong. The home is eerily quiet, the kind of quiet that makes you jump at the drop of a pin. My paranoia is in overdrive, amplifying the lack of noise. When the ice maker in the fridge sounds loudly, indicating a new cycle, my pulse spikes. Normally I'm able to keep my overactive mind from racing when I'm on the job, but nothing about this situation is normal, and nothing threatening Ellie's safety will ever have me reacting calmly.

Moving on from the main level, I check upstairs, the bedrooms and bathrooms appear untouched. One guest room is being used as a closet—overflowing with clothes—and the other an office. I try not to let my mind wander into inappropriate places when I get to her bedroom, where her bed sits in the middle, sheets crumpled from where she was curled up before all hell broke loose. I can't help put look at the smooth spot next to it, where someone else would be if she shared her bed—where I would be if I was lucky enough to sleep next to her. The idea feels as far-fetched as it could possibly be. And now, more than ever, I can't afford to let myself get distracted by my feelings for her—not with so much at stake.

After checking every closet, and any space someone could slip into and appear undetected, I'm satisfied no one was in the home or is hiding in it now, and head back downstairs to the living room.

Through the front window I can see Ellie is right where I left her—seated in the passenger seat of my cruiser, wearing a stony expression.

When I reach the cruiser, and open up the passenger door for her to step out, she doesn't acknowledge me. Her body moves as if it's going through the motions. She's so deep in her head I'm not sure she knows it's me who's guiding her to the front porch.

I prop open the door for her to pass through. "All clear," I tell her as I toss a wave to the deputies, indicating they can leave.

She passes, not once looking my way.

I close the door behind me, latching it at the same time, and watch her move through her home. Tossing her purse on the entry table, she walks to the kitchen, where she opens a cabinet and pulls out a wine glass.

There's a half-finished wine bottle on the counter. She yanks off the rubber stopper and pours a generous glassfull.

I twist my wrist, checking the time. It's six in the morning.

"Kind of early for wine, don't you think, Ellie girl?"

The glare she aims my way could light a fire. It's also the most emotion I've seen her show since she broke down hours ago.

She raises the glass as if to cheers me. "My house. My wine. My coping mechanism. You're welcome to leave."

My head shakes as I approach her. I risk my pride and stand closer than I should. Now that I've had her in my arms, I'm nothing if not a fiend, seeking my next fix of her. She keeps her feet planted, not moving, and trying like hell to not look affected.

"You're going to have to pry this glass from my cold, dead hands." Once she's done speaking, her eyes close with a wince, like she's regretting her poorly worded phrase. "You know what I mean."

I wrap my hand around the stem of the glass, covering hers. "Never joke about your death. You're not dying. You're not allowed to."

Our eyes lock and her chest rises with a big inhale. "There you go again, trying to tell me what to do."

Even though I know now isn't the time, my body leans closer, brushing up against hers as I dip my head to hover above her ear. "You used to like it," I whisper.

She visibly shivers, causing my chest to swell. I want her reactions. I *need* her reactions. Anything besides her blank stare.

But as quickly as it dropped, her blank expression is back, and she breaks eye contact, putting distance between us as she pulls her hand away from mine. The pang of loss is immediate.

Setting down the wine glass, she begins rifling through a junk drawer, haphazardly tossing things on the floor, looking for something.

"Where are they?" she hisses under her breath.

"What are you looking for?"

"Cigarettes," she grumbles while continuing to search the overflowing drawer.

My head rears back. There's no way I heard that correctly. Right?

"Since when do you smoke?"

Ellie never smoked. Not even weed, let alone a cigarette. I can't even picture it, the image is so far removed from the girl I knew.

She shrugs, not bothering to look at me. "Only sometimes. Like when I'm drinking or stressed." Her gaze darts to the wine glass. "In this case, it's both."

After tearing apart the drawer and still coming up empty, she lets out a frustrated groan, slams it shut, and swipes the wine glass up.

"Definitely wasn't expecting that," I say more to myself than to her.

Her lips crest the rim of the glass before she tips her head back and takes a big gulp, swallowing the wine like it's water. "That's the nice thing about getting older, you change."

I laugh with a huff. "Whatever you say, Ellie girl." If my presence is grating on her now, then she's really not going to like what I have to say next. "Better get used to me, because we're about to become really close."

She snorts as if I said a joke. "What makes you think that?"

Instead of answering her, I turn my back and walk into the living room. She lets out an exasperated sigh as I sink down onto the couch and get settled.

Stomping in, she stops just short of the coffee table in the middle of the room. "What are you doing?"

My shoulders lift. "Getting comfortable."

Her spine straightens, and she remains standing, staring at me with pure ice. "Don't you have work or something? Or better yet, a house to go to?"

The corners of my lips twitch before a smile fully takes over. I'll take whatever anger she wants to throw at me, it doesn't faze me a bit. "Oh, I'm not leaving."

She crosses her arms, causing the wine in her glass to swirl around. "What do you mean, you're not leaving?"

My grin widens. "I'm. Not. Leaving."

She's out of her mind if she thinks I'm leaving her alone after this. Her car getting destroyed could just be the beginning, and I'm not going to sit back and act like this is nothing. Even if it's not related to the Delmar case, which I hope to hell it's not, someone has it out for her. Until this is resolved, they're going to have to get through me first.

If smoke could blow out of her ears, it would be happening right about now.

"Until the situation is handled," I continue. "And the perp is in custody, you're never left alone. Either I'm here, and sleeping on your couch, or there's a patrol car parked out front. Until I know your life is no longer in danger, you're going to be protected. I'd gladly do it twenty-four seven, but I have a job, so when I can't be here, patrol will take over. I already spoke to Under Sheriff Doyle and got the approval.

"And while we were at the station, I spoke with your family. Your dad agreed that I should stay with you, and your brothers are on board with keeping an eye on you, escorting you home if needed. Everything has been handled."

Her eyes bulge as she rapidly shakes her head. "Absolutely not! And why are you talking to my family behind my back? My car was vandalized, no one held a knife to my neck and threatened me. This is a massive overreaction."

I stand and walk up to her. She responds by stepping back until her back hits the wall that divides the kitchen and living room.

"Someone has been trying to get your attention and taking pictures of you without your knowledge. Someone has been *watching* you. And who knows how long this has gone on before they got brave enough to make it known. They're stalking you. Now they've escalated to vandalism. It's only going to get worse. If I'm here, I can protect you."

With our eyes locked, and her scent floating between us, I can no longer keep my hands to myself and cradle her face in my hands. When she doesn't flinch, I stroke my thumbs over her cheekbones. If I'm not mistaken, she leans into the touch.

"If I have to burn down the world to find this fucker, I will. I'll do anything to keep you safe, even if it means pissing you off. There isn't anything I wouldn't do to protect you. I would kill for you without a second thought, do you understand?"

Her sea glass eyes stare at me, shocked, and her only response is to nod.

Realizing I got carried away, I stagger back and release her from my hold.

Knowing what I know about Victoria Delmar is enough to send me spiraling, especially imagining the same happening to Ellie. I didn't give it a second thought. I'm staying, and it's final. We're past the point of me giving her space.

The Delmar case had some interesting revelations this week. One being that we're suspecting the perpetrator held Victoria captive, keeping her alive until she no longer served him. There were signs of assault and malnourishment. Ellie doesn't know any of this because the details haven't been released to the public. Unfortunately, I know too much. And I'll be damned if the same happens to her. It might not be the same guy, this might be an isolated incident, but I'm not willing to risk her on a bunch of maybes and mights.

"Whatever," she says flatly, before tossing her head back and chugging the remainder of wine in her glass. She strides away, not looking back. "I'm going to bed; I'm exhausted. Don't bother me."

I expected a little more of a fight from her, but it's been a long morning.

Fuck, I'm exhausted, too.

As tired as I am, I have no plans to sleep for a while. Not with this shit going on. While she rests, I'll be spending the remainder of the day focused on the house and the surrounding area. Watching.

CHAPTER 29

Elyse

NOT SORRY FOR IT

PRESENT

"Oh. You're still here?"

Dominic's lips curve upward as he surveys me, eyes full of way too much amusement. "Good morning to you, too."

My eyes swivel to the clock on the microwave. It's noon.

"I made a fresh pot of coffee, help yourself," Dominic says before taking a sip from the mug in his hand.

Rolling my eyes, I drag my feet over to the coffeemaker and work at making myself a cup. My back is to him, but his eyes are burning a hole through my robe.

"I see you've made yourself at home. Not like I said you could stay, or anything."

He chuckles, and the sound vibrates against the ceramic mug. "It's cute that you think you have a choice."

At that, I spin to face him, and tip my chin down, making sure to pin him with my stare. "I don't need a babysitter. And if I did need one, I can think of plenty of other guys I'd rather have stand guard than you."

I don't want to lash out at Dominic, but it's pouring out of me, and I can't stop it. My mind is a collision of emotions, all crashing together at once. I feel angry and violated and vulnerable and out of control. It's like I can't get a handle on myself, and need to scream. It feels oddly good to take it out on him, which is so fucked up; I'm trying not to think about it too deeply.

With a calculated calmness, he keep his gaze latched with mine and sets his mug on the coffee table, moving to stand. His shoulders square as he straightens.

It's as if in that one single move, he's declared his command. His imposing height swallows up my small living room. His arms cross, emphasizing the bulge of his biceps, and I have to clench my jaw to keep it from dropping open. Even my inability to navigate the storm raging inside of me isn't enough to detract from how fucking attractive he is.

God, it's annoying.

I didn't think it was possible to feel so out of sorts, yet fight to keep my thighs from squeezing to feel any semblance of relief. His presence has me more twisted up than a pretzel. And worst of all, I think he knows it.

"Ellie girl, fight it all you want. I'm not going anywhere. The sooner you accept it, the sooner we can figure out how to coexist without starting a war. We were just starting to get along. What happened to that?"

The more he spoke, the closer he got. Now, he's inches from me, and I have to decide if breathing is really worth it if it means breathing his air, and risking my resolve crumbling under the weight of everything I've been trying to ignore.

His eyes hold mine, refusing to let go, as if he's daring me to look away. I can't. I'm frozen, caught somewhere between wanting to step back and wanting to close the small distance between us.

My pulse is a traitor, hammering in my throat. I know he can see it—in the way my chest rises and falls too quickly.

"Ellie," he whispers as his face softens from the hardened expression he was wearing moments ago. I ignore the little flip in my stomach and clear my throat. "I know you hate this—but I'm not capable of walking away from you. You can try all you want to make light of this, it won't work. I've seen awful, vile things in my line of work; the depths of humanity. You have no idea what it's like in my head, the images I live with. I won't survive anything happening to you."

Heat rises from my neck and washes over my face. The pain in his voice paired with his penetrating gaze; it's enough to put another chink in my armor. All the chinks belong to him, each one going deeper than the last.

I open my mouth to respond, but nothing comes out. The words I want to throw at him—snarky, dismissive, anything to regain control—die on my tongue.

"Dominic..." I finally whisper, my voice more fragile than I'd like. "You can't just...come back. We don't know each other anymore. You can't treat me like—"

"Like you're everything?" he interrupts, his tone unwavering, as if the words were begging to come out. "Because you are, Ellie. You can pretend we're strangers, if that helps you sleep at night, but make no mistake, querida mía; I know you better than anyone. And I know you're scared. I also know I'm the only man in your life qualified to keep you safe."

I shake my head, backing up a step. The intensity in his voice, in his eyes, it's too much, and I feel myself retreating, both physically and emotionally. "This isn't fair. You don't get to take control of everything. You don't get to—"

"Yes, I do," he says without hesitation. Stepping forward, he closes the space I just created, his presence swallowing me whole. "I'm going to protect you and take care of you—and you're going to let me, because I need it too. I need it so badly, Ellie girl."

"Don't call me that," I snap, more out of self-preservation than actual anger. "The nicknames; no one calls me either of those."

Dominic tilts his head, a ghost of a smirk playing on his lips despite the storm brewing in his eyes. "What? Ellie girl? Querida mía? Why not? Because it reminds you of *us*? Because it makes you feel things you don't want to admit?"

I glare at him because I have nothing to say in defense. He's not wrong.

"You're being annoying."

"And you're stubborn," he fires back, his voice softening but not losing its edge. "But I'd rather deal with your stubbornness than the alternative. Because at least that means you're alive. And that's all that matters to me."

My throat tightens, and I turn away, gripping the edge of the counter to steady myself. I hate how much of what he says affects me, how much his words weave their way past my defenses. I hate that he's right—about my heart racing, about me feeling things I'm not ready to acknowledge.

"I don't need you." My voice is barely above a whisper—so weak I don't believe it myself.

Dominic moves closer, his hand brushing against mine where it grips the counter. It's a featherlight touch, but it sends shockwaves through me. "Maybe not," he murmurs, his voice low, but rough enough to make me shiver. "But I need you, Ellie. And I'm not sorry for it."

"Scottie, please stop crying."

Her tear-filled eyes get closer to the screen. "You almost died!"

I sigh, running a hand through my hair, still damp from the shower I took to calm my nerves. "I did not almost die! My car is fucked, but nothing happened to me, okay? I'm fine. I already have a rental. The cops are on it. And Dominic is here..." I trail off quietly, hoping she didn't really hear it.

Scottie narrows her eyes, suspicion cutting through her tears. "Dominic? Can you repeat that? I'm not sure I heard you correctly. You said Dominic, right?" Her tears are practically nonexistent now, replaced with a knowing smile.

I groan, already regretting mentioning him. "I don't know why I tell you anything."

Scottie giggles, wiping her nose on her sleeve. "Wait, wait, wait. So, you're telling me you're holed up with Dom, who's, what, sleeping on your couch now? Or, wait—your bed? Is he just wandering around without a shirt on?"

I huff. "Focus. He's not walking around without a shirt. He's overreacting, and annoyingly making himself right at home."

"Wait! He's there right now?"

I toss my head back, exhaling loudly. "Have you been listening to me?! Yes, he's here! He won't leave."

The phone crashes, causing the image to distort, but I can still hear her. She's in a fit of laughter.

A few seconds pass before the phone gets pick back up and her face fills the screen.

"Sorry! I lost my shit for a minute there."

My eyes roll. "No, really? I couldn't tell."

She leans closer to the screen, her dramatics fully back. "How am I supposed to focus when you have a whole romantic movie situation brewing over there? What's next? You're forced to share a bed and one thing leads to another?"

"Scottie."

"I'm serious, Elle. If he ends up in your bed, I'm going to need all the details!" She thinks for a moment. "Well, maybe not *all* the details, but you know what I mean."

I let out an exasperated laugh despite myself, shaking my head. "That won't be happening." It feels good to laugh, even when the cause is Scottie's wild imagination.

She smirks. "Yeah, sure. Remind me to text Ariana and Layla so we can get another bet going."

"Not you too. Why is everyone betting on us? It's embarrassing."

"You know what they say," she sings. "Only bet on a sure thing."

Before I can retort, her expression shifts, her playful tone gone in an instant. Her voice mellows, cracking slightly. "But seriously, Elle. You need to promise me you'll stay safe. It could be nothing—just a couple crappy kids—but what if it's not? Promise me you'll be careful. Maybe I should drop out of the show and come stay with you for a bit."

My chest knots at the worry in her cloudy blue eyes. I blink quickly and look away. "I know. I promise, I'm being careful. I'll call you every day if it'll make you feel better. But you can't drop everything—you've worked too hard for this show."

She pauses, clearly torn. "Fine. But if anything else happens, I'm on the next flight."

I smile faintly. "Deal."

She points a finger at the camera. "And don't think this gets you out of keeping me updated on the Dom situation. I have a very specific interest in this subplot."

I laugh, my heart feeling lighter for the first time all day. "Goodbye, Scottie."

"Bye babe, love you," Scottie blows a kiss, winking before the screen goes dark.

Releasing a breath, I set my phone down and lean back

against the headboard. My gaze flicks toward the door—Dominic is probably still downstairs, wide awake, keeping watch.

After our little kitchen moment—where I basically unleashed all my personalities at once—I avoided him for the rest of the day.

It helps that my family's been blowing up my phone. The group chat got so overwhelming, I muted it. By some miracle, I managed to keep them from coming over, claiming I was resting. When really, I just didn't have it in me to pretend I'm okay. I can fake it over the phone. But in person? That's a whole different level of draining.

It should bother me more that Dominic is still here, but the truth is, I've never felt safer. I could get used to this feeling—and that's the problem. Letting myself rely on him is dangerous. I used to rely on him for everything. Somewhere along the way, I lost the ability to exist without him. I didn't know who I was without his presence, and realizing that was terrifying. I felt stunted.

When everyone in college was exploring themselves, testing their boundaries, I was crumbling—trying to piece together a puzzle with too many missing parts. I swore I'd never let it happen again. I told myself I'd never mold to someone so much that I disappeared.

But the longer Dominic is here, the more I want to lose myself.

CHAPTER 30

Elyse

ENJOY THIS TIME

18 YEARS OLD

"**D**o you think anyone's going to notice we disappeared?"

Dominic shakes his head as he continues driving. "Who cares? We graduated; we're done."

He's right, but a flicker of guilt still pricks at me. We're supposed to be with our class, celebrating at the senior party hosted by our school. Instead, we snuck off together.

Scottie is really the only person I care about hanging out with, but she was the one practically pushing me out the door.

"If I had someone to go sneak off and have sex with, do you really think I'd be hanging out with these people?" she'd said while looking around the packed gym with her nose scrunched.

I couldn't really argue with her, so while the chaperones weren't paying attention, we slipped out the non-working emergency exit and drove straight to Sullivan Ridge House.

Dominic isn't usually one to break the rules, but after prom, I think he's trying to make it up to me. I had no idea part of the deal with us getting to spend more alone time together included both sets of our parents chaperoning prom.

Even though I'm not a big drinker, I'd hoped to have at least one drink—preferably through a flask that matched my dress. We didn't even get to go to the after party at the Benton's house. Despite embarrassingly winning prom king and queen, the night was pretty much a bust.

Tonight, though, it's just us and the beginning of our last summer before reality kicks in. Thinking about the fall, and starting college, terrifies me, and I'm doing everything I can to enjoy this time while we still have it.

Dominic pulls up alongside the house. The cloudy night sky only emphasizing how much darker it is out here without any lights to speak of. He guides me inside, more by memory than by sight.

Using our cell phones, we light our usual candles and get settled on the pile of blankets I brought over earlier, just in case.

We've never spent a full night together, and I can't help the warmth that stirs low in my belly thinking about sleeping in Dominic's arms.

I wrap my arms around him, bringing his lips down to meet mine. Slipping my tongue in, I instantly deepen the kiss. He opens up, taking more of me as his hands skim down my sides, and he crawls on top of me.

"We have all night, we don't have to go fast." He kisses along my jaw and down my neck, sending waves of heat down my spine.

My thighs fall open, making room for him. "Exactly," I giggle. "We have all night. Think about how many times we can go."

He laughs against my lips. "Querida mía, don't set me up for failure."

We continue making out, Dominic trying to go slow while

I do the opposite. He slides the straps of my graduation dress down slowly, revealing the swell of my small cleavage. My back arches, aching for him to go faster.

When my breasts are finally free, the sound of a car door slamming brings everything to a screeching halt.

Dominic slides my dress back in place like it was never down to begin with. He scrambles off me and crawls over to the window.

"Shit," he hisses. "Cops."

What!

When he spins to face me, there's panic in his eyes. "You have to hide," he whispers.

I shake my head. "No, I'm not hiding."

He grabs me by the shoulders and starts pushing me into the parlor room. "Stay in here, and no matter what, don't come out. Okay?"

"But—"

"No, Ellie. I'm serious. Don't come out. We can't both get in trouble."

That's when the seriousness of the situation hits me. We're not supposed to be here.

When I don't say anything, his eyes widen, waiting for my answer. "Promise me you won't move."

"I promise," I tell him.

The moment he leaves me alone, hidden in the dark parlor, the front door opens and the beam of a flashlight comes through.

"Police," a male voice calls out. "Anyone in here?"

From where I'm standing I have a perfect view of the foyer.

I watch as Dominic comes out with his arms raised. "Just me," he calls out.

The officer has his weapon ready to draw. "You armed."

"No, sir."

"Are you aware this is private property?

"Yes, sir."

I gasp and then slap my hand over my mouth.

It never occurred to me that Sullivan Ridge House is private property. I just thought it was in some limbo since it's right on the border of the vineyard.

The officer holsters his gun.

"What's your name, son?"

"Dominic Alvarez."

"Not sure if you're aware, but trespassing is a misdemeanor. I'm going to have to take you in."

Dominic says something I can't make out and then he's turning.

"Dominic Alvarez, you're under arrest..."

My heart jumps in my throat, waves of panic crashing over me.

As the officer reads out the Miranda rights, the same ones I've heard on TV, Dominic looks right at me.

I don't think he can see me, but has a pretty good idea where I'm standing, just out of sight. My throat tightens hearing the handcuffs lock, and Dominic shakes his head, silently telling me to keep my promise.

I stand there, frozen, watching as my boyfriend gets arrested.

The officer blows out our candles and moments later, they're gone, leaving me a shaking mess. I don't know what to do. I'm not sure what the right response is. The one thing I know for certain, is that I have to save him. I have to do something.

So, I do the only thing I can think of.

I call my dad.

CHAPTER 31

Dominic

THE STRAIGHT AND NARROW

18 YEARS OLD

I 've never been in the back of a police car. Can't say I'm a fan.

"If you knew you were on private property, why were you there?" the officer asks, meeting my gaze in the rearview mirror.

I shrug, knowing whatever I say could make things worse.

Considering all things, the officer has been pretty decent. He wasn't rough with me; he didn't yell. It could've been worse. Much worse.

"You eighteen?" he asks.

"Yep, just turned eighteen, actually."

He sighs, studying me for a moment before his eyes return to the road.

"I wasn't trying to cause any trouble," I say under my breath. "Just wanted to go somewhere quiet."

He nods slowly. "Don't stress too much, kid. It's a minor offense, and you don't look like a troublemaker."

Up until now, the worst thing I've ever done is get a tattoo before turning eighteen, which is nothing.

The rest of the drive is silent. All I can think about are the impacts this could have on my future. Suddenly, I'm wishing I had read the fine print on my scholarship. Something like this could go on my record and fuck up the rest of my life.

I knew we shouldn't have been going there, but the house has sat abandoned for so long it seemed harmless. Now, it could be the one thing that ruins any chance I had at a decent future.

I'm so fucked.

We pull into the Clore County Detention Center.

I swallow, looking at the building, knowing it's packed full of people locked up for a hell of a lot more than trespassing. It's just now hitting me I could end up in a bad situation quickly if I'm not careful.

The officer turns off the ignition but doesn't move.

He twists in his seat to face me through the partition. "Here's how it's going to go. I'm going to take you to booking. You'll fill out some paperwork, get your mugshot taken, you'll be fingerprinted, and then they'll search you. There're a few more things after that, but that's the gist of it. And try not to shit your pants, you're not going to be placed in a holding cell with some hardened criminal. Probably a DUI case, if anything."

I guess my expression made it pretty obvious how scared out of my mind I am.

"Why are you being so nice to me?"

He breathes out a laugh. "Because you're just a kid, and you're shaking like a leaf."

I didn't realize I was shaking so badly, but when I look down at my knees, they're trembling.

"Thanks," I mutter.

He helps me out of the back, since it's awkward with the handcuffs still on and escorts me through the front doors.

The second we get past the lobby, I see a familiar face and freeze.

It's Jack.

And he's not alone.

Beside him is a stocky, short man I don't recognize.

Jack approaches the officer escorting me and greets him with a handshake. "Jack Ledger."

"Officer Diaz," he responds, with confusion in his words.

"I already spoke with your captain," Jack continues. "He agreed to release Dominic into my custody. The Sullivans won't be pressing charges."

Officer Diaz looks at me like I had something to do with it. I'm just as confused as he is.

"Let me give my captain a call first," he looks between me and Jack. "Just a moment."

The officer moves a few feet ahead and makes the phone call, keeping his eyes on me as he does.

Jack approaches me with a smile.

"How did you—how." I shake my head, trying to gather my thoughts. "How?"

He lets out a chuckle, as if we're not standing in a jail in the middle of the night. "Elyse called me. Told me everything. Told me you protected her—made her hide so she wouldn't get in trouble too."

I look down, my face heating in shame. "It's my fault. I didn't mean for any of this to happen."

"Listen—I'm pissed because somehow you two keep finding ways to send me into an early grave. Nothing like your daughter calling you crying in the middle of the night because her boyfriend's been arrested—"

"I'm sor—"

Jack raises his hand to stop me. "Let me finish. I'm not

going where you think I am. You sacrificed yourself for Elyse. And I'm proud of you."

"You're proud of me for getting arrested?"

He laughs, shaking his head. "Not exactly. I'm just proud of you for being a good man. But don't get me wrong, I'm livid. Not sure I'll be letting Elyse out of the house all summer. And you two will be hanging out in the living room, where I can keep my eyes on you."

"I understand." Unsure of what to say, my eyes land on the guy Jack was standing with. "Who's he?"

Jack glances back and then meets my eyes. "My lawyer in case things got out of hand. For some reason people seem to listen to me around here, but I thought it'd be wise to bring in some legal backup."

"So, I'm not going to jail?"

"Nope. As far as your record is concerned, this never happened."

Officer Diaz approaches us with a smile. "Well, kid. You've got some luck on your side or," his eyes flick to Jack as he unlocks the handcuffs, "friends in very high places. Either way, you're off the hook." He lets out an exhale, looking on either side before speaking. "If you've got a minute though, I'd like to have a chat."

My gaze flies to Jack and he nods, stepping back to join his attorney.

"I swear I had nothing to do with him coming, my girlfriend—"

"It's cool, kid. I'm glad you've got good people looking out for you. The reason I wanted to talk to you is because I was wondering what your plans are for the future."

My shoulders lift. "I start WSU in the fall, but I'm not really sure what to major in yet. I'm hoping I'll figure it out while I'm there."

Officer Diaz reaches in his pocket and hands me a business

card. "This is my last week with RMPD. I'm transferring down to LA to be close to family. You ever think about becoming a cop, you give me a call."

I look down at the card, confused how I was just arrested and asked if I was interested in becoming a cop all in one night.

"Do you usually ask guys you've arrested if they want to become cops?"

He laughs, throwing his head back. "No, not usually. I don't know, just got a good feeling about you. It's really easy to go down the wrong road if you're not careful. Once you cross over certain lines, it's a hell of a lot harder crossing back. Tonight, you got close, and I'd like to see you continue walking the straight and narrow. And I like to see a little color on the force, if you know what I mean. The leaders of the community should look like the residents, and that's not always the case."

He claps my shoulder. "Anyway, think about it. We could use more guys like you."

As Jack and I walk out to his car, he puts his arm around me. "Come on, son. Let's get you home."

CHAPTER 32

Dominic

SHE SEEMS KIND OF CRAZY

PRESENT

"He's not your guy."

Detective Kincaid gives me a flat smile, knowing the news is disappointing.

When Ellie told me she'd been having problems with a guy she met online, it took everything in me not to hunt him down myself and break every damn law out there. In that moment, my oath was out the window.

Stuart Hollis.

They'd met on a dating app, went on one date—which Ellie described as the most uncomfortable thirty minutes of her life. She said she let him down gently, sensing he was a little off. But the guy refused to take no for an answer, and wouldn't leave her alone. When I asked her why she never filed a report, she told me she almost had, but he'd gone quiet in the last few weeks, so she figured he'd finally moved on.

To say I'm furious is an understatement. There isn't a word in the English language strong enough to express how fucking angry I am. Angry at myself for ever letting her go in the first place, angry that some piece of shit thinks he's entitled to her after she clearly turned him down, but most of all, I'm angry with time. Angry that so much time has passed— enough for Ellie to put herself out there and try to find love when no one could ever or will ever love her the way I never stopped.

Every time I picture her being woken up in the middle of the night by the sound of her car being vandalized, all I can think about is how she was alone. How she had to handle that by herself.

I knew something was going on with her. I never could've imagined it was this.

I scrub a hand over my face, approaching Kincaid. "How do you know it's not him?"

He slides a report over to me.

With a quick glance, I fold it shut, throwing it back on the desk.

Stuart was in custody the night Ellie's car was vandalized.

Brought in on suspicion of a DUI.

This has to be a fucking joke. If it's not him, then who the hell is it?

Kincaid bumps my shoulder with his knuckle. "Relax. We'll find him. That's what we do. In the meantime, we've got a big case on our hands."

I nod, but there's a knot in my chest that keeps getting tighter.

Returning back to my desk, I start combing through the latest statements on the Delmar case.

According to some of her friends, Victoria had recently broken things off with a boyfriend none of them had met. They suspected he was married, and that's why she kept him hidden.

I continue reading through, getting lost in the case

file when Morales strolls over, a to-go cup in hand and an extra pep in her step.

She plops herself on the corner of my desk.

I don't look up, hoping she takes a hint and leaves.

"So, I had an interesting run-in with your ex and she threatened me. Elyse, right?"

Now she has my attention. Ellie hasn't mentioned anything about running into Morales.

I look up to find Morales's lips lifted in a satisfied smirk.

"What did she say?"

She lets out a dry laugh. "She basically told me to stay away from you and implied that you two are together. It was pathetic, really."

Interesting.

I rub a hand down my face to conceal my smile.

Ellie got territorial.

"She seems kind of crazy," Morales continues.

I'm getting the sense she isn't telling me the full story. "Why do you say that?"

Her shoulders lift and she takes a slow drink before answering. "Because clearly you're not interested in her. It's sad."

Now I definitely know Morales isn't telling me the full story.

I don't give a shit though, because all I'm hearing is Ellie staked her claim on me and it's the best news I've heard all day.

"It's not sad." I rise to stand, ready to be done with this conversation. "We're together."

Morales gasps, and I wonder if she realizes how loud it was. "You are? But why?"

Instead of indulging Morales, I look at the clock and count down the minutes until I'm off shift and back with my girl.

She still feels something.

CHAPTER 33

Elyse

YOU'RE STARING

PRESENT

I t's been six days. Six long, exhausting days.

After the first night, Dominic worked two straight twelve-hour shifts. For a while, I almost felt normal—just a single patrol car parked out front while I went about my usual business. I barely noticed it.

Dominic did little more than eat and sleep when he wasn't at work, and I kept myself locked away in the safety of my bedroom, pretending not to notice his presence.

But then came day four.

I came home from work, Ethan following me to make sure I made it safely. I hadn't been in for more than two seconds when I heard a loud thud in the garage.

Dominic's patrol SUV was parked out front, so I wasn't necessarily scared, more curious.

I opened the door to find him shirtless and sweaty. He'd moved over some weights and set up a workout area in my garage.

I've seen him shirtless before, but that was back when he was barely more than a boy.

I can confirm he's not a boy anymore.

He's a man. A muscled, tattooed, delicious man.

My gaze instantly caught on the trail of hair running down the center of his abdomen, disappearing beneath the waistband of his shorts. I couldn't stop staring at the bulge there, my mouth watering at the thought of what I already knew he was packing.

"You good?" Dominic asked, smirking as he wiped the sweat off his forehead with a rag, veins visible along his forearms.

"Huh?" I swallowed. "I heard a noise."

"Just me." He winked, knowing full well what he was doing.

I was barely resisting him in uniform. But nearly naked? That was decidedly harder.

"I'll be inside in a minute. Didn't mean to scare you."

I almost didn't hear him, too distracted by the ripples of muscles running across his stomach, taut and defined, as if they'd been sculpted from stone. There were eight.

Eight.

The man had an eight-pack.

His shoulders were broad, leading down to chiseled biceps that were massive. I'd seen them strain against his shirts, but seeing them bare was something else entirely. I couldn't help but blatantly ogle him.

He stalked toward me, cocky smile in place, sweat dripping down his body, causing his olive skin to gleam. The gold chain around his neck was almost my undoing.

As he got closer, I caught a whiff of his scent.

Even his sweat smelled good.

"You're staring, Ellie girl," he whispered, his eyes roaming over me.

My cheeks burned. "No," I lied. My shoulders squared as I tried to look unaffected. "I don't remember you asking if it was okay if you turned my garage into a gym."

He chuckled. "My mistake. I should've ran it by you. Is it a problem?"

"No," I said weakly.

I rarely used my garage for anything more than housing a few totes full of Christmas decorations.

"Good to know." His smile grew. "You seem distracted."

Distracted didn't even scratch the surface. I was ensnared. I was trapped. He was quicksand—and I was sinking.

I only knew one way to fight this losing battle—and that was to walk away.

So I did, without another word.

On the fifth day, he cooked.

I hadn't realized his schedule was two days on, two days off. But since he'd appointed himself my live-in bodyguard, I found myself spending more time holed up in my bedroom than ever before—leaving for work early, staying late. Part of it was because of Dominic, but mostly it was because work was one of the only places I still felt in control.

Since the incident with my car, nothing else had happened. No more notes, no weird flowers, no photos. Nothing. I was starting to think the whole thing had been blown out of proportion. Maybe it had been the interns, who eventually realized their pranks had gone too far. Or maybe someone else with the same make and model as my car had pissed off the wrong ex. Either way, it was starting to seem like whatever had been happening was over.

When I walked in, my house smelled amazing. It smelled familiar. It smelled like the house Dominic grew up in.

"Hey," he called out casually. Like this was normal.

"Hi," I replied.

"Hungry?"

245

I would've lied, but then my stomach growled loudly, answering for me.

"What did you make?"

"Barbacoa. My dad's recipe."

Dominic's dad was an amazing cook. I couldn't recall a dish of his that I didn't absolutely love. I've even attempted to replicate some, using the internet as my guide, but I've never come close.

I joined Dominic in the kitchen, and lifted the lid off the pressure cooker, inspecting the inside.

He looked nervous. "I cheated and used a pressure cooker, but it should taste similar." His gaze dropped to the floor. "Probably not as good."

A lump sat heavy in my throat. Food was probably how he felt connected to his dad.

I gave him a soft smile. "I bet it tastes exactly the same."

He smiled back, like he needed to hear that.

We ate dinner together in the dining room. The conversation was light, surface level, but so easy I almost forgot all the reasons it was a bad idea.

We cleaned up the kitchen together. He tried to shoo me out, but I insisted. Wiping countertops, washing pans, loading the dishwasher—it all felt so normal. It felt couple-y. It felt right.

Later that night, all I could think about was how much I wanted to do it again.

And that was a problem.

So, tonight, I'm redirecting things. I have a plan.

Girls' night. It also happens to be my birthday, even though I never celebrate it anymore.

All I know, is I need some space from Dominic, and I need some time with my girls. A night where I don't have to think about some stalker who may or may not exist, or my ex, holed up in my house, or the fact that said ex is getting harder and harder to resist.

I'm dragging Ariana and Layla out to The Jackalope, and Marisa is joining us.

I need this. Desperately. Some time to breathe—to feel normal again.

There's only one small obstacle.

I have to convince Dominic to let me go without locking me in here, or worse, tagging along.

I find him in the kitchen, leaning against the counter drinking an energy drink. His head is tipped back, working down a swallow. His dark eyes stare at me as I approach, immediately narrowing in that way that makes my skin tingle when he notices my outfit.

"What?" I cross my arms, my defenses rising.

"Is that my birthday present?" he asks, eyes giving me a heated once over. "Because if it is, I approve."

His burning gaze roams over me again. It lingers on my exposed legs before slowly dragging up to the deep V of my dress. I'm not wearing a bra, not as if there's much to look at in that department anyway, but it still sends my stomach into a dive.

"No," I scoff. "It's girls' night. I'm going out with Marisa and my sisters. And you can't come."

He straightens, all six-foot-two of him radiating disapproval. "Not happening."

I blink. "I'm sorry, what?"

"You're not going out."

"Yes, I am." My voice hardens. "Last I checked, I'm a grown ass woman who can do whatever the hell she wants, and the last person I'm going to let tell me what to do is you."

"Are you suffering from amnesia? Did you forget someone has been stalking you and vandalized your car?" His voice is infuriatingly calm. "I'm trying to keep you safe."

I scoff. "Safe from what? It's been a week. Nothing's happened. Whoever it was is likely gone. I refuse to put my life on hold just because you're paranoid."

A muscle in his jaw tics, and I can tell it's taking everything in him to not boil over. "A week of silence doesn't mean shit. I'm not being paranoid. I'm taking it seriously, which is what you should be doing instead of putting yourself at risk. It's foolish behavior."

Foolish.

"If you weren't so quick to jump to conclusions and treat me like an idiot, you'd know that my brothers are coming. I'm not so reckless, I'd actually go out with all the shit that's happened without some sense of safety."

He rubs the back of his neck, a hint of guilt sweeping across his features. "I didn't mean it like that. I just—fuck— I'm sorry."

Well, shit, now I feel guilty.

"I'm sorry for snapping," I admit.

"It's okay," he breathes. "You can go. I won't try to stop you."

My brows lift. For some reason, I thought he'd go as far as handcuffing me to the radiator to stop me from going. Or maybe handcuffing me somewhere else...

My eyes squeeze shut as I shove the intrusive thought away —before I end up liking the idea a little too much.

"But I'm coming with you," he adds.

The Jackalope is loud and crowded. I thought it would be exactly what I need, but I can't seem to let loose.

Three drinks in, and I don't feel drunk at all. I don't even feel tipsy.

Layla is beside me, throwing back a shot. Meanwhile, Ariana's still nursing the same drink she ordered an hour ago. Knowing her, she'll slip out the second she thinks no one will notice. And Marisa has been eye-fucking my brother since we got here. At this point, I'd rather they both leave to prevent me from having to witness it.

Speaking of leaving, there's one man who definitely should...

Dominic is parked at the guys' table near the corner, sandwiched between Ethan and Gavin, with Cole Benton across from him. His arms are crossed and his gaze is zeroed in on me, making it incredibly difficult to actually relax. He hasn't moved or sipped on anything more than water since we got here. I get that he's trying to protect me, but I'm in a bar, surrounded by people I know. Nothing is going to happen here.

Ignoring him—or at least trying to—I down the rest of my cocktail, hoping it finally does the trick. It's been so long since I've gone out, I'm not going to let Dominic ruin it.

"Another round?" Layla asks, waggling her eyebrows.

"You read my mind. But make it something stronger. I need something strong enough to make me forget my problems."

Marisa gives me a side-eye that's equal parts amused and concerned. "You mean the guy who can't take his eyes off you, or...you know, the other thing?"

"Both. And I want to dance!" I declare, tossing my hair over my shoulder.

Ariana lets out a groan. "And that's my sign it's time to leave."

I give her a good-natured eye roll, not surprised at all, and slide off my stool, smoothing down the short hem of my dress.

The black fabric clings to my minuscule curves in a way that makes me feel like I actually have some.

Ariana gives me a hug and whispers "happy birthday" in my ear before handing me her drink and leaving. I finish the remainder of her lukewarm lemon drop in one gulp. My face pinches as the sour burn works its way down my throat.

Layla returns, and hands me a shot. We clink our glasses to cheers, tossing them both back at the same time.

It's cheap tequila, but I feel it almost instantly. Exactly what I needed to tip me over the edge. I've been chasing that sweet-spot kind of drunk—where my thoughts go fuzzy and my limbs feel light.

The bass thumps through the floor as we make our way onto the dance floor, weaving between sweaty bodies. The moment we find a spot, I start moving to the beat, letting the music take over.

I grab on to Layla to steady myself while she does the same. Together, we dance, holding on to each other to keep from stumbling.

I don't have to look to know Dominic's watching.

Even though he hasn't taken his eyes off me all night, this is the first time since we arrived that maybe I actually want him to watch me.

When I wear something sexy, it's for me—because I want to feel good in my own skin. When I dance, it's not to get anyone's attention. It's because I'm caught up in the moment, because it makes me feel alive.

But with Dominic's gaze locked on me, I know the truth. Tonight, my choices aren't just for me.

I'm not just dancing for me anymore. I'm dancing for *him*. And I didn't wear this dress just to feel good. I wore it because I wanted *him* to see me in it.

I want his attention. Even when I tell myself I don't.

So when I glance over my shoulder and find his dark eyes on me, I give him a little smirk and keep dancing.

I know this dress is driving him wild and the devil on my shoulder is loving every second of it.

The music shifts to a sultry beat, and I let my hips sway a little slower, a little more deliberate.

A guy I don't recognize slides in behind Layla at the same moment a pair of male hands settle on my hips and begin to move with me. I'm normally not one for dancing with random men, but decide to just go with it. I just know Dominic's going to lose his shit.

The Jackalope doesn't get many tourists so there's a high likelihood I know the person dancing behind me.

Layla sinks back into her guy, and starts grinding her ass. He responds by pulling her tighter, lowering his head to the curve of her neck, and sucking on her skin.

Okay, then.

My guy's a bit more of a gentleman—or at least he's trying to be. His hands rest lightly on my waist, giving me space, so I keep moving my hips, keeping just enough distance between us.

Suddenly his mouth is near my ear, breathing heavily. "God, I missed you."

I freeze.

His voice is familiar.

Alarm bells flash in my head.

Immediately, I pull away, turning to face him.

The moment I realize who was behind me—who I let touch me, my stomach rolls.

It's Stuart.

"What the hell!" I snap loud enough to turn a few heads.

His lips curl into an off-putting smile as his eyes scan me in a way that makes me feel naked. "You look even better than I remember."

I shuffle back, bumping into a solid chest.

"Back the fuck off."

The voice comes from behind me.

Dominic.

He steps around me in one swift, protective motion, placing himself directly between Stuart and me. His shoulders are squared, fists clenched, biceps bulging and for the first time tonight, there's nothing restrained about him.

Stuart lifts his hands in mock innocence. "Hey, man. I was just dancing. No need to get all—"

Dominic grabs him by the collar before he can finish his sentence.

"Touch her again, and I'll break the hand that does it. I'll break every fucking bone."

"Jesus, relax," Stuart says with a laugh that's anything but amused. "She was dancing with me. Maybe you should take it up with her. She wanted it."

I open my mouth to shut that shit down, but Dominic's already moving.

He shoves Stuart hard, enough to send him stumbling into the sticky wood-paneled wall. Marisa rushes up to us as Layla clings to my arm. Chaos breaks out all around—people shouting, phones going up, the music skipping. My brothers have Stuart pinned to the wall, and based on the look on his face, they're not holding him back gently.

Dominic's already on his phone before I've had a moment to wrap my head around what the hell just happened.

"This is Deputy Alvarez, Charlie-Four-Eight. I've got a trespasser in violation of a no-contact directive. Requesting immediate pickup."

"What?" I choke out. "That's not—there's no—"

Dominic doesn't look at me. Doesn't even blink.

He knows there's no official order. He's lying through his teeth.

But he doesn't care.

Stuart's wide-eyed now. "You're full of shit, man. There's no restraining order."

Dominic's voice drops so low, I hardly recognize it. "There will be."

By the time RMPD shows up—faster than I expect—Stuart's near tears. Maybe it's because he's terrified of being arrested or it's because Gavin's massive hand has likely dislocated his shoulder.

Dominic stays by my side the whole time, acting as a barrier between me and Stuart.

The cops don't question him. They take one look at Dominic, take one look at me, and slap the cuffs on Stuart.

As they haul him out, Stuart shoots me one last look. It's pleading and apologetic, making me question what's real and what I've built up in my head.

Dominic already told me he was ruled out as a suspect for vandalizing my car, but that doesn't necessarily mean he's innocent of the other incidents.

I should feel relief. Maybe I do. But mostly, I feel my pulse pounding and my legs unsteady.

When Dominic finally turns to me, the hard edges of tension in his expression have softened.

"You okay?"

I nod slowly, unable to look away from him.

"Good," he says. "Because I'm not. Time to wrap it up. We're leaving."

I cross my arms, hating the control he's trying to place over me, even if it's justified.

"What if I don't want to leave?"

His eyes skate down me briefly—so brief I almost miss it—and when they come back up, they're darker, more intense.

He steps closer, invading my space. "Was that nightmare not enough of a reason to leave? I just had to watch some piece

253

of shit put his hands on you. I had him arrested for *touching* you. Don't make me break every law because I can't keep my jealousy under control. When it comes to you, I'm fucking weak. Cut me some slack. Please, querida mía."

All the fire drains from my body, leaving me a useless puddle on the floor.

He steps in close. "Go wait by the bar with the others. Don't go anywhere alone, okay? I'm going to check in with RMPD, make sure he actually gets booked."

I can't find words—just a tiny nod that barely feels like enough—and turn toward the bar, legs moving on autopilot.

Rhonda sees me coming and doesn't say a word. She just slides two double shots across the counter.

"On the house, princess. The good stuff—99 proof. What a fucking night."

I knock them back without a second thought.

CHAPTER 34

Dominic

DEPUTY ALVAREZ

PRESENT

llie is giggling as I help her out of the passenger seat. The sound so sweet and carefree, I close my eyes for a moment just to let it wash over me. After tonight, she deserves to have a moment not laced with all the shit that's going on.

I haven't seen her like this in a while. She's drunk, way too drunk, and I can't let myself enjoy it. Not tonight.

She seemed somewhat sober when we left the bar, but by the time we pulled into the driveway, the drunk haze was back in her eyes. Either the alcohol she'd been tossing back all night finally hit her, or she had something while I dealt with the Stuart situation.

"Dominic," she slurs, gripping my arm as I guide her to the door. "You saved me. You saved me, and it was so hot."

Yeah, she's definitely shit-faced. Sober Ellie would never admit that.

She's swaying on her feet, clinging to my arm so tightly,

her nails are digging into it. Her nearness is doing something dangerous to my self-control.

Inside, the air is quiet and still. I set up security cameras around the perimeter of her property and didn't get one alert while we were gone.

While it's only been a few days, her space is already feeling like home. Maybe it's because my house is in massive disarray, or maybe it's because this is Ellie's home, and wherever she is feels like exactly where I need to be.

She leans into me, her body warm and soft, and I hate myself for noticing, especially when she's too drunk to realize what's she's doing. I want her touch, but only when her mind is clear, and she wants it as much as I do.

"Come on, let's get you some water." I steer her toward the couch.

"Water's boring," she mumbles, pulling away. She stumbles slightly, and I catch her by the waist, steadying her before she can fall.

Fuck, she feels good. What I wouldn't give to be able to bury my face in her neck and suck on the pulse jumping out of it. Lick down it, suck on her—

"You're not boring, though," she teases, brushing her breasts against me. "You're all...big and muscly and..." Her fingers trail up my chest, and I grab her wrist gently, stopping her movements.

"Ellie," I warn.

This is torture.

"What?" She blinks up at me, her wide, pale green eyes full of mischief. "I'm just saying you're sexy. Is that a crime now? Are you going to arrest me, *Deputy Alvarez*?"

I close my eyes briefly, fighting for composure. I'm not going to survive this. "You've had too much to drink. You don't know what you're saying."

"So?" she counters, leaning closer. "I know what I want,

and I want you." Her breath is warm against my neck, and I can feel her smile. "We've had sex drunk before."

I swallow down a choke.

We have had sex drunk before. But we were young and stupid, and *both* drunk. This is different.

"You know," she continues. "You don't have to sleep on the couch. My bed's big enough. I think you earned it tonight."

I laugh, despite myself, and step back, putting some much-needed space between us.

I'm being punished. I've been wanting her since I moved back. Hell, I've been yearning for her from the moment I lost her. Now, the one time she can't keep her hands off me, I have to push her away.

"Maybe you should sit down."

She pouts but obeys, collapsing onto the couch in a flurry of dramatic sighs that cause my dick to jerk to attention. "You're no fun."

"You'll thank me in the morning." I grab a bottle of water from the kitchen and hand it to her.

She takes it begrudgingly, twisting the cap off clumsily. "You should've had some drinks tonight. Maybe then you'd stop being such a buzzkill."

Setting aside the water, she stands, and her dress rises dangerously high. Enough for me to get a peek at her underwear. Red lace. So fucking sexy my mouth starts to water.

"Since you're so hell-bent on staying here and protecting me," she says, stepping toward me. "Maybe you can take care of some of my other needs, too."

"Like what?" My voice croaks.

She moves closer, her gaze fixed on mine, and I can see the fire in her eyes—the same fire that's had me hooked on her nearly my entire life.

"I'm so wet," she purrs. "Take care of me."

Fuck me.

"I know you want me."

"Ellie—"

"Don't deny it," she cuts me off, her hands pressing against my chest. "I can feel it. Every time you look at me; every time we're in the same room. You want me just as much as I want you. Let me reward you tonight for protecting me."

I swallow hard, my resolve shattering to pieces at the same time my cock presses against my zipper.

Of course I want her. But not like this. Not when she's drunk and vulnerable and not thinking clearly.

"You need to sleep," I say, my voice strained.

"I told you what I need, and it's definitely not sleep. So I had a little to drink—who cares? I can handle myself, and I can handle you."

Fuck, do I remember how well she handles me. I remember it so well, it's been playing on repeat for ten years, every time I've wrapped my hand around my cock, it's only Ellie. It's always only been her.

I close my eyes, taking a deep breath. "I'm staying down here. Go upstairs. Please."

Her expression falters, just for a moment, and I hate myself for putting that flicker of hurt in her eyes. But then she huffs, crossing her arms over her chest. "Fine. Be boring. See if I care."

I don't respond. I can't.

"I'll just be in bed taking care of myself."

It takes me a moment, and then I realize what she said—at least what I think she said.

Her footsteps stop when she reaches the top of the stairs. "You're welcome to watch."

CHAPTER 35

Dominic

STRAIGHT TO HELL

PRESENT

I'm frozen, stuck on the bottom step. If I go up, something will happen. What? I'm not entirely sure. I can't touch her—I won't. I waited ten years, and I'm not going to fuck it up just because my dick can't listen to my brain. But would watching be so terrible?

"Are you coming?" Ellie calls out at the top of the stairs, laughter in her voice.

Something tells me I'll be coming at some point. At this rate, probably in my damn pants.

I'm going straight to hell for this. As I take the first step up, my index and middle fingers glide across the chain around my neck, tugging at it like it might make me feel better about what I'm about to do.

Hell it is.

I walk slow, my limbs heavy with hesitation.

When I get to the top, her bedroom door is propped open and all the lights are off, save for the flicker of a candle.

I should turn back around, be a better man. I just know

there will be fallout from this come tomorrow when her mind is lucid, but right now I don't want to be a better man. I want to storm in there and strip that dress off, and sink into her like I've been dreaming about.

Thankfully, I have just enough resolve to not indulge in my fantasies tonight. My brain is on repeat, screaming: *Don't touch her.* Yet, my feet still drag me in.

When I finally make it inside her bedroom, my mind goes completely silent. No warning bells, no rationality to speak of. Because Elyse Ledger is sprawled out on her bed in nothing but a red, lace thong. No bra, no sheets, nothing.

My knees shake on their own accord.

Definitely hell. Fucking worth it.

I've seen her body countless times, but we were younger. This—this is different. She's a grown woman now. Her hips flare out more than they used to and her breasts look like they would fit in my hands perfectly. Not to mention her nipples are pierced—that's new. She tugs on one of the studs when she catches me staring.

"Do you like them? It was kind of an impulsive decision."

"Yeah." My voice cracks. I swallow roughly. "They—they look really good."

While toying with her breast, her eyes meet mine. "Want to touch them?"

Holy shit. I'm not sure I'm strong enough for this. Is any man strong enough to watch the woman of his dreams play with herself and beg to be touched? I deserve a fucking award right now.

"I can't," I croak out.

She giggles, and it morphs into a sexy little sigh. "Fine. Suit yourself."

While one hand continues to play with her beautiful, pierced pink nipple, the other caresses down her abdomen, before dipping into her panties. Her back arches, followed by a moan, as her palm cups over her pussy.

I drag a hand down my face while my lungs squeeze, trying to find air. This may be the death of me.

"Dominic, baby, I'm so wet."

I haven't heard those sweet words leave her lips in so long, I nearly forgot how much they affect me. Stepping closer, I teeter on the edge of crossing some major lines.

"Show me," I rasp.

She smiles up at me, and obliges by lifting her arm and fluttering her fingers in my face. They're glistening, drenched from her soaking pussy. I catch a whiff, and like a goddamn drug addict, wish I could grab hold of her hand and inhale deeply, before licking them clean.

"Want a taste?" She wiggles her fingers again, and my mouth opens, so fucking hungry for her.

"Come on," she teases. "Be a good boy and lick your reward."

I can't resist her, not when she's like this. I'm only a man.

My hand wraps around her wrist, and her back bows like I touched between her thighs instead.

"Yes, please. Do it. Lick me."

Fuuuuck.

Keeping my eyes locked onto hers, I dip my head and bring her fingers to my mouth. I hesitate, only because I know this is wrong. She's drunk. It's so wrong, but it feels so right too.

Her drenched fingers just so happen to be attached to the wrist with my name across it—a reminder that she's always been mine.

Making the decision for me, Ellie shoves two fingers into my mouth. Instinctively, I suck on them, letting my tongue lap up the moisture.

My eyes roll back in my head. She tastes like honey; sweet,

addictive. I want her taste on everything I consume for the rest of my life.

She pulls her hand away and laughs a sexy, husky sound. "I think you've had enough."

Not even close to enough.

"Take off your panties. I want to see you," I grit, blurring the lines of my morals.

She twists her hips and hooks her thumbs on the sides of her underwear, sliding them down. "Hmm," she hums. "I love it when you get all commanding and tell me what to do."

She tosses the red scrap of fabric at me, and I ball it up in my hand, rubbing my thumb over the wet spot she left behind. With her eyes anchored to mine, she spreads her legs, revealing her perfect pussy. Even from where I stand, I can see how wet she is, how swollen and pink her lips are from being so aroused. It's the best fucking view.

"Look at you," I whisper, amazed. "So pretty."

My mind has gone fuzzy, trapped in the fragile space between a dream and disbelief.

I'm still not going to touch her, but I'm going to enjoy the show. "Got anything in that nightstand, Ellie girl?"

"Yes," she answers without hesitation.

That's my girl.

"Pull out your favorite and let me watch you fuck your pretty little pussy. Show me how you touch yourself in bed, alone. Show me what no one else gets to see."

She reaches in her nightstand and pulls out a thick, purple vibrator with a clit massager attached to it.

"Is this one okay?" she asks, looking amazingly doe-eyed and innocent for a naked woman holding a vibrator.

"You tell me, querida mía. Is that the one you like?"

The corners of her lips lift slightly. "It's the one I use when I miss you. Makes me come every time, just like you did."

I'm never going to be the same after this. She may have

regrets tomorrow, which I'll deal with when they come. I'm never walking away. I didn't have plans to, but now my intentions are cemented. I'm completely ruined. She owns me.

"Show me, Ellie girl. Show me how you like it."

She turns it on and presses the button until she reaches the setting she wants, a steady vibration.

A faint ringing in my ears tangles with the sounds of the vibrator. I may pass out from this. It's too much to take in, and I want her so badly I have to keep my fists balled to stop from touching her.

The head of the vibrator disappears between her swollen, wet center at the same time a relieved moan escapes her throat.

Holy fuck!

When she was mine, we were still learning so much about sex—about what we liked. We explored and our sex life was adventurous. But we never did this. This is new territory, and it's the hottest fucking thing I've ever witnessed.

"Dominic," she sighs. "I wish it was your cock."

Me too. Me fucking too.

She pushes the vibrator in and out, fucking herself. I clench my jaw to fight a moan of my own.

"Do you like watching?" There's a hint of vulnerability in her voice, of unease. Despite how drunk she likely is, she's still unsure, and it pinches at my heart, painfully.

"I could watch you do this all day, every day, for the rest of my fucking life, and my life would be full. You're the most beautiful woman I've ever laid eyes on. I'm never going to forget this, it'll be the last image I'll think of before I leave this earth."

Her lips twitch before a full-fledged smile takes over. "And people say I'm dramatic. Power of the pussy, huh Dominic, baby." She rolls her lips between her teeth, but there's nothing hiding that smile.

"Power of *your* pussy, querida mía." She must like my answer, because her cheeks flush like I paid her a compliment.

"Are you turned on, too? Or is it just me?"

I shake my head with a laugh. I thought my tented jeans were evidence enough. "Harder than I've ever been before. How could I not be? You're a fucking fantasy brought to life."

She pauses moving the vibrator, holding it inside herself. "Show me. I want to see it."

I really should've had a drink or two, I'm not sure I'm brave enough.

"Please," she begs, flopping her bottom lip in a pout. "I need to know you want me as badly as I want you."

I guess we're doing this because no way in hell am I saying no to her.

With unsteady hands I undo my top button and slide my zipper down carefully, making sure to not hurt my already throbbing cock. She watches me with wide-eyed fascination.

I don't think dicks shrink with age, but now I'm nervous as hell my nineteen-year-old cock won't hold up well against the thirty-year-old version.

"Don't be shy," she giggles, since I'm clearly hesitating.

I take a deep breath. *Fuck it.* My hand reaches inside my boxer briefs and wraps around my shaft, giving it a firm pump for good measure before I whip it out.

Her mouth drops open at the sight of it, and I'm not sure if it's a good thing or a bad thing.

What the fuck am I doing?

"It's even bigger than I remember," she says with a sigh before licking her lips.

My shoulders drop some of the tension that had built up. Better than saying it got smaller, at least.

She shoots me a sly smile. "If you want to keep watching me, then I get to keep watching you. We do it together. It'll be our birthday gifts to each other. And if you're a good boy, you'll come at the same time as me."

Best birthday gift I've had in years.

She never used to say "good boy," and now she's said it twice.

I think I like it.

"I'll fuck my fist, if that's what you want querida mía. Anything for you."

"Good." She tosses her head back as she pushes the vibrator in deeper. "Come with me."

I pump my cock, already so close it's embarrassing. "Tell me when you're close," I say through a clenched jaw. "I'm not going to last long. My cock has been hard for you for so goddamn long," I admit.

"I'm close. I've been touching myself every night you've been here just to stay sane."

Jesus Christ. Now she tells me? She's trying to kill me. I've been sleeping on the couch downstairs for almost a week, meanwhile she's up here touching herself.

I jerk my cock faster. "Next time, tell me. Might as well use me if I'm here."

"Dominic, baby." She gasps. "I'm going to come."

Thank God. I'm going to come any second. "Me too, I'm right there with you," I rasp.

She spreads her legs wider, pumps the vibrator harder. "Come on me. I want your cum on my skin."

The woman isn't real, she's a fantasy I created. I had to have. I'm dreaming.

"Please come on me," she begs as her body arches off the bed, the orgasm ripping through her.

Please.

I walk the two small strides it takes to stand over her on the bed, and just as I do, cum spills out of my cock in ropes and lands over her breasts and stomach. Her hooded eyes watch, transfixed.

Just when I think my mind can't be anymore blown than it already is, she takes a finger and swipes at my cum that's landed on her nipple. Spreading it, she paints it over her breasts, before bringing the tip of her finger to her mouth and tasting it.

"Mmm," she moans. "So good."

I'm so fucked, it's not even funny.

"Ellie girl, you're better than any fantasy I've ever had. And I've had a lot of fantasies about you."

Her eyes morph from lust to something else—something softer. "Me too," she says quietly.

For a moment neither one of us speaks. I cut through the silence first.

"Let me clean you up," I say under my breath, tucking my dick back in my pants.

She stays quiet, and watches me as I step into her en suite and dampen a washcloth under warm water.

When I return, she's still like she was when I left her, but her eyes look tired.

Wordlessly, I clean her up, and she lets me.

After dropping the washcloth in a nearby hamper, I pause, unsure of what my next move should be. It doesn't feel right going back downstairs and sleeping on the couch like nothing happened, but it also feels wrong to stay, even though I already went too far.

As if she can read my mind she says, "Stay."

Her hand pats the left side of the bed, the side I just so happen to already sleep on.

For once in my life, I don't question if this is right or wrong. Nothing about getting to share space with Ellie could ever be wrong. So I nod, and take off my jeans and shirt, leaving me in nothing but my boxer briefs. She stares, her eyes full of heat.

Honestly, I'm already getting hard again. But I know we crossed a boundary thanks to some alcohol, and shouldn't keep going.

I slip under the covers and reach for her, way past stopping myself from touching her. Especially, after tonight. She stiffens for a second, before completely melting and cuddling against me, her back to my front.

God, she feels so good. She feels like she was always meant to be in my arms. And I can't believe I've survived so long without her.

Never again. I don't care what it takes, but I'm never going back to the man I was without her. I fell for her hard, and I never got back up. She's mine. She's my everything.

I kiss the back of her head, snuggling her closer. "Happy birthday, querida mía."

"Mmm," she hums, sleepily. "Happy birthday, Dominic."

CHAPTER 36

Elyse

HANDLE IT LIKE ADULTS

PRESENT

I wake up alone.

My body jackknifes, sitting up so fast the room spins.

Maybe I dreamt it. Maybe it was just a really vivid dream.

I pat my hand over the left side of the bed. It's still warm. Sheets twisted.

Fuck!

Oh my God. Oh my God. Oh my God. It wasn't a dream.

As panic grips me, the smell of chorizo wafts through the air. I can faintly hear the crackling of it frying downstairs. My head is pounding and my mouth feels like I swallowed a bucket of sand.

I don't know if I can face him. He must think I'm insane. I've been all over the place—cold and bitchy one moment, friendly the next, and then practically threw myself at him.

I let him see me *naked*!

Mortification burns my face, and I turn, tossing my head into the pillows, muffling my groan.

I want to die.

Forcing myself, I shuffle out of bed and glance at myself in the mirror. My mascara is smudged, my hair looks like a small animal nested in it, and at some point in the middle of the night, I put on Dominic's T-shirt. Perfect. I look like the most stereotypical image of a one-night-stand.

Just as I'm about to spin around, my eyes snag on something shiny hanging around my neck.

It's the necklace Dominic gave me on my eighteenth birthday.

The one I left behind on the day I broke up with him.

My fingers toy with the initials dangling from it, and for a moment I consider taking it off but instead, for some reason, I can't bring myself to do it.

I have two choices, I can stay in my room and hide, or grow a pair, go down there, and face him.

With some deep breathing and lots of dry swallowing, I make it a few steps before seriously considering getting back in bed and hiding until the end of time.

Dominic starts to whistle. He knows I'm awake, I'm not sure how. Maybe it's my back and forth steps as I have a mini meltdown. Or maybe he can sense I'm awake, because I'm utterly predictable.

If I go down and face the music, at the very least I need to look presentable. I strip out of Dominic's shirt, and definitely don't inhale it a few times before tossing it on the bed. Rifling through my drawers, I pull out a pair of leggings and a sweatshirt, something comfortable but not sloppy. I'm trying to not look like the train wreck I feel like. Once dressed, I finger comb my hair into a messy bun, swipe a makeup wipe under my eyes to clean up what's left of the mascara.

I give myself one last look in the mirror. "Acceptable," I mutter to the disheveled version of myself.

Dominic's whistling continues, cheerfully grating on my

nerves as I make my way down, each step feeling like I'm walking to my doom. My heart pounds in my chest as I inch down the staircase, pausing halfway to listen. The clink of a spatula against a pan. The scrape of a chair on the hardwood floor. The unmistakable low hum of Dominic singing.

Singing.

Singing in Spanish. It's "Mujeres Divinas" by Vicente Fernández. His dad used to sing it all the time.

Suddenly, my reaction—more like overreaction—feels silly. We're both adults, and we can handle it like adults. It was nothing. No big deal.

I square my shoulders and take the last steps down, rounding the corner into the kitchen like I don't have a care in the world.

Dominic's back is to me as he crumbles the chorizo, still singing quietly to himself, his shoulders swaying slightly. He's wearing gray sweatpants and a fitted green T-shirt. His muscled back is clearly defined through the cotton, and my fingers itch to touch the skin underneath, to drag my nails down it.

Life is incredibly unfair because even casually dressed he can look like *that* while I still feel like a raccoon caught in a dumpster fire.

He turns as I step into the room, spatula in hand, and flashes me a grin so dazzling I nearly turn around and run straight back upstairs.

"Morning, querida mía." His voice is way too chipper for someone who watched me masturbate just a few hours ago.

I narrow my eyes at him, trying to play it cool. "I thought we talked about not calling me that."

"Why not?" He shrugs, scooping chorizo con huevo on a plate. "You didn't seem to mind it last night."

I freeze, my face burning hotter than the stove. "Oh my God, shut up."

His grin only grows. "Relax. I'm only teasing. We don't have to talk about it. Yet."

"Or never," I mumble, slinking over to the coffee maker, desperate for caffeine to dull the embarrassment clawing at my insides.

He sets the plate on the island and leans back against the counter, crossing his arms over his annoyingly broad chest. "You're cute when you're embarrassed."

I whip around to glare at him. "I'm not embarrassed. I was drunk and it's nothing you haven't seen before." I shrug to add how much I really don't care about the whole thing. Easy breezy.

"You know it's a crime to lie to a member of law enforcement, might have to cuff you for that," he says and then hits me with a wink.

"Does that line work on all the girls?" I pour the coffee aggressively, willing myself to not make eye contact.

Why the hell would I even ask that? Imagining him flirting with someone makes my stomach turn.

He laughs, a deep, rumbling sound that makes my heart betray me by skipping a beat. "No, just you."

"It really doesn't," I sing, irritated.

A beat later I feel the heat of him behind me, his hot breath on my neck. "Careful, querida mía. I think you like the idea of me cuffing you more than you're willing to admit."

I freeze with the coffee mug halfway to my lips. Flames creep up my neck as I force down a swallow, my mind immediately imagining Dominic using his cuffs on me.

I should've stayed in bed.

Turning to face him, keeping my mug on my lips, his wry smile says it all. He knows exactly where my brain went. Before I can formulate something witty to say to save face, he drops a plate in front of me and nudges my shoulders until I'm forced to sit on a barstool.

"I figured you could use a hearty meal to soak up all the alcohol. How are you feeling?"

In an instant he's gone from flirty to caring. I hate the way my heart squeezes. I'm not used to this—to someone trying to take care of me.

"Fine," I say quietly.

His brows raise like he doesn't believe me.

"Small headache. It'll go away soon."

"And what about everything else that happened?"

Since I'd been pounding back excessive amounts of alcohol, the memory of Stuart and everything that happened is a hazy blur. Which is maybe for the best, because the little I do remember, makes my skin itch. Violated. Vulnerable. Weak.

"I'm okay. I think."

Dominic swallows, his eyes distant for a moment as if he's recalling the events. "He's in custody. And I suspect he'll be there for a while. His prints matched a Peeping Tom case in Coyote Creek Junction."

"Good," I say, unsure about how I should feel.

Stuart isn't who vandalized my car, so even though he's behind bars now, nothing about my current situation is resolved.

Dominic's eyes flash down to my uneaten plate. "Eat up. You'll feel better."

I pick up my fork as he's about to walk away, but he stops, and instead reaches for me, cradling my face in his hands while brushing his thumbs over my cheekbones. It happens so fast, by the time I'm in his hold, I'm too stunned to pull away. The fork drops from my hand and lands on the plate in a loud clatter.

"You're beautiful, you know that?"

He used to do this all the time—out of nowhere he'd grab my face and tell me something sweet, and every time it would melt even the hardest parts of me. Apparently, I'm still not immune to it because I'm a puddle on the floor.

His eyes hold mine captive, refusing to let go. So dark and warm, the safest abyss. The warmth of his skin radiates, so hot I imagine there's heat waves coming off him. And his smell... he smells like my pillows this morning—cedarwood, clean, masculine. The urge to brush my nose against his neck is so overwhelming I'm not sure I can bear it.

I lick my lips and watch him track the move.

He leans closer and my breath hitches. I think he's going to kiss me, and I think I'm going to let him.

"Fuck, Ellie," he whispers, his breath fanning across my lips. "If something had happened to you last night, I'm not sure what I would've done." My heart is pounding so loudly there's no way he doesn't hear it—feel it.

Just when I think he's going to close the distance, instead his lips brush against my forehead, where he plants the softest kiss before walking away.

"Necklace looks good on you," he calls out.

I walk around my living room, my phone clutched in my hand as I FaceTime Scottie. She's sitting cross-legged on her couch with a steaming cup of tea in her hands.

"Alright," she says, smiling like the cat that ate the canary. "Spill. What happened last night? And don't you dare hold out on me. I'm living vicariously through you."

I sigh, knowing she's going to absolutely freak out.

I give her a replay of everything. The drinking. Seeing Stuart. Dominic having him arrested. And finally, my drunken attempt at seducing Dominic, which turned into mutual masturbation.

She stares at me silent for the first time in her entire life.

"Are you there? Did the screen freeze?"

Her throat clears, eyes wide, before swallowing loudly.

"I'm here. Just processing."

I breathe out an exhale. "I know, it's a lot to unpack."

"I'm coming back. I can't stay here knowing someone is after you. It's getting scary, Elle."

I stop pacing, my heart tugging at the sound of her concern. I love her for it. But I can't let her put her life on hold for me.

"No. You can't. You've got shows almost every night— you're finally living your dream!"

She frowns. "There will be other opportunities."

"You've worked too hard to let all of it go to waste now. I swear, if things get worse, I'll tell you. But Dominic's on it, and my family is looking out for me too."

She glares at the screen like she wants to fight me on it. "I hate this."

"I know you do."

"I hate that I'm not there. I hate that this freak is still out there. And I really hate that I'm missing out on watching Dominic wear you down."

I let out a half-laugh, half-groan.

She smiles, but it doesn't quite reach her eyes. "Promise me you'll keep your location on. And text me when you get home. From anywhere."

"I promise," I say softly. "I'll be safe."

She hesitates, then nods slowly. "Okay. I'll stay. For now. But don't make me regret it."

"Never."

There's a beat of silence, the kind that says everything without needing to be said.

"Okay," she murmurs. "I'll let you go."

"Love you."

"Love you more."

The screen goes dark, and I sit there for a second, staring at my reflection in the black screen.

Then I toss the phone on the couch, and I immediately dive into stress cleaning. Dominic is working night shift and left a few hours ago. It'll be my first time staying alone at night since this whole thing started, and despite the patrol car parked out front, I don't feel nearly as safe as I do when Dominic is home.

After breakfast, I had a couple to meet with. We did cake tastings and met with the florist to pick out their centerpieces.

I assumed Dominic would tag along, but instead a deputy, whose name I didn't catch, patrolled the winery. I was oddly disappointed.

I felt like maybe he was avoiding me, and after what happened last night, it was kind of messing with my head.

By the time I got home, he was already on his way out the door, leaving me unsure of what to do with myself.

I feel antsy—and when I'm antsy, I clean.

I start with the dishes, scrubbing them with more force than necessary. Then it's the counters, the floors, the bathroom—every surface I can reach. The physical activity helps me burn off some of the restless energy buzzing under my skin, but it doesn't quiet my thoughts.

No matter how hard I try to push Dominic out of my mind, he won't budge. I'm questioning myself, regretting what happened. I was drunk but I wasn't *that* drunk. If anything I was using it as an excuse—permission to do exactly what I wanted. And maybe after what happened with Stuart I needed something good. I needed something not tainted. I needed Dominic. Now, I don't know what to think.

By the time I've cleaned everything twice over, I'm physically exhausted but my mind is wide awake. It's two in the morning, and I don't see myself falling asleep anytime soon. Not with my thoughts racing the way they are. Not with my life in this weird limbo of constant surveillance. I just want this to be over.

I can't be here right now. I need to go somewhere I can think.

CHAPTER 37

Elyse

YOU'RE JUST SO WISE

PRESENT

"Are you lost?"

Gavin's voice cuts through the silence, making me nearly jump out of my skin.

"Jesus Christ!" I exclaim, pressing a hand to my chest. "I didn't think anyone would be here this late—or early, I guess."

The lab is located on the edge of the winery estate, near the bottling facility. It's where the wine is actually made— more science lab than picturesque winery. And much like my brother, it's tucked away and isolated from everything else.

Gavin descends the metal staircase, pulling off his gloves and hairnet as he goes. "Lily's at a sleepover, so I thought I'd get some work done. Spring Release is right around the corner."

When he reaches the bottom step, he pauses, raising an eyebrow. "But the real question is, why are you here? Especially at this hour?"

He steps off the last stair, his boots scuffing against the concrete floor as he walks toward me. Tossing his gloves onto a nearby table, he leans a hip against it, folding his arms across his chest.

I shrug, not entirely sure why I came here. I just started driving and ended up at the winery, and instead of turning back around, I kept going until the road came to a stop at the lab.

"What's going on? Are you alone? Why are you alone?" He has a concerned look on his face, the same kind our dad gives us, and for some reason it makes me feel guilty. I know what's going on isn't my fault, but I can't help but feel like all it's done is cause my family unnecessary stress.

"Patrol is parked outside. And I'm fine, it's nothing to do with that." I reassure him.

He nods slowly, silently probing me to continue with what's really bothering me.

Rather than answer him right away, I busy myself with straightening the papers on a cart next to a rack of new barrels. "Well, you know how Dominic has been staying with me the past few days?"

He blows out an exhale. "Yeah, it's the only reason any of us can sleep at night, knowing someone's watching over you. And after last night, I feel indebted to the guy."

There goes that pang of guilt again, hitting painfully.

"It's just that it's been confusing. You know the history. I don't know..."

I'm close with all my siblings, each in their own way, but I've never been very open about sharing details about my love life, especially with my brothers.

"I remember," he chuckles. "Hard to forget. It was the first time I ever wanted to fight one of my friends."

"What?" I laugh. "What are you talking about?"

Gavin shrugs. "I mean, he was younger than me and Ethan, but we liked him, liked hanging out with him. Then you two started dating, and we didn't fucking like that one bit."

My forehead scrunches. "Why?"

He cocks his head, staring down at me. "Because we're guys. We knew what all teenage boys want—shit, what all men want. And we knew it was likely going to happen." He pauses, shaking his head with a laugh. "It's different when it's your sister. We liked him, but we love you, and if he hurt you, we knew what we were going to have to do."

A corner of my heart tugs. Not everyone is close with their siblings—some of my friends barely speak to theirs. Mine might drive me crazy, and we don't always see eye to eye, but I know how lucky I am to have them.

"You guys were wrong," I mutter. "He never hurt me. I hurt him."

"So, what's the problem?"

Playing with the string of my hoodie, I avoid Gavin's gaze. "I think he wants to try again, and I don't know if I can. He hasn't really said it, but it's not like he's subtle."

"I see." He moves toward one of the barrels on the rack, giving it a tap. "Sometimes you do everything right, perfect balance, right ingredients, but for whatever reason the wine doesn't age properly in the barrel. Could be for a variety of reasons—temperature, environment, pressure. The list is endless."

I look at him, confused as hell how we're now on the subject of wine. Knowing Gavin, it's best to just let him him process through.

"When that happens," he continues. "Sometimes we transfer it from one barrel to another, giving it the chance to pick up new characteristics. Other times, we blend two different wines—each with their own strengths—and something entirely new is created. Flavors deepen, complexities emerge, and sometimes, what we end up with is even better than what we started with."

"You lost me," I tell him, huffing a laugh.

Gavin does this—nerds out on wine.

"That's what these are." He gestures to the barrels. "They're in the double barrel process."

It's then that I realize what he's doing, and roll my eyes, though I can't stop the slight tug at my lips. "Are you seriously comparing Dominic to wine right now?"

"I'm comparing *you* and Dominic to wine," he corrects, drumming on a barrel. "Think about it. Your relationship was aged in one barrel, and yeah, maybe it wasn't perfect. Maybe it needed more time, more care. But now you have the chance to start fresh. To let things develop in a new way."

In any other situation, I'd probably be laughing—making fun of Gavin for going too deep with the wine analogies, doling out unwarranted advice, but since it's my life we're talking about, I don't find it quite as funny.

"And what if the second barrel doesn't work? Maybe one wine is better off without the other—because the other's gone rotten. What if the wine ends up ruined?"

Gavin turns to face me fully. "Sometimes that happens. But more often than not, if you choose the right barrel and you're willing to put in the effort, the result is worth it."

I'm not sure how he's managed to turn this conversation into some kind of profound lesson. For someone who hasn't been in a relationship in years, he sure has a lot to say. Lucky for him, I'm not going to call him out for it. At least not today.

"This is what Ethan was talking about," I say with a laugh, trying to steer the attention off me. "He told me you went off on some tangent about blending wines when Marisa went back to Seattle."

Gavin nods with a proud smile. "He still hasn't thanked

me. If I hadn't given him such wonderful advice, he'd still be crying about letting her go. No one in this family appreciates my lessons."

"You're just so wise," I tease.

A stretch of silence passes between us, his smile settling into something serious again.

"We weren't meant to walk the earth alone, Elle. I don't know the full story, that's between you two, but I know I've never seen anyone else make you that happy—love you that much. You wouldn't let anyone even if they tried. You're so afraid to tell him whatever it is you've been keeping hidden away all these years, but I bet you'll feel a million times better just speaking your truth."

"I'm scared," I say around the growing lump in my throat.

"So be brave."

I laugh because it's that or cry. "Such a dad thing to day." Sighing, I lean against the rack. "It's not that simple. It's not as easy as throwing all of our shit in a new barrel. I did a shitty thing. I don't know how to explain myself. And I don't think he'll forgive me once he finds out the truth."

"You'll never know if you don't try." His voice is softer now. "The best wines come from grapes that have been through a lot. Harsh weather, tough soil—they survive, and they come out stronger for it."

Before I can respond, a yawn sneaks up on me, reminding me I haven't slept at all.

"Go home, Elle. Get some rest." He pulls me in for a one of his signature bear hugs, kissing the top of my head. "And be brave."

On the drive back to my townhouse, the sun is beginning to rise. I didn't expect to run into Gavin, but I think talking to him was exactly what I needed. Maybe he's right. Maybe the second barrel will be better.

Maybe it's worth finding out.

CHAPTER 38

Dominic

WORSEN THE STATE OF MY DICK

PRESENT

L eaving Ellie's bed was torture.
I knew she needed space—to process everything that happened, both at the bar and between us—and I figured waking up next to me wouldn't exactly help.

I'm not even sure I actually slept. I just lay there, perfectly still, holding her as if the smallest movement might make her disappear.

Something in me shifted the moment I saw another man's hands on her. Not just because they belonged to that pencil-dick prick—though that didn't help—but because I realized I never wanted to witness that again. Not now, not ever.

This time, it was unwanted. Uninvited. But what if one day, she wanted someone else's touch—and I had to stand there and let it happen?

So, while she slept, I let myself hold her, silently begging to any higher power listening that it wouldn't be the last time I'd get to.

She sleeps just as I remember; making the softest moaning noises that did nothing but worsen the state of my dick.

Once morning came, she was embarrassed, but in an adorable way. I could hear her pacing back and forth, likely having an internal debate about facing me.

When she came downstairs, I tried to play it cool—when really, all I wanted was to pull her into my arms and kiss her until she couldn't take it anymore and dragged me back to her bed.

Unfortunately, I know she's not there yet.

I wanted to spend the day with her. Instead, I had an on-duty deputy patrol her while I gave her space. She needs to think about what happened between us. Drunk or not, clearly she still feels something for me, even if it's only physical. At this point, I'll take her any way I can have her. I'll be her damn boy toy if that's what it takes.

We crossed paths as I was leaving for work, and she looked almost disappointed to see me go. She gave me a small, unsure smile—so unlike her I almost called in, hating being unable to decipher her thoughts.

Now I'm at the station and can hardly focus. Unlike day shift, it's eerily quiet on nights.

It doesn't help that Morales is on shift with me, and acting stranger than usual. She hasn't said a word to me all night. Instead, she's been glued to her screen, laser-focused, and for once, not trying to get my attention. I guess she finally got the message that I'm not interested.

Still, somehow, I'm the one who feels like the asshole.

As I search my email for the surveillance footage I've been waiting on, my phone dings and I scramble for it, immediately thinking it's Ellie.

It's not.

It's a picture of a sonogram.

And it's from Adrian.

ADRIAN

Got some exciting news today...

Is that what I think it is?

ADRIAN

Baby Alvarez coming in February

You're gonna be an UNCLE

I swore I'd never be the kind of person who can't be happy for others, but I can't help feeling envious. Just last year, Adrian was sleeping his way through dating apps and swearing he'd never settle down—now he's married with a baby on the way. It's hard not to get whiplash.

Congratulations! Happy for you guys.

ADRIAN

We told Mom earlier and that's all it took to convince her to move up here.

The relief I feel knowing my mom is moving closer is over-shadowed by the tight pressure building in my chest—the ugly head of jealousy starting to rear. And it makes me feel like the worst kind of person.

We go back and forth for a while, but once I tell him I'm on shift, the conversation winds down, and we call it a night.

My workload has doubled in size the past couple weeks.

Ever since my temporary assignment under Vorheis began, I've been consumed by the Delmar case. On top of that, I've been quietly working my own investigation into Ellie's situa-tion. Technically, I was pulled from the case for being too close to it—but I can't help myself.

What makes it worse is that whoever's behind it has gone completely silent. Her car turned up with zero evidence, and the note, the picture, and the flower haven't led us anywhere.

If Ryker were around, I'd bounce some ideas off him—but he's been on leave all week. His wife's pregnancy took a turn that landed her in the hospital, and he didn't hesitate to step back from work.

The station's felt off ever since.

"Alvarez," Vorheis calls from his office.

I push up from my chair and head his way. "Yeah, Sarge?"

He's holding a case file, flipping it open as I step in. "Patrol got called to a convenience store robbery just outside city limits—technically our turf, but RMPD responded first."

I nod slowly. "So, you want me to play jurisdiction tug-of-war?"

"Get eyes on the scene so we can figure out who the lead is. Keep it clean. If it's ours, we take it. If not, don't waste time getting territorial. You think you can handle it?"

The last time I responded to a call at a convenience store, I got shot.

I swallow against the anxiety lodged in my throat. "Yeah, I can handle it."

CHAPTER 39

Elyse

CAN WE PRETEND

PRESENT

"Hey," Dominic says quietly as he passes through the front door.

It takes me less than a second to realize something is wrong. I stayed up, waiting for him, and he doesn't seem at all surprised to see me wide awake at six in the morning.

Standing, I approach him cautiously. I've never seen him so sullen looking, and I'm not sure what the right response is. "Everything okay?"

He looks at me as if he's just now noticed I was speaking. His eyes sweep over me, lingering on my breasts for a moment. I'm not wearing anything exciting; a black tank top and lounge pants. No bra, which is probably why his gaze snagged there.

A few heartbeats of silence pass before he lets out a sigh. "Shitty night."

My lips twist, teeth tugging on my bottom lip. "Am I

allowed to ask why? I don't really know the rules, what you're allowed to tell me."

His eyes lose some of the hardness they held when he walked through the door as they settle with mine. "You're allowed to ask me anything you want, about anything. Sometimes I can't answer, and sometimes I won't because you don't need your head filled with evil shit. But ask anyway, I won't keep anything from you I don't have to."

I nod, words escaping me. I can feel his turmoil like it's my own. It's like a twisted coil, uncomfortably tight.

"Can you do me a favor, querida mía?" His voice is strained, raspy almost.

"What is it?"

He threads a hand through his hair, causing some pieces to stick up on end. Messy. Ruffled. So much more attractive than it should be given the cloud that's hanging over him.

"Can we pretend, just for right now, that we're not still figuring this out?" He points between us. "Can we skip to the part where I'm allowed to hold you after a bad shift? Please."

Something cracks open inside me, a warmth that spreads through the uncomfortable pressure that's been pressing against me since he got home. Dominic isn't the type to ask for comfort, which means whatever happened is worse than I could imagine.

I nod before I even fully process his words. "Yes."

He closes the distance between us in two steps, his large hands finding my waist with a gentleness that doesn't match the rawness in his voice. He tugs me toward him, his arms wrapping around me like they've done it a hundred times before, though this feels different. He's holding me like I'm the anchor he's been searching for; like if he lets go, he might fall apart.

I sink into him, resting my cheek against his chest, listening to the rapid rhythm of his heart. For a moment, there's nothing but the sound of our breathing—his, heavy and strained, and mine, steadying.

His chin drops to the top of my head, and I feel him exhale, his body sagging just slightly. "This okay?" he murmurs, his lips brushing my hair.

"Yeah," I whisper. "This is okay."

His grip tightens, just a little. "Good," he whispers. "Because I needed this more than I knew."

We stand like that for what feels like forever, his body slowly losing the tension it carried through the door, his weight shifting as if he's letting me bear some of it. I don't mind. I'd hold more if he let me.

After a long stretch of silence, I say softly, "You want to talk about it?"

His fingers press into my lower back in a way that feels like a no. "Not yet," he says finally. "Just...not right now."

"Okay," I reply easily. I don't push. I don't need to. Whatever it is, he'll tell me when he's ready.

"I'm going to shower. Wash work off me." He untangles himself from me and is up the stairs before I can process what's just occurred. But before my mind can grasp it, my body is in protest, missing the feeling of being wrapped up in him.

My defenses are weak, armor cracked, walls crumbling. He's breaking through everything I built so much faster than I thought possible.

Once the water in the shower starts, I'm able to snap out of whatever daze Dominic left me in. I'm used to his humorous, mischievous side, but I'm completely unprepared for the serious realities of his job.

The sound of water gets louder as the creak of the door squeaks.

"Hey, Ellie," he calls out. "Can you grab me a towel, please?"

"Coming," I yell, already jogging up the stairs. I grab a fresh towel out of the dryer and knock on the bathroom door.

Steam pours out as he opens it, the heat curling around him like a soft mist. He's removed his shirt and is only in tactical pants and a gold chain.

"Here," I say, holding the towel out toward him. Anything else I might've said gets clogged in my throat.

I don't think I'll ever get used to the sight of Dominic shirtless. It's worse now that I know what he feels like. All it took was one night in his arms and I've already memorized the hard planes of his chest, the muscled curve of his pecs, the pattern of his abs as they molded to my back. Smooth skin in some places, scruffy hair in others. I could spend hours dancing my fingers across his chest and stomach, exploring.

He's beautiful.

My gaze moves over him, and I can't help but take in the way his chest rises and falls, each breath emphasizing the dip of his collarbones. The muscles of his abdomen are a perfect arrangement of hard lines and ridges, cascading in an unreasonably symmetrical formation down to where his pants sit low on his hips.

It's ridiculous, really—how a human body can look like that.

"Ellie girl." Dominic's voice pulls me from my stupor, the faintest trace of amusement lacing through it.

My eyes snap up to his, heat rushing to my cheeks as I realize I've been staring far too long.

"Uh, towel," I stammer, thrusting it toward him again, as if he's not already reaching for it.

The corner of his mouth quirks up just enough to hint at a smirk. "Thank you."

He grabs it, and I turn on my heels, heart pounding in my chest, and blurt, "You're welcome," under my breath, but it comes out a little strangled.

As I flee back into the hall, his voice stops me.

"Wait."

I pause, glancing over my shoulder, avoiding looking directly at him. "Yeah?"

"Don't go." His voice is quieter now, softer, almost hesitant. "Just...stay for a minute."

I falter, only because there's a vulnerable undercurrent to his request. It tugs at something deep in my chest.

"Okay." I walk in the steamy bathroom and lean against the sink, arms crossed, trying to act casual even though my pulse feels anything but.

It's only when he steps to turn off the shower that I see it —just barely at first—a mark on his left shoulder.

My brow furrows as I lean closer, my casual pretense forgotten. "What's that?"

He glances past me, staring at his reflection in the mirror, his expression is blank, but his jaw is tight.

"What's what?"

"That scar." I point, my finger shaky, almost like I'm afraid of the answer. There's no mistaking it now—a circular scar, about the size of a dime, marred and pale against the tanned and tattooed skin of his shoulder.

Dominic doesn't answer right away. Instead, he sighs and leans a hand against the counter, his head dropping forward slightly. "It's nothing."

"Dominic," I push, stepping around him until I'm close enough to see the faint edge of a matching mark on the back of his shoulder—a through-and-through. My heart tumbles in my chest. "That's not nothing."

His eyes finally meet mine, something raw flashing in them. "It was a few months ago. When I was still working for the LAPD."

"A few months ago?" I echo with a crack. "You—you got shot?"

He straightens, looking away. "It was a robbery gone bad. I wasn't even supposed to be there, I just happened to be a block away and responded. The call was for a convenience store hold-up. I went in, and...it escalated." He gestures vaguely to his shoulder, as though it's explanation enough. "Dispatch said it was a robbery at knifepoint, but one of the robbers was armed. I didn't even see it until —" He stops, exhaling hard through his nose. "It missed the artery by less than an inch. The doctors said I was lucky."

Lucky. My stomach knots, bile burning up my throat as I stare at the scar—proof of how close he came to dying.

"You almost died," I whisper, barely audible, as if saying it quietly will make it less true.

Dominic shrugs, trying for nonchalance, but it doesn't reach his eyes. "Comes with the job."

"You almost died," I repeat, louder, blinking rapidly, but it does nothing to stop the sting of tears brimming in my eyes. "You almost died—" My words catch again as I break, and I press a hand to my chest, trying to breathe through the ache building there.

The more I said it, the more real it became. What if he had died? What if I never got this chance with him? What if I never saw him again? I can't breathe. I can't see. I can't—

"Ellie. Hey, hey, hey," Dominic soothes, his brows pulling together as he takes in my reaction. He steps closer, his large hands gathering my face. He rests his forehead to mine. "I'm okay. I'm okay." It's a whisper that blows over the dampness running down my cheeks.

"But you almost weren't," I choke out. "That's not okay to me. You—" I stop, forcing myself to meet his dark penetrating eyes. "You're not allowed to die."

It's the same thing he told me just a few days ago—and now saying it back, I finally understand just how heavy those words really are.

His thumbs brush over my skin in a quiet, grounding motion. So tender and careful, I think my heart might burst.

"I'm not going anywhere."

"Promise?" I let out a trembling breath, my tears spilling heavily as I look up at him.

His head moves against mine, nodding, eyes closing as he exhales. "I promise."

My mind whirls back to him showing up at my parents' anniversary party when he first moved back. How rude I was, how cold and awful I've been to him.

It was my defense mechanism.

I knew I didn't deserve his kindness, let alone more.

If I could take it all back, I would. There's so much I wish I could take back.

"Your job scares me," I admit. "I know Red Mountain isn't LA, but bad things can happen anywhere."

His hand moves to gently settle on my neck as his thumb glides along my jaw. "Now you know how I feel. Why I freaked out. There are bad people everywhere, and now one is after you."

"We don't know that. Nothing else has happened."

"Yet. I won't rest until I know you're safe."

"Okay," I relent, too consumed by him in this moment to do much else but agree with everything he says.

He pulls back, inching his face from mine, but continuing to cradle my jaw.

"I saw you," he says softly. "Right before it all went black. Your face was the last thing I saw—your eyes, your smile. People say your life flashes before your eyes, but there was no montage for me. Just you."

I'm trapped in his gaze, his dark eyes locked on mine. I swallow roughly as my heart threatens to jump out of my throat.

"Then what happened?"

"When I finally saw the sun again, I asked for you." He lets out a quiet, sad laugh. "I wasted so many years trying to get over you, trying to accept that our story was over. I figured you would've reached out if you wanted to see me again, and when you never did, I decided I wasn't going to make more of a fool of myself than I already had."

"Dominic—"

"No, let me get this out," he breathes. "Almost dying was the best thing that ever happened to me. I survived, but it killed my pride. It killed my fear of rejection. And all that was left was determination." He grabs my hand and places it over his chest, right over his thundering heart. "Feel that? Feel how steady it is?" It hammers against my palm at an even rhythm. "My heart still beats because I couldn't leave this life with so much unfinished. I couldn't let go, knowing the other half of my soul was still missing."

Panic crawls up my spine. If he knew what an awful person I am, he'd change his mind. He would never look at me the same. "I need to tell you something," I start, but he shakes his head, stopping me.

"Querida mía, what are you so afraid of? Push me away all you want, make me work for it, give me your worst—I'm not going anywhere. I came here for you, and I won't let you slip through my fingers again."

My heart is a racing, chaotic storm. I don't know what to

say because nothing feels sufficient, nothing feels big enough in comparison to everything he's just told me.

It's overwhelming.

There's no way to grasp the surging emotions coursing through me. I need an anchor. I need to feel him.

Reaching for Dominic, my hands move up his arms with a slow drag, traveling over new and familiar tattoos. The continuation of roses that started on his forearms has now spread up and over his biceps, a multitude of pieces all connected, creating one image. Years of stories on his body, each one I'm desperate to know.

"Feels good," he breathes as the skin beneath my palms prickles with goosebumps.

On their own accord, my hands move to his stomach, tracing the ripples. He shivers, his head falling back, eyes closing with a groan.

"Is this okay?"

He works down a swallow. Huskily, he says, "It's more than okay."

I snake up his abdomen, looping my arms around his neck, resting them on his gold chain.

He leans in, slowly, hesitantly, giving me every chance to pull away, but I can't. I don't want to. His breath mingles with mine, warm and intoxicating, and my resolve finally shatters.

I close the distance.

Our lips meet, and the world falls away.

It's instinctual; it's familiar yet entirely new. It's ten years of longing and heartbreak crashing together in one perfect, all-encompassing instant.

His tongue curls against mine as his hand sinks into my hair, cupping my head. He opens his mouth wider and an embarrassingly desperate whine escapes me. He groans in response and deepens the kiss, stealing the air from me. His free hand moves to my waist, pulling me closer, and I melt into him, my arms tightening around him. The heat between us is combusting, a mounting pressure that's been building for so long there's nothing left for it to do but explode.

He kisses me like he's been waiting his entire life for this moment, and I kiss him back with just as much fervor.

When we finally break apart, we're both breathless, foreheads pressed together as we try to steady ourselves. His eyes search mine, edged in concern, as if he's worried he'll find signs of regret.

"I meant what I said," he murmurs, low and thick. "You're the other half of my soul, Ellie. Don't make me live without you again."

I brush my fingers over his jaw, marveling at the way he looks at me, like my mere existence is as vital as the air he breathes.

"Okay," I whisper against his lips.

And when he kisses me again, it's anything but hesitant. Rougher. Messier. Frantic.

CHAPTER 40

Dominic

TAKE WHAT YOU NEED

PRESENT

One taste of her and I'm done for, unable to continue holding back. My hands hungrily grip at her waist, lifting her onto the edge of the sink in one fell swoop.

Her breath hitches, but she doesn't pull away. Instead, she arches into me, spreading her thighs wide as she molds her body to mine.

She moans, tilting her head back, making room for me.

Part of me can't believe this is happening and the other part of me can't believe it took us so long to get here.

The elegant curve of her neck is stunning, flawless, and I ache to claim it. To mark her as mine. My lips press against the wild rhythm of her pulse, feeling the quiver as her throat shifts with a sharp swallow. When my tongue traces a slow, deliberate path along her skin, a tremor courses through her, and her nails sink into my back. I bite down, nipping at the smooth skin, leaving a trail of possession along her neck. With a teasing gentleness, my teeth graze to the other side, drawing out a gasp.

Her hands begin to roam over me, pointed nails drag down my back, marking me just as I'm marking her. With my grip still firmly cradling her head, my other hand slides under the hem of her top, my hands skimming over her smooth stomach, pausing before I reach her breasts.

"Is this okay?"

She nods against me, pushing her chest out further. "God, yes."

I take a nipple between my fingers, tugging on it, toying with the stud.

I can't get over them. I never would've guessed she had them pierced.

Her thighs fall all the way open, inviting me.

"Touch me," she cries. "I need you."

"I got you, Ellie girl."

My fingers dip into the waistband of her pants. Tugging at the fabric of her underwear, I push it aside and drag my middle finger down the smooth center of her pussy. She's already so wet, so warm, drenching my hand. I sink in, adding a second finger, slowly curling them inside her. Her head falls back as her hips buck, seeking more.

"Dominic, baby. I need—"

"I know what you need," I grit. No time apart could keep me from knowing her body—knowing every touch and stroke it takes to make her come.

My fingers pump inside at a rapid pace, curling further, as my thumb circles her clit. Her knees start to shake on either side of me and using my shoulders as leverage, she lifts her hips to grind against my fingers.

"That's right Ellie, ride my hand, take what you need."

Her walls tighten, gripping my fingers like a vise. She's close.

Our gazes catch. I watch her lips part, tongue darting out the corner before my name tumbles in a sigh.

Her breath, her moans, they're the sweetest melody. A song I could listen to until the end of time and never tire hearing it.

Angling my hand, I flatten my palm just above where she's hot and wet, pressing lightly while continuing to pump in and out of her. The pressure of it has her chest heaving, back curving.

"I'm coming," she moans.

I crush my mouth to hers, craving to feel every piece of her come apart against me. The waves of her orgasm rip through her, and feeling it, knowing I'm the one responsible, fills me with a suffocating swell of pride.

Not ready for the moment to end, I continue kissing her, letting my hands rediscover her body.

"Let me learn you." I press a gentle kiss against her mouth, leaving my lips a ghost's breath from hers. "Let me explore."

She smiles as I suck on her bottom lip.

"You've seen me naked. What more is there?"

I let out a groaning laugh. "Everything. Are you kidding me? Look at you."

She blushes, shyly.

Fuck, is it sexy.

I hold her jaw. "Like these gorgeous lips of yours." My mouth presses against hers, branding her with a searing kiss. "And these eyes." I brush my thumbs under her bottom lashes. "Most beautiful eyes I've ever seen." Tugging at the flimsy straps of her tank top, I drag them down until her breasts are free. "And don't even get me started on these." I take a nipple in my mouth, letting my tongue play with the stud, sucking lightly. Her back bows toward me, feeding me more of her perfect tits.

"I got them pierced on my twenty-first birthday," she says through a sigh.

"I love them," I tell her, taking the next one in my mouth, making sure it's given the same attention.

When my hands wander south, she stops me. Her gaze passes over me, eyes bright. "My turn."

The corners of her mouth lift into a smile as she reaches for the top button on my pants.

Her slender hands pop the button and fiddle with the zipper. My dick is painfully busting against it, even more so now with her hands so close. When she finally tugs it down, my cock springs free, standing at attention for her. Her wine-red painted nails wrap around the fabric of my briefs as she grips me, stroking me with a measured firmness. When the smooth skin of her palm slips between the slit of my briefs, the air is knocked right out of me. Her thumb spreads the pre-cum that's gathered at the tip and rubs it down my length. My cock starts to jerk in her grasp, on the edge of coming.

In an attempt to stall the inevitable and save myself the embarrassment of coming in less than a minute of her touch, I grip her thighs and lift her off the counter. Her legs wind around me instantaneously.

She lets out a squeal, laughter mingling with it. "What are you doing?"

With one hand holding her, I use the other to turn the shower back on. "I'm gonna wash your beautiful body, and then I'm going to lay you down on your bed and fuck you all day. You good with that?"

Instead of answering me right away, her teeth tug on my ear, her hot breath dusting over the delicate skin. "All day? Kind of ambitious, don't you think? You might be too old to last that many rounds."

She shoots me a wicked smile.

I swat her ass before setting her back on the ground, where

I start stripping off her clothes. "Oh, Ellie girl, when it comes to you, I have endless reserves."

She giggles, lifting her arms for me so I can remove her top.

Her nipples are pebbled, a flushed pink, and I nearly drool. The studs on either side draw me in like a moth to a flame.

"Suck on them, they need more attention."

Her eyelids flutter shut as I lean down to capture one in my mouth, the cold metal of the studs paired with heated, puckered skin have my eyes rolling back in my head. A growl I didn't know I was capable of crawls out of my throat. If I don't rein in some control soon, I'm going to fuck her fast and hard right this second, and I can't let that happen. I've waited ten years for this. I want to savor her, take my time, drive her wild to the point she's an absolute, aching mess for me. I need her so desperate she can't think straight.

She holds onto my shoulders to steady herself, arching into me. "Dominic."

I nip at the nipple, taking it between my teeth. She gasps, digging her hands into my hair and pulling me closer.

This is how I remember her, she was never shy about her pleasure. She was greedy in the sexiest way, never holding back. I loved it then, and I still fucking love it.

Steam from the shower clouds around, wrapping us in a warm, intimate fog that blurs everything but each other. I snake my arms around her waist and lift her, pressing her body against mine to stand under the water. Intentions to wash her go out the window with her bare breasts brushing against my chest, and instead, I crash my mouth to hers. As the water falls over us in a veil, my tongue devours her, hands cupping her jaw, completely consuming her.

Her hands eagerly drag down my chest before she grips my cock. I moan into her mouth, her touch is almost too much, enough to make me lose my goddamn mind.

I'm always controlled, always thinking one step ahead, but with Ellie I want to be daring and let go of all the hard-held restraint. I want to lose myself in her and never come out.

She strokes my cock with one hand and caresses my balls with the other, squeezing her thighs while she does it.

"Is your pussy craving me, querida mía? Aching to be filled?"

"Yes," she breathes. Her eyes snap to mine, so beautifully clear.

"You're going to have to wait just a little longer," I tell her as I swipe a finger between her soaking slit. "I'm taking my time with you. I didn't wait this long for a quick fuck."

She pumps me faster, firmer. "What if I want a quick fuck?"

I laugh, and press a soft peck to her lips. "You're not the kind of woman who would ever be satisfied with quick." I let my hands smooth down her soft skin and our gazes meet, her lashes heavy with water droplets. Time doesn't feel real, nothing feels real, there's only her. The sexy smile she was wearing fades, arms dropping to her sides.

I gather her face in my hands. "How did I ever live without you?"

Her throat bobs, lips rolling with nerves, but her stare never wavers. "The same way I did. Like something was always missing."

I brush my thumbs over her cheekbones, my chest tightening at the truth in her voice. "If we do this, there's no going back. So, I need you tell me right now if you want to stop." She's quiet, simply staring back at me. "Ellie girl, do you want this?" I rest my forehead against hers. "I'm going to need your words, because I won't survive waking up tomorrow with you full of regret."

Seconds pass, each one like a pinch to my heart. She closes

her eyes and nods her head against mine. "I want this—I want you. All of you."

I inhale deeply. "And what about tomorrow? And the day after that?"

My breath stills in my chest, preparing for the pain of her rejection.

"Everyday," she says softly.

She straightens and rises onto her tiptoes, pressing a featherlight kiss to my lips.

"You should step out and go wait for me in the bedroom."

Her lips quirk up. "Are you kicking me out?"

Even though I need her to leave, my hands can't stop touching her, trailing around her body, keeping her pressed against me. I need her to be stronger, and disentangle.

"I need to shower, and you're too tempting. All I want to do is bury my cock inside you."

She laughs, a sexy smile splitting her face. "You're the one who dragged me in here, with promises to wash me, and now you're trying to make me leave." Her hands slide up my shoulders and wrap around my neck. "A little rusty in the seduction department, huh?"

I groan, my head dropping to her shoulder as her fingers toy with the back of my neck, sending shivers down my spine. "You have no idea what you do to me."

Her laugh softens, turning into a hum that vibrates against my chest. "I can't help myself." She leans back, her eyes sparkling with mischief.

"So, what's it going to be? Are you kicking me out, or are you going to be a good boy and wash me?"

With one swift motion, I turn us under the spray of the shower, water cascading over her as her gasp turns into a laugh. My mouth captures hers, silencing any more teasing words.

She laughs against my lips.

The water pours over us, warm and soothing as it runs

down her body. I reach for the soap, lathering it in my hands, never taking my eyes off her. Her teasing smirk has softened, turning more tender, more intimate, and it makes my chest tighten.

"Turn around," I murmur, my voice low.

She hesitates, her gaze holding mine for a moment before she complies, turning her back to me. My hands find her shoulders first, gliding the suds across her skin in slow, deliberate strokes. She shivers under my touch, and I can't tell if it's the temperature of the water or me that's making her tremble.

"I like the way you touch me," she says softly, tilting her head to the side as I work my way down her arms.

"Good," I tell her, "I like having an excuse to touch you." My hands dip lower, brushing over the curve of her back.

She turns her head, glancing at me over her shoulder with a small, knowing smile. "You don't need an excuse."

That smile wrecks me.

She shifts in the space between us, taking the soap from my hands. "Your turn." Her voice is softer now, almost shy.

I stay still as her hands move over my chest. Her fingers trace over the lines of my muscles, her touch more intimate than playful now. I close my eyes, letting her take her time, feeling the tension unravel from my body with every pass of her hands.

"I like the way you touch me, too," I murmur, my eyes opening to find her watching me, her lips parted.

"Good," she echoes, her smile widening.

Elyse

FITS PERFECTLY

PRESENT

I never knew a shower could be the longest foreplay of my life.

By the time we're out and Dominic is wrapping me in a towel, I'm frantic. I've never felt so worked up, and I've already orgasmed.

Holding the towel tighter around myself to grab onto something as my sanity crumbles, Dominic's brown eyes work their way down and back up my body. The towel may as well be nonexistent with how heated his stare is.

His gaze travels the same path it did before, but this time he stops where I'm pressing my legs tightly together. My pussy clenches, the anticipation mounting.

"You're dry enough. Drop the towel."

I quirk a brow. "Don't tell me what to do." My lips threaten to curve into a smile, betraying any attempt I made at sounding difficult. "And I'm definitely still soaking."

He gives me a slight head shake, and makes a ticking noise with his tongue. His arms cross, drawing my eyes to his bulging biceps, veins branching, ink shiny from the sheen of moisture still coating his skin. The towel around his waist slips, and drops to the floor, where it gathers at his feet, but he keeps coming toward me, unbothered. My gaze holds on his hardened cock. I lick my lips and swallow deeply.

God, it's bigger than I remember.

"You're gonna put an eye out with that thing."

His head falls back and a barking laugh escapes from his throat. "Jesus Christ, querida mía."

I swallow hard, trying to force down the giggle bubbling in my chest, but it spills out anyway.

It was never like this with anyone else; the ease between us, the way it can be heated and lighthearted. He has me laughing and desperate in the same breath.

"Drop the towel," he repeats. "I want to look at you."

The rasp in his voice, the way he's looking at me with so much intensity, so much dominance. I love it. Dropping the towel, I keep my eyes latched onto his.

Bared before him, a wave of vulnerability creeps in, and my hands move to cross over my chest, an uncharacteristic surge of self-consciousness hitting me.

Before I know it, he's inches away, carefully unraveling my arms. "Nope, none of that. Arms at your sides, where I can see them." He shakes his head, his hand skimming down the side of my waist and leaving a trail of goosebumps in its wake. "Do you have any idea what you do to me?"

I give a small shake of my head, lost in his gaze as his hand travels back up, grazing my breast before taking my nipple between his thumb and forefinger, giving it a slight tug. A needy whimper escapes my lips. I'm coming undone, powerless under his commands, already addicted to the way he strips me of every defense with nothing but his voice and touch.

He nudges his thigh between my legs, the swell of his hard cock brushing against me as he does. "Don't bother squeezing those pretty thighs together when we both know I'm the only one who can give this needy pussy what it craves." His fingers tease me, barely dipping inside. "Spread 'em, Ellie girl. Don't make me tell you twice."

Liquid heat floods through me, turning me into absolute putty, and he smirks, fully aware of the effect he has on me.

"Yes, officer," I manage to whisper, breathlessly.

His chest visibly puffs, his tongue swiping across his bottom lip, eyes brewing with hunger. He likes it.

He dips his head, crowding me with his body as his hot breath fans over my neck. "It's deputy."

I angle my head to meet his stare. "Mmm, doesn't have the same oomph as officer. I like officer better."

In an instant, the room spins as Dominic tosses my naked body over his shoulder, a squeal escaping my lips. My wet hair leaves a trail of water as he moves. His long strides eat up the distance to my bedroom, where he deposits me on the bed. In the next motion, he's crawling over me, settling his body over mine.

Our bodies fit together perfectly, curving to one another like we've never been apart.

His weight on mine, hard length pressed to my thigh, his scent everywhere; it's consuming. I squirm, rolling my hips. "I can't take it anymore, please Dominic."

He huffs a laugh. "I love it when you beg, querida mía."

I spread my thighs to make my point and reach between us, my hand guiding his cock. He nudges forward, barely, before pausing.

I answer the silent question in his eyes. "I'm on birth control, and I haven't been with anyone...in a while."

He nods slowly. "Same. And I had a physical recently. All clear."

A beat passes, our positions held but unmoving.

Dominic caresses my cheek with the pad of his thumb,

running it softly down to my jaw as he pushes through my entrance, only the tip, before stopping.

I exhale and it comes out shaky. My body is slowly opening up for him, and my heart is doing the same.

His eyes lock with mine, brows creasing. "Do you want me to stop?" There's concern and care and so much familiarity it makes my chest ache. I feel alive for the first time in a long time—like I've just woken up from the longest slumber.

I shake my head, barely more than a twitch, but he catches it. Of course he does. He always does. My hips lift, taking more of him. "Don't stop," I breathe. "Just give me some time to adjust—I'm not used to your size."

He smirks, resting his forehead against mine as he slides in further. "If I remember correctly, it fits perfectly."

The snarky reply that was about to leave my lips, escapes me the moment he fills me completely. My head falls back with a moan.

"Ohhh."

Dominic thrusts before pulling nearly all the way out, and then coming forward once more, filling me to the hilt.

"So full," I say through a clenched jaw.

"Fucking right you are." He adjusts, sitting up straighter, and stares between us. "Fuck, Ellie, you still feel so good, just like I remember. Same tight little pussy, wrapping around me like a glove." His eyes are wide, mesmerized by our connection as he thrusts in and out of me achingly slow, driving me higher and higher. "I love watching my cock disappear between those pretty pink pussy lips."

His hands grip the back of my knees, spreading my thighs wider and pressing me harder against the bed, forcing my lower back to lift with each push of his body against mine. He's so deep, hitting the spot that has my body shaking uncontrollably.

"You're taking me so well. Look at you—getting used to it."

"Don't stop," I moan. Just when I think my orgasm is going to hit, it keeps rolling, keeps building.

"Never stopping." He moves harder, more frenzied. "Gotta remind this pussy who it belongs to. You're going to feel every inch of my cock until you can't remember anyone but me."

His possessive jealousy should have me pulling away, but it only makes me clench harder around him. I'm his—I belong to him, and I always have. "You own my pussy," I say between gasps. "It's always been yours."

"Right answer, Ellie girl. Mine to fuck"—*thrust* — "mine to fill"—*thrust*— "mine to make come."

He smiles down at me wickedly as the most powerful orgasm of my life ripples through me. My lips part, head falling back. I'm possessed as my back curves off the bed, a ringing in my ears dulling even my own cries and whimpers.

In the midst of my orgasm, he moves his hand between my thighs, using his pointer and index fingers to rub steadily at my clit, dragging out my pleasure until the build begins again before I've even fully come back to ground.

"Yes, just like that," I sigh, my hips lifting to meet his touch.

Dominic chuckles, watching me start to come apart again. "I know what my girl likes."

Fuck, he really does.

He crashes his lips to mine, our bodies molding together as we move in sync, anticipating the other's needs. A kiss to my neck, where he licks at the spot my pulse races. A palm to his ass, pushing him in even deeper. Hands roaming, lips tracing, a dance that moves like muscle memory. Soon we're both coming, together. The slapping of our skin mingles with the heaving breaths escaping us, a pandemonium of noise so familiar, yet new all at once.

When it's over, Dominic rolls off me, and we stay silent, save for the sound of our ragged breathing, both staring up at the popcorn ceiling.

"That was—holy fuck I don't even have words," he says as he slides his arms around me and drags me against him, nuzzling my neck.

I tuck myself into him like I've always belonged in this spot—notched just for me. "It was alright," I murmur, capturing my bottom lip to keep from giggling.

His arms squeeze around me tighter as he slaps my ass. "Lying brat." He slaps my ass again, and this time a needy sound claws up my throat and my nipples pebble, brushing against his skin. He notices it immediately and looks down and then back up at my eyes with a knowing smile. "I bet your pussy is already ready for more, even with my cum still running down your thighs." Before I can protest, his fingers smooth between my legs, dragging the cum that's leaked, and pushing it back inside me, leaving his fingers sunk. "That's what I thought."

I can't help myself, I'm so needy for him again, and my hips swivel, silently begging.

He indulges me and lazily pumps his fingers, too fast to go unnoticed but too slow for relief.

"Dominic." I squirm. "Faster."

When our eyes meet, the corner of his mouth lifts, his eyes hazy with lust. "Think I can still do it?"

I don't need to ask; I know exactly what he's referring to. It's the thought that consumes me whenever I'm alone, imagining his hands, his mouth, bringing me to the edge and beyond. He used to make me squirt, and as much as I've tried, I've never been able to accomplish it alone.

I roll my hips, challenging him. "Probably not."

Rather than argue with words, he lets his actions speak. He pushes two fingers roughly inside me with a deftness that makes my breath hitch, curling them just right. A gasp escapes my lips as he finds that spot, the one that makes my vision blur and my thoughts scatter. His eyes lock onto mine, a silent question in their depths. I bite my lip, refusing to give him the satisfaction of a verbal response, but my body betrays me, arching into his touch, seeking more.

He smirks, leaning in to brush his lips against my ear. "Just for that, I'm going to make this pussy gush like a goddamn waterfall."

And true to his word, he delivers. I feel completely out of control in the best way—my body entirely his as he draws out every last drop of pleasure. My skin is slick, hair matted, limbs boneless, and my heart so full it might just burst.

He gazes down at me, his smile a mirror of mine. His eyes trace the length of my body, finally landing between my thighs.

"Oh, querida mía, you're a mess. Let me clean you up... with my tongue."

"Wake up. "

"Hmmm," he hums.

He's still half-asleep even though I've been awake for hours, just staring at him.

My limbs ache, muscles I didn't even know I had are sore. If I didn't know better, I'd think I had run a marathon—and in some ways, I guess I did.

Dominic kept true to his promise and fucked me all day

long. We have a lot of time to make up for, and hardly made a dent.

His eyes are still closed, but I know he's awake. I nuzzle his neck and dart my tongue out just a bit, giving him the tiniest lick.

He moans, and it vibrates against my mouth. "Insatiable," he mutters.

I give him a mock gasp in response. "I was just trying to wake you up, not seduce you."

Warm hands reach for me, wrapping around my waist and roll me until I'm settled over him, my necklace hanging between us. I squirm, but make no real attempts to actually escape his hold.

"Best sleep I've gotten in a long time," he mumbles into my neck—the small amount of scruff on his face scratches against me.

He mindlessly plays with my hair while I rest my cheek on his chest. "Well, yeah, I'm sure a bed is more comfortable than the couch."

He laughs. "Ellie, it's because I got to sleep next to you. Hold you."

My stomach dips at his admission, and I curl my body to him, snuggling closer. "Oh." I lift my head to meet his gaze. "That was really sweet."

He smirks, his hand trailing lazy circles on my lower back. "For you, always. Just don't tell anyone, I'm not trying to ruin my reputation. I play a really convincing bad cop."

I laugh, pressing my forehead to his chest for a moment to hide the flush creeping up my cheeks. "I would love to see you play bad cop." My face heats, imagining being restrained by him.

The look on my face must give me away because he grins. "I handcuffed you once, maybe next time we can have some fun with it."

I try to scowl but fail. "I still haven't forgiven you for that."

He chuckles and then presses a kiss to my forehead. I can't even attempt to act like I'm angry, never knew I was such a slut for forehead kisses.

"Good. Don't. I would rather spend a lifetime earning it."

A whoosh of air exhales past my lips. "That's a long time."

One of his hands reaches to cradle my jaw. "Yeah." His palm smooths over my cheek. "Almost like that's the plan."

My heart squeezes as I nuzzle into him. "Do you like it?" I ask cautiously. "Being a deputy?"

"Most of the time," he says quietly. "Last night was hard."

I angle my face to meet his eyes. "What happened?"

"Nothing," he huffs. "I just—I got stuck in my head for a bit. Had to climb my way out."

He pauses, like he needs a second to gather his thoughts.

"I started on patrol in L.A. Not the best neighborhood. There was this kid who used to hang around. Good kid. Didn't get a lot of attention at home, so I'd keep an eye out for him. Bought him lunch a few times. Nothing major—just small stuff."

I nod, even though he's not really looking at me.

"He got older. I got transferred, working my way toward detective. We lost touch." He swallows roughly. "That night, at the convenience store…"

He looks at me then, eyes distant.

"It was him. He recognized me. And he still pulled the trigger."

I don't breathe. I can't.

"I was so stunned I froze. I didn't even reach for my weapon. I just stood there. Long enough for him to take the shot."

He pauses again, sifting through the memory.

"He ended up in juvie, and somehow got his hands on a

phone, and managed to find me online. He sent me a message."

My eyes widen. "What did it say?"

A bitter laugh escapes him. "I don't know. I haven't opened it yet. I don't know if I want to. But last night, the scene just reminded me of that day, and it's not a day I like to think about. Those are the moments that break you a little—make you question why you do the job in the first place. I think my faith in the goodness of people took a big hit after that. I can see why some of the older guys are so jaded." His thumb brushes softly over mine. "But coming home to you was exactly what I needed. And everything else that followed was more than I could've ever hoped for."

I smile against him and melt just a little. "It was everything for me. I don't have any regrets, I promise. But I think we should go slow with this—with us."

"No," he shakes his head. "We're not going slow, querida mía."

I still, staring back at him with my brow raised. "Dominic—"

"Don't do that. Don't run away from us. There's no sense in going slow when I already know you're the one. I'll give you time to wrap your beautiful, brilliant mind around it, but make no mistake, every future plan I have has you at the center."

"But we've barely just—it's too soon to talk like this."

He scoffs, tossing his head back in laugh. "Too soon? More like almost too late. Were you not listening to what I said? I came back for *you*. I'm here for *you*."

"We can't just skip all the steps. We don't know each other like we used to. We need to start over."

"I've seen what I needed to see. I've already decided, Ellie girl. It's time for you to catch up."

"This is crazy!"

He pulls me tighter against him. "You know what's actually crazy? That we've been living apart for ten years. I've wanted to marry you since I was seven years old. Do you really think I'm going to waste more time? Fuck that, time is up."

My heart begins to race uncontrollably. "I—I don't know what to say. You just threw so much at me, it's a lot to process."

His thumb glides across my bottom lip, his brown eyes staring deeply into mine. "I'm not proposing right this second. We're not making any decisions, but just know that it's coming."

I turn my chin, breaking eye contact, too overwhelmed by it all.

But he doesn't let me get away. Gently, he brings me back to face him. "Talk to me."

"I'm scared." The words tumble out like a hiss.

He stares back at me, patiently waiting for me to elaborate.

"I'm scared of relying on you too much. Of losing myself, of needing you to function."

They're things I never admitted out loud. And what I was never able to communicate to him when we were younger.

The tension in his body hardens as his grip on me loosens. "Is that why?" His question is quiet, almost a whisper.

I nod slowly, darting my eyes away because I can't handle looking into them and seeing the hurt so clearly looking back at me. Hurt that I caused.

"Part of it," I admit. "I was so codependent on you I didn't even know who I was anymore. And you weren't. You were fine without me."

"What the fuck do you mean I was fine? I wasn't fine. I hated being apart from you. Holy shit," he breathes, anger vibrating off him. He starts to move, and I think he's going to stand and leave, but instead he turns us, pinning me beneath him.

When I finally meet his gaze, I realize I was wrong. It's not anger, it's sadness.

"Is that why you broke up with me? Because you thought I was fine without you? And because you weren't? Why didn't you talk to me?" he's voice rises with each question. "Please don't tell me a simple conversation would've saved us years of having to live without each other."

I have no choice but to look at him; I can't hide. Not anymore.

"There's something I need to tell you. There's more."

CHAPTER 42

Elyse

HATE MYSELF A LITTLE MORE

25 YEARS OLD

"**R**emind me again why we're here," Scottie says, raising a brow, her face twisted in disgust.

I tip my shot back, the burn of the tequila warming me almost instantly. While sucking on a lime, Scottie casts me an unimpressed look.

"There isn't enough tequila on the shelves to make this place any less divey." She squirms in her seat as if bugs are crawling on her skin.

"So, you move to the big city, and suddenly you're too good for the local watering hole?" I tease.

"I am not too good," she defends. "I'm just not a bar girl. They're so loud and sticky."

I sling my arm around her shoulders, sliding a shot toward her. "We're here to celebrate you landing a spot in that improv group you never shut up about and the fact that you're visiting, which is reason enough."

She reluctantly picks up the shot glass, eyeing it like it's poison.

I bite down on my bottom lip to keep from laughing. Scottie isn't a big drinker, but that's never stopped me from peer pressuring the shit out of her.

Closing her eyes, she takes a few deep breaths, and then downs the shot in one gulp, immediately slapping her hand over her mouth to keep it from coming right back up. I'm already prepared with a lime and shove it in her mouth the second her hand slips.

"See," I shout over the buzzing bar. "That wasn't so bad, was it?"

She chokes on a cough. "That was vile. Why do people drink this stuff?" She coughs a few more times, her skin taking on a red tint, matching her hair. "Jet fuel," she croaks.

"Oh, stop. You're fine." I lift my hand to Rhonda to get her attention. She sees me and makes her way over after sliding beers across the bar to a group of rowdy guys. On a quick glance it looks like they're cops. They're not in uniform, but in a town this small, I recognize nearly everyone.

"What can I get you, princess?"

"Water—"

"Two Palomas—"

Scottie and I speak simultaneously.

"Palomas," I repeat. "No water."

Scottie's shoulders slump. "I'd prefer water," she grumbles.

"You can have water *after* you finish your Paloma."

While Rhonda works on our drinks, my eyes wander around the bar, landing on several familiar faces. It's Saturday night, and with not much else to do since it's off-season, the bar is packed with locals and people in town visiting family for the holidays. The group of guys are louder than ever, obviously celebrating something. They're all surrounding one guy, but I can't seem to make him out. After staring long enough,

317

someone in the group moves, revealing Ryker at the center of attention.

"When did the Ken doll move back?" Scottie asks, looking in the same direction I am.

I shrug. I haven't seen him in years. "I guess recently. First time I'm hearing about it."

When a few more guys in his circle disperse, I notice he's not alone. Tucked under his arm is a pretty brunette.

He must sense our blatant staring because his eyes meet mine, narrowing with a smile on his face. He pushes past the crowd, keeping his arm around the woman and coming straight for us.

"Elyse Ledger and Scottie James, the dynamic duo."

"Hi, Ryker," Scottie says with a dismissive half-wave. For whatever reason she's never liked him.

"Hey," I say with a slight slur, the tequila hitting me.

My gaze flits to his date, who looks adorably shy. Ryker shakes his head, like he's just now realizing he needs to make introductions.

"Honey, this is Elyse and Scottie, they were a few years behind me in school.

She smiles sweetly extending her hand to me and then to Scottie. "Claire."

As they claim the barstools next to us, I catch sight of something shiny, finding a generously sized diamond on Claire's left hand.

"Are you guys engaged?!"

Claire beams as Ryker nods. "Yeah, I asked her last week. I just accepted a job as a deputy sheriff, and decided it was time to make things official."

Claire and Ryker proceed to explain that they met in college and had been living in Bellingham, but just moved back for Ryker to start his new job.

"So when is the big day?" I ask.

Claire's smile eases slightly. "We're hoping soon, but we haven't been able to find the right place. Every venue we look at is either booked up or too expensive. And I recently started grad school, so I don't have a ton of time to focus on planning." A small frown curves her lips, her eyes looking defeated as they meet Ryker's. "Maybe we'll just elope."

"Let me plan it!" I burst. "I just took over as the event coordinator for my family's winery, and we're offering full-planning services."

Technically, I haven't discussed this with my dad yet, but I know he'll agree. Weddings are a huge moneymaker, and it's a corner of the market the winery has been neglecting to nurture. Maureen, the former coordinator, retired last month, and she'd really been dropping the ball these last few years. I was itching to takeover but had to wait for her to retire before my title could become official.

Claire's face lights up. "Wait! Really? Because I will seriously hire you right this second."

Ryker lets out a breath. "Honey, you haven't even seen the winery. What if you don't like it?"

Sensing Ryker's hesitancy, I rifle through my purse for one of my newly-printed business cards. "Here." I hand it to her. "Call me on Monday, and you two can schedule to come take a tour. If you like what you see, we'll move forward."

Claire jumps out of her barstool, and wraps me in a tight hug. "Thank you so much! I can't wait to see it."

"Hey, Ryk!" someone calls across the bar. "Got a boiler maker with your name on it."

Ryker stands, putting his arm back around Claire. "Let's go rejoin them. The guys are trying to get me shit-faced as some kind of hazing ritual."

We wave our goodbyes, Scottie shaking her head with a smile. "Look at you, hustling after hours." She lifts her glass to mine, cheersing. "You might've just booked your first solo wedding."

I'm trying not to get my hopes up, even though Claire seemed really excited. Ryker not so much, but guys are rarely excited when it comes to wedding planning.

"Hopefully," I say, shrugging while taking a sip of my drink.

Scottie cocks her head, her eyes trained on Ryker and Claire. "Was it just me or did she look familiar? She kind of looked..."

She trails off, her sentence dying as I feel her stiffen beside me, nearly dropping her drink.

"Uh, you know what?" She stands. "Suddenly I'm not feeling so great." Her hands visibly tremble as she puts on her coat. "Let's go."

Her voice is shaky, laced with panic. Leaning back slightly, I gaze around the bar, trying to find the source of Scottie's sudden shift, but I come up empty.

"What has gotten into you? Did one of your exes walk in, or something?" I say with a laugh.

She shakes her head quickly. "Nope! Not one of mine."

I pause, my eyes pinching. "What are you talking about?"

Placing both hands on my shoulders, she forces my eyes on hers. "Babe, I'm gonna need you to take some deep breaths for me and don't look over at the entrance."

Without thinking, my head starts to turn, but she stops it with her hand on my cheek. "Who just walked in? You're scaring me."

I already know, I'm not sure why I'm acting as if I don't. Maybe a small part of me is hoping Scottie is being dramatic, but there's only one person she would be this freaked out about me seeing.

"Dominic," she begins and my chest caves in, heart jolting.

"He just walked in. He's with his brother. Looks like they're joining Ryker's group."

The tequila churns in my stomach, slowly rising. I'm going to be sick. I take an unsteady breath, swallowing burning acid as I do.

I haven't seen Dominic since the day I broke up with him. It's been over six years. And every day since then, he's occupied corners of my heart and brain I actively work to not acknowledge. Over time it got easier to live with him at the fringes, just lingering there. But now, everything is in full force, coming to the surface all at once.

I take a deep, gasping breath. "I can't see him. I can't see him."

She strengthens her grip on my shoulders. "I know, okay. Let's leave. We can slip out the back."

"We need to pay!"

Scottie scoffs. "I'll swing by tomorrow and close out our tab."

As I fight the nausea threatening to expel at any moment, I put my coat on, willing myself to not look for him.

Why is he here? After his parents moved I truly didn't think I'd ever see him again. He has no reason to be here.

"Jesus Fucking Christ," Scottie says under her breath. "Like damn magnets."

She's staring behind me. I don't even have to ask. I know it already. He's spotted me, and he's coming this way.

"Ellie girl?" His voice is in disbelief, but still so warm and velvety I might just disintegrate on the spot.

I close my eyes, trying to wake up from this dream. It has to be a dream. This isn't real.

"Ellie," he repeats. "I know you heard me."

Gnawing on my bottom lip, I already feel the pressure of moisture stirring behind my eyes. I can't cry. That would be silly. I can't cry over things that are my own fault.

I breathe deeply, past caring if he can see the rise of my shoulders if I do, and spin to face him.

My knees give out the second our gazes collide, and it's only because I'm holding onto the bar that I don't completely collapse.

Adrian is next to him, but I can barely see him. I can barely see anything—anyone but him. It's all a blur, only Dominic is clear.

"It is you."

He steps closer.

I step back.

The disappointment that flashes on his face may as well stab me.

"Hi," I say, my voice too bright and breathless. "We were just leaving."

I move to walk past him, but his hand wraps around my elbow softly. Soft enough for me to pull away, but I don't.

"Stay." His voice is quiet, just for me. "Let me buy you a drink. Maybe we can talk..."

I don't want to talk. I'm not ready to talk. And I'm not sure I ever will be.

"I don't think that's a good idea," I tell him with a force in my voice I don't feel. Maybe if I come off as a bitch, it'll be better. It's better if he hates me. It's easier.

"Feels like déjà vu. Me begging you to stay, you leaving anyway."

I clench my jaw, tears fighting to come out. "I don't have time," I grit, barely holding myself together.

He tilts his head, his eyes raking over my face, seeing too much. I jerk my face down, hating his eyes on me.

"You don't have five minutes?"

Yanking my elbow out of his hold, I step back. "Not for you, I don't."

And then I'm pushing through the crowd, not caring if

Scottie is behind me or not. I can't breathe in here. I need to get out before I suffocate. The second I'm out the back exit, I lean over the railing of the stairs and puke, the tequila projectiling out of me in angry spurts. A few moments later, warm hands are soothing my back.

"Get it all out, babe," Scottie says in a hushed, motherly tone that's so unlike her. She's usually even worse at comforting than I am.

"Why is he here?" I ask, still leaned over the railing. With nothing left to vomit, hot tears start falling down my cheeks.

"I don't know," she whispers.

For a while, we're both quiet. Scottie continuing to rub my back, while I stay suspended, not ready for anyone to see me cry, not even Scottie.

Eventually I have to straighten, too much blood having rushed to my head.

Scottie's sympathetic eyes meet mine. "Maybe you should talk to him. This isn't normal. Most people don't puke after running into an ex. Especially with how long it's been."

"He's different."

"You're literally so sick over the breakup that it makes you physically ill. Don't you think you'd feel a hell of a lot better just telling him what happened and getting it all out in the open? There's no way this is healthy."

A sharp pang of anger hits me. "There's no point in telling him. You know I hate talking about it; I can't believe you would bring it up right now."

"I can't keep watching you not deal with this. Deal with it! Face him!"

I turn, walking down the steps that lead into the narrow alley, my shoes echoing against the pavement, breath fogging in my line of vision. I don't need Scottie—of all people—judging me and my decisions.

"Elle!" She calls out. "Real mature, walking away. You're a fucking pro at it. Too afraid to handle your shit."

I keep going, ignoring her. I'm not in the right headspace to deal with anyone, not even my best friend. And the worst part, is she's not wrong, which makes it hurt so much more. Her words cut to levels I don't let anyone past. I don't want to feel this—any of this. I want to forget.

As I turn the corner toward Main Street, I nearly collide with a curly-headed blonde woman. "Sorry, Sherry," I say as my steps falter. Apparently, there's still some tequila lingering in my system.

She's leaning against the brick building, a cigarette between her lips as she takes a long drag. She turns her head to exhale the smoke, but keeps her eyes fixed on me.

"Rough night?"

"Something like that," I tell her, lifting my shoulders. I'm not about to divulge it all to Red Mountain's queen of gossip.

"Here." She nudges a box of cigarettes at me. "Have one, it'll take the edge off."

I shake my head, eyeing the box. "I don't smoke, but thanks anyway."

She nudges it again. "Come on, looks like you've been through it. Trust me, it'll help."

I'm not sure why, but I reach for it, taking a cigarette out, and handing the box back to her.

"Like this." She demonstrates, lighting a fresh one for herself and then lighting mine. "All you gotta do is inhale and then blow it out."

I do as she says. I've never smoked anything before and it takes me a few tries to get it right, but when I do, the rush of calm is indescribable. The cool menthol fills my lungs, immediately relaxing me—ridding the taste of vomited alcohol still in my mouth.

"Feels good, huh?" she says, raising her brows. "Always does the trick for me."

Joining her, I lean against the brick wall and text Shane to come pick me up. Oddly enough, he's the only one who never bothers me about the breakup, never asks questions about Dominic. As soon as I told my family we had broken up, Shane accepted it without a second thought, and he's had my back about it ever since.

Sherry tells me she suspects her husband is cheating. I only half listen, but nod my head along to her story.

What a weird fucking night. With another drag, I close my eyes, tipping my head back, and all I see is him. His eyes, how much more grown up he looks now than he did the last time I saw him, how the regret that weaves through me feels like a knot that will tighten enough to kill me one day.

And I hate myself a little more.

CHAPTER 43

Dominic

MY ONLY PLAN

PRESENT

"You're going to hate me," Ellie whispers as she moves to sit up.

Despite my stomach sinking like a weight in the ocean, I try my best to reassure her. How could she think I'd ever hate her. I'm not capable of it.

"I'm not going to hate you; just talk to me. We can't move forward if we don't talk about the past."

She takes a deep, shaky exhale. To soothe her, I cradle one side of her jaw and run soft brushes down her cheek.

"I—I—It's not easy to explain."

"So try anyway."

She goes quiet for a long beat, her eyes flicking around the room before finally landing back on me.

"I just felt...lost." Her voice trembles. "We were always such an *us*. But the second I got to school, I couldn't figure out how to be *me* without you."

I knew she struggled with the adjustment—I did too. But I stay quiet.

"The more time that passed, the more I realized I didn't like the version of myself I was becoming. I lived for the weekends, because that's when I got to see you. I didn't make any real friends because that would've meant cutting into the little time we had together. My grades were slipping. Yours were too. Everything felt like it was moving around me—fast—and I was stuck. Everyone else seemed to know what they wanted, what came next. And all I had was...you."

She swallows, her fingers curling in her lap.

"You were my only plan. I didn't know what job I wanted, or what I even liked anymore. Everything I did was for us, around us, because of us. That's when I started thinking maybe I needed a little space. Just a break. It was never supposed to be permanent."

She glances at me, eyes so full of pain, it physically hurts to look into them.

"But I knew if I told you it was temporary, you wouldn't really let go. You'd wait. You'd call. You'd show up. And I needed the kind of space that meant figuring things out on my own."

She blows out a long, heavy breath.

"You make one choice, thinking it's just a pause, a breather —and you don't realize it's the thing that changes everything. I thought maybe I needed a few weeks. A month. Just until study abroad started. I didn't mean for it to be forever."

Her voice breaks just a little, and when she meets my gaze again, it's devastating.

"When you're young, everything feels like the end of the world. Every choice feels bigger than it is, and every mistake feels permanent. I didn't mean to lose you. I was just trying to find myself."

I swallow hard, the burn creeping up my throat like acid. There's more. There has to be. Ellie's always been quick to make rash decisions, sure—but *that* being the reason we ended? Just her needing space? I'm not buying it. Not completely.

She drops her elbows to her thighs, burying her face in her hands. When she speaks again, her voice is muffled and tired.

"About a week in, I knew I'd fucked up."

She lets out a dry, humorless laugh, lifting her head just enough to look at me.

"I realized what I really needed was to talk to you—*really* talk to you. So I made this whole plan to come visit you that weekend and basically beg you to take me back."

She pauses, eyes glassy now.

"But I wasn't feeling well. I figured it was just stress at first. My period had started, and it was bad. Heavy. Cramping that wouldn't let up. Or at least—that's what I thought it was..."

She trails off and my heart lurches.

"I could barely move," she continues. "The pain was indescribable. I was pale; I was shaking. Scottie threatened to call my mom if I didn't go to the hospital. So we went to the hospital."

My lungs deplete all their air. I'm choking on nothing, suffocating in the void.

I was holed up in my dorm room trying to figure out where it had all gone wrong, meanwhile she was hundreds of miles away, and she wasn't okay. And I wasn't there.

"What was happening?" My voice is barely audible.

A shuttering exhale passes through her lips, her green eyes meeting mine, and my heart compresses.

"I was having a miscarriage. A very early miscarriage." It comes out like a strangled breath, yet glaringly clear.

My vision blurs as my stomach drops in a free fall. One where it never lands, it just continues falling and falling and falling.

"I—I didn't even know I was pregnant." Her voice cracks, and the words seem to catch in her throat, but she forces them out. "By the time I found out, it was already... over."

Her gaze drops and when it lifts to meet mine, it's shiny with tears that spill over in silent waves. My chest constricts, my heart struggling to pump under the magnitude of her confession.

"It was yours, obviously," she whispers. "We were going to have a baby, and I didn't even know. I was so self-absorbed and wrapped up in my own shit, I didn't notice I had missed my period. It was like the universe knew I was already a bad mom, and took the baby away just to show me how unworthy I was to begin with.

"I never told you because at first I couldn't even process it. It was like I left my body. I wasn't—I wasn't there. I had completely disassociated." A hollow, tear-laced laugh escapes her as she wipes under her eyes. "You were the first person I wanted to call, but I didn't know how to handle what was happening while also taking back the breakup. It was like something in me fractured that day."

Her tears continue to fall, heavy droplets cascading down her cheeks.

"My professors' pity passed me, thanks to my mom and some carefully worded threats, and then she took me home for the summer. I was like this ghost of a person. I hardly remember it, yet remember it so vividly it hurts. I'm sure that makes zero sense—"

"No, I get it." I clear my throat. "I understand. In my own way."

Our gazes hold, a small sliver of time stretching between us. Life, losses, years slipping by, it's heartbreaking. Something to grieve all on its own.

"I was there...that day you showed up. And I just couldn't. I couldn't see you when I was still so gone, so far away from myself I felt like a stranger, just going through the motions of what felt like someone else's life. I didn't know how to be the girl you loved anymore. I knew if I saw you, it would break me. It would break me to have to explain, and I wasn't strong enough to do that. I didn't want you to know, because even saying it out loud made it so much more real. I couldn't. I'm sorry. I couldn't do it." Her voice grows thicker, barely coherent. "I'm a terrible person. I'm a coward," she chokes. "You have every right to hate me. I shouldn't have kept it from you. And then I was such a bitch because even ten years later, I still didn't want to tell you—didn't want to deal with it. I'm not a good person."

I can't take this anymore. Watching her punish herself. It's torture.

Instead, I gather her in my arms and hold her. Feel the tremors of her cries pass between us, absorbing them.

"I don't hate you." My hand runs up and down her spine. "I don't hate you," I repeat.

Maybe if I repeat it enough times, she'll actually believe me.

CHAPTER 44

Dominic

I'LL WAIT

19 YEARS OLD

They say time heals all wounds, but whoever came up with that was either delusional or had a hell of a lot more patience than I do.

The last month has been the slowest, most agonizing stretch of time in my life. Ever since Ellie ended things, it's like I've been moving in slow motion, trapped in a fog so thick I can barely see in front of me. The sun rises and sun sets, the world keeps turning, but I'm stuck. Stuck in the exact moment she told me we were over. I can't focus, can't make sense of anything. Everything feels hollow. Ellie isn't just in my thoughts; she's everywhere. In every song on the radio, every laugh I hear in passing, every memory that surfaces when I least expect it. And at night, when I close my eyes, she's waiting for me. Her face lingers, haunting and comforting all at once. And the worst part? I crave it. I ache for those moments when I can see her again, even if it's only in the fragile space between waking and dreaming.

If losing Ellie wasn't enough, life decided to hit me with

another punch to the gut. A week after everything fell apart, my parents dropped the news; they sold the house. The house I grew up in, the one they promised they'd never leave. Now they're packing up and moving to Arizona. Which leaves me with one final trip to Red Mountain, one last chance to get my things—and maybe get Ellie back.

That's how I ended up here, pacing the driveway of the Ledger family home like some kind of stalker. For an hour now, I've been working up the nerve to knock on the door. My heart's racing, my palms are sweating, and every logical part of my brain is screaming at me to turn around and leave. But I can't. I can feel her here, like she's an extension of me. It's irrational, I know, but it's the kind of irrational that makes me certain I can't give up just yet.

Before I can convince myself to act—or run—the front door swings open. Leanne steps out like she's been watching this pathetic display long enough. She walks toward me with purpose, and I freeze, rooted to the spot like a kid caught stealing cookies before dinner.

"I take it you're here for Elyse," she says. It's not a question.

I nod, shoving my hands deep into my pockets to hide the nervous tremor. My eyes flick to the upstairs window, where the curtain sways ever so slightly, as if someone had just been there.

"She doesn't want to see me, does she?" I ask, my voice hoarse.

Leanne doesn't answer right away. Instead, her smile fades, replaced by a look of pity that twists something deep in my chest. "Come on," she says, nodding toward a stone bench overlooking the vineyards. "Let's sit for a minute."

Reluctantly, I follow her, the crunch of gravel beneath our feet the only sound. The view from the bench is beautiful, the hills stretching out endlessly, rows of grapevines glowing under the afternoon sun. But I can't appreciate it. Not when I'm this close to the only person who can tell me what the hell went wrong.

Leanne waits a beat before speaking. "I'm sure this feels like the end of the world, but I promise you, it's not."

"She's my world." The words tumble out before I can stop them. "I love her, Leanne. I don't think I'll ever stop. I just—I don't know what I did wrong. If I knew, I'd fix it. I'd do anything."

She smiles gently, her gaze softening. "Oh, honey, I know you love her. And don't doubt for a second that she loves you, too. Watching the two of you fall in love has been one of the greatest joys of my life.

"Elyse has always been fiercely independent, almost to a fault. She's never been one to lean on anyone, not even me. But with you? She lets you in. That's not something she does lightly."

"Then why did she breakup with me?" I hate how raw I sound, how pathetic.

"She's going through something right now." Her hand reaches out to give mine a reassuring squeeze. "She needs time to figure things out on her own. It's not my place to say, but one day she'll tell you—explain everything. But that doesn't mean you need to wait around, holding your breath. You've got dreams, a future ahead of you. Don't let this define you."

"But the only future I want is one with her in it."

"I know," she says with a breath. "But sometimes the best thing we can do for the people we love is to give them the space they need."

"What if I lose her? What if she meets someone else, gets married, and forgets all about me?"

Leanne lets out a wistful sigh. "I can't predict the future, but I do know this; a love like what you two have is special. And if it's meant to be, life has a way of working things out.

333

But you can't put your life on hold waiting for that day to come."

I glance back at the house, at the window where the curtain is now still, and feel the weight of her words settle on my shoulders.

"My parents sold the house," I say quietly. "Once they move, I won't have any reason to come back here."

Leanne smiles gently. "You'll always have a reason to come back. But for now, give her the time she needs. Trust that what's meant to be will find its way."

And though her words offer a glimmer of comfort, the ache in my chest remains. Because the truth is, letting go—even temporarily—feels impossible.

I drag myself back to my car, gravel dragging beneath my feet like nails on a chalkboard. The sun dips lower on the horizon as I drive away from the Ledger house, the sprawling vineyards slowly giving way to the open road. My chest tightens the farther I get, the view of her home shrinking in the rearview mirror until it disappears entirely.

The house I grew up in, just down the hill and around, isn't much farther, but I drive the longest way possible. Not ready to face reality. When I left, my parents were busy sorting and boxing up their lives, ready to leave behind every corner of this place that feels stitched into me. It's unsettling, how easily they can move on, while I'm here, stuck in this cycle of waiting and wondering if I'll ever be able to let her go.

By the time I pull into the driveway, the pain in my chest is unbearable. The old porch light flickers as I step inside, every creak of the floorboards grating at me. My room is almost bare now, stripped of the posters and awards and pictures that used to litter the walls. All that's left are a few boxes stacked in the corner, waiting to be loaded into the back of my car.

I toss my keys onto the dresser and collapse onto the edge of my bed. The silence in the house feels deafening. My parents must be in their room, too tired from packing to notice I've come in. I'm not in the mood to talk to either of them anyway, still pissed they're selling the house.

My phone sits heavy in my hand, my thumb hovering over Ellie's name. I've stared at her contact photo so much lately it's seared into my brain. It's a selfie she took at the beach last summer. I couldn't stop staring at her then, and I can't stop now.

The rational part of me knows I shouldn't call. That I've already done enough. But my heart is louder than my head tonight, and before I can stop myself, I hit the call button.

It rings once. Twice. Three times. My breath catches when the line clicks, but it's not her. It's her voicemail.

"Hi, this is Elyse. I never check this, leave a message at your own risk."

The tone beeps, and for a moment, I can't speak. My throat feels thick, my thoughts racing, but then the words pour out like a flood.

"Ellie, it's me. Look, I know you don't want to talk to me right now, and I get that. I do. I just...I wanted to say that I'll respect your wishes. If you need space, I'll give it to you. I'll leave you alone. But I'm not giving up on us. I can't. I don't care if it takes years, querida mía. I don't care how long it takes. One day, when you're ready, I'll be here. Waiting. Because you're it for me. You've always been it."

My voice breaks, defeated. I'm way past trying to mask it from her. I hate the way the silence on the other end makes me feel like I'm talking to a ghost. But I keep going, because this might be my only chance to lay it all on the line.

"You're my future, Ellie girl. You always have been. And even if I have to let you go for now, I'm not letting go forever. I love you. I just...I needed you to know that."

I end the call before I can say anything else, dropping the phone onto the bed beside me. The room feels too small, too quiet, and I press the heels of my hands against my eyes, trying to hold myself together.

I know I said I'd leave her alone, and I will. But as much as it hurts to walk away, I meant what I said. I'll wait. For her, for us, for whatever the future holds. Because if there's one thing I know for sure, it's that she's worth it, no matter how long it takes.

CHAPTER 45

Dominic

THE FUTURE THAT NEVER WAS

PRESENT

"I thought you'd hate me for leaving in the first place. And then, after it happened, I hated myself enough for both of us. I thought it was my punishment for walking away from you."

My mind immediately goes back to walking in on her in the bathroom, hunched over the sink like she'd been puking. "You were pregnant when you came to visit. That's why you were sick."

She shakes her head, gnawing on her bottom lip. "I was sick because I knew I was going to breakup with you. I think I was still too early to have those kinds of symptoms. It might've added to it, but I truly had no idea. I wouldn't have broken up with you had I known. I would've been more terrified than anything and would've needed you."

The silence between us extends, suffocating and unbearable. She's still trembling, and I don't think she even realizes it.

"Ellie..." I begin, but my voice pauses. What could I possibly say? That I should have been there? That I wish I

337

could have stopped her pain? That I'm furious she went through this alone?

Instead, I pull her into me. She stiffens at first, but when I wrap my arms around her and press her to my chest. She collapses, breaking apart in my arms. Her sobs come hard and fast, and I let her cry, cradling her like she's fragile.

"You didn't have to go through that alone," I finally whisper, my voice shaking as much as hers. "You didn't deserve to carry that by yourself. And fuck, you were just a kid. *We* were kids."

Her fingers clutch onto my shoulders like they're the only thing keeping her tethered to the earth. "I thought...I thought you'd never forgive me."

I gently pull back just enough to tip her chin up, forcing her to meet my gaze. My own tears blur my vision, but I don't wipe them away.

"There's nothing to forgive." My voice breaks under the weight of my emotions. "You were hurting, Ellie. And clearly I was being a piece of shit boyfriend for not realizing how much you were struggling. You made the best decision you could at the time. But I wish you had told me—about what happened. I wish I could've been there for you."

Her lip quivers, and she shakes her head. "I didn't think I deserved you."

I press my forehead to hers, closing my eyes as the pain between us hums like a windstorm. "You've always deserved more than you think, querida mía. You always have."

Her sobs quiet, replaced by shallow, uneven breaths. "I'm so sorry," she whispers again, like she can't stop herself.

"Stop apologizing."

"I was so awful to you." She swipes the tears on her cheeks. "It was easier—to be mean. I didn't want you to like me; I wanted you to hate me, to hate me like I hated myself."

I brush my lips to her forehead. "I could never hate you."

We're quiet as we hold each other. I have questions, most for another time, but one I can't contain.

"Do you know what the baby was?"

Silently, she shakes her head. "It was too early."

"What happened afterward?"

The question slips out before I can stop myself. Realizing how invasive I sound, I quickly backtrack. "You know what? Never mind. I'm sure it's not something you like talking about."

She gives me a soft smile, but her voice is laced with sadness.

"I had to have a D&C, which is standard after miscarriages. It's a procedure that just kind of...clears everything out." She stops for a moment, her eyes falling shut, before taking a breath. "My mom took me. A few months later, we went to the doctor for a full checkup, just to make sure everything was okay. It was. The doctor said I shouldn't have trouble having kids one day—but you never know."

"Is that something you want? Do you want kids?" I ask, hesitantly, unsure if I should've asked it in the first place.

"Yeah, I think so. My family is huge, so probably just one or two. But kids, someday—when the timing feels right."

"I want kids, too," I admit. "More than a couple, actually."

She laughs lightly and nudges my shoulder. "If they're coming out of my vagina, I get to decide how many."

Her playful tone makes me smile, but my thoughts slip into a deeper place. "It kind of turns me on, thinking about trying. Getting you pregnant, watching your stomach grow with our baby..."

Her eyebrows shoot up. "Never took you for a breeding kink guy," she teases, and her cheeks flush faintly.

"Querida mía, I have every kink for you." The moment lightens for a second before I sober again. "I want you to know —If you hadn't miscarried back then, I would've stepped up. I

339

would've been excited, even if it would've completely changed our lives. I need you to know that."

She looks away for a beat, her voice quieter when she speaks. "After I had some time to process it, I fell into a depression. I'd never been depressed and didn't recognize what it was at first. It felt hard to do anything. Existing felt exhausting. I was grieving someone I never even knew, yet I felt so connected to them. And I felt guilty—because sometimes, I was relieved it happened. How messed up is that?"

"It's not messed up. You were young, scared, and dealing with a lot. That's normal. I just—I should've been there. I should've come after you. Fuck, I screwed up so badly."

Her eyes swivel to mine, full of understanding I feel I don't deserve. "It's not like I made it easy for you. I blocked you on everything, shut you out completely. And honestly? I wouldn't have responded well if you had come after me. I was in such a dark place back then. Scottie and my mom were the only people I let in. They're the only reason I even made it through school."

I hold her closer, probably too tight, but I don't care. My heart hurts for her, for us, for the loss of a baby I didn't know existed.

I don't like to buy into the *woe is me* mentality, but it's hard not to in this instance. Our lives could've been so different, and I think a part of me will always mourn the future that never was.

CHAPTER 46

Dominic

IS THAT A GUN IN YOUR PANTS?

PRESENT

I f it were up to me, we wouldn't leave the bedroom for at least twenty-four hours. But Ellie wants to see the house; so we're going to see the house, even though I'd rather keep her away from it for now.

It's not that I don't want her to see it; I do. I just don't want her to see it like this. I imagined showing it to her closer to being finished—perfect—not in its current state.

A pile of garbage.

Ever since Ellie's incident, I've all but neglected anything to do with the house. For all I know, we're about to walk into an even bigger disaster than I can remember.

The drive is quiet, but comfortable. Ellie's been staring out the window for most of the ride, her thoughts clearly elsewhere. Something about her looks lighter. As if no longer carrying the burden of her secrets has finally let her take a full breath.

I steal glances at her when I can, catching the way the sunlight dances through her hair and the way she bites her lip absentmindedly when she's lost in her own head. Her face is bare of makeup, and while I find her stunning with or without, there's something special about getting the stripped-down version of her. She's beautiful in every light, but like this, she's almost impossible to look away from.

We pull up to the house, and my chest constricts, preparing for the disaster. It's so far from ready, the urge to turn around and hide it from her increases more and more the closer we get. It's got potential, but right now it's a far cry from the home I want it to be.

I kill the engine and step out, grabbing the keys from the console. Ellie follows me to the front door, her arms crossed against the crisp breeze, her eyes scanning the exterior.

"Still looks the same from the outside," she says, a faint smile tugging at her lips.

"Hopefully not for long," I reply, unlocking the door and pushing it open.

Inside, the place smells like sawdust and paint, and a combination of old wood and must. I've gutted most of it, but there's still a long way to go. Exposed beams stretch across the ceiling, and half-finished drywall lines the hallways.

I almost forgot how behind I really am.

Ellie steps inside, taking it all in. "You've been busy," she says, running her fingers along the edge of a workbench I set up in the foyer.

"Yeah, well, it feels like a lot of work and very little progress." I shrug as I watch her move through the space.

Her eyes fall on the blueprint tacked to the wall, and she tilts her head, studying it. "Is this the layout?"

"More or less," I say, walking over to stand beside her. "Some things are set, others are still up in the air."

"What's this?" she asks, pointing to a room marked off in the corner.

I glance at the spot she's pointing to and smile. "That's the library."

Her head whips toward me, eyes wide. "The library?"

"Yeah," I say, shoving my hands into my pockets. "You always talked about wanting one. Remember? Back when we used to come here?"

Ellie stares at me for a moment, her expression unreadable. Then she laughs, shaking her head. "I can't believe you remember that."

"I remember everything."

Her soft gaze meets mine as she flashes me a mesmerizing smile. "I read now, in case you were wondering. Though, I'm not sure they're quite the intellectual novels I'd imagined reading—more like dark mafia romances and monster smut."

"Something tells me I'll reap some benefits from those."

Her eyes regard me with mischief. "If you're a good boy, then maybe."

My hands itch to touch her, and now, after everything we've shared, I finally let myself give in, and wrap my arms around her, pulling her close. She melts into me without hesitation, her back resting against my chest in perfect alignment.

"Mmm," I murmur against her. "Querida mía, I'll be the goodest boy for you."

She wiggles her ass against my hardening length. Being around her, holding her, it's enough to make me come in my pants.

"Is that a gun in your pants, or are you just happy to see me?"

My head falls back, as a laugh tumbles out. "That was terrible."

She sticks her ass out further, bumping me with it. "I've had that one banked since you pulled me over."

My hand trails up her abdomen, brushing against the side

of her breast before I grab it, squeezing my palm around it. A throaty little moan escapes her.

"Checking me out, were you?"

She pushes her breast into my hand more. "I can't be held responsible for my reactions to you in uniform."

I brush my lips against the shell of her ear, causing her to visibly shiver. "Is that what does it for you, Ellie girl? Do you want me to fuck you with it on? Cuff you to the bed, and make you scream my name?"

"Yes," she moans while rubbing up against me.

Just when I think we're about to start ripping each other's clothes off, she spins out of my grasp and flashes me a knowing smile.

"Give me a tour." Her hand reaches out for mine, and I grab it, intertwining our fingers. "If I like what I see, I'll give your cock a tour of my mouth."

I nearly choke on my own spit. "Jesus Christ, Ellie."

Her smile is wicked, and I make a mental note to punish her for that later.

Hand in hand, we walk around the house. I tell her about my plans for the kitchen, for redoing all the fireplaces, for the flooring I plan to install.

She shakes her head. "No, don't do that. Light oak is not meant for this house. It needs to be a rich, warm brown."

"You think?"

Her forehead creases in the most adorable way. "Thank God we came today. You need a woman's opinion, badly."

I shake my head. "I don't need a woman's opinion. Only yours. Yours is the only one that matters."

She raises a brow. "Not even your mom's?"

"Querida mía, I love my mother. But you trump everyone. You always have."

Her lips roll, smile disappearing. "Being here reminds me of who we were back then." She looks around, admiring the old and the new. "I really don't want to ruin this."

I drag her toward me, snaking my hands around her waist. "Nothing is getting ruined. I don't care how long it's been, it's always been you." I pause, questioning if I should bring up our time apart, but I don't want secrets either. "I tried to move on from you. I tried seeing other people. And I couldn't. No one lasted more than a couple months, and even then I was never fully in it, always had one foot out the door. You are the standard; no other woman could ever measure up."

Her head tilts, an odd expression on her face, and I worry it was a mistake to bring up other people.

"I tried too," she says quietly. "And look how that turned out." She huffs a laugh. "You heard Marie at the diner. Even before that psycho, none of them were very great."

I opened this nightmare of a door, which I'm now regretting, because despite not wanting secrets between us, imagining her with anyone else but me has a green slurry poisoning my insides. The thought of another man seeing her, touching her body, kissing her, it's enough to drive me insane.

The corner of her mouth quirks up. "Jealous?"

There's no sense in hiding it, when it's obviously written all over my face. "Fuck yeah, I'm jealous. I was your first everything, and I'd planned on being your only."

She presses her lips against mine, placing a soft kiss before pulling away slightly. "So be my last."

I grab onto her jaw with both hands and kiss her possessively, slipping my tongue in, letting my hands wander her body. Breaking our kiss, I rest my forehead to hers. "Gladly, querida mía. I'll be anything you let me be."

She stares at me, a question in her eyes. "Did you buy this house to Noah me?"

My face scrunches. "Is that some new term the kids say?"

She giggles, fanning my damp lips with puffs of air. "Like

in *The Notebook*." Her smirk grows. "He rebuilds that big, fancy house to win Allie back. Is that what you're doing?"

I can't help it—I laugh, the sound loud and unexpected in the quiet house. "Yeah, I guess I am."

She blinks a few times, turning to cough like she's masking her emotions.

"There's still a lot to do," I say, gesturing around the room. "I've been trying to handle it myself, but it's slow going."

Ellie bites her lip, glancing around the space again. "You should talk to Ethan," she says after a moment. "He's got a great contractor for the house he's building with Marisa. They've been moving fast, and the guy's work is solid."

I nod, considering it. "Might not be a bad idea. This place deserves better than what I can do alone, even though my plan was to do it all solo."

"Stop being so stubborn and let someone help you for once."

I grin, leaning back against the wall. "You're starting to sound like me."

CHAPTER 47

Elyse

MI CAMA ES TU CAMA

PRESENT

"Your bedroom is depressing. No wonder you've been sleeping on my couch."

Dominic's eyes roam over me, heating me from the inside out. "Am I still on the couch? I thought I'd graduated to your bed."

I laugh, and he smiles back. The kind of smile that makes my stomach dip.

When I walk over to stare at one of the only pieces of furniture in the room—his bed—he moves to stand behind me, and I drop my back to his chest.

It's funny that it's only recently we started touching this way again, and already it feels instinctual, like my body just knows how to fit against his.

His arms wrap me tightly, and a little sigh floats up my throat, both from comfort and from something else.

"Tell me, querida mía. Am I allowed in your bed?"

His mouth tickles my ear as he trails nips down the shell of it.

"Yes," I breathe, relinquishing my weight onto him, because I know he'll carry it. "As long as I'm allowed in yours."

"Mi cama es tu cama." *(My bed is your bed.)*

I glance at him over my shoulder, finding his eyes light with amusement.

"As long as you're naked," he adds.

Twisting in his arms, I bring us face to face.

"If I'm naked, you're naked." I brush a kiss against his neck, feeling his rapid pulse beat against my lips.

"Of course." He swallows.

I step back. "Do you want me naked now?"

Without giving him a chance to answer, I strip off my top and step out of my jeans, leaving me in nothing but a bra and underwear.

"Fuck," he groans as his gaze travels over the length of me. "You're fucking beautiful."

I could hear the same phrase a million times from a million different people, and it would mean nothing. When Dominic says it, it's everything.

I unhook my bra, dropping it with the rest of my clothes.

He licks his lips, eyes fixated on my hardened nipples.

His hands reach for me, tugging me forward. He dips his head and buries his nose in the hollow of my collarbone, inhaling me like I'm a drug. One of his hands grabs my breast, kneading it.

"I love just getting to touch you. You have no idea how much I missed you."

My head falls back, a needy noise escaping me. The faint stubble on his cheeks scratches the tender skin and a bolt of heat ignites at the base of my spine.

"I missed you too," I admit. "So much."

He dots tender kisses up the column of my neck and across my jaw.

"Yeah?" His voice is rough with disbelief.

I thread my fingers through his hair, encouraging the journey his mouth is on.

"Always."

His lips slam against mine. It's a demanding, urgent kiss, like he's trying to make up for lost time—or punish me for it. His hands grip my waist, pulling me closer, until there's not an inch of space left between us.

I kiss him back just as fiercely.

We're unmoored, breathing each other in like we've been starved.

He pulls his mouth from mine and the wet heat of his mouth warms the side of my cheek.

"Prove it," he whispers.

His challenge starts a bloom of pressure low in my belly.

I grasp the hem of his T-shirt and slip my hands beneath it, letting my nails lightly scratch up his abdomen as I pull it off.

Starting at his neck, I drag a lick down to his chest, tasting salt and skin.

His hands dig into my hips, a quiet whimper sliding past his teeth.

"I would love to prove it," I murmur against his stomach, slowly making my way down his body.

There's no mistaking what I want.

His half-lidded eyes stare down at me. "Yes, Ellie girl," he hisses. "Get on your knees and give my cock some attention."

My thighs press together as my knees meet the cold hardwood floor.

I work to unfasten his pants, feeling the bulge of his cock battling the restraint of his zipper.

Once his jeans are bunched at his ankles, he sucks in a harsh breath. "Touch it, please," he rasps.

The *please* melts me. So polite. So dirty.

I give him an intentionally slow stroke over his boxer briefs, watching his jaw clench and chest rise with an inhale.

Looking up at him through my lashes, my lips curl into a smirk. "Since you asked so nicely."

My hand dips beneath the waistband, dragging them down until they join his jeans. He steps out of them, kicking them away, as his cock springs free. My mouth waters.

He's hard and thick and veiny, with a bead of pre-cum, shiny and ready to be tasted.

"The prettiest cock," I praise.

My hand wraps around it, and works a long stroke. Staring at it, it's hard to believe it fits inside me so well.

I lick his tip, and then glide my tongue down his shaft, my eyes falling shut as I savor his earthy arousal, before sinking my mouth around it.

"Take all of it," Dominic grits. "Show me how badly you missed me."

His demand sparks a frenzy within me. My lips surge forward, taking more of him. The tip of his cock down my throat chokes me.

It's his undoing.

"Así, así, así." *(Like that, like that, like that.)*

His hips thrust, fingers tangling in my hair, digging into my skull. He uses me, fucking my mouth. It's rough and controlling, forcing obscene choking gags out of me. My panties grow wetter by the second, my thighs are sticky and wet, my core achingly needy.

"You like the way I use you? That pussy's dripping, isn't it?"

I moan a garbled yes around his cock, continuing to let him control the rhythm.

His ragged breaths quicken. "I'm going to cum," he says, biting down on a moan.

And then he's spilling down my throat, grunting through his orgasm.

When he's finished, he helps me stand, gently smoothing my tangled hair. He wipes the dampness from my cheeks and around my mouth with his discarded shirt—tending to me with a softness that stirs warmth in my chest.

Gathering my face in his hands, he caresses my cheeks with his thumbs.

"Was I too rough?"

I smile, leaning into his touch. "I liked it." Color rushes to my face, admitting the truth.

He chuckles before pressing a quick kiss to my lips. "I thought so, but wanted to make sure. I was never very rough with you before..."

"Well, we're older now. Nothing wrong with trying new things."

He smiles, satisfied with my answer.

"Speaking of new things..." He grabs me by the waist, spins me around, and tosses me onto the bed—crawling over me in one seamless move. "This bed is brand new, needs to be broken in."

I barely catch my breath, before he's stealing it, pressing his mouth to mine and driving in his tongue.

I groan, opening up for him, crossing my ankles around the small of his back.

We're messy. Our kissing is wet and sloppy, all tongue and teeth. An impatient ache builds at my core, and I grind my hips against his already hardening length. It's digging a bruise into my inner thigh.

I tear my lips from his, arching my back.

"Your recovery time is nonexistent," I muse, swiveling my hips.

He sucks on my neck. "Ten year hard-on, querida mía."

His answer makes me giggle.

I'm still sore from him but my pussy clenches, ready to be filled.

Reading my mind, his fingers slide my panties down, throwing them on the floor beside us. He spreads my arousal around, massaging my clit.

"Want to try something?" he asks quietly against the dip in my shoulder.

"Like what?"

He licks his way back to my mouth before answering. "Cuffs," he murmurs. "I have a backup pair in the closet."

I nod, curling my tongue to his. "Mmm hmm." He tugs on my bottom lip with his teeth. "Yes," I gasp. "We need a redo."

He's out of bed in a flash, leaving me a panting, squirmy mess.

When he returns just as fast, the gleam in his eyes is shy and hot. My pulse spikes when I spot the silver cuffs dangling from his fingers.

"On your stomach," he says in his on-duty voice.

I obey, rolling over, turning my face to watch him.

He's gentle as he puts my hands behind my back and clasps the heavy bracelets to my wrists. He gives them a soft tug.

My anticipation mounts, wondering how he'll take me. How I'll feel being controlled this way. How he's the only person in the world I'd trust to do this with.

His hands grip my waist, forcing my ass up as I rest my weight on my knees.

It's an awkward position. Hands behind my back, ass high in the air, cheek pressed into the mattress.

Dominic tugs on the cuffs again, harder this time, and my chest lifts off the bed.

"How does that feel?"

"Weird." I laugh.

"Good weird or bad weird."

"I don't know," I admit. "Both."

His weight causes the bed to dip as he settles behind me. "If anything doesn't feel good, just tell me." He caresses my ass cheek and my skin prickles in goosebumps. "Your pleasure is the only thing that matters."

"Okay."

I expect to feel the nudge of his cock at my entrance, but instead his palms flatten on the swell of each ass cheek. He spreads them apart and blows on the sensitive hole.

I shiver, gasping in surprise that morphs into a moan when his tongue laps at the area, swirling and teasing.

Two fingers sink into my soaking center, pistoning in and out of me at a relentless rhythm as his mouth continues to eat my ass.

My orgasm builds quickly, thighs shaking, stomach trembling, the most delicious twist of heat unraveling inside of me. I come loud, Dominic's name flying with a string of mangled sighs.

The head of his cock drags at my wet seam, gathering my release before he slots himself inside. One hand holding the chain of the cuffs as leverage while the other is settled on my hip. He slams his hips. *Once. Twice. Three times.*

"Fuck," he breathes. "Nothing sexier than seeing you cuffed and stuffed full of my cock."

I moan, pushing back against him. "More. Harder."

Our bodies slap together as breathless murmurs tangle with gasps and unintelligible words. It's mindless and unfiltered and fervent.

I can sense his impending orgasm. The frenzied grunts, the frantic pace at which he rocks into me. Together, we climb higher and higher, reaching the peak in a shaking, wild, strangled string of cries.

Before my body comes down from its high, he's removed

the cuffs and has me tucked at his side, rubbing at my wrists in delicate soothing circles.

We lie there, wordless and satiated, until a memory bubbles up.

"I forgive you," I say, half-slur, half-laugh.

Dominic lets out a confused hum. "For what?"

I smile into his chest. "Arresting me."

CHAPTER 48

Dominic

HE'S NOT GOOD ENOUGH FOR HER

PRESENT

"**B**ruh, I need you to know I don't fucking like you," Shane says, his eyes blazing into mine.

I choke on my water, coughing.

Ellie groans. "Shane! Knock it off."

"This meathead's been back in town for two seconds and you took him back like nothing—"

"Mom!" Ellie yells. "Do something."

"Shane," Leanne warns. "Can you please behave?"

"No," he grits, moving to stand. "How are you all okay with this?"

"Because it's her life," Ethan says calmly as Marisa nods along with him.

"You weren't there—neither of you were." Shane points between Ethan and Gavin. "Dom showed back up a few years ago, and when I picked her up after seeing him, she was a goddamn mess. I've never seen her so upset, and I never want to see her that upset again."

The room quiets, save for the sound of someone biting

into a carrot stick—probably Gavin, based on the loud crunch. Ellie, sitting beside me, drops her head into her hands. I glance at her briefly before turning back to Shane, who looks about five seconds away from lunging across the dinner table.

"We've already talked through everything," Ellie says to everyone. "And frankly, it's no one's business but our own."

"She's right," Jack booms loudly, his voice piercing through the tension. "You all need to be supportive of your sister the way she supports all of you and your countless bad decisions." I place a hand over my mouth to keep from smiling. Everyone looks stunned, staring at Jack. "Dominic's been keeping her safe in the midst of some maniac on the loose. Protected her at that bar. Maybe go a little easy on him." His eyes meet Shane's across the table. "Right, Shane?"

"He's not good enough for her," Shane huffs. "I'm just saying what everyone else is thinking."

Ethan clears his throat. "I'm not thinking it. I'm minding my own business. Leave me out of it."

"Same," Gavin pipes up, gesturing toward Lily. "Can we table the yelling until curious ears leave the room? Or at least until after the lasagna? I'm starving."

"Lasagna's just about done," Leanne calls as she walks toward the kitchen. "So behave, all of you, or I'll be forced to send you all home with empty stomachs."

When Ellie invited me to Sunday dinner, I definitely didn't expect it to go like this. I knew Shane didn't like me; I just didn't realize it was this bad.

Ariana leans forward, resting her elbows on the table. "I think everyone needs to take a deep breath." She turns her focus on Shane. "And you need to calm down. You have no room to judge. I've lost friends because you had your fun with them and never called. That's not cool."

Shane dips his chin. "That's different," he mutters. "They're not my sisters."

"I love you, but you're kind of a pig, Shane," Layla chirps up.

Shane throws up his arms. "You know what? I'm not even hungry." He storms off, slamming the front door loudly behind him.

I start to stand, to go after him, but Ellie stops me.

"No, you're not going after him. He's the one in the wrong."

"She's right." Leanne walks back in and sets the lasagna in the middle of the table. "He owes you an apology, not the other way around."

"It's kind of sweet, in a messed up little way, how protective he's being," Ariana, says.

Ellie scoffs. "It's not sweet, it's embarrassing."

I scrub a hand down my face. "I can't just let him keep hating me. We have to work it out."

Jack lets out a breath. "He'll come around. Kid's all out of sorts because his brain is maturing faster than his behaviors. Give him some time."

Gavin looks around the table. "Well, now that we got that over with, can we eat and pretend we're a normal family?"

Dinner commences and conversations resume, but I can't relax.

I'm not going anywhere, and the last thing I want is for one of Ellie's siblings to have a problem with me. I'm not sure how, but I'm going to have to figure out how to make peace with Shane. The last thing Ellie needs is worrying about something this petty, when she has real shit going on.

"Shhh." Ellie giggles. "Quiet."

As soon as the dinner from hell ended, she grabbed my hand, and sneakily dragged me up the stairs.

For as many times as I've been in the Ledger home, I stopped being allowed upstairs when we began dating. We snuck around a few times, but I was too terrified of Jack to break his rules. Now, I'm a fucking adult, and I think I'm even more terrified.

Everyone is still downstairs, their voices drifting up to the second floor, fading the farther we get, but not enough to drown out completely.

"Where are we going?" I whisper.

Ellie looks back at me over her shoulder, her cheeks sporting the sexiest blush. "My old bedroom."

I was worried she would say that.

She pushes the door open, pulling me in with her.

When the light flicks on, I'm transported to a different era. Her bedroom is a time capsule. Same black and white checkered bedding, a furry black rug at the center, posters and pictures covering the cherry-red painted walls.

"Looks the same, huh?"

My eyes dart around, landing on all the pictures of us. I'm in disbelief she kept them up after all this time.

Us as gangly little kids, awkward preteens, awkward teenagers, slightly less awkward teenagers, and then the pictures end.

She sits on the bed, her eyes traveling the length of me. "There's something I've always wanted to do in here, and we never got the opportunity."

I work a swallow down and rub the back of my neck. I can still hear everyone downstairs. There's no way.

"We can't. They'll hear us."

Her red lips turn down in a little pout that makes my cock twitch.

Fuck me.

She comes up to me, crossing her arms around my neck, dotting kisses along my jaw.

I'm still tense from dinner, but the more she trails her lips along my skin, the more malleable I become.

I can't fuck her up here. Not with her entire family one floor away. Right?

"I can be quiet," she whispers against my neck, causing the puff of her breath to travel straight down to my dick.

She backs up, dragging me along until we reach the bed, where she sits, scooting back until she's at the center.

"Don't you want me?" she asks, while stripping off her top and bra at once.

I bite down on my knuckle to keep from groaning too loud.

She shifts to her knees, crawling across the bed until she reaches where I'm standing at the edge. She peers up at me with the clearest doe eyes. When she rises to sit up on her knees, her hands immediately start working on my belt buckle.

"We can't," I repeat, with barely any strength behind it.

"We can." Her hand wraps around my painfully hard cock, and she starts stroking it over my boxer briefs.

My neck rolls back as I clamp down on my jaw to keep from whimpering.

Hearing her family's hum of conversation while she works my dick, is somehow only making me harder.

"Please, Dominic baby." Her voice is a velvet purr. She knows exactly what she's doing. I'm defenseless—so weak for her.

And my resolve cracks.

I strip off my shirt, and gently push her so she falls back on the bed. She lands with a satisfied sigh, but the moment I start to settle over her, the bed squeaks loudly.

"Fuck," I say, easing out of the lust fog I was just in. "That's way too noticeable."

Ellie squirms, pressing her thighs together. "No, no, no. It's fine."

I shake my head. "I won't be able to walk out of here knowing your family heard us."

"Please," she begs. "I need you."

My eyes rake over her. Over her pink-pebbled nipples adorned with shiny studs, her chest rising and falling, the haze in her eyes.

I might not be able to fuck her right now, but I can definitely make her come without alerting the entire house.

Moving to stand, her face is full of protest until I start tugging at her pants, removing them roughly.

"Lie back and relax. I'm going to take care of you."

Once she's free of clothing, I pull her by the ankles until her ass is almost hanging off the edge of the bed.

Her eyes light up as she watches me get on my knees.

"What are you doing," she says through a sigh.

My hands pry her thighs apart, revealing her glistening center.

"I'm going to devour this pussy."

"But what about you? I want you to feel good, too."

I shake my head, already running my nose through her arousal, inhaling her addictive scent.

"I'll live." I suck on her clit, releasing a gasp from her lips. "But if I don't eat your pussy right this second, I might die."

She giggles, liking my answer as her back arches off the bed.

My tongue flattens, lapping up all her sweetness. I suck and swirl just how she likes it, sinking my fingers in and curling them to hit the right spot. I know her body like it's my own

"Yes," she hisses. "Just like that."

Her hips move, grinding her soaking pussy against my tongue, and I bury my face deeper, flick my tongue harder.

She grabs onto my hair, pulling it painfully, and my cock jerks.

I love it when she's greedy, when she just can't stand it and has to chase her pleasure.

"Such a good boy," she praises.

Her words only further encourage me.

The more I drown between her thighs, the louder she gets.

"Shhh," I tell her before giving her clit a light nip.

"I'm sorry," she whispers. "It's too much." She gasps. "It's too good."

Pulling back, I keep my fingers inside her, the cool air brushing my soaked face.

"Put a pillow over your face now, or I won't let you come."

She laughs softly, her skin flushing pink. "So commanding." Reaching behind her head, she places one over her face.

"Good," I tell her. "Bite the pillow, querida mía. No one gets to hear you scream but me."

I push her thighs farther apart, and eat her pussy like I'm starved. Swiping my tongue at her center, circling her clit, lapping up every drop pouring out of her. Soon, she's shaking, thighs trembling against my palms, back bowing. She's so fucking beautiful when she comes, I can hardly stand it, and wish more than anything we were in our bed so I could sink my cock in her.

Her muffled cries are still loud, but I don't give a fuck. They're the best damn sound, and knowing I'm the cause gives me a surge of pride.

As she's coming down, she lies there, boneless and satisfied, her chest heaving. So fucking sexy.

Eventually she removes the pillow, tossing it aside. She looks at me, her smile spent and satiated.

"You good, Ellie girl," I ask, biting my smile.

She sighs, stretching her naked body like a cat. "So good."

CHAPTER 49

Elyse

ALMOST FEEL NORMAL

PRESENT

"Which one? Sage or celadon?"

Paisley's eyes squint as she looks between the two ribbon color swatches. "Those literally look exactly the same."

"No," I drag, trying to hold back my laugh. They really are nearly the same color, and I'm mostly just messing with her. Mostly. "The celadon pulls more gray undertones, whereas the sage is warmer."

She stares at me, looking more confused than ever. "You're starting to make me think I'm color blind. They look identical."

"They are very close. The more you look at colors, the more you're able to tell them apart."

"Is this a test, and I'm failing it? Am I getting fired?"

I laugh at her questions. "Why on earth would I be firing you?"

She crosses her arms. "Because you called in yesterday, and

362

you never call in. We all assumed you were getting ready to fire us or something."

A heated blush blooms on my face, so I cough in an attempt to conceal it. She's right, I never call in. I'm not sure what came over me, aside from the fact that leaving my warm bed, with Dominic draped over me like a weighted blanket, seemed like the last thing I felt like doing. So I didn't. Instead, I fired off assignments via email to Paisley and Faith and Ben and stayed home.

It was easily one of the best decisions I've ever made.

It's been three weeks since Dominic and I officially got back together, and it's been fulfilling to say the least. While the sex has been great, and there's been plenty of it, it's been so much more than that. We've fused our lives together.

Gone are the days of coming home to an empty house and sad leftovers. Even when Dominic isn't home—because he's on shift or tending to something work-related—his presence is everywhere. His shoes are gathered next to mine at the entry, his clothes hang in my closet, his toiletries are in the bathroom. I didn't realize how much I would like it.

He took my advice and contacted Ethan's contractor, who quickly got to work. The renovations became more of an undertaking than anticipated, forcing Dominic to move in with me. He was already staying with me as much as possible, but this made it more official.

Things almost feel normal. Almost.

Though it's been weeks of silence from whoever was trying to get my attention, we still don't have any answers, leaving a dark cloud hanging over everything.

Under Sheriff Doyle made the call to pull back on patrol surveillance due to resources and lack of evidence that it was still needed. Dominic was pissed about it, but understood. Since then, the most we get is a patrol drive-by each shift. I still don't go anywhere alone, and we take as many precautions as necessary, but it's starting to feel pointless.

Maybe it was Stuart, and because he's locked up, the threats have stopped.

Either way, it's hard to fully embrace all the good things that have happened lately without feeling the looming shadow that it could all be taken in an instant.

But for every stress and worry about what comes next, Dominic is by my side.

Sometimes it's hard to imagine I wasn't always sharing my life with him. It's only been weeks, but it feels like it's been longer than that. We fit together so seamlessly, I'd never guess we were ever apart.

As I'm about to put Paisley out of her misery, there's a double tap on my door. When I look over, Dominic is standing in the doorway, in his work uniform, looking way too delicious. He shoots me a grin while lifting a bag.

"Brought you lunch."

"Hey," Paisley greets, already on her way out.

Dominic lifts his chin to her, and as soon as she's past him, he closes the door. In three strides he's on me, the takeout bag tossed on my desk. My back is pressed to the wall and his hands are cupping my face.

"Fuck, I missed you," he breathes, and then captures my mouth, planting a consuming kiss on my lips, which I quickly deepen.

"We saw each other this morning," I sigh, as he trails kisses down my neck.

His lips pause against the curve of my neck, his breath hot on my skin. "Not the same," he murmurs, low and rough. "Morning you is a grumpy brat. Midday you? In charge and fucking sexy. Drives me wild."

A laugh bubbles out of me, though it's cut short when his teeth graze my collarbone. "Dominic," I scold, but my hands betray me, gripping the front of his shirt and pulling him closer. "You're going to wrinkle my blouse."

His palms slide down my sides, settling on my hips as he leans back just enough to meet my eyes. "You say that like I'm supposed to care."

"You're supposed to care because I have a meeting soon," I remind him, trying to sound steadier than I feel. "One where I'll need to look professional and not like I've been thoroughly kissed in my office."

A slow grin spreads across his face, the kind that always makes my stomach flip. "Thoroughly kissed, huh? Would you rather look thoroughly fucked instead?"

I swat at his chest, laughing again. "What are you doing to me?"

"The same thing you do to me," he counters, leaning in for another kiss, this one slower, softer, like he's savoring me. My resolve wavers for a second—or maybe ten seconds—before I finally plant my hands on his chest and push him back.

"Lunch," I say, a little breathless. "You said you brought me lunch. Stop distracting me before I get hangry."

His grin widens, and he grabs the takeout bag from the desk, holding it out like a peace offering. "Fine, fine. Food first. Eat your lunch, and then I'll eat you."

I roll my eyes, taking the bag from him. "Not here. You can do that last part at home."

He leans against the edge of my desk, watching me open the bag. "Gladly, querida mía."

In the middle of eating, Jenna, my bride, taps on the door.

"Hi," she calls out as Dominic stands, knowing it's his cue to leave.

She frowns when she sees the food spread out on my desk. "Sorry, I can come back. I know I'm a little early."

"You're fine," I tell her, wrapping up my sandwich. "Come on in."

She sinks down onto a chair and Dominic leans down to give me a quick kiss.

"I'll see you at home. Don't forget to wait for Gavin to follow you."

"I won't forget."

With one more quick kiss he's out the door, leaving me with Jenna.

"Is that your boyfriend?" she asks, her face bright with a curious smile.

I laugh, a flush creeping up on my cheeks. "Yeah. He's pretty affectionate. Sorry if that made you uncomfortable."

She shakes her head. "No, I think it's cute." Her smile fades slightly. "Sometimes I wish Matt was a little more affectionate. He's not big on PDA."

The last few times Jenna and I have met to go over wedding details, Matt has been noticeably absent. I've been meaning to ask, but I try my best to stay out of my clients personal lives. There are a variety of reasons the groom would choose to skip out on meetings, but I don't have a good feeling about any of Matt's reasons. I haven't had a good feeling about Matt from the start.

Just as I'm about to begin showing Jenna the latest mockup for the table layout, a knock sounds.

Dominic hesitantly walks back in with a shy grin.

"Sorry for interrupting." He lifts two small takeout containers. "I forgot to give you dessert."

He sets a box down in front of me and one in front of Jenna. "It's nothing fancy, just pie from the diner."

Jenna looks up at Dominic, "Oh. Don't feel obligated to give me one."

"It's fine," he tells her. "I have to go back on shift, and don't have time to eat it. It'll go to waste."

She smiles with a creased forehead, like it's the nicest thing anyone has ever done for her. "Thank you."

"No problem."

"Thank you," I tell him, craning my neck to give him another goodbye kiss.

He cradles my jaw and kisses me softly. "Okay, now I'm really leaving."

Once he's gone, I try to get back on task with Jenna, but she seems unfocused, distracted.

"Everything okay?" I ask her, worried I've offended her somehow.

She lets out a long exhale. "No—I mean yes." Pausing, her eyes get slightly misty. "Things have been a little strained with Matt lately, and seeing you and your boyfriend, and how sweet he is with you, just made me feel a little sad about my own relationship."

My lips stretch into a straight line. "As your wedding planner, I can tell you it's perfectly normal for your relationship to be strained during wedding planning. It's stressful, and you're blending your families together. It's a big undertaking. But," I hesitate, "as your friend, woman to woman—the right guy won't ever make you wonder. The right guy shows up. Your future husband never makes you feel like your wants and needs are a burden."

She nods slowly, the worry in her brows deepening the longer I speak.

"Marriage isn't just a wedding," I continue. "It's one of the strongest, most legally binding contracts you'll ever enter into. The person you pick as your partner needs to be someone, who even at their absolute worst, is still better than anyone else you could've chosen."

Tears start to shine in her eyes, her bottom lip trembling. "I'm—I'm not sure if I should go through with it."

My shoulders rise as my gaze settles with hers. "So don't."

Tonight is my last free Friday evening for a while. With my schedule packed full of weddings to prepare for, I fully intend to make the most of it. And because of that, I can't wait to get home and have Dominic all to myself.

As I step out of the winery, the excitement to get home has me quickening my pace toward the parking lot.

I'm supposed to wait for Gavin to finish up, but he has at least another hour left of work, and I don't have an hour of patience left in me.

It's been so long since anything has happened, I'm reaching the point of accepting Stuart was the one behind everything. It makes the most sense.

I'll just text Gavin when I get home. No harm, no foul.

With the winery in my rearview mirror, I let out a breath, relaxing into my seat. It's a short drive home, and I finally got my car back from the shop. The sun is still out, my favorite playlist is blasting through the speakers, and soon enough I'll be jumping into Dominic's arms, giving him my favorite greeting.

At the stop sign that acts as the divide between the viticulture area of Red Mountain and downtown, my phone buzzes with a new message. Glancing at the screen, I see it's from an unknown number.

> UNKNOWN
> I'm done waiting for you.

My stomach drops. I look around the vacant road with nothing but acres of vineyards stretched before me and not a car in sight.

I shake my head, willing away the panic rising in my chest.

The message isn't necessarily nefarious. It could be nothing.

Determined not to let myself spiral before I've had a chance for Dominic to determine if it's something to worry about, I continue the drive home, gripping the steering wheel tighter than usual, and ignoring the pit that's now taken residence in my stomach.

Halfway home, I notice a dark sedan in my rearview mirror. At first, I think nothing of it, but every turn I make, the car follows. My heart rate accelerates. I take an unexpected left; the sedan mirrors my move.

My phone buzzes with another message.

UNKNOWN

Time is up.

A frenzy grips me, my chest tightening as my breaths come in shallow gasps. I press the accelerator, weaving through traffic, taking random turns in an attempt to lose them. The sedan matches my every move, its headlights glaring in my mirrors.

I remember a narrow alley behind The Jackalope, barely wide enough for a car. Swerving sharply, I enter the alley, scraping the side mirrors against the brick walls. The sedan hesitates at the entrance, unable to follow.

Emerging onto a different street, I make a series of quick turns, finally losing sight of the sedan. My hands tremble as I navigate the remaining streets home, constantly checking the mirrors for any sign of pursuit.

Pulling into the driveway, I barely take the time to turn off the engine before jumping out. Dominic is exiting his patrol SUV, having just gotten home.

He takes one look at me and rushes to my side.

"What's wrong? What happened?" His words are hurried.

I collapse into his arms, the adrenaline finally catching up to me.

"Someone followed me," I manage to say between gasps. "They were texting me while it was happening."

His stance goes rigid. "And where the fuck was Gavin?"

My shoulders start to curl in, as if making myself smaller will somehow lessen the magnitude of my reckless decision.

"I left without him," I say quietly.

Dominic takes a step back, his stare sharp and cold. "What do you mean you left without him?" He runs both hands through his hair, exhaling so loudly it sounds like a hiss. "One rule. One fucking rule, Ellie." He stalks off toward the end of the driveway. "Fuck!" he yells. "Fuck!"

And then he's on his radio, barking out calls and commands to whoever is on the other end of it. The entire time, his grip is on his service weapon, ready to take it out at a moment's notice.

Within a matter of minutes, the front of my townhouse is littered with patrol cars, my phone has been confiscated, and Dominic hasn't looked my way once.

CHAPTER 50

Dominic

ONE MISSTEP

PRESENT

The drive to the station is a blur. Visions of worst case scenarios rotate through my mind. What if she had gotten in a car accident? Gotten ran off the road? Gotten hurt? Or worse?

Dropping Ellie off at her parents' house was the right thing to do—keeping her somewhere safe where I know she's not alone—but the look on her face when I left was enough to make my chest feel like it was caving in.

I lost my temper.

I couldn't see. I couldn't think. One look at her, and I was ready to kill someone. Had that sedan even dared to drive by, I would've shot the driver and anyone else in it at point blank range without a second thought.

But I know I fucked up. I fucked up in the worst way imaginable. I made her feel like it was her fault, and I could tell it broke her the moment I raised my voice.

I've never spoken to her that way.

And it feels like shit.

As upset as I am that she went directly against our plan and drove alone, I'm more upset I wasn't there. This situation has dragged on for way too long.

I'm fucking furious. At whoever is behind this, at the situation, and at myself for not protecting her better.

Parking my cruiser, I slam the door hard enough to rattle the vehicle.

Heads turn as I stomp through the station, a few casting me sympathetic glances. By now, everyone is well aware of the situation. And even more aware that it's not even close to being solved.

Morales lifts her chin at me as I walk in her direction. "Sheriff's in his office. He's waiting for you."

Ryker's been out for a while now. I was fully expecting to handle this matter with Doyle and Vorheis.

When I push the door open, Ryker is leaning over his desk, papers scattered everywhere. He looks up as I enter, and his eyes narrow.

"Deputy Alvarez," he says, too professional for my liking. "Close the door."

I do as he says, but the tension in the room is suffocating. "Talk to me. Tell me what happened."

"Ellie was followed tonight," I begin, pacing the room as the words pour out of me. "She got these cryptic text messages from an unknown number, and then some jackass in a sedan tailed her halfway home, trying to scare her. She managed to lose him, but—" I stop, clenching my fists. "This is escalating. He went silent, and now he's back in full force. Whoever this is, they're not just sending threats anymore—they're acting on them."

Ryker listens, his face unreadable, but I can see the gears turning in his head. He's always been good at staying calm under pressure.

"Tell me what happened afterward."

"Kincaid interviewed Ellie and then sent her phone to get analyzed. That's it, that's all we got."

Ryker sighs. "What do you need from me?"

I place my hands on my waist, trying to get my breathing to slow. "I want access to every traffic camera, every doorbell camera, anything that could get us a visual on a plate."

Ryker nods. "Done." He clasps his hands over the desk. "But it's all going to Kincaid. You're too close to this. I can't have your emotions messing with the investigation. This isn't coming from me, it's a direct order from Sergeant Vorheis."

"You've got to—"

Ryker raises his hand. "Look, I get it. If it were Claire, I'd be losing my shit. But you've got to let the investigation roll out properly. One misstep, and you could lose the chance to put whoever is doing this behind bars."

I nod, balling up my fists to keep my frustration under control. "Understood," I grit.

"Good," Ryker says, his tone leaving no room for argument. "Now go home and get some rest. You're no good to anyone running on fumes."

Rest is the last thing on my mind, but I nod and head for the door.

CHAPTER 51

Elyse

ONCE-IN-A-LIFETIME

PRESENT

This is by far the worst outfit I've ever worn to a wedding. I'm wearing my signature all-black, but my pants are wrinkled, my blouse is faded and looks more gray than black, and my hair is in a messy top knot. If my appearance is any indication as to how things are going, it's clear they're not going well.

After Dominic picked me up from my parents' house last night, there's been an undercurrent of tension. Dominic is on edge, and I'm barely keeping it together. Before, I was able to brush aside what was happening, but I can't anymore, and I think it's starting to fracture my psyche piece by piece.

Life goes on though; we can't stop everything because of what's going on. And today I need to focus on my job.

Behind me, I can feel Dominic's presence. He's leaning casually against the wall near the entrance, his arms crossed, but I know better than to think he's relaxed. His eyes are scanning the room constantly, pensive and alert, taking in every detail. Even when he looks at me, his gaze softens for only a second before focusing back to the crowd.

We still haven't talked about how he reacted when he found out I left without Gavin. I understand his anger, but it doesn't mean I'm going to put up with being spoken to that way. I would've preferred to discuss it after he picked me up, but it was already late, and I was way too exhausted to have a real conversation by that point.

So now we're doing this weird tiptoe—being overly polite, talking around the problem, but very aware it needs to be dealt with.

He hasn't left my side all morning—only adding to the tension between us. After what happened, I can't bring myself to be annoyed. If anything, I feel safer knowing he's here, even if his watchfulness is a constant reminder of the fear curling in the pit of my stomach.

"Elyse!" My bride Valerie's voice pulls me out from my thoughts. She's walking toward me, her perfectly curled hair bouncing slightly with each step. She's holding her bouquet with her nose scrunched. "Do you think the florist has anything fresher? These look a little...wilted."

I offer her a reassuring smile, stepping closer to inspect the flowers. "Let me check. We'll make sure everything is just right."

She nods, her panic easing slightly, and I head toward the table where the florist is putting together some last-minute arrangements. As I walk, Dominic falls into step behind me, his long strides matching my shorter, brisk ones.

I glance over my shoulder. "You know you don't have to follow me everywhere, right?"

His lips quirk into a faint smile, but his eyes are sad, worried. "I do, actually."

My gaze scans the room, looking around for anyone listening. "Nothing is going to happen here," I say under my breath.

"Between you and security and the gate being closed to outsiders, the likelihood of an incident is small."

He lets out a breath, and all it does is reveal how tired I know he is. "Small or not, I think if I let you out of my sight, I'd have some kind of breakdown. Right now, it's more for me than it is for you."

My lungs squeeze around the sudden rush of warmth. Even when I'm mad at him—even with all this shit going on— he still manages to send my heart thrumming.

"Okay," is all I manage.

If I said much more, I think my emotions would get the best of me, and now isn't the time. I have a wedding to run.

So I do what I do best, and shove all my issues into a nice, neat box, and get to work.

The ceremony is flawless, the bride and groom exchange vows near the vineyard while their guests watch with misty eyes.

Last spring, I had roses planted between the rows of vines that backdrop the ceremony space, and now that spring is in bloom, the roses beautifully color the space, adding a layer of romanticism to the ambiance.

After the ceremony, I assign Paisley, Faith, and Ben to handle the finishing touches in the ballroom while I monitor cocktail hour in the tasting room.

By the time we transition to the reception, I feel like I've been running on empty for hours. The band plays a soft, melodic tune as guests drift toward the dance floor, their laughter and conversation filling the air.

I'm busy double-checking the seating chart when Dominic appears beside me. He's been hanging back the last few hours, giving me space to work.

He doesn't say anything at first, just watches me.

"What?" I ask, feeling my cheeks heat. "Why are you staring at me like that?"

He shrugs, smiling. A real smile this time. "I'm just impressed, that's all."

I laugh. "Impressed about what?"

He comes closer, resting his hand on the small of my back. The contact sends a tingle up my spine. "You, querida mía." His eyes roam the ballroom and then come back to meet mine. "When I first moved back, I kind of wondered why you became a wedding planner. I just assumed it was because it allowed you to work with your family. But now I get it."

"Get what?"

"You're magic." His voice is hushed, but he sounds almost amazed, in disbelief. "I don't know how you took all these blank walls and turned it into something out of a movie. I always knew you were creative, but this is a whole other level of talent."

I'm used to being complimented by my clients, but very rarely do I hear it from anyone else.

"Thank you," I say quietly.

"Seriously," he continues. "I'm not sure why I'm so surprised when it makes perfect sense—the way you take care of everyone, and notice all the little details—you were meant to do this. I'm just glad I got to witness you in action."

"You're making it very hard to stay mad at you right now," I tell him, biting my smile.

His hand trails up my spine, rubbing soothingly. "I know we need to talk, but right now let's take a pause on the anger and the stress and the world crumbling around us—and let's dance."

My head is already shaking before I can get the words out. "Oh, yeah, no. I don't dance at my weddings. I'm the behind-the-scenes person; I'm supposed to be invisible."

His head dips, hovering over my ear. "Nothing about you could ever be invisible. It doesn't matter what room you walk into, you're the center of it."

Pieces of my heart warm like dominoes falling, until eventually my entire heart is warmer and fuller than I thought possible.

"Dance with me. I need everyone to know the wedding planner is taken. Can't have any of these guests thinking you're single."

I laugh despite myself, and let Dominic lead me out onto the dance floor.

His hands rest on my lower waist, mine crossing around his neck, and together we sway to the music like teenagers.

His breath is warm on my neck as I let my head rest on his chest, finally giving myself permission to let go of some of the weight on my shoulders.

"I know you want us to go slow, and I want to go at lightening speed." He chuckles. "But there's something I've been meaning to tell you, and I've been wanting to say it from the moment I first saw you after I moved back. I don't think I can keep it to myself anymore."

I angle my head to meet his gaze. "What is it?"

"I love you." His voice is barely above a whisper, but unmistakably clear. "I never stopped. I've loved you since before I knew what it really meant, and I'll love you into the afterlife."

I stay quiet, my bottom lip trembling as I stare into his eyes.

"After we broke up, I used to tell myself, *maybe in another life*. Maybe in the next one, we'd get it right. And somehow, that thought made it easier—that somewhere out there, some version of me didn't lose you."

A tear slips down my cheek.

"I'll always look for you. In every parallel. On every plane. Every version of me is made to love you. You're a once-in-a-lifetime, Ellie girl. So, in our next life, meet me at the fence—

because that's where I'll be, hoping lightening strikes the same place twice."

My tears are more like sobs now, as they fall in hot streams down my face.

I spent years doing everything I could not to cry, only to cry more the past month than I have my entire life.

"I—I—"

"You don't have to say anything. I just wanted you to know." His thumb swipes under my eye. "I didn't mean to make you cry."

"They're the good kind," I choke out.

"Good," he says, kissing my forehead.

We continue swaying to the song, and once it's over I have to sneak off to the restroom to make myself look presentable. Normally, I keep a bag of emergency makeup and other odds and ends for my brides and the bridesmaids. Tonight is the first night I've needed to use it on myself.

After I've tamed the mess of mascara that was streaking down my face, there's still plenty more wedding left before I can call it a night.

The bride tosses her bouquet, the groom wraps the garter around a football and tosses it into a crowd of unruly men, and the cake cutting goes smoothly, the song "Sugar Sugar" by The Archies playing as the bride and groom feed each other a bite.

While the dancing continues, Paisley and Faith work on gathering the floral arrangements, preparing them for donation to local nursing homes tomorrow.

Near the buffet table, I spot Ben, lingering awkwardly. He's holding his phone, angled slightly toward me, and I feel a strange prickle of unease. Before I can think too much about it, Dominic moves from behind me.

I watch him approach Ben, and my stomach twists. I

follow, but a guest stops me with a question, and by the time I catch up, Dominic has cornered Ben near the coat check.

"What are you doing?" Dominic growls.

Ben stammers, holding up his phone. "I—I was just taking pictures of the event. They're for my final."

"Really?" Dominic's tone is sharp, his eyes narrowing. "Then why do you keep pointing it at Ellie?"

Ben pales, his eyes darting between Dominic and me. "I— I wasn't—"

"Don't lie to me," Dominic snaps, stepping closer. "You've been following her around all night."

"Dominic," I say softly, placing a hand on his arm. "He's supposed to be following me around. He works for me."

Dominic doesn't look away from Ben, but he takes a small step back, his jaw still tight.

"I don't give a shit. I don't trust him." He shifts his focus back on Ben. "Hand over the phone."

CHAPTER 52

Dominic

I LIKE HER

PRESENT

I knew I didn't like that little punk.

I pace the hallway outside the interrogation room, summoning all my strength to not go in there and torture the truth out of him.

Through the one-way glass, I can see Kincaid sitting across from Ben, who looks every bit as uncomfortable as I want him to feel.

Ryker steps up beside me, arms folded in a similar stance. "You need to let him handle this," he says through a clenched jaw.

I don't look at Ryker, instead I keep my eyes firmly planted on Ben. "I don't trust him to ask the right questions."

Detective Kincaid is seasoned and experienced, and in any other circumstance I'd trust him. The problem is, when it comes to Ellie, I don't trust anyone.

Ryker exhales slowly, clearly trying to keep his patience contained. "You're too close to this. That's exactly why I'm not letting you in there. You know that."

Finally, I turn to face him. "That kid is hiding something. You saw his phone. He's been taking pictures of Ellie for weeks. And he's got no damn business doing it. That's not just weird—it's predatory."

After Ben turned over his phone, the digital forensics revealed countless images of Ellie.

"And that's why he's being questioned," Ryker replies evenly. "But we don't have enough yet to hold him. He hasn't committed a clear crime, at least not one we can prove."

I clench my fists, turning back to the glass. Kincaid is leaned back in his chair, his posture relaxed as he tosses out a few seemingly casual questions, trying to put Ben at ease. My eyes zone in on him.

Vorheis steps in beside me, casting a glance at Ben through the one-way. "You think this kid's got the balls to follow her in that sedan?"

"Maybe," Ryker admits. "But we need more than maybes. Right now, all we have is suspicion, and we all know that's not enough."

My gaze doesn't waver. "We need to tie him to the sedan. Get fingerprints, cross-reference his phone GPS with the locations Ellie was at when she got the texts."

"And we're working on it," Ryker says. "But you need to cool down, or you're going to blow this case wide open and give him an excuse to lawyer up."

I shake my head, my frustration boiling over. "She doesn't think it's him."

Ryker raises an eyebrow. "And you?"

"I'm more convinced than she is. He's been watching her. I think he's obsessed with her."

Ryker sighs, rubbing the bridge of his nose. "Let Kincaid do his job. We'll see if anything concrete comes out of this interview."

I don't respond as I watch Kincaid lean forward, his

expression turning more serious. Through the glass, I can hear the muted sound of his voice.

"Ben, we found a series of photos on your phone. Can you explain why you were taking them?"

Ben fidgets in his chair, his hands clasped tightly together. "I—I told you. It's for my internship requirement. I'm just documenting proof so I can get credit."

Kincaid tilts his head slightly, his tone even and calm. "Why didn't you ask her permission? It's standard practice, isn't it? Getting the subject's consent before taking photos?"

Ben swallows hard, his gaze darting to the door. "I didn't think she'd mind. I wasn't doing anything wrong. I've been openly taking photos my entire internship. I don't get what the big deal is."

"Except you weren't just taking work-related photos," Kincaid says, sliding a printed image across the table. It's one of the shots from Ben's phone—a candid photo of Ellie taken from behind, clearly focused on her rather than the event. "This doesn't look like her work. This looks like you're following her."

Ben's face goes pale, his hands trembling. "I—I wasn't following her."

"Then explain this," he presses. "Why are there so many pictures of your boss? Why just her?"

Ben looks down, his voice barely audible. "I like her. She's...pretty."

Kincaid doesn't let up. "Pretty enough to follow her after work? To vandalize her property? To send her threatening messages?"

Ben's head snaps up, his eyes wide. "No! I'd never do that! I swear, I didn't send her anything."

My breathing gets heavier as I watch the kid squirm. "He's lying," I mutter, more to myself than to Ryker and Vorheis.

MICHELLE MOSLEY

Ryker shoots me a warning look. "We don't know that yet."

Inside the room, Kincaid continues. "Where were you Friday evening, Ben? Around 6 p.m.?"

Ben hesitates, his gaze darting around the room. "I—I was at home. Studying."

"Can anyone confirm that?"

He shakes his head, his voice growing smaller. "No. I live alone."

Kincaid leans back in his chair, letting the silence stretch. "You know what I think, Ben? I think you've been watching Elyse for a while now. And when that wasn't enough, you started following her. Maybe you thought the texts were a way to get her attention. Maybe you thought scaring her would make her notice you."

Ben's voice cracks as he shakes his head vehemently. "No! I didn't send those texts! I don't even have her number. She only communicates with us through email."

Kincaid's expression doesn't change. "But you have her picture. Plenty of them. And we're pulling traffic cam footage from Friday evening. If we find a sedan matching the one Elyse described near her route home, and it ties back to you, we'll know."

My stomach knots as I watch the kid shrink further into himself. I'm not sure what I'll do if this kid ends up being who I've been after this whole time. All I know is he's lucky I'm not the one interrogating him. Kincaid is going easy on him, too easy for my liking.

Ryker's voice breaks through my thoughts. "We'll keep him here as long as we can, but if we don't find anything concrete, we'll have to let him go."

I turn to him. "And what if he's the one? What if we let him go, and he comes after her again?"

Ryker meets my gaze evenly. "Then we'll make sure he

doesn't get that chance. But we don't have enough to hold him indefinitely. You know that."

I clench my jaw, my agitation simmering just beneath the surface. Turning back to the glass, I watch as Kincaid continues to press Ben when a knocks sounds.

Morales walks in, a grin stretched across her face. "You guys are going to wanna see this."

CHAPTER 53

Dominic

I'LL DO ANYTHING

PRESENT

"Who the fuck is that?"

The image Morales has pulled up is a still from a traffic cam—a sedan matching the one that chased Ellie—alongside the DMV photo of the registered owner tied to the plates.

After Morales informed us we got a hit from the traffic cams, we gathered in the conference room to go over her findings.

"Name's Matt Pagio."

The name rings a bell. I stand, walking closer to the screens to get a better look at his picture.

"I think he was in my class," I mutter.

Morales nods. "Based on his age, he likely was."

Vorheis clears his throat. "Do you know of any ties he has to Elyse? Has she mentioned him recently?"

I shrug, unable to recall her ever bringing Matt up in conversation.

"Let's ask her," Morales chirps in. "She's still in the lobby."

Guilt twists low in my gut. Ellie's got to be exhausted—working all day to pull off the wedding, only to end up at the station afterward.

If this doesn't get resolved soon, it might kill us both.

I walk out to the lobby, where Ellie is passed out, sitting straight up in a chair. She looks so uncomfortable it physically hurts me to see her this way.

I cast a glance at the night shift clerk, and she smiles politely.

"She fell asleep about thirty minutes ago," whispers the clerk—Nora, according to her nameplate.

"Thanks," I whisper back.

I crouch down in front of Ellie and start stroking her thighs in soothing motions. "Ellie girl. Time to wake up."

She stirs for a moment before her eyes fly open. A sharp gasp bursts from her lips as her chest rises in a sudden, panicked breath.

I gather her face in my hands. "You're fine. You're okay. It's just me."

It takes her a moment, but soon there's clarity in her gaze.

"What's going on?" she asks, groggily.

"We might have something," I tell her, pulling back and helping her stand. "If you're up for it, we'd like you to look at some traffic cam stills."

She nods. "Yeah. At this point I'll do anything."

With my fingers threaded through hers, we walk into the conference room.

The moment her gaze lands on the screens, her eyes widen.

"Matt?" Her head whips at me. "It's Matt?"

Vorheis steps forward, extending his hand. "Sergeant Vorheis, but you can call me Dennis."

She smiles, years of being a Ledger kicking in—her manners on autopilot. "Elyse."

Vorheis returns her smile and gestures for her to have a seat.

As she gets settled, Ryker nods at her. "Are you thirsty? Do you need anything?"

She shakes her head. "I'm fine, Ryker. Thank you."

Morales moves to stand near the screens. "Okay, let's get started." Using the remote, she changes the image. "At 6:18 p.m., the traffic camera at Main and Third captured this image."

It's of a black sedan.

Ellie nods. "That's it. That's who followed me."

"According to the plates," Morales continues, "it's registered to Matt Pagio."

My attention turns to Ellie. "Has he been giving you problems? You never mentioned him."

She huffs a dry laugh. "Well, up until yesterday afternoon I was planning his wedding. That woman you saw me meet with was his fiancé."

Vorheis leans over the table. "Is there any reason he would have something against you?"

Ellie shrugs. "I guess so. I'm the one who convinced her to call it off."

"Well, there's your motive," Ryker says, twisting in his chair.

I shake my head. "That doesn't explain everything prior. If he didn't have a reason to be angry with her before Friday, then he's probably not who's responsible for the other incidents."

"Alvarez is right," Vorheis says. "We'll need to bring him in for questioning. We'll have patrol pick him up in the morning, but as of right now, his overall motive is shaky at best." He points between me and Ellie. "You two should go home, and get some rest. We're not getting any further tonight."

Ryker stands. "Agreed. I'll have full-time patrol surveillance reinstated, and you'll have an escort home."

I shift my focus to Ellie. "Ready to go home?"

Her gaze settles with mine. "You have no idea."

"Have you ever been so tired that you can't fall asleep?" Ellie asks in the darkness as we lie in bed.

"All the time," I admit. "Sometimes I'm afraid to fall asleep, and it keeps me up no matter how hard I try to relax."

"Why?" Her voice is hushed, like she's worried about waking someone up even though we're the only ones home.

I turn to face her, propping my head up on my palm. "Bad dreams. Bad memories."

The blankets rustle, and I feel her body reposition, mirroring mine. "You never told me you have bad dreams."

Ever since I started sleeping at Ellie's, I haven't had one. "It's been a while, but sometimes I have one creep up. Same one every time."

She swallows. "What happens in the dream?"

I don't like talking about it, but there's a layer of comfort in the darkness. If I can't see anything, it makes it less real. And if there's anyone who's ever going to know all of me, it's her.

"The shooting, but in my dream I shoot him, and I always wake up before knowing if I killed him or not."

Her hand reaches out, smoothing over my cheek. I can only see her eyes as they stare back at me. "That sounds terrible." She pauses for a moment. "Is that how you would've preferred it went? Do you wish you'd killed him?"

"No." I shake my head. "Never. He was just a kid who made some bad decisions. I'm not sure I could live with myself if I'd killed him—or even shot him in the first place, justified or not."

She sighs, moving against me. "Maybe that's why you wake up. Your brain is protecting you."

"Maybe," I admit.

Her arm drapes across my stomach as she cuddles up to me. I immediately pull her closer.

"You should probably talk to someone," she murmurs against my chest. "Might help."

I let out a sigh. "I know."

She's quiet for a long moment—so long I'd think she might've drifted to sleep, but her breathing isn't even enough.

"I'm sorry." My hand glides up and down her arm softly. "I'm sorry for getting angry and raising my voice. I was just scared—scared of all the bad things that could've happened to you."

She blows out a humorless laugh. "It's not like you were wrong. It was a stupid move on my part."

I shake my head. "No, it wasn't. Nothing about you is stupid. None of this is your fault."

"Doesn't mean I don't still feel like it is."

"This was part of the problem, wasn't it? Me trying to control everything—be everything, and not giving you the space to make your own choices and mistakes."

She twists her neck, resting her chin on me. "You weren't controlling of me, it wasn't like that. I think I just got too used to doing everything with you, I didn't know how to do anything alone."

A beat of silence stretches between us before she takes a breath. "I don't feel like that this time, though. I'm more inde-pendent, sometimes too independent, depending on who you ask." She laughs quietly. "I'm not worried about not being able to function without you. I *can* live without you, I just don't want to anymore."

"I never want to again. It wasn't great."

"What was it like? When you were working in California? What did you do besides work?"

"Exist."

She snorts. "That's not the answer I was looking for."

"It's true," I defend. "I mostly worked, did a lot of overtime. Sometimes I would hang out with the guys, but mostly it was just me. Alone."

"I bet you left a string of broken hearts down there."

"Nah, I never got that close." I tilt my head to kiss her forehead. "You see, there was this girl I could never get over, and I left my heart with her a long time ago. No one could hold a candle to her, so why bother trying."

"You're very swoony when you want to be."

"Only for you. Always for you."

We stay wrapped in each other, the only sound coming from the whir of the ceiling fan above us.

Ellie starts running her hand up and down my stomach. I think she's trying to be comforting, but the more she does it, the less I feel comforted and the more my dick hardens.

I close my eyes, willing it to go away.

Now isn't the time, but my body doesn't know that.

I take a few deep breaths, hoping it does the trick.

"Are you okay," she asks. "Why are you breathing so hard?"

There's laughter in her voice, and now I'm thinking maybe her touch isn't so innocent after all.

"It's very difficult when you're touching me, and I'm trying to be a gentleman."

She giggles, nuzzling her face into the crook of my neck. The heat of her breath skirts across my collarbone, and I get a little harder.

"Maybe I don't want you to be a gentleman." She nips at the skin just under my ear. "Maybe I want to end the night on a good note." She sits up, and even though I can't make out her expression, I know it's more serious than it was a moment ago. "I want to forget for a little bit." She bends to kiss my chest. "Distract me." Her lips trail kisses down to my stomach. "Please."

I feel like I'm failing her, not being able to catch the person behind everything. But this? This I can do. I can distract her. I can love her until she's mindless. Until all she feels is us, and how good we are together.

Gripping her thighs, I flip us to settle her beneath me. Her legs cross behind my lower back like it's second nature.

Thrusting, I nudge at her entrance even though we're still clothed. "Is this what you need?"

Her back arches. "Yes, I need you."

My heart squeezes, overwhelmed by how much I love her —how much *I* need her.

Together, we strip off the layers between us, and soon we're tangled with my cock pressing into her thigh.

Ellie lifts her hips, silently begging for it.

"Do you want it quick and rough?"

Through the faint light filtering in from the stars, I see her lips quirk up. "You know I'm never satisfied with anything quick."

I laugh against her mouth before slipping my tongue in. "Slow and rough it is."

CHAPTER 54

Elyse

HOLDING OUR BREATH

PRESENT

I wake up alone, the spot beside me cold.

When I get downstairs, Dominic is leaned over the kitchen island with his back to me. He glances back as I approach.

I can tell by the way his shoulders are high above his neck, that something is wrong.

"What's going on?"

Before answering me, he cradles my jaw and plants a soft kiss on my lips.

"Vorheis just called me." He pauses, taking a breath. "Matt confessed to following you, but denied having anything to do with the other incidents. They arrested him for reckless driving and attempted vehicular assault."

I can't say I'm surprised. As soon as they showed me the proof that Matt was the driver, my gut was telling me he wasn't the one responsible for vandalizing my car.

"And Ben?" I hesitate.

If Ben is behind anything, it might break my heart a little.

He's been a hard worker, and he's a sweet kid. I would hate to be wrong about him.

Dominic drops his head as he rubs the back of his neck. "All clear. According to the GPS on his cell, he was home when your car was vandalized, and Paisley and Faith said they were with him the entire time when the flower and photo were left on your car."

It's both good and bad news. I didn't want it to be Ben, but all that means is we still don't have answers.

I look at Dominic. At the worry creased on his forehead, at the hollowness under his eyes. He's stressed, and I can't help but feel responsible.

"So, what now?"

He shrugs, the kind of shrug that looks defeated. "Back to square one, I guess." He moves toward the living room and slumps onto the couch, resting his forehead in his hands. "On top of that, the Delmar case keeps getting colder and colder. All our leads have dried up."

I wish there was something I could say to make things better, to ease the burden he's carrying, but I come up short. Some cases take years to solve. Some never get solved. There's nothing I can say to make him feel better about either situation. It's a helpless feeling.

"You know what we need?" I jump up to stand.

His neck rolls to meet my eyes. "What?"

I extend my hand out to him, and he grabs it, letting me pull him up. "Breakfast."

He smiles, tucking a strand of my hair behind my ear. "You're right, Ellie girl."

We spend the day together, avoiding discussing the heaviness surrounding us. We're just going through the motions—holding our breath until something comes along to knock the wind out of us again.

I woke up this morning, determined to be brave, and to

tell Dominic the truth. After he told me he loved me, the words were on my tongue, desperate to come out. I love him. Of course, I love him; I've always loved him.

But as much as I want to tell him, now isn't the time. Not with how sullen he's been, not with how unsure our lives feel right now. When I tell him I love him, I want the moment to only be about us. So, until the timing is right, I'll wait.

CHAPTER 55

Elyse

DO YOU REMEMBER?

PRESENT

The house feels too quiet once Dominic leaves for work.

As much as I hate it when he's on nights, I feel oddly energized despite the sun beginning to drop behind the mountain. I grab my laptop and a fresh notebook from the kitchen counter, then set up at the dining table, switching on a nearby lamp and lighting my favorite candle.

One of the weddings I have booked for June has a massive budget, and with everything that's been going on, I haven't had the bandwidth to give it the attention it deserves. But tonight, I'm forcing myself to drown everything out and focus on it.

The latest developments on my case have made it hard to focus. Every new discovery is dead end after dead end.

Throwing myself into something creative is just what I need to stay distracted until Dominic gets home.

I scroll through the bride's Pinterest board for inspiration, jotting down notes as ideas begin to form. With one click, I queue up one of my throwback playlists, soft but just loud enough to fill the silence. The rhythm helps steady my thoughts, and soon I'm sketching centerpiece arrangements and brainstorming color palettes.

The notes of a familiar song drift through the room, and I hum along, my pen moving quickly across the paper.

I'm mid-thought, writing down an idea for floral runners, when a knock at the door startles me. The pen skids across the page, leaving a long, jagged line. My heart jumps, but I take a calming breath. With patrol surveillance back on, there's not a chance of anything happening. It's probably just a neighbor or one of my siblings dropping by unannounced.

I glance at the clock—Dominic's only been gone for an hour.

Cautiously, I walk to the door, peering through the peephole. My twisted stomach unravels in relief when I see Ryker standing on the porch, his tall frame silhouetted by the porch light.

"Ryker?" I say, opening the door partway.

He gives me a small smile. "Hey, sorry to bother you. Mind if I use the bathroom? I didn't get a chance to stop at home before coming here."

I blink, confused. "I thought Gerard was going to be patrolling tonight?"

Ryker shrugs, a tired smile barely lifting the corners of his mouth. "He was, but he called in sick, and I happened to be free."

I open the door wider and step back to let him pass through. "Sure. Come on in."

Based on how tired and worn out he looks, I think he just got off shift, only to have to come here and patrol me. A pang of guilt hits me. This situation isn't just impacting my life, but now everyone in the department.

He steps inside, his boots thudding softly against the hardwood floor as he glances around. His eyes settle on my laptop and sketchpad. "Working late?"

"Just catching up," I say, brushing a loose strand of hair behind my ear as I make my way back to the dining table. "It's been a busy week." I point toward the hallway. "Bathroom's the first door on your left."

Ryker nods, and turns on his heels.

A few moments later I hear the toilet flush and the sink run, before he reappears.

Standing just outside the dining area, his gaze flashes to the speakers. "You always did have good taste in music."

I let out a dry laugh. "Gosh, can you believe we're old enough now to hear music from our teen years on old-school stations? Makes me feel ancient."

Ryker comes closer, exhaling a laugh as he sits. "How do you think I feel? I'm three years older, practically a senior citizen."

I roll my eyes at him with a smile, double-checking that my project is saved. Before I can respond, Ryker's strained gasp grabs my attention, forcing me to turn to see what's happening.

"This song," he says, his voice quieter now. His eyes fall shut as he listens, like he's lost in a memory. When they reopen they settle on mine. "Do you remember?"

The playlist just switched from an upbeat Bruno Mars song to "Stay with Me" by Sam Smith. Besides being one of the many songs on my chaotic playlist, I don't know the significance of it.

"Remember what?" I ask, tilting my head.

His smile morphs into an expression I can't quite place. "Prom. We danced to this song."

My eyes flit to my screen, a wave of awkwardness crashing against me. I often forget we went to prom together.

Sensing his stare, I force my focus back to him, despite

how incredibly uncomfortable I feel. I never know how to react when he brings up our one and only date.

A strange chill runs down my spine when our gazes meet, but I try to keep my expression neutral. "I guess I forgot. That was a long time ago."

He stands and walks around the table, now hovering over me, his eyes drilling into mine. "How could you forget? It was such a special night. The one time it felt like you were mine, even just for a little while."

My ears snag on the word *mine* as my stomach starts to knot.

When Ryker asked me to prom all those years ago, it was a bit of a scandal for our small town. He had recently broken up with his longtime girlfriend, and I was just a freshman. The age difference between us is nothing now, but back then I was newly fifteen, and he was a very grown eighteen-year-old. Luckily, the scandal died as quickly as it made the waves, because nothing came of it. We were casual friends, nothing more. I started dating Dominic, and Ryker graduated and went off to college.

In all honesty, I never think about prom with Ryker because it's completely overshadowed by the memory of coming home that night and finding Dominic waiting for me. I had told myself if he was waiting for me, then there was hope—that maybe he did like me as much as I liked him. He did.

It was a huge turning point for us, all the details leading up to it are insignificant by comparison.

Maybe I should've given that night more thought.

Ryker is still looming over me, watching me.

I rise from my chair, needing to put distance between us.

He moves toward me. "Don't tell me you forgot. I think about it all the time."

I take an involuntary step back, my pulse quickening.

"Ryker, that was a long time ago. We went as friends; it wasn't like that."

"Not for me," he says, his voice tightening. Then, he holds out a hand, a strange look in his eyes. "Dance with me. For old times' sake."

The request sends alarm bells ringing in my head. I force a shaky laugh, trying to deflect. "I don't think that's a good idea."

His hand drops, his expression darkening. "Why? It's not like your boyfriend is here. No one has to know."

I falter, unable to come up with an excuse fast enough. His smile vanishes, and the air grows thinner. I can't take in a full breath.

"Fine," I say quickly, trembling. "One dance."

His smile returns, but it doesn't reach his eyes. He steps closer, placing one hand on my waist while his other hand takes mine. I feel trapped, my mind racing as I try to make sense of the unease clawing at my chest.

As we sway to the music, his grip on my waist tightens slightly, and I fight the urge to pull away.

Being in his arms feels wrong. It's nothing like the dance I shared with Dominic. Nothing about Ryker feels right. It didn't back then, and it definitely doesn't now.

"You know," he starts, "I never told you this, but Claire and I were having problems for a long time. Things were bad, really bad."

I stay quiet, unsure of where this is going.

"She found out about Victoria," he continues, casually, as if he's discussing the weather.

My breath catches. "Victoria?"

"Delmar," he clarifies, his gaze piercing into mine. "She was...well, she was a mistake. She didn't know her place. When she found out I was married, she ended it, and then threatened to tell Claire."

My body stiffens, my mind reeling. "What are you saying right now?"

He lets out a soft chuckle, the sound sending shivers down my spine. "I couldn't let her ruin everything. So I handled it."

I feel like I've been doused in ice water. My heart pounds as his words sink in. "Are you telling me *you* killed Victoria Delmar?"

It's not possible. There's no way.

His grip intensifies, and I can feel the strength in his fingers, the sheer force he's holding back.

"I didn't have a choice. That whore was going to destroy my life."

I can barely breathe, my mind racing as I try to piece everything together. "But Claire's pregnant. You guys seem so happy. "

"She left me," he says, almost bored. "Can you believe that? That bitch thinks she can leave me and take my kid. I told everyone she's sick because it's easier than answering questions about where she is. She's been staying with her parents since she confronted me about the affair. Fucking gold digger was following me. She thinks she'll be free after I sign the divorce papers, but I have plans for her once my son is born."

I try to move backward, but his hand on my waist keeps me firmly in place. My heart thrashes as the pieces click together, the realization hitting me like a thunderclap.

"It's you," I whisper, shaking. "It's been you this whole time."

His eyes regard me with a menacing stare. "You were always supposed to be mine. I saw you first!" He yells, forcing me to jump in place.

Like the draw of a curtain, his facade slips, revealing a person I don't know. I've never seen Ryker yell or lose his temper. Ever.

"You were so fearless back then." He chuckles, as if the

story is heartwarming. "You came right up to me and pushed me to the ground because I'd accidentally shoved Scottie. I think I fell in love right then and there. Years later, when I finally worked up the nerve to ask you out, Dom came along, and everything got ruined."

I try to pull away again, panic surging through me, but he doesn't let go.

"I planned everything," he continues, his voice rising slightly. "Prom night. I was finally going to have you. All you needed was a little liquid encouragement, laced with something to loosen you up a bit. Instead, the drinks got mixed up, and I ended up sick. You were such a little cocktease back then —but I knew you wanted me." He presses his cheek against mine, his hot breath like fire on my ear. "You were so innocent, so pure. Untouched." Moisture slicks across my earlobe as his tongue drags over it. It takes everything in me to not vomit. "I was going to be your first. Instead, you had to be a slut and let that 'spic touch you."

Goosebumps spread across my body, rising like individual needles stabbing all at once as his confession spills out.

"You're insane," I manage to say, my voice barely above a whisper.

He shifts me, forcing our eyes to meet, his icy stare piercing through me like a blade. "I'm not insane. I'm in love with you. I always have been."

I shove at his chest, trying to break free, but he's too strong. He grabs my wrist, pulling me toward the door with terrifying ease.

"Ryker, stop!" I scream, struggling against him.

"Elyse, I'm done waiting," he growls, dragging me out onto the porch. "Time is up. You've tortured me enough— flirting with me, wearing sexy outfits just for me, but you open your legs for *him*. I'm done fucking sharing you."

In a swift motion, he's lifting me, and hauling me outside.

I scream so forcefully the taste of metal floods my mouth just as his hand slaps over my lips, muffling me.

I twist and kick, desperate to break free, but his grip is like iron, his fingers digging into my arm as he drags me toward the vehicle. The unmarked patrol car sits in the shadows, its dark windows reflecting the faint streetlights above. He opens the rear door with a practiced motion, yanking it wide as I thrash in his grasp.

"Let go of me!" I scream, my voice raw, but he doesn't flinch. His hand shoves me forward, and I stumble into the back seat, the slick leather cold against my skin. The door slams shut with a hollow thud, and the sound reverberates through my chest, stealing my breath. I lunge for the handle, tugging frantically, but it's locked. No matter how hard I pull, it doesn't budge.

He slides into the front seat, glancing at me through the rearview mirror with cold, lifeless eyes. I scream again, the sound a piercing cry, but it's swallowed by the heavy silence as the engine growls to life.

The car jolts forward, tires crunching over gravel, and panic consumes me. The dim glow of streetlights fades as we speed into the darkness, each second stretching into eternity. A sharp pang flashes across my chest as I take in my surroundings—a partition separating the front and back seats, no divider with trunk access, no way out, no one around to hear me. My nails claw at the door's edge, the leather, anything, as my mind races.

I press my forehead against the window, watching the world blur past, and a terrifying realization settles over me; I have no idea where he's taking me or what's waiting for me at the end of this ride. One thing is clear—I have to find a way to escape, and fast.

CHAPTER 56

Dominic

THE BASTARD CHEATED

PRESENT

Morales waves me over the second I enter the station.

"Guess what! Guess what! Guess what!"

She's been keeping things professional lately, so seeing her act this friendly throws me for a loop.

"What is it?"

"Well," she starts, practically bouncing. "I've been trying to prove myself to Vorheis—prove that I'm good enough to make detective. And before his shift ended today, he asked me if I'd thought about taking the exam!"

"That's great," I tell her.

As much as she's annoyed me and crossed a few lines, I'm genuinely happy for her. At the end of the day, she's good at what she does, and deserves to be recognized for it.

Her smile evens out, turning serious. "I owe you an apology. You and Elyse. I know I said and did things that probably made you think I was a little nuts." She laughs, nervously. "It's just hard to meet a nice guy, and you're a nice guy."

I nod, feeling my face heat. "Well—uh. Thanks." Awkwardness prickles beneath my skin. "There're plenty of nice guys out there. You'll meet the right one."

She tosses her head back, laughing. "God, you should see the look on your face. Relax, Alvarez. You're just pretty to look at. And just so you know, I did meet someone. It's only been a few weeks, but I have a good feeling about him."

The tension in my shoulders eases, but before I can respond, the sound of the station door opening catches my attention. A woman walks in, her steps hurried. At first glance, she looks vaguely familiar, but it only takes me a second to place her; Claire, Ryker's wife.

"Is Ryker here?" she asks, her voice edged with unease as she glances around the room, rubbing at her rounded stomach. It's obvious she's been crying—her face is puffy, green eyes shiny and red.

"No," Morales says, standing up. "He left about an hour ago. Something wrong?"

Claire's face crumbles, and she takes a shaky breath before blurting out, "I need to find him, now!"

Morales gestures for her to take a seat, but Claire shakes her head, refusing. "We can have someone radio him. Are you feeling alright? Is it the baby?"

Claire looks at her confused. "I'm fine. The baby is fine. It's him; he's the problem."

Despite how upset she is, Claire looks great. She looks healthy. I know looks can be deceiving, but with how long Ryker was out because of her health, I was expecting her to look sick. She doesn't.

"Ryker's mentioned you've had a tough pregnancy," I say.

Her glassy eyes meet mine, her expression pinched. "What are you talking about?" She rubs her stomach. "I mean it's no walk in the park, but I've been managing it fine. What has he been saying?"

Morales's gaze flicks to mine before flashing Claire a polite smile. "He said you have HG and had been hospitalized."

Claire shakes her head, laughing in disbelief. "He's lost it," she says under her breath. "No, I don't have that. I don't know why he would say that."

Why would Ryker lie and say his pregnant wife is sick?

"We've been in mediation for weeks," Claire continues. "I thought it was going fine, and that he would sign the divorce papers willingly. I was wrong. I just found out now he's trying to prove I'm unfit and wants to fight me for full custody."

My stomach starts to twist. "Did you say divorce?"

She nods, wiping away the last of her tears.

"Yeah, the bastard cheated on me."

My breath stills as my gaze collides with Morales's, both of us caught off guard. Divorce? Ryker hadn't said a word about it.

"Divorce?" Morales echoes, as if the word is foreign.

"Yes," Claire snaps. "Have you two met his little girl-friend? Victoria? I should've noticed the signs earlier."

The name lands like a wrecking ball. My muscles tense, and I see Morales freeze beside me.

"Victoria?" Morales asks carefully. "Victoria Delmar?"

Claire blinks, clearly confused by her reaction. "I don't know her last name. She's got dark brown hair, tall, pretty, younger..."

Morales reaches for her tablet, pulling up a photo of Victoria Delmar from the case file. She turns the screen toward Claire. "Is this her?"

Her eyes widen, and she nods, her hand flying to her mouth. "Yes, that's her. That's Victoria. The woman he was cheating on me with."

My stomach sinks. Morales shoots me a glance, and I can see the same dawning realization in her eyes.

"Claire," I start, almost unable to continue because I'm in

such disbelief. "Victoria isn't Ryker's girlfriend. She's missing. Or, she was. Her body was found a few weeks ago. She was murdered."

Claire gasps, staggering back slightly before catching herself on the edge of the desk. "Oh my God," she whispers. "I had no idea. I've been staying with my parents in Seattle. I didn't hear anything about her being missing."

She turns to me, her eyes round and questioning. "You don't think he...You don't think Ryker...He would never— he's not like that. I mean, he's a cheater, but he's not a..."

The unsaid words hang in the air like a dark cloud. My instincts scream at me, the bad feeling in my gut turning into a full-blown storm.

"We don't know anything yet," Morales says carefully. "But we're going to find out."

I can barely hear her over the pounding in my ears. My thoughts are racing, pieces clicking into place that I hadn't thought to connect before. Ryker's disinterest in calling in the feds when we're clearly not equipped to handle the investigation properly, his insistence that it didn't look like a setup. Thinking back on our conversation about Ellie, him telling me I was on borrowed time. It always bothered me that he wasn't quiet about his attraction to her, as if I'm not aware of how badly he wanted her in high school.

Ellie, home and alone, immediately comes to mind.

I look between Claire and the photo of Victoria—same type, dark brown hair, fair skin, and green eyes...

Fuck!

I grab my phone, dialing Ellie's number as fast as my fingers can move. The line rings once, twice, three times before going to voicemail.

"Ellie, it's me," I say, trying to keep the panic out of my voice. "Call me back as soon as you get this, okay? It's important."

I hang up and immediately redial. This time, the call doesn't even ring—it goes straight to voicemail.

"She's not answering." Consuming panic takes hold of me as I try to rein in my thoughts. "Something's wrong."

Quickly, I pull up the live footage from the security cameras, and they're all black.

The security cameras I installed were recommended by Ryker.

Fuck!

I call Gerard, and he answers on the second ring. "Hello," he says, sounding groggy.

"How's Ellie? Is she okay?"

He's silent for a beat. "I called in. Came down with something nasty. Sheriff told me he'd fill in for me. Kind of surprised he'd take on such a menial task, but who am I to judge, right?"

I hang up, not bothering to respond.

"It's Ryker. He has her, and I fucking know it." I look to Claire. "Is there anywhere you can think of he would go if he didn't want to be found? Even if it seems insignificant."

Claire's chest heaves in quickened breaths. "He—He," she stammers. "He used to meet up with Victoria at some hunting cabin off the highway between Badger Canyon and Red Mountain. I followed him there once."

While Claire writes down a description of the location, Morales is already grabbing her keys and a jacket.

"Let's go," Morales calls out.

Before leaving, I spare a parting glance at Claire. "Go somewhere safe and call your lawyer."

She stares at us, open-mouthed.

There's no time to explain further; we can't waste another second.

I follow Morales, my heart pounding as we rush out of the station and into the night. The car ride to Ellie's house feels like an eternity, even though Morales is driving at full speed with the lights flashing and sirens blasting.

"We've got to be wrong," I say, though it sounds more like I'm trying to convince myself. "Ryker wouldn't—"

"Wouldn't he?" Morales cuts me off. "His wife just told us he's been lying about their marriage, cheating on her, and now the woman he was cheating with is dead. You really think that's a coincidence? There are no coincidences."

I grit my teeth, my fists clenching in my lap. "I don't know. I just know we need to get to Ellie. Now."

When we pull up to her house, the lights are still on, the energy pulsing in the air unsettling. The door is closed, but it's not locked.

I push it open, my voice ringing out. "Ellie!"

Silence. The kind of silence that feels like an empty void.

My hand instinctively moves to my hip, fingers curling around the grip of my service weapon. I don't draw it yet, but I'm not about to walk in unprepared.

Stepping inside, my heart hammers as I take in the scene. Her laptop is still on the dining table, a colorful sketch beside it. The music is playing quietly, but there's no sign of her.

I draw my gun, holding it low as my eyes dart around. With careful steps, I clear the kitchen and living room while Morales takes the hallway and starts making her way upstairs. We move in calculated motions, wordlessly clearing every room of the house until we meet back on the main level in the kitchen.

"She's not here. Her car's still here, though."

My vision goes black for a second and my hands begin to shake. I glance at the table again, my eyes catching on Ellie's sketch. There's a harsh line across it, as if something—or someone spooked her.

I'm done ignoring the signs that have been screaming at

me something wasn't right. Ryker is looking more suspicious with each passing second, and Ellie is missing.

"We need to get an APB on Ryker."

Morales shoots me a look. We both know the consequences of raising the alarm on the sheriff. If we're wrong, it's career-ending.

Morales nods after a beat before reaching for her radio.

I scrub a hand over my face, trying to get a grip on the crippling fear that's about to suffocate me. I can't lose it. Not now.

We didn't come this far for it to end this way.

"We're going to that cabin. If they're not there, I'm burning down the whole fucking county until I find her."

Morales starts the engine. "And if it's him, then what?"

"Then I kill him."

CHAPTER 57

Elyse

WORSE THAN DEATH

PRESENT

The room is dark, the only light coming from a single, flickering bulb suspended from the ceiling. It swings lazily, casting shadows that crawl up the walls and stretch long across the floor like they're reaching for me.

My hands are tied behind my back. The rope digs roughly, deep into my skin. My heart pounds so hard it feels like it might crack through my ribs. I try to focus, to breathe, but the fear is coiled tight in my throat, consuming me.

The only thought that brings me back, over and over again, is Dominic will find me. He has to.

Footsteps echo across the floorboards—slow and deliberate. My pulse spikes, and I hold my breath.

Ryker steps into view with a calm, unnerving smile.

"Comfortable?" he asks casually.

I glare at him. I won't give him the satisfaction of my fear, even if it's clawing at my insides.

He chuckles low in his throat and the sound slithers down my spine.

"Still feisty. I've always liked that about you, Elyse. Always thought it was so sexy."

"Where are we?"

Smiling, his gaze roams the space. "Somewhere no one will find you, and that's all you need to know."

I grit my teeth. "What do you want?"

He crouches, dragging a finger down my cheek. My stomach lurches, and I fight the urge to throw up.

"I want you."

The words land like ice water on my skin.

My body shakes—trembling, twitching, completely out of my control. I can't breathe. The thought of him touching me, of him doing everything he's hinting at, makes me want to tear my own skin off just to escape it.

There are things worse than death. And right now, I know exactly what they are.

A tear slips down my cheek before I can stop it. He catches it with his thumb, and I flinch away, repulsed.

He grins. "It kind of turns me on, seeing you cry. Not so tough now, huh?"

He stands, and for a second, my body loosens just enough to breathe.

"Don't you want to be fucked by a real man?" he adds with a twisted smile.

I don't answer. I can't. One wrong word, one twitch, and I don't know what he'll do. He's not stable—he's a match already lit, ready to burn.

His fingertip traces my collarbone, causing bile to rise in my throat, before wrapping around my necklace. He yanks at it, hard, and I scream from the pain. "You won't be needing that anymore." He tosses it aside, and it lands somewhere in the darkness.

The back of my neck burns, and my body is throbbing

from the fear and tension coursing through it. Every second that passes, my hope dies a little more.

I just need to keep him talking. If he's talking, maybe it'll stall him. Maybe it'll stall him long enough that he doesn't—

No. I cut the thought off before it finishes.

"Why me?" I ask, voice trembling. "You could have anyone. Why me?"

His smile falters, just barely.

"Because you were the one I couldn't have. You were always out of reach. You never saw me—really saw me." His voice rises, his pacing turning erratic. "I watched you, protected you. Scared off the string of losers you tried to date. And I waited. I waited so long for you to realize I was the one who could give you everything you needed."

"You're married," I whisper. "We've been friends. Why now?"

He crouches again, hands on my thighs. My entire body goes cold.

"I thought I could let you go," he murmurs. "But I can't. I lost Victoria. Then Claire. I wasn't going to lose you, too."

I can barely hear over the sound of blood rushing in my ears.

"What about the note? The flower? All the other weird shit?" My voice breaks. "Why?"

He stands again, and I suck in a breath the second his hands are gone.

"Dom," he says simply. "I needed him distracted. The man has impeccable timing, moving back just as my life crumbles to pieces. I put him on Victoria's case because I wanted him busy. And once I started messing with you, I knew he'd spiral. He couldn't help himself. When people are overworked, emotional, desperate, they make mistakes."

He steps closer again, and I press myself back against the chair, wishing it could swallow me whole.

413

He leans down until he's close enough that I can smell his cologne—my stomach sours.

"With Victoria and Claire out of the picture, it was finally time for me to have you. The plan was perfect. If he hadn't moved back, we'd finally be together. He ruined everything."

He's delusional. There isn't any scenario in which I'd ever be with him.

"You know what the best part is?" he whispers. "He's never going to touch you again. I bet he'll kill himself knowing he lost you for good. He's weak like that."

"He's not weak," I grit out, before I realize the mistake I've made.

The veins at Ryker's temples start to bulge, popping one by one. "Stop fucking defending him!"

His hand rises above me, casting a shadow across my cheek, before snapping down like a whip crack.

And then it all goes black.

When I come to, Ryker is pacing the perimeter of the room, his movements calculated as his eyes sweep over me.

Without windows, I can't gauge how long I was out for.

I try to keep my breathing steady, but the painful sting on my cheek only makes me more panicked. My mind scrambles for an escape plan, anything to get me out of this nightmare. The more I move, the more the ropes around my wrists bite deeper.

He's talking, mumbling so low I can barely understand him. I'm only catching pieces of his words because my ears are ringing with panic.

"...tried to be subtle," he says, leaning against the wall with a casualness that makes my stomach churn. "But you were always so focused on him. It was frustrating, really. I gave you every chance to see me. To notice me."

The Ryker I'm familiar with, the one I've known most of my life, is gone. The man before me is unrecognizable. He's twitching and speaking in circles and moving his hands frantically. My mind is struggling to make sense of how we got here.

"Just let me go," I plead. "I won't tell anyone. We can pretend it never happened."

He shakes his head erratically. "It's too late for that."

I need to get him to calm down—I need to pull him out of whatever this is.

"You're getting divorced, right?"

He stills, his head turning to me slowly. "I already told you that. You never listen to me."

"We can be together." I try to smile, but I can't. It's as if my body is refusing to allow it. "Me and you. We can be happy." My voice is shaking uncontrollably, and I'm praying to anyone listening that all he hears are my words and not the fear making them spill out.

I'll say anything I need to—anything he needs to hear to survive this.

"You mean that?" He asks in a hushed whisper, so hopeful it makes me want to shudder.

"Yes! You're right, I've been so blind."

He bends down in front of me, a chilling smile splitting his face. "I've been watching you for so long." His voice is distant, like he's recalling a memory. "I used to watch when you'd come home from work. You always looked so sad, and I just wanted to be there for you—to hold you. I shouldn't have married Claire. It was a mistake—she was a mistake. Please tell me you forgive me."

"If I forgive you, will you untie me?"

My heart pounds, waiting for his response.

"How do I know I can trust you?"

I rack my brain trying to come up with a response I think will satisfy him. I need to get loose. It's one step closer.

"Because you know me. You know me better than anyone. You trust me, don't you?"

The back of his hand travels over my injured cheek, and I flinch from the pain. His pupils are huge as he stares, without truly looking at me. "You're right." His voice is faint. "I do know you."

He moves behind me and it takes everything I possess to stop shaking. I need him to think I'm not scared.

When I start to feel the rope unravel, an entirely different type of panic overcomes me. Once I'm loose, I'm not sure what comes next.

As he's untying me, the faintest sound reaches my ears—a muffled thud, almost like a door being opened somewhere outside. My heart jumps, hope flaring in my chest.

Ryker doesn't notice at first.

"I can't wait to touch you," I tell him, hoping it encourages him to continue.

He frees one wrist, but then he pauses.

Moving, he stalks toward the lone door, tilting his head slightly, his hand drifting toward his waistband where his service weapon is holstered.

"Looks like we have company," Ryker murmurs with a smile. "If it's who I think it is, I'll get rid of him, and you'll never have to worry about him again."

I try to keep my face blank, but inside, I'm screaming.

Using my free hand, I try to work on the other wrist, but I can't seem to reach the right angle.

Time stretches. Minutes or seconds pass, my vision fading in and out of darkness. It's like I'm going into shock, drowning in fear.

Ryker has his gun drawn, waiting.

In an instant, the door bursts open, light bursting through. Dominic charges through first, his gun raised, with Morales right behind him. Seconds later, more uniforms enter the room. My breath catches, relief and terror colliding in my chest.

"Ryker!" Dominic shouts, his voice booming. "Drop the weapon. Now."

For a split second, everything is still. The air is heavy, so thick I can't see through it.

Everything happens so fast. Screams, commands, so many voices I can't make sense of it all.

A shot sounds, piercing through the air, followed by my blood-curdling scream as I watch Dominic's lifeless body fall to the ground.

CHAPTER 58

Elyse

A FEW SCRAPES AND BRUISES

PRESENT

I t smells like pee.

My legs bounce, knees jittering in a rapid rhythm as I sit in the hard chair next to Dominic's bed.

He's hooked up to all kinds of monitors, but the only one keeping me from spiraling is the steady beep of his heart rate.

He's alive.

He's alive, and that's all that matters.

Maybe if I repeat it enough, I'll actually believe it.

The doctors said he's okay. The bullet grazed him, on the edge of his vest, and didn't do any serious damage. They've said it enough times, but it's like my brain can't process it. My lungs burn with anxiety, and every breath feels like I'm choking.

Nervously, I twist the necklace around my neck. The one that Morales—of all people—managed to find in the rubble. I forced her into a hug after she gave it back to me, and I think that means we're friends now.

Dominic's been drifting in and out of consciousness from

the pain meds. About an hour ago, the nurse said they were starting to ease him off the morphine drip and expected him to wake up soon.

I stare at him. At how pale his skin looks, at the thick white bandage stretched across his shoulder—what was formerly his good shoulder. His lashes rest against his cheeks, unmoving, his chest rising and falling slowly.

My eyes have been stuck in a constant haze of moisture. I keep blinking, wiping them away, but they continue coming. Not the kind that fall in heavy sobs—the quiet kind that leaves your skin raw.

Reaching out, I wrap my hand over his, needing to touch him, to feel his warmth. The moment our hands meet, he stirs.

His fingers twitch beneath mine, a small, almost imperceptible movement. Then his brows pull together, a faint crease forming between them.

"Dominic?" I whisper, leaning in, holding my breath.

He blinks slowly, lashes fluttering, and then—finally—his eyes open. They're hazy and unfocused, but they're open.

He's awake.

"Hey," I say, a watery smile breaking across my face. "Good morning."

He groans in response.

"Do you know where you are?"

"Hospital," he says hoarsely.

I smooth his hair back in slow, soft motions. "Yes, but everything is okay. You're going to be just fine."

He squints at me, groggy. "Why're you crying?" His voice is rough, barely more than a rasp.

I laugh—more of a sob—and shake my head. "Because you scared me. You're not allowed to die, remember?"

His hand curls weakly around mine, and his eyes slip shut again, but not before I hear him mumble, "Sorry, Ellie girl."

I start to move, pulling my hand away, but he won't let me go.

"I'm just going to tell your nurse that you woke up."

"Stay." His eyes reopen, heavy-lidded. "Please."

"Okay," I whisper, brushing my thumb over the scruff on his cheeks and press the call button instead.

There's a hospital-issued water bottle sitting on the rolling table beside his bed. I grab it and hold it up to him, guiding the straw to his lips. He manages two big gulps, his throat bobbing with each one, before sinking back against the pillows with a quiet groan.

"Thanks," he murmurs, scratchy, but clearer. "And don't worry about me dying, because me and you are dying on the same day."

I set the water bottle aside, careful not to let go of his hand. Breathing a smile, I say, "You say shit like that and then pretend you haven't seen *The Notebook*."

He smiles with his eyes closed. "If I'm a bird—"

He drifts to sleep for a moment before suddenly, jerking upright, his whole body tense, and the heart rate monitor spikes in response, beeping frantically.

"Ryker," he rasps, eyes wide, panic flooding his face.

"Hey, hey—look at me," I say quickly, tightening my grip on his hand. "He's in custody. It's over. You got him."

He lets out a relieved exhale, sinking into the pillows.

When his eyes land on my cheek, he winces. His breathing sounds shaky as he tries to inhale. "I should've killed him. I should've fucking tortured him."

I shake my head, sweeping my thumb over his knuckles. "No. You're better than that. You got me out. That's what matters."

His eyes find mine, darker, more alert. "Did he—"

"He didn't." I cut him off gently. "And I'm okay. Only a few scrapes and bruises."

Once the doctors convinced me Dominic was stable, I finally let them check me out. I didn't have any serious injuries —at least none that were visible. Just some bruising along my ribs, minor cuts on my wrists where the rope dug in, and the split in my cheek where Ryker slapped me. It didn't even need stitches.

Physically, I'll recover quickly.

It's the rest I'm not so sure about.

Dominic goes quiet, and I can see the war still playing out behind his eyes. The guilt. The fear. The anger. I lean forward and press my forehead lightly to his.

"You saved me," I whisper. "That's all I'll remember." Lifting my head, my gaze locks with his. "I love you, you know. I love you so much, and I can't believe I almost lost you."

A tear streaks down my face, and Dominic catches it. His smile is weak and tired, but it's there.

"Took you long enough."

I snort through my crying. "I should've told you sooner."

His head shakes. "I already knew. I don't need your words, I can feel them."

He closes his eyes again, but not from exhaustion this time —it's more like relief.

Moments later, the nurse strides in with a smile. "Looks like someone's awake."

Dominic nods. "Barely," he groans.

She laughs and proceeds to check his vitals, recording each one as she does. When she's done, she points to a poster on the wall with smiley faces, each one different based on the number.

"On a scale of one to ten, one being the lowest, ten being the highest, can you tell me what your pain level is?"

"Three," he grits.

I snap my head at him. There's no way his pain is at a three.

He flops his head back onto the pillows, huffing. "Seven."

The nurse places her hands on her hips and sighs with a smile. "Seven is on the high side, so we don't want that."

"I want to be alert," Dominic says.

She nods and types into the computer. "We can try to manage your pain without narcotics and see how it goes." When she's done typing, her attention turns to me. "The doctor will come by in about an hour to check on your husband and answer any questions. He'll probably be released in about a day or two."

Once she's gone, Dominic gives me a tired, but very cocky smile. "She thought you were my wife, querida mía."

I breathe out a laugh. "I told the staff we're married so they'd keep me informed on everything."

He laughs and moans at once. "My little criminal."

"I am not a criminal."

Grabbing my hand, he laces our fingers together, giving me a squeeze. When his eyes settle with mine, they're soft around the edges. "We're going to have to make it legal, then. Can't have you getting in trouble. I heard they take HIPPA violations pretty seriously."

Before I can react, a soft knock sounds, and a second later the door opens. Silvia steps in first, eyes already glassy, followed by Adrian. They arrived yesterday, and we've been trading shifts, sitting by Dominic's side.

"He's awake," I tell them as they walk in.

"Ay, dios," his mom breathes, hurrying to his other side. Her hand trembles as she reaches for him, wrapping her arms around him. Adrian doesn't say anything right away, just nods at me before gently bumping his fist against Dominic's shin.

"I'll give you guys a minute," I say, standing.

Dominic glances at me, reluctant to let go, but he doesn't

protest. His mom needs to know he's okay. Between the two of us, we've cried enough to fill a well.

I slip out into the hallway, rubbing my hands together to shake off the nerves still buzzing under my skin.

The waiting room is packed. My family, Dominic's coworkers, friends, neighbors, acquaintances—it's like the whole town has taken up residence in the hospital.

My mom's sitting stiffly in a plastic chair, a coffee cup cradled between her palms with my dad pacing beside her. Layla's curled up next to Ariana, both of them looking like they didn't sleep. Gavin has Lily resting on his lap while she watches something on his phone. Ethan and Marisa are next to them having a quiet conversation. Scottie is conked out on a bench, exhausted after flying in on a red eye. And Shane is standing near the back, arms crossed, looking more stressed and tense than I've ever seen him before. When he sees me, he walks straight over.

"How is he?" he asks.

"He just woke up."

His shoulders drop, and he lets out an exhale. "Thank fuck."

Any resentment Shane felt for Dominic disappeared the moment he found out he took a bullet for me, and ever since then he's been riddled with worry. I have a feeling they'll be making up fairly soon.

After I update everyone, letting them know Dominic's awake, the crowd starts to filter out, leaving with hugs and promises to visit once he's up for company.

Silvia and Adrian return, looking relieved. It's been a stressful twenty-four hours, and despite not having seen or spoken to each other in years, we fell right back into sync.

Silvia's English has amazingly improved. So much so, that she told me she teaches ESL online. Adrian gushed about his pregnant wife, who stayed behind in Portland because her morning sickness couldn't withstand the three-hour drive. We met over FaceTime though, and I'm excited to get together once things calm down.

Silvia and Adrian leave to go back to my townhouse to whip up Dominic a home-cooked meal. Something Raúl would've made.

We say our goodbyes, and I return to Dominic's room.

"Hey," I say, slipping back into the chair beside him.

"Hey." He looks so much livelier, and I feel myself relax.

"Your dad still out there?"

"Yeah, my parents said they wanted to see you before they left. Why?"

He shifts slightly as he tries to sit up straighter. "Think I could talk to him? Alone?"

My heart does a ridiculous little somersault. "Alone?"

He smiles, a shy, adorably handsome, contagious smile. "Yeah. Got a question I've been meaning to ask him."

CHAPTER 59

Dominic

JEWELRY AND PAPERWORK

6 MONTHS LATER

"Sheriff Alvarez has a nice ring to it."

Ellie's arms are looped around my neck, her body pressed against mine, making it nearly impossible to keep my dick from twitching in a room full of people. I clear my throat and glance around the station, packed with the majority of the sheriff's department, city staff, and a few local reporters here to celebrate my new position. Tomorrow we're celebrating with friends and family, but today is for the official stuff.

"Have I told you how sexy you look in that dress, Mrs. Alvarez?" I whisper in her ear, letting my hand travel to inappropriately low levels on her back, resting on the swell of her ass.

She blushes, still getting used to the name, even though I call her by it all the damn time.

As soon as I was coherent enough, I asked Jack for permission to marry his daughter. I'd learned my lesson—no more wasting time.

He laughed and told me when he said he didn't want me to rush into marriage with Ellie, he never meant for me to wait this long. Then, without hesitation, he gave me his blessing.

He told me I never needed his permission—that he'd always seen me as a son and couldn't wait to officially call me family.

I might've cried.

He might've too.

We blamed it on the dry hospital air.

After I got released, it felt silly to wait to get married. So, two months after we survived the worst ordeal of our lives, we finally did it, and it was fucking perfect. But one of my favorite parts of the entire day happened right after we left the courthouse...

"This marriage better last, because I don't do refunds," Ray grumbles as he finishes the tattoo on my wife's left ring finger.

My wife.

Fuck, I love the sound of that. Wife. The word I've been wanting to call her nearly my entire life—it's surreal. I keep waiting to wake up because if this is a dream, I never want it to end.

Ellie laughs, shaking her head as she inspects the ink. "You sure about that? What if he turns out to be a terrible husband?"

Ray snorts, eyes flicking to me briefly. "Then you call me, and I'll straighten him out. I may be an old man, but I ain't that old."

He aims a wink my way as I squeeze Ellie's knee, my thumb brushing the inside of her thigh. "Not happening. It's lasting. Forever."

Her gaze lifts to mine, her eyes soft, smile sure—like she already knew what I was going to say. Because she did. Because for all the ways we've gotten things wrong in the past, this—us— is the one thing we're finally getting right.

Instead of the grand, over-the-top wedding everyone prob-

ably expected—the kind Ellie has famously spent her career planning—with a fancy cake, opulent floral arrangements, and hundreds of guests—we walked into the courthouse, signed a few papers, and walked out as husband and wife.

I would've given her anything she wanted. A ballroom, a beach, a destination wedding on a mountainside. But what she wanted was this. Quiet. Just us. No fuss, no audience, no pressure to put on a show.

She told me that after years of planning other people's happily ever afters, she realized the performance of it all wasn't for her. That a big wedding would've been for everyone else—not for us. And after all this time, after everything we'd been through, we weren't interested in waiting any longer.

So we didn't.

But before the honeymoon can begin, I wanted to make our union a little more permanent than paperwork and jewelry. And luckily, Ray was more than happy to come out of retirement for one more job. For the right price, of course.

Ellie admires her hand, staring at the simple black band now permanently on her finger.

"Well, does the husband approve?" Ray asks me.

Tipping my face down to Ellie, I cradle her jaw in my hands. "Fuck yeah, I approve." I crash my lips to hers, branding her with a kiss.

Ray groans. "Jesus, I'm gonna hurl. Get out of here, lovebirds."

My beautiful wife laughs against my mouth and turns to give Ray an apologetic shrug. "Sorry, Ray."

In her distraction, I move to scoop her up, carrying her bridal-style. She squeals as I do. "You're supposed to carry me over the threshold, not just randomly," she argues, even though I know she loves it.

Despite my shoulder still healing, I barely feel it, too excited, too happy to give a damn.

Ray kindly holds the door open for us, giving us a good-natured eye roll as we pass. I jog with her in my arms, loving the feel of her smooth legs in my hands.

We may have kept the wedding low-key, but Ellie looks absolutely stunning. Her short white dress hugs her waist before flaring at the hips, the thick straps slipping off her shoulders just enough to draw attention to her delicate neck and cleavage. It shows off her long, lean legs, and the second she walked downstairs, all I wanted to do was throw her over my shoulder and strip her out of it.

It was a long road getting here, but we finally got it right, because she's mine forever now, and I'm never taking that for granted.

When we reach my patrol SUV, I set her down, holding the back door open to see if she notices.

She does.

"No way. I'm never getting in the back of that thing again."

I laugh, remembering how angry she was when I arrested her. "Not even for old times' sake?"

Stepping close, her chest brushes against mine. "The only way I'll crawl back there, is if you join me." She grabs the collar of my button-down, drawing me down, our lips nearly touching. "Preferably in uniform."

"That can be arranged, querida mía." I dissolve the distance between us, planting a hot kiss on her gorgeous mouth.

Ellie smiles, glancing down at her ring finger again. I put my own hand out next to hers, the skin around the fresh ink still red from the needle. Out of everything, for whatever reason, this makes it feel the most official. Permanent.

"So, husband, what now?"

I pull her in, pressing my lips to her ear. "Now, Mrs. Alvarez, I take you back to our house and show you exactly how good of a husband I can be."

She grins, circling her arms around my neck. "Hmm. I don't know. You might have to work pretty hard to convince me."

I smirk, lifting her off her feet. "I promise I'll be a good boy."

In a few weeks we're leaving for Western Europe for a month-long honeymoon, the trip we never took all those years ago. But tonight, we're celebrating in the house we're making a home. An old house that looked like it was well past salvaging, but underneath it all, the foundation was solid.

With my wife by my side, I look around the room at the deputies and staff happily chatting. Gone is the dark cloud that plagued the department in the aftermath of Ryker's crimes. Instead, there's a sense of excitement—of new beginnings.

Six months ago, I wouldn't have believed this moment was possible.

Ryker's arrest shattered Red Mountain, and putting the pieces back together has been slow, painful work. People were left feeling betrayed and confused. Beneath the polished exterior he presented, there was a closet overflowing with skeletons. According to information from the FBI and a few psychiatric evaluations, they believe Claire leaving him was his breaking point. When the illusion of his perfect life began to unravel, something in him fractured.

A part of me had always known Ryker harbored feelings for Ellie, but I never could've imagined the depths of his fixation or the darkness it would unleash. When he lost both Claire and Victoria, his long buried obsession with her worsened. The investigation is ongoing, but Claire and Victoria's resemblance to Ellie doesn't feel like a coincidence.

It's been hard not to feel some level of blame. There were signs, and I failed to see them until it was too late.

Ellie's been drowning in guilt ever since everything came

to light, blaming herself for Victoria's death. For that reason alone, I wish I'd just killed him.

She has nothing to feel guilty about. Ryker was sick. This was his fault—his alone. I don't know if she'll ever fully move past the trauma he inflicted. But I'll be by her side, every step of the way. We started therapy, both separately and together. I'll do whatever it takes to make sure this doesn't consume her.

And through all of it, crime didn't stop. Clore County still needed a sheriff. The Board of County Commissioners appointed Doyle as interim sheriff, but with his retirement around the corner, he had no interest in keeping the job long term. To my surprise, he encouraged me to run. So I did, not thinking I'd actually win.

I didn't take into account how the media would spin things, making me look like the hero who took down a sheriff who'd gone off the rails.

When the emergency special election was held, I ran unopposed. Today, we're celebrating. And while it feels strange to celebrate something I was practically handed, I'm trying to embrace it and show up with the kind of presence this role deserves.

Ellie, still wrapped around me, pulls back slightly, her grin fading when she notices my expression. "You don't look like you're having fun."

"It's uncomfortable," I admit. "Hard to celebrate something when it doesn't feel like I truly earned it."

"Hey," she protests. "You absolutely deserve it." Her voice softens, and there's warmth in her eyes that makes my chest tighten. "Look at everyone here, happily celebrating your big win. They're proud of you."

"Maybe." I let my hands slide from her waist and step back, though it takes more willpower than I'd like to admit. "But right now, I'd rather be celebrating with you—alone."

She doesn't need more encouragement.

Taking my hand, she tugs me toward the hallway.

"Where are we going?" I ask, even though I have a pretty good idea.

"You'll see."

We slip out the back, the noise from the party fading as we step into my new office.

She shuts the door behind us, locking it with an audible click.

The old me would not be down for this, but Ellie's impulsive streak has started to rub off on me.

Sneaking away with my wife on my first day on the job, is probably a terrible idea. But if there's anyone worth breaking rules for—even laws—it's her.

"You know, this is how rumors start." I lean against my desk as she eats up the distance between us.

Her fingers toy with the new, shiny badge pinned to my chest. "Let them talk."

"You say that now—"

She silences me with a kiss, her hands tangling in my hair. It's slow and teasing, just enough to drive me wild without giving me what I really want.

"This is criminal behavior," I say under my breath as she pulls away.

Her brow arches, lips curling into a smile. "Maybe you should do something about it."

Fuck, this woman. A goddamn dream girl.

I reach for my belt, unclipping the handcuffs. Her eyes flick to them, curiosity and amusement sparking.

"Are you going to arrest me, *Sheriff Alvarez*?"

God, I love it when she calls me that. Her voice is like velvet, teasing me. Fucking intoxicating.

"Is that what you want, Mrs. Alvarez? Have you been breaking the law?"

I move around her, clasping one cuff around her wrist.

"So many laws," she breathes. "I need to be punished."

If anyone is on the other side of this door, they probably think they're listening to a cheesy porn, but I don't give a shit. I'm just weak enough to admit that this totally does it for me. And she knows it.

"Don't worry, querida mía, I'll punish you so good." I tell her, brushing a strand of hair from her face. "You've been a bad girl, dragging a law enforcement official behind closed doors, against his will."

Her laughter fills the room. "Against your will? Hardly. What are you going to do about it?" She raises her brow in challenge, but her body is already more pliable against mine.

I grab the wrist that's cuffed and press it up against the wall and lean closer, my lips hovering just above hers. "Do you want me to fully cuff you? Restrain you where you can't move?"

She nods as her body curves to me. "Yes," she says breathlessly. "I need it."

In one fluid motion, I spin her to face the wall, and cuff her other wrist, just like I did when I actually arrested her. She tests the restraint, and looks at me over her shoulder, her smirk growing.

"Did you wear this dress for easy access?" I start lifting the hem, letting my hands drag over the round of her ass.

She responds by sticking it out further.

"You know I did." She moans as I drag her thong down and let a finger glide at the center of her pussy."

"Estás tan mojada." *(You're so wet)*

Her legs begin to shake. "Dominic, baby, give me what I want."

With her dress gathered at her waist, I let my hands wander around her hips and to the front, near her pussy, but not close enough.

"Beg more, querida mía."

"Please," she squirms.

I tug on the cuffs, forcing her to arch back. "If I fuck you in here, you have to be quiet."

"I can be quiet," she sighs.

My head shakes, and even though she can't see me, I know she feels the movement.

"I don't think you can. That mouth of yours doesn't know how to be quiet."

The panties she was wearing are in my pocket, so I retrieve them. "Open those pretty red lips for me."

She does it without hesitation, letting me stuff her mouth full of lace.

The sight of her cuffed and gagged, her body trembling with anticipation, sends a surge of heat straight through me. I take a steadying breath, my fingers grazing the curve of her ass as I lean in close to whisper against her ear. "You look so fucking pretty like this," I murmur low and husky. "You better hope no one catches us, because I can't have anyone seeing my wife in this state." She writhes, fighting the cuffs. "Can't let anyone find out what a filthy girl you are. No panties, cuffed, pussy so wet it's running down your legs."

She lets out a muffled whimper, her body pressing back against mine, begging.

Her muffled protests vibrate against the lace in her mouth, her wrists straining lightly against the cuffs. I smile, knowing she's not going anywhere—and knowing she loves every second of this.

"Patience, querida mía." My hands glide over her hips, brushing close to where she aches, but not giving in. "You know I like taking my time."

Her legs tremble again, and I can feel the heat radiating off her as she rests her cheek to the cool wall. I press my lips against her shoulder, taking in the sight of her. She's beautiful, desperate, and entirely mine.

433

I finally let my fingers drift to where she's wet and waiting, stroking her lightly. She moans around the gag, her body melting in response, and I can't stop the growl that escapes me.

"Quiet," I remind her, using my on-duty voice. "Unless you want someone walking in and seeing you like this."

She glances back at me over her shoulder, her eyes widening slightly. The spark of excitement in them tells me she's not entirely opposed to the idea.

I unfasten my pants, my cock rock hard and ready for her. "Damn it, Ellie," I mutter, half-laughing as I give myself a firm stroke before sliding into her completely, filling her to the hilt. Her muffled cries threaten to break my resolve, and I have to steel myself to keep the pace slow and controlled. "You're pussy has ruined me."

Her body responds to every thrust, and the sound of her soft moans—despite the gag—drives me closer to the edge. I pull her hips back against me, my grip straining as I move deeper, harder, savoring the way she shudders.

When I finally let her come undone, her cries are an intoxicating muffle. I watch as her body goes taut, shaking with release, and I follow soon after, my breath ragged as I press my forehead to her shoulder.

For a moment, we're both still, the only sound our heavy breathing. I reach for the cuffs, unlocking them with a quick click, and she slumps against me, her legs barely holding her up.

I pull the gag from her mouth, and she gasps, a soft laugh escaping her lips as she turns to look at me.

"That was fucking hot. We're definitely doing that again."

I chuckle, brushing a strand of hair from her face. "One-time deal, Ellie girl."

She pouts, but there's nothing behind it. I think we both

know having sex in my office was a little too reckless, even for us.

"Come on." I straighten her dress and tuck her panties back into my pocket with a smirk. "We should get back before anyone notices we're missing."

She nods, still catching her breath, and I help her steady herself before unlocking the door.

Stepping into the hallway, the noise of the party greets us. I glance at her, a satisfied smile tugging at my lips, and hand in hand, we head back to the celebration, leaving our little secret behind.

I've been keeping a secret.

Ellie's head rests on my chest, her body nestled against mine, our legs a comfortable tangle beneath the sheets. She's breathing steady and slow, already drifting to sleep. Meanwhile, my heart is doing the opposite—racing with excitement.

While we were celebrating me becoming the new sheriff, Ariana texted me to let me know the finishing touches were complete.

I'd hired Ethan's contractor to finish the bulk of the renovations on Sullivan Ridge House—most of which are still in progress—but there was one room I kept off-limits. One space I didn't trust to anyone but me. I may not be as skilled as my dad was, but I wasn't about to let anyone else build my girl her dream library.

Keeping it from her was a gamble, and I'm lucky it worked out. I blamed it on asbestos, told her the contractor had to keep the doors sealed for safety. A total lie, considering I'd already had the house treated months ago. But Ellie bought it. Between her work days and my late shifts, I carved out hours where I could—building shelves, sanding, staining—doing as much as possible with very little time.

Once the room was done, I called in Ariana. I figured with her book-themed coffee shop, she was the perfect person to help me furnish and decorate the space.

I took a peek at it when we got home, and even though I told myself I would wait until tomorrow morning to surprise her with it, I'm not sure I can wait that long.

Ellie stirs slightly, in that hazy in-between state where she's awake, but only barely. She's tired—completely wrung out from my inability to keep my hands off her.

"Mmm," she hums, stroking her hand up and down my bare chest, nuzzling my neck. "You're so warm."

Probably because I'm close to sweating, worried she won't like it.

My mouth opens and closes a few times, debating whether I should force her out of bed, when it can definitely wait until tomorrow.

It's not like it's an emergency.

"I have something to tell you…"

She goes rigid in my arms, and I immediately wish I had worded that differently.

"Shit, sorry. That came out wrong."

Seconds pass before Ellie moves to sit up, the sheets slipping off her naked body, revealing her breasts. Two perfect handfuls. For a moment, I forget why she sat up in the first place.

Her pinched, sleepy face looks at me, adorably confused and maybe a little angry.

She's so sexy when she's mad.

"Spill. Because not a lot of good things start with *I have something to tell you*."

I laugh. "Nothing bad." My chest constricts. She's probably going to like it, but just the thought of disappointing her has my nerves standing on end. "I have a surprise for you."

In a flash, her face morphs, a delighted smile lighting it up. Her chin dips, almost shy. "What kind of surprise?"

"Come on." I move to stand. "Let me show you."

She practically jumps out of bed, and much to my disappointment, slips on a black silk robe, covering up all her delicious creamy skin.

I drag her out by hand, guiding her through the darkness of our home.

The main level is mostly done, aside from a few finishing touches. We've got a working kitchen, a real dining room, and a living room that finally has more than just lawn chairs.

When I bought this place, I hoped it might help pave a path back to Ellie. But it wasn't until she actually came back that things started to turn around. The house went from a mess to actual potential. Like maybe it had been waiting for her—just like I was.

Sometimes it felt like the house had a life of its own, and no matter how hard I tried, I couldn't put it back together until things were right with us. It was never supposed to be just mine. It was always meant to be ours.

"This house is still kind of spooky," she says quietly.

"Shhh," I hiss. "It'll hear you."

Her breath is on the back of my neck as she giggles, pressing a palm to my shoulder.

When we reach the closed pocket doors, I step in front of them and blow out an exhale.

Even in darkness, I can see the bright excitement in her eyes, glowing from the moonlight shining through the stained glass windows.

"Before I show you," I start, trying to stall. "If you don't like it, we can change it. Nothing is permanent. And go easy on me, I did this one myself. No contractors. Just me."

The edges of her smile soften, and her head tilts. "I'm going to love it." Then her face twists with amusement. "Is it a sex room? Trying to determine what my excitement level should be."

I huff a laugh. Only my Ellie girl. I think she has a pretty good idea what I'm about to show her, but she's trying to put me at ease.

We both know what I always promised this room would be.

Rather than answer her, I move my hands behind me and slide open the double pocket doors.

The sound that follows can only be described as shock.

She gasps loudly, and her hands immediately fly to her mouth, cupping it in disbelief.

I flick on the chandelier light, revealing the library—wall-to-wall built-in bookcases to match the home's architecture. The rich wood shelves stretch from floor to ceiling. A rolling ladder rests along one wall. The shelves are adorned with books and touches of decor Ariana meticulously picked out with Elyse in mind, all anchored by a dark beautiful antique rug and a velvet arm chaise lounge in the middle.

"How?" She turns to face me. "When?"

I shove my hands in the pockets of my sweatpants. "Do you like it?" I swallow roughly.

"Like it?" Before I register her movement, her arms are around my neck, yanking me down as her lips crash to mine. Her kiss is deep and slow. When she breaks it, our foreheads stay resting against each other. "I can't believe you did all of this."

The thickness in her voice makes my chest swell. "I promised you I would."

"I know, but I never expected you to do it with your bare hands. You already work so hard."

I tuck a loose strand of her hair back and gently smooth over her cheek. "A promise is a promise."

She flashes me her gorgeous smile before going to inspect the mostly empty shelves. Ariana moved in Ellie's books but there's still plenty of room to grow.

"This is it," she calls out. "I found the spot."

My eyes narrow, confused. "What spot? Did I miss an area? It can be fixed."

When she spins to face me her eyes are bright with anticipation, lips caught between a smile and a smirk. She points to the bottom row of the bookshelf closest to the window seat. "This is where we can put the nursery rhymes. It's the perfect spot, don't you think?"

Now I'm even more confused. "Since when do you read nursery rhymes? Is that some new kinky genre I don't know about?"

She laughs, shaking her head. "And you call yourself the sheriff."

It takes me a moment, and then it dawns on me. I feel like an idiot for not catching on sooner. My gaze lands on her flat stomach and then back to her eyes. "Are you—are we?"

Her lips lift in a small smile. "No, not yet. BUT," she drags me close, snaking her arms around my neck. "I was thinking we should start trying." The light behind her eyes dims slightly. "See if we can. If I can."

I hate the flicker of fear there, of the worry she carries. I don't want her to blame herself if it's not easy.

"Hey," I start. "There are so many ways to grow our family. We can do it the old-fashioned way," I rock my hips into hers, eliciting a faint laugh. "If we need a little help, that's okay, too. There are supplements and treatments and surrogacy and adoption—we have plenty of options."

439

My answer doesn't seem to soothe her the way I hoped it would.

"Yeah," she nods. "You're right." Her voice is small and quiet, and I'd give anything to make it go away.

I kiss her softly, trying to dissolve some of the worry. "We're a family with or without kids. You're my family; you're my whole fucking world. We're going to figure it out, and no matter what I'll be there every step of the way. You'll never go through anything alone again. Never, querida mía."

Her eyes fall shut. "I know," she whispers.

"I love you, Ellie girl."

"I love you, too."

A stretch of silence passes between us before I glide my hands down her waist and under her ass, lifting her.

She yelps, laughing. "What are you doing?"

"You said you wanted to start trying." I smash my mouth to hers as I walk us against a bookshelf, pressing her back into it. "No time like the present."

Epilogue

ABOUT 10 YEARS LATER

I didn't realize these pants weren't going to fit until it was too late. Now I'm lying on the bed, defeated and out of breath.

I run a hand over the swell of my belly, feeling the familiar weight of the baby pressing against my palm.

We weren't even trying, perfectly happy with our three girls, but a well-timed weekend away paired with playing fast and loose with any form of birth control, and I got knocked up with our fourth.

This has been my hardest pregnancy yet—and, of course, it's our first boy. Because naturally, it had to be a boy—men are always difficult.

Being pregnant at forty is no joke. More appointments, more strain on my body, and if I'm honest, a little fear. I'd just gotten used to the girls being older, more independent, needing me less. And now, here I am, starting over. Back at square one.

I worry I won't have the same energy I once did. That I

won't keep up the way I used to. But ready or not, in about three months, he'll be here.

"Ellie girl, you up there?" Dominic calls out as he climbs the stairs.

I turn to face him as he stands at the threshold of our bedroom, finding his jaw clenched to keep from laughing. I'm sure I'm quite the sight right now in nothing but a bra and these jeans squeezing the life out of my hips.

"What's going on in here?"

I groan, letting my head fall back against the mattress. "I thought I could still wear my regular jeans. I thought wrong."

Dominic leans against the doorframe, arms crossed, his eyes sweeping over me with amusement and barely contained heat. "I can see that."

I shoot him a glare. "Don't laugh at me. This is your fault, you know."

His mouth twitches, but he plays along. "Oh yeah? How's that?"

I gesture vaguely at my belly, which is currently acting as a blockade between me and my favorite jeans. "You and your stupid face. And your stupid hands. And your—"

He's already moving, crossing the room in a few easy strides before he reaches the bed and crawls over to me, hovering his body over mine. He places a warm hand over mine, palm pressing against my rounded stomach.

"What was that about my hands?" He leans down, placing a kiss on my neck as his hand travels between my thighs. My hips lift on their own accord, grinding against his touch.

"I think your greedy pussy is what got us in this predicament."

He dips his hand inside my unfastened pants and starts rubbing circular motions over my underwear, right where my clit is, forcing a needy sigh to float out of me.

I try to spread my legs wider for him, but the pants won't allow me to move.

"Take them off," I groan, trying to do it myself, but can't.

He chuckles, shifting to help me. "Querida mía, if you wanted me to take your clothes off, you could've just said so."

I smack his arm, laughing as he finally frees me from the denim prison, taking my panties with them. He leans in, tucking a loose strand of hair behind my ear, his voice quieter now. "The girls are playing outside. Your mom is watching them for a bit before Lily's competition starts." He crawls back on top of me, settling some of his weight down on me enough to feel his hardened cock. "I'd say we have at least ten minutes."

I roll my hips, seeking relief. "Then stop wasting time."

My eyes meet his in challenge, and he shakes his head, breathing out a laugh.

"If we had more time, I'd have your hands restrained behind your back for that comment. Guess I'll have to fuck the brattiness out of you instead."

He dips his head, sucking softly against the wild pulse in my neck.

"Please do, Sheriff Alvarez," I moan.

His cock twitches against my thigh. He loves it when I call him that, never gets old. I scratch my nails up and down his back, lifting his T-shirt to feel more of his warm skin. He drags my bra down and captures one of my nipples in his mouth. The piercings are long gone, but that's never stopped him from showering them with attention. It helps that I'm at the stage in pregnancy where my breasts are heavy and sensitive.

A throaty groan crawls up his throat as he tugs on my nipple with his teeth, a delicious combination of pain and pleasure.

"Fuck, your tits are so massive right now, makes me want to slip my cock between them."

"I need your cock somewhere else." I spread my legs for him, proving my point, and like a good husband, he immediately slips two fingers inside me.

"Nice and wet." He curls them just how I like, languidly thrusting them in and out, spreading my arousal.

"You have too many clothes on," I tell him between breaths.

He moves back, stepping out of his jeans and stripping off his shirt. My mouth starts to water, taking him in.

If there's one perk to his job, it's the shape he stays in—strong, solid, incredibly fit. My body has changed in so many ways over the years, sometimes I hardly recognize it. But Dominic has always been steady, all strength and sculpted muscle, layer upon layer. So ridiculously hot sometimes I catch myself staring, and can't believe he's mine.

His eyes roam over me, tracing every curve, every change—over the c-section scar, the stretch marks I try to ignore, the beach ball of a belly that's taken over my frame. But all I see in his gaze is appreciation.

He's loved my body in every phase of life, through every transformation, and I've never once doubted it. Not when I was young and unmarked, not when I carried our daughters, not now, with our son stretching me to my limits.

His hands follow where his eyes linger, slow and reverent, as if memorizing me all over again. And when he angles closer, pressing a kiss to my stomach, I fall a little more in love with him.

"So fucking pretty," he says under his breath as he joins me on the bed, sliding in behind me. Since this isn't our first rodeo with pregnancy, we're already familiar with all the best positions, and me on my side with Dominic's chest to my back, is one of my favorites. He lifts my thigh to line up at my entrance and my breath hitches, waiting for the moment of relief when he's finally inside me.

He enters me slowly, as if he's savoring every second. Once he's filled me to the hilt, I moan, tossing my head back into the crook of his neck.

"Feel good, Ellie girl?"

"So good," I admit.

His hands travel over me as he pushes his cock in and out, his breath hot on my ear, one hand squeezing my breast, the other cradling my stomach before sliding further down and rubbing right where I need him. I feel consumed when we fuck like this, and it's such an addictive feeling it's no wonder I've been pregnant for almost half our marriage. I can never get my fill of him.

"God, I love your pussy," he says in grunt. "So desperate for my cock, gripping me like a vise."

His words are my undoing, so filthy, they unravel me completely. I come with a vengeance, screaming his name as I do.

He follows right behind me, moaning into the back of my neck.

Afterward, the house is still quiet, and we take advantage of the alone time, cuddling until one of the girls will no doubt burst through the front door any minute now.

I curl around him as he soothingly rubs my lower back. I trail light kisses on his bare chest, right over his heart, where he has our girls' names tattooed. I kiss each one, already envisioning the day he adds baby boy's name.

We're still deciding on a name. My vote is Raúl, in honor of his dad. Dominic would rather give him an original name and make his middle name Raúl. We'll see who wins the battle.

"Our son in there giving you any trouble?" he asks, kneading at the ache around my tailbone.

I sigh, shifting so he can reach more of me. "He's just like his daddy, always wants my attention." I let out an appreciative moan when he rubs just the right spot. "Unfortunately, he likes kicking my ribs so I know he's there."

"That's my boy," he says with pride. "Probably going to be an athlete with all the moving he's doing." His hand moves in slow, careful motions, and already the dull pain eases.

I thread my fingers through his hair, letting my nails scrape gently against his scalp. "You gonna survive a house full of girls and one very spoiled baby boy?"

Dominic's expression turns serious for a moment. "I don't know. Might be tough. The girls have already got me wrapped around their fingers." Then he smirks. "But baby boy? He'll have you wrapped around his whole damn fist. Us Alvarez men have a way with the ladies." He waggles his brows at me, and I laugh while rolling my eyes.

"And who are these so-called ladies?" I ask, feigning jealousy.

His hand cups the side of my face, thumb sweeping over my cheekbone. "Only you, Ellie girl. It's always only been you."

He pulls me against him tighter, and I sink into his hold, molding myself to him. We rarely have the opportunity for a middle of the day quickie and some naked cuddling. I didn't realize how badly I needed this.

"We're going to be okay, you know that, right?" Dominic whispers.

I angle my head to meet his gaze. "What do you mean?"

"The baby. I know you're worried things will be different this time."

I hadn't voiced my worries, but I'm not surprised he picked up on them. He knows me better than I know myself.

"What if I'm too old? Too tired?"

He lets out a soft chuckle. "Ellie girl, you're not old. And yeah, we're gonna be fucking tired—but I got you. We're a team."

His thumb sweeps gently over my cheekbone.

"Sometimes, in those first few seconds after I wake up, I forget," he says quietly. "I forget that I got you back, that we built this beautiful life together. For a moment, I think I'm back in L.A. Alone. But then I feel you against me, or I hear the girls, and I remember.

"I've loved you my whole life, but loving you as my wife, as the mother of our kids—carrying our son—that's my greatest privilege. I'm scared too. But I'm also excited. He's already the luckiest kid, having you as his mom.

"The way you go to battle for our girls, the way you protect them—I just know he's going to be so loved and cared for by us and by his sisters. We're going to be okay. We'll be tired as hell, but we'll be happy."

My tears fall heavily. Motherhood and therapy changed me into a cryer. Now I cry about everything, but it's especially worse when Dominic is the cause. He wipes them away with a tenderness that makes my heart squeeze.

"Thank you," he says.

I swallow. "For what?"

"For letting me love you."

I scoot up and press my lips to his, placing a slow, soft kiss. "I love you, too. Always have, always will."

We stay intertwined, Dominic's chin resting on the crown of my head, my arms wrapped around him like I never want to let go.

We've traveled all over the world, visited some of the most beautiful places on earth. But in his arms, in our home, with our kids safe and playing outside—this is paradise.

After a long beat, he stirs. "Think we have time for round two?"

Before I can reply, the creaking of the downstairs door swinging open sounds, followed by the pitter patter of three pairs of feet and the sound of my mom's car descending our driveway. Time is up.

Dominic moves to sit, helping me along as he does. "Well, that was fun while it lasted."

Together, we get dressed and join the girls. It's nearly dinner time and sometimes they get a little feral when they're hungry. They take after me in that regard.

Once we get downstairs, Dominic gets started on dinner while our two younger girls run around like little hellions, working off the last of their energy. Our oldest sits at the dining table instead, likely about to draw until it's time to eat.

"Who wants pancakes?" Dominic calls out, standing at the stove, flipping one.

Thea and Esme simultaneously shout "Me!", but Stella stays quiet. She's moving past the little kid stage, slowly morphing into a dreaded preteen.

"Stella, baby girl, do you not want pancakes?" Dominic asks her, barely concealing the hurt in his voice. He's having a hard time with her growing up.

"I guess," she murmurs, more fixated on her drawing. My little artist.

It's funny how different and alike the girls are. Thea is Dominic's twin, taking after him so completely I'd doubt she has an ounce of my DNA if she wasn't so strong-willed. Esme looks more like me, but with a wise quietness that reminds me of my mother-in-law. Then there's Stella, the perfect mix of us both, not just physically, but even her personality. She's funny and perceptive like Dominic, but has a streak of wild impulsiveness just like I had at her age.

Stella catches me staring and looks like she might roll her eyes, but thinks better of it. For a moment she looks to her dad and then to me, a question lighting behind her green gaze.

"Is it okay if my friend comes over after dinner?"

"Of course, you know your friends are always welcome

here," I tell her. "Do you want me to call Hazel's mom and ask if she can come?"

I stand to grab my phone. Stella and Hazel have been best friends since kindergarten. The moment I reach my phone, Stella's voice has me pause.

"Not Hazel. Asher," she murmurs, focused on her drawing, her voice much smaller than I'm used to. "I told him he could come over."

Immediately, I sense Dominic go rigid hearing *him*.

Dominic spins from the stove, spatula in his hand, his eyes impossibly wide. He absentmindedly hands the spatula to Esme, leaving our seven-year-old to take over pancakes. Thankfully, Shane is her favorite uncle, and she knows her away around the kitchen.

Choking on a cough he says. "Stell, who's Asher?"

She shrugs, already uninterested. Or at least pretending she's uninterested. "He lives in one of the new houses. He was playing with us before Grandma left and made us come back inside."

Last year, the winery sold some acreage to a developer after the soil had degraded to the point it no longer produced good crop. Since then, our quiet home has been joined by neighbors down the hill.

Dominic's chest rises and falls as he takes several breaths. Likely to calm the panic attack he thinks he's having.

"Sure," he croaks. "Bring the *boy* over."

I meet his stare and silently mouth, "Stop."

His skin blooms red. He's on the edge of a spiral.

Before the situation escalates, I move toward him. "Girls, set the table. I need Daddy's help really quick."

Grabbing his hand, I drag him out of the kitchen and into the library down the hall. The moment the pocket doors shut behind me, he lets out a ragged breath.

"She's too young. Nine. Ellie! She's nine!"

I cover my mouth with my hand to stifle a laugh. He sees the amusement on my face and shakes his head.

"How are you laughing right now? Our baby girl is bringing home a boy." He starts to move past me, but I put my arms out to stop him. "I'm just going to change into my uniform. He should know I'll arrest his little ass if he lays a hand on her."

"Dominic," I say through a laugh. "She's not sixteen. He's her friend."

His nostrils flare as he runs a frustrated hand through his hair. "Yeah, well I was that nine-year-old boy once, and my thoughts were anything but innocent. Even then."

Coming close, I loop my arms around his neck, pulling him against me. "You need to be nice. We're only going to chase her away if she doesn't feel safe coming to us. My parents were very supportive of our friendship as kids."

He huffs. "Your dad would've wrung my neck if he knew I had a big fat crush on you."

I giggle, bringing my lips to hover over his. "I think he knew. We have to be welcoming to all her friends, even the ones who are boys. Besides, we don't even know if she likes boys."

Dominic huffs. "So now I have to worry about *all* her friends?! I don't like this. I'm not ready."

To distract him, I brush my lips to his, kissing him softly, and giving a little nip to his bottom lip as I pull away.

"I know what you're doing," he says with a moan before kissing me again, this one slightly rougher. "And it's not going to work."

Exhaling a sigh, I lock eyes with him. "She has lots of friends. No need to get worked up over this one." My words have no effect on him, but I continue on. "Besides, if our daughter gets to experience a love like ours one day, would that be so bad? I think we turned out pretty great."

Some of the strain in his jaw releases. "I'm overreacting. I know I'm overreacting. But, fuck, Ellie, you have no idea the torture it is to know what all these little boys are thinking about my baby girls. We made beautiful daughters, and now I'll have to suffer through them growing up and dating, and I fucking hate it."

I roll my lips, but a smile still slips out. "She's nine. We have plenty of time before she's even close to dating. You need to calm down."

He shakes his head. "I kissed you when we were twelve. And I would've done it sooner had you let me."

I toss him a pointed stare. "Exactly. You followed my lead. Trust her, she's a smart girl."

He rubs the bridge of his nose. "Between you and the girls, I'm going to be full-on gray by the end of the year."

"Me?" I gasp. "What did I do?"

His hands run down my sides and then back, to cup my ass. "You just keep getting so goddamn sexy I can't keep my hands off you."

I giggle like I would have when we were teenagers, my skin flushing pink. Even after all these years, he still makes me feel giddy—like I'm fifteen again, crushing on the boy next door.

It hasn't always been easy, but it's always been worth it. Through the mess I was during my pregnancy with Stella, terrified I'd miscarry. Through the stress of every election cycle when Dominic re-runs for sheriff. Through the worry of aging parents, the chaos of raising kids, the whirlwind of summers packed with sports and wedding season. Life never really slowed down.

I glance up at him—the boy I loved, the man I married, the one person who has always had all of me. I was right all those years ago when I got his name tattooed on my wrist. Even then, I knew he was permanent.

With a soft sigh, I lace my fingers through his and give his hand a squeeze.

Together, we step out of the library and back into the warm hum of our kitchen, where our girls are waiting. The scent of maple syrup and butter fills the air, the chatter of our daughters drifting through the room. Breakfast for dinner. A simple tradition, but ours.

Life has a funny way of working out. Sometimes all you need is a little time to age. Maybe some pressure. Definitely the risk of giving it another try.

Some things are simply better the second time around.

The End

Curious about whose story is next?
Read the Bonus Epilogue for a sneak peek!

Thank you so much for reading *Double Barrel*. If you enjoyed this story, please consider leaving a review. Reviews are instrumental to the success of indie authors. Scan the QR code below to leave a review on Goodreads:

Also by Michelle Mosley

RED MOUNTAIN SERIES

Rare Blend (Ethan & Marisa)

Double Barrel (Elyse & Dominic)

Bottle Shock (Gavin & Scottie)

Blush Crush (Ariana & Cole)

Perfect Balance (2026)

Bright Finish (TBD)

RED MOUNTAIN SERIES NOVELLAS

Last Call (Hillary and Archie)

Find signed books and merch at

www.authormichellenaomimosley.com/

Xo, Michelle

Newsletter Sign-Up

Do you want to stay up to date with Elyse, Dominic, and the rest of the Red Mountain crew? Scan the QR code below to sign up for my newsletter, where I'll be sharing exclusive updates on the Red Mountain Series and future projects.

Stay Connected

Want to chat all things Double Barrel and the Red Mountain Series? Consider joining my Facebook Reader Group. Scan the QR code below for unhinged commentary, bonus content, and exclusive sneak peeks.

Content Warnings

Please review the following content notes before continuing and proceed at your own discretion:

- *PTSD - specifically related to a law enforcement-involved shooting*
- *Law enforcement shot in the line of duty (on and off-page)*
- *Miscarriage (*see note below)*
- *Mentions of a difficult pregnancy (specifically HG)*
- *Depression*
- *Stalking (not between MCs)*
- *Incel ideologies and terms*
- *Racial Slur*
- *Sexism and misogyny in the workplace*
- *Gun use and violence*
- *Attempted sexual assault*
- *Kidnapping*
- *Death of parent (heart attack, off-page)*
- *Homicide (off-page)*
- *Mentions of blood*
- *Mentions of sex work (*see note below)*

- Minors engaging in consensual sex (closed door, off-page)
- Strong language/profanity
- Alcohol consumption
- Sexually explicit content (consensual restraint, rough sex, degradation & kink play)

Miscarriage: While the miscarriage occurs off-page, it is discussed between the main characters. Approximately 1 in 4 pregnancies end in miscarriage, and I felt it was important to reflect the emotional impact of such a personal loss. Your mental health matters to me. If this subject feels too triggering, please know you are absolutely welcome to skip this book without fear of missing out—you can continue with the series at any point that feels right for you.

Sex Work: This book contains a minor reference to sex work and sex workers. Based on conversations with law enforcement professionals, the term "sex worker" is used as it is most commonly recognized in that context. While it is widely accepted as a neutral and respectful term, I acknowledge that some view it as controversial or insufficiently representative. Please read with care.

Acknowledgments

This book was **HARD**. I thought after writing one full-length novel and a novella, this book would be a breeze. It was, in fact, not a breeze—more like a Category 5 hurricane. Elyse and Dominic had baggage, and they were messy. Wanting to give their story the justice it deserved, paired with an insurmountable level of imposter syndrome, made the writing process feel like pulling teeth. There were also parts that were incredibly emotionally taxing to write—I almost couldn't do it. But somehow, at the eleventh hour, the story finally came together. As hard as it was to complete Dominic and Elyse's story, I'm deeply proud of everything it became.

To my betas—Rose, Corinne, Ada, Sydney, Danie, Rachel and Izabela—thank you for reading this book in its roughest form and still seeing all the potential beneath the surface. Your notes, suggestions, and unhinged comments kept me going when I was very close to giving up.

Lauren, you're an amazing sounding board and the keeper of all my author secrets. Thank you for the endless voice messages and input. Even when I'm rambling, I always walk away from our chats fueled with inspiration.

ROSE! I would be lost without you. Also, every time you message me "MICHELLE!" I have a mini heart attack. Thank you for keeping me organized, and for never hesitating to bridge the gap between authors when we need advice. Getting this book to publication was a roller coaster, and you made the ride smoother than I could've managed on my own.

Kayla, thank you for listening to all my meltdowns and for always being honest with me. I didn't always want to hear it, but I *always* needed it. When I sent you the final draft of *something that shall not be named*, you were the voice of reason I needed to make sure it never saw the light of day.

To my agent Dani (that's still wild to say)—thanks to you, this baby, along with the rest of the *Red Mountain Series*, is coming to audio. I CANNOT wait to hear it! I know we're going to do some big things together, and I'm so lucky to have you in my corner.

Lemmy, thank you for not blocking me when I threatened to post feet pics to entice ARC reader signups. I didn't—which is probably why I still have ARC readers! You've created an amazing community of authors and creators, and I'm blessed to be part of your circle.

Dad, you know nothing about the book world, but your excitement makes me giddy. Just promise me you won't read this—or anything else I publish!

To my mom—every year that passes without you makes it all the more real that you're truly gone. So much of Elyse was inspired by you. Your boldness, your fearlessness, your take-no-shit attitude. I'll never be as tough as you, but every time I'm faced with a challenge, I think of you—and it gives me the courage to take it head-on.

Kari, thank you for not charging me. I give you a lot of work and only pay you in treats and Amazon gift cards. Best big sister ever!

To my mother-in-law, Marie—you're an amazing cheerleader and always hustling to sell my books! Forever grateful to have you in my life.

To my husband—thank you for setting up two different office spaces for me because I couldn't decide...and for not saying anything when I still worked from the couch.

Litzuli, where would I be without you? Thank you for being there through every phase of my life. I look forward to our *Golden Girls* era, telling sordid stories from our youth to anyone who will listen. I love you like a sister!

To my editor Andrea, I know I always promise not to send you multiple drafts after a deadline, but we both know I'm lying. Thank you for not dropping me. LOL!

To my content team, you all are **AMAZING**! The shares, the likes, the posts—I feel so undeserving, and I'm beyond thankful for each and every one of you!

To my ARC readers—I'm writing this before you've read the book, but thank you for taking a chance on me and my stories. Your support sets the tone for this book's release, and I appreciate your time more than you know. I hope you love Dominic and Elyse's story as much as I do!

Thank you to Michelle and all the members of law enforcement who let me pick their brains and helped me make Dominic's career and experience with PTSD accurate and respectful. I know it's a career filled with controversial opinions, but I'm grateful for all that you do and for your willingness to share the realities of law enforcement and the sacrifices you make for your communities.

And lastly, to my readers—I had no idea how much my life would change after releasing *Rare Blend*, and because of you, it's changed for the better. Thank you for reading my books and flooding my DMs with encouragement. I'm overwhelmed by your love for my characters. Being an author comes with a lot of tough days, but you guys make it more than worth it!

I battled my health and my brain in 2024 and 2025, and this book was along for the ride. I think I'll always doubt myself in some ways, but with every project I grow a little more confident. I'm incredibly thankful for my team of doctors at Swedish Thoracic—you quite literally gave me my life back.

If you've made it this far, know that I'm probably writing my next project and drinking way too much coffee. Love you all!

About the Author

Technical writer turned romance author Michelle Naomi Mosley writes small town romances with relatable characters and heartfelt narratives, incorporating humor and open-door spice in all her stories.

Michelle lives in Washington State's wine country with her husband. When she's not writing, she's reading, cooking the latest viral recipe, or redecorating her home for the millionth time. Since deciding to take the plunge and finally make her writing dreams a reality, it's been a whirlwind of late nights crafting stories and trying to keep up with the countless book ideas that strike her at any given moment.

You can follow her on Instagram and most socials @authormichellenaomimosley. For more information on books, merchandise, and newsletter sign-ups, visit authormichellenaomimosley.com.